D0397410

queen

BOOKS BY TIMOTHY ZAHN

DRAGONBACK SERIES

*Dragon and Thief**
*Dragon and Soldier**
*Dragon and Slave**
*Dragon and Herdsman**
*Dragon and Judge**
*Dragon and Liberator**

QUADRAIL SERIES

*Night Train to Rigel**
*The Third Lynx**
*Odd Girl Out**
*The Domino Pattern**
*Judgment at Proteus**

STAR WARS® NOVELS

Heir to the Empire
Dark Force Rising
The Last Command
Specter of the Past
Vision of the Future
Survivor's Quest
Outbound Flight
Allegiance
Choices of One
Scoundrels
Thrawn
Thrawn: Alliances
Thrawn: Treason
Fool's Bargain

COBRA SERIES

Cobra
Cobra Strike

Cobra Bargain
Cobra Alliance
Cobra Guardian
Cobra Gamble
Cobra Slave
Cobra Outlaw
Cobra Traitor
Cobras Two (omnibus)
Cobra Trilogy (omnibus)

The Blackcollar
Blackcollar: The Judas Solution
A Coming of Age
Spinneret
Cascade Point and Other Stories
The Backlash Mission
Triplet
Time Bomb and Zahndry Others
Deadman Switch
Warhorse
Conquerors' Pride
Conquerors' Heritage
Conquerors' Legacy
The Icarus Hunt
Soulminder
Cloak
*Angelmass**
*Manta's Gift**
*The Green and the Gray**

SIBYL'S WAR

*Pawn**
*Knight**
*Queen**

*A Tor Book

TETON COUNTY LIBRARY
JACKSON, WYOMING

queen

A CHRONICLE OF THE SIBYL'S WAR

timothy zahn

TOR

A TOM DOHERTY ASSOCIATES BOOK

NEW YORK

This is a work of fiction. All of the characters, organizations, and events
portrayed in this novel are either products of the author's imagination
or are used fictitiously.

QUEEN

Copyright © 2020 by Timothy Zahn

All rights reserved.

A Tor Book
Published by Tom Doherty Associates
120 Broadway
New York, NY 10271

www.tor-forge.com

Tor® is a registered trademark of Macmillan Publishing Group, LLC.

The Library of Congress Cataloging-in-Publication Data is available
upon request.

ISBN 978-0-7653-2968-4 (hardcover)
ISBN 978-1-4299-5146-3 (ebook)

Our books may be purchased in bulk for promotional, educational, or
business use. Please contact your local bookseller or the Macmillan Corporate and
Premium Sales Department at 1-800-221-7945, extension 5442,
or by email at MacmillanSpecialMarkets@macmillan.com.

First Edition: April 2020

Printed in the United States of America

0 9 8 7 6 5 4 3 2 1

queen

one

"The hopes and fears of all the years
 "Are met in Thee tonight."

The last strains of the old Christmas carol were still drifting through Nicole Hammond's mind when she started awake.

For a pair of heartbeats she blinked furiously, driving the stickiness from her eyes, trying to pull her brain out of the wild dream she'd just had and sort out where she was. Through the gloom and the flickering of her eyelids she could see a set of bars angling across her view. Had one of Trake's schemes or one of Bungie's stupid fights gotten her tossed in jail? She could hear footsteps coming toward her . . .

Then the fog cleared, and her vision snapped back, and she remembered.

She wasn't in a jail cell in Philadelphia. In fact, Philadelphia and human jails were far, far behind her. She was out in space, a million billion miles from nowhere, in a huge alien ship called the *Fyrantha*. What her sleep-fogged mind had taken to be bars were in fact the slender, chest-high cylinders of memorial pillars, the *Fyrantha*'s version of a cemetery, where the hundreds or thousands of human workers who'd slaved away aboard the ship through the long years were honored and their lives recorded.

Nicole wasn't sure how many years they'd been working and

dying. She had no way of knowing how many of them had held on to hopes, or given in to fears, or had given up and let themselves sink into blank weariness.

But whatever they'd felt, and for however long, it was all focused in Nicole now.

Are met in Thee tonight . . .

She'd been brought aboard as just another slave, a Sibyl who could listen to the *Fyrantha*'s telepathic damage-repair instructions and relay them to the work crews. But then she'd seen things she shouldn't, and done things she shouldn't, and somewhere in its alien heart or mind the *Fyrantha* had decided that Nicole Hammond should be elevated to the role of Protector.

Protector. Nicole winced at even the mental sound of the word as it echoed across her brain. Protector of the ship? Not doing a very good job. Protector of the men and women in the work crews? Doing even worse. Protector of her whole world?

Disaster. Complete, utter, horrifying disaster.

"Nicole?" a soft voice came.

She winced, blinking the last fogginess from her eyes. "Sorry," she said, pushing herself up into a sitting position. "I guess I fell asleep."

"No apology needed," Jeff assured her. "You needed the rest. Kahkitah? Anything from that end?"

Nicole turned her head to see the hulking, shark-faced Ghorf coming from the other direction through the gloom. He gave off a series of birdcall whistles—"I saw no signs of anyone," the translation came in Nicole's mind. "I don't know, though. Something feels odd."

"I know," Jeff said, stopping by Nicole. He sat down in front of her, his eyes still sweeping across the huge darkened space around them. "Open spaces with no cover except a bunch of pillars make me nervous."

"I understand," Kahkitah said, sitting down beside Jeff. "But that's not what I meant."

"You think the Shipmasters know where we are?" Nicole asked.

"Hard to tell," Jeff said. "You said you can't talk to the Caretaker this deep in the ship, and if the Caretaker can't see or hear you the Shipmasters might not be able to, either. Probably means no personnel sensors or boosters down here."

"What are boosters?" Nicole asked.

"Relays and echo transmitters," Jeff explained. "All the metal in the *Fyrantha*—not to mention all the electronics and electrical systems—will interfere like crazy with radio communications. They'll need boosters to get the signals where they're going."

"Do they even *have* radios?" Nicole asked. "I've never seen anyone use something like that."

"They have to have *something*," Jeff said. "A ship this size? You're sure not going to want to rely on a messenger service." He made a face. "On the other hand, if they know you've disappeared, and if they know this is a spot where you'd be invisible to the Caretaker—" He shrugged.

"Still, there's a great deal of space down here for them to search," Kahkitah reminded him. "And the open space also prevents them from easily sneaking up on us unless they come pillar by pillar."

"Or drop through one of the heat-transfer ducts," Jeff pointed out. "Never mind—it's still the best place for a quiet meeting. So. Nicole, you have the floor."

"What?" Nicole asked, frowning.

"Means we're ready to listen whenever you're ready to talk."

"Oh." Nicole took a deep breath. *The hopes and fears of all the years* . . . "All right. What we know is that Fievj and the rest of the Shipmasters now know humans are—how would you put it? Organizers? Persuaders?"

"Leaders, basically," Jeff said. "They still don't know if anyone besides the two of us can fight—"

"The two of you plus Bungie," Kahkitah corrected.

"Yeah. Plus Bungie," Jeff agreed, making a face. "But whether or not we can actually pull triggers and throw grenades isn't important anymore. The fact is that they see us as leaders; and unless the universe is full of George Pattons and Erwin Rommels, they're definitely going to want a good, hard look at Earth."

"Right," Nicole said, wondering who Patton and Rommel were. "But remember they're trying to sell us to other aliens. Unless you're stupid, you don't start working a deal until you know exactly what your product is worth."

"I agree," Kahkitah said. "That implies they'll still wish to settle the question of combat spirit before they approach anyone about selling your world."

"As Nicole said, that assumes they're not stupid," Jeff said. "But okay, let's go with that."

"Okay," Nicole said. "Now, Ushkai told me—"

"Ushkai's the Caretaker?" Jeff asked.

Nicole nodded. "He told me that the *Fyrantha*'s mind or computer or whatever was fragmented into four pieces: the piece that controlled him, the piece that controlled the Wisps, the part the Shipmasters control—I guess that's also the part that steers the ship and everything—and the part that talks to the Sibyls."

"And unfortunately, the part the Shipmasters control seems to be bleeding over into the part that controls the Caretaker," Jeff said. "Which could be a problem. All the Wisps they control are in Q1. But the Caretaker seems to have eyes and ears all over the ship." He looked at Nicole. "Crucial question: If the Caretaker can see everything, and the Shipmasters are controlling him, how are we ever going to make an effective move against them?"

"I've been thinking about that," Nicole said. "I don't think they're controlling him, exactly. If they were, they could have made him give us the wrong formula for the Sunset drug. I think they can just listen in on what we're saying to him, and talk through him. But that's all."

"Not sure how that helps," Jeff said. "If they can listen through him, they can presumably see through him, too."

"Maybe," Nicole said. "Maybe not. I mean, even if they can see, it doesn't mean he has to be looking."

"Ah," Kahkitah said. "You're saying that they can ask to see you"—he turned his head to the side—"but the Caretaker can deliberately choose to look away?"

"That's what I'm thinking," Nicole said, nodding. "Or, well, maybe just hoping. But it makes sense. There are things the Shipmasters could have done to stop us or capture us if they'd known everything we were doing. And remember, the *Fyrantha* picked me as Protector. Why do that unless it thought it needed protecting from something?"

"Not sure the logic completely tracks," Jeff said doubtfully. "But if the Shipmasters know everything we're screwed anyway, so we might as well keep this as our working theory."

"So we can speak in assured confidence down here," Kahkitah said, "and trust the Caretaker to limit the Shipmasters' access to our actions and words elsewhere."

"Right," Nicole said. "And we *don't* specifically ask him anything, because he probably can't ignore that or pretend we're not there." She looked at Jeff. "You're right, it's not a great position to be in. But I think we're stuck with it, unless we can figure out a way to cut the Caretaker completely out of the *Fyrantha*'s systems."

"Yeah," Jeff said. "And we might want to look into that, too."

Nicole winced. "Don't know if that would be a good idea until we know more about how everything works together."

"Desperate times," Jeff said. "Anyway, if we break something the ship can always tell us how to fix it."

"Assuming we don't damage the Oracle," Kahkitah warned. "That's the part that communicates with the Sibyls, correct?"

"Right," Nicole said. "And the Shipmasters also use it to talk to the people they put into the arenas."

"I've been thinking about it as a sort of a multipurpose intercom system," Jeff said.

"Sounds about right," Nicole said. "Hmm."

"Hmm what?" Jeff asked.

"I was just wondering," Nicole said. "If the Caretaker isn't giving the Shipmasters everything we're doing, maybe one reason is that the Oracle is fighting against it."

"So the ship's now not just fragmented, but is actively fighting itself?" Jeff shook his head. "Doesn't exactly brim me over with confidence."

"Would you rather it was united against us?" Kahkitah asked. "It is what it is."

"Always hated that phrase," Jeff said. "But yeah, you're right. Just remember that whatever's going on with the *Fyrantha,* it could change in a snap. We need to be prepared for the Shipmasters to be able to tap into the whole surveillance system at any time and without warning."

"In addition, the Caretaker may be making permanent records of everything," Kahkitah said.

"Good point," Jeff said, making a face. "Even if the Shipmasters aren't listening in now, if they do get in they might be able to rewind the tapes and hear what we were saying earlier."

"There seems little we can do about that except be careful," Kahkitah said. "Let us move on to the Wisps. You said you were able to give some orders to those in Quadrants 2 and 3?"

"It was mostly in Q3," Nicole said. "Some in Q2. But I'm not sure it's me *in* control so much as it is the Shipmasters are *not* in control. Which may be good enough. Right now, I'll settle for being able to go into those quadrants without getting attacked and grabbed."

She looked at Jeff. "But you're right about Ushkai giving them eyes and ears. Worse than that, losing Ushkai also means losing our own best information source."

"You say *best*," Kahkitah said, his birdsongs going thoughtful. "Don't you mean *only?*"

"Maybe not," Nicole said. "That's what I wanted to talk to you both about." She braced herself. They were *not* going to like this. "There's still the part of the *Fyrantha* that talks to the Sibyls."

"No," Jeff said flatly. "Absolutely not."

"Agreed," Kahkitah seconded with equal determination. "Using the inhaler leads to premature death."

"And going up blind against the Shipmasters doesn't?" Nicole countered. "I don't like it any better than you do. But pretty much every time I've been able to bluff Fievj it's been when I said the *Fyrantha* told me to do something and him not knowing whether or not I was lying. That tells me that so far they haven't been able to get into the Sibyl part of the ship. I'm not even sure they can."

"Because that section is most closely associated with the humans aboard?" Kahkitah suggested. He still didn't sound happy, but there was a reluctant thoughtfulness now in his tone.

"That's kind of what I was thinking," Nicole said, though she hadn't thought about it in exactly those words. "Remember, we think the *Fyrantha* is on our side, or as much on our side as it can be."

"*You* think that," Jeff murmured. "I'm not convinced the Ghorfs' little back-door communication system is bothering it in the first place."

"If Nicole says the *Fyrantha's* on our side, then it is," Kahkitah said firmly. "She understands the ship far better than any of us."

"Hold it," Jeff said suddenly. "Did you feel that?"

"No," Nicole said, tensing. "What was it?"

"Pressure change," Jeff said. "Like a door somewhere just opened."

"Such as the door into a heat-transfer duct?" Kahkitah asked, his birdsong going grim.

"Could be," Jeff said. "Did you feel it, too?"

"Unfortunately, our skin is more sensitive to pressure changes in water than in air," the Ghorf said. "But I have no reason to doubt you. No—stay seated," he added as Nicole started to stand up.

"He's right," Jeff said, swiveling around to face left. "Movement attracts the eye. Stay cool until we have a better idea where they're coming from."

If they're coming at all, the hopeful thought flickered through Nicole's mind. Jeff *might* just be jumping at shadows.

But the hope was futile, and down deep she knew it. The Shipmasters had found them, all right, and they were coming.

She looked around the dim space. The only lighting came from wide-spaced ceiling lights, with much of the view blocked by the orderly array of floor-to-ceiling support pillars. The perfect setup for an ambush, or for a game of cat and mouse.

And with the Shipmasters controlling the only serious weapons aboard the *Fyrantha,* there was no question as to which of them was the mouse.

"There," Jeff said, dropping his voice to a murmur as he flicked a finger a little ways to his left. "Movement."

"I see them," Nicole said, her heart sinking. The figures were barely visible, right on the edge of one of the pools of light. But from the glimpse she'd gotten before they disappeared behind a couple of the pillars they looked too big to be Fievj or any of the other Shipmasters. Almost certainly they were the two Koffren she and her team had tangled with in the Q1 arena.

Tangled with, beaten, and humiliated. And Nicole had seen enough bruised egos and petty revenge in Trake's gang to know how mindlessly nasty a person could get when he'd been embarrassed.

Maybe the Koffren were different. Maybe they took defeat calmly and didn't go in for payback.

She didn't believe that for a second.

Neither, clearly, did Jeff. "Time to move," he murmured. "Where's the nearest duct in the other direction?"

"Over there," Nicole murmured back, pointing away from the approaching figures. "There should be one over there, too, past the edge of the cemetery."

"Let's go with Door Number One," Jeff said. He eased out of his sitting position, rising up into a crouch facing the distant Koffren. "Not much room to maneuver in there."

"The Koffren might not be able to move through the memorial cylinders," Kahkitah said. "That could give you an advantage."

"Yeah, but if *they* can't get through, neither can you," Jeff said.

"My life and safety aren't important."

"*Everyone's* life and safety are important," Nicole put in. "We're going out the other way, okay?"

"Anyway, the Koffren may have ranged weapons," Jeff said, offering a hand to Nicole. "Or might just knock over the cylinders on their way through."

"You see where they went?" Nicole asked as she took his hand and levered herself up into a crouch.

"They're being coy," Jeff said. "But I think—there they are," he interrupted himself as a pair of shadows suddenly lumbered across the open space in the distance and disappeared behind another pillar. "They know we're here, all right. I wonder how they got down here without killing themselves."

"Some kind of parachute, probably," Nicole said. That was twice the Koffren had done the same run-and-hide routine. If they did it the same way a third time, that might be their chance to make their own run for it.

Jeff was clearly on the same page. "Okay, get ready," he said. "As soon as they hit the next pillar, we go. You two first; I'll bring up the rear. Nicole, as soon as we're moving shout out to the Wisps."

"Bring them into as many of the nearest heat-duct access points as you can," Kahkitah added, rising into a half crouch. "The more escape options we have, the better."

Nicole nodded. Ahead, the Koffren again appeared and crossed the open space. Jeff took Nicole's arm . . . the Koffren disappeared from sight . . .

And with a squeeze on Nicole's arm, Jeff stood up, helping her to her feet and giving her a push toward the distant heat duct. She'd barely gotten herself turned around when Kahkitah grabbed her other arm, steadied her, and pulled her into a dead run.

She filled her lungs with air. "Wisps!" she shouted. "All Wisps! I need you down here. Please," she belatedly added, remembering that politeness seemed important to the Wisps in Q3. She stumbled, briefly off balance as Kahkitah steered her behind one of the pillars—

There was a sudden sharp slapping noise, like a slush ball hitting someone's head. Something grabbed at the shoulder of her jumpsuit, trying to pull her to a halt. The grip spun her halfway around—there was a small tearing sound from her shoulder—

And as she looked back in the direction of the Koffren she saw a spiderlike clump of something on the edge of the pillar they'd just passed. It looked like a small dark glob sticking to the pillar, with a dozen tendrils stretched out across the pillar's surface and one attached to her shoulder.

The tendril's grip was incredibly strong. Fortunately for her, so was Kahkitah's. He pulled on her hand, sending a jolt of pain through the arm. There was another tearing sound, a louder one this time, and the Ghorf's momentum pulled her free from the tendril, leaving a small patch of her jumpsuit behind. Something shot past her face, and as Kahkitah got her turned forward again she saw another glob hit the next pillar ahead and explode into the same mass of tendrils.

"There!" Kahkitah said, pointing with his free hand.

"I see them," Nicole said. In the distance ahead, right where Nicole had expected, four Wisps came into view, floating down through the heat-transfer duct's updraft on their stretched-out butterfly wings. A quick glance to both sides showed similar groups landing on the deck beneath the other ducts.

"No good," Jeff said grimly from behind her. "We can't go that way. Too much clear space—they'll nail us long before we get there."

"Agreed," Kahkitah said. Abruptly, he let go of Nicole's arm. "Take her," he said. "I'll lead them away. Bungie den."

"What?" Nicole gasped, stumbling a bit before Jeff's steadying hand closed around her upper arm. "No, wait. You can't go alone."

"He has to," Jeff said. "Don't worry, they want you, not him."

"Thanks," Nicole growled.

And nearly lost her balance yet again as Jeff suddenly swerved them sideways toward the rows of memorial pillars. "Wait—where are we going?"

"The cemetery," Jeff said. "There's a group of Wisps over there—see them?"

"Of course I see them," Nicole gritted out. They were also nearly twice as far away as the group she'd originally been leading them toward. "What about the Koffren?"

"I think we've got enough of a head start that if we keep low they won't be able to get us."

Nicole clenched her teeth. Not a single bit of that sounded re-assuring.

But they had to try *something*. He was right about too much empty space along their original path, and even a glancing blow from one of those spidery things would stop them dead in their tracks. "I hope you're right."

"Me, too. Come on."

Four more spider globs slapped into pillars or shot harmlessly through the space in front of them as they ran. The rows of memorial cylinders loomed ahead—Jeff shifted his grip from her upper arm to her hand—

And then they were there, Jeff leaning forward and ducking down, stretching his arm behind him to continue guiding and pulling Nicole through the rows. She leaned over, too, matching his posture as best she could, painfully aware that the leaning and the need to stay between the close-set cylinders was slowing them down.

But it seemed to be working. The spider globs were still spitting through the air all around them, but most of them were hitting and getting hung up on the pillars before they ever reached their targets. The only one that even came close shot between her and Jeff and snagged itself on a cylinder three rows away.

And then, suddenly, the cemetery ended. Jeff gave her an urgent tug and poured on a burst of speed. Nicole did the same, struggling to keep up. The Wisps were waiting for her fifty feet ahead—

"Two of you: come here," she called as a sudden idea struck her. "Quickly. Please."

Two of the Wisps glided forward. They passed her and Jeff— "Stand behind us and open your wings, please," she ordered. She glanced over her shoulder, saw their wings unfurl in all their magnificent colors.

A second later the wings began to jerk and twitch as a barrage of spider globs slapped into them.

Three more seconds, and she and Jeff were at the two remaining Wisps. Nicole turned and backed into the nearest one's chest. Its arms folded around her—

Welcome, Protector, the familiar voice came in her mind. *How may I serve?*

Take us to level 4 as quickly as you can, please, she thought back.

Yes, Protector.

Nicole sensed the wings unfurl.

And then she was rising up in the duct, leaving the cemetery and the *Fyrantha's* basement behind. There was a small jolt as another spider glob slapped into the Wisp somewhere, causing a brief wavering in their ascent.

With the Wisp's touch completely paralyzing her Nicole couldn't tell where the glob had hit, or whether there'd been a serious injury. But to her relief, the wavering faded away and they continued smoothly upward. She couldn't see Jeff and his Wisp from her position, and of course couldn't move her eyes to look. All she could do was hope that he'd also gotten safely away.

Jeff, and Kahkitah.

She couldn't wince in the Wisp's grip. But that didn't prevent a double wince's worth of guilt from trickling through her. Jeff had been right about the Koffren and Shipmasters wanting her and not Kahkitah. But that didn't mean they wouldn't settle for second prize if that was all they could get.

After all, the Cluufes she'd first faced in the Q4 arena had been perfectly willing to use Jeff as a hostage to get her to do what they wanted. Even if the main Lillilli culture that the Shipmasters came from didn't go in for that sort of thing, the Shipmasters themselves had certainly watched the Cluufes' strategy and seen the result. They might well think that capturing Kahkitah would force Nicole to give herself up.

They might be right. The *Fyrantha* was counting on Nicole to protect it, but she was supposed to protect everyone inside, too.

She and Kahkitah had been through a lot together, and there wasn't much she wouldn't do for him.

Especially since leaving him in Shipmaster hands might reveal to them that the Ghorfs aboard the ship were far more than the strong but simpleminded creatures they'd pretended to be all these years.

And that would be disastrous. Right now, the Ghorfs were her—and the *Fyrantha's*—secret weapon, a group of willing soldiers the Shipmasters had no idea were sitting there under their noses. The last thing Nicole could afford was for that secret to be exposed.

She brooded about it all the way up the ship, knowing there was nothing she could do about it, but brooding just the same. Finally— the trip felt longer than usual—the door slid open and the Wisp floated through it onto the solid deck.

Have you any further orders, Protector? it asked into her mind.

No. Thank you, Nicole thought back at it.

The Wisp opened its arms, and Nicole was once again free to move. She turned around just as the second Wisp floated through the doorway and set Jeff down on the deck. Both Wisps turned and glided down the corridor, furling their wings as they went.

But not as smoothly or as neatly as usual. Both Wisps had a pair of spider globs on their wings, which kept them from folding properly. "Damn it," Nicole muttered under her breath. "I hope to hell the *Fyrantha* has something that can get that out."

"The *Fyrantha*, or the Shipmasters," Jeff agreed as he stepped to her side. "You saw him, right?"

"Saw him who?"

"The Koffren weren't alone," Jeff said sourly. "There was a Shipmaster tagging along behind them."

"No, I didn't see him," Nicole said. "Where was he?"

"About fifty meters back," Jeff said. "I didn't even know he was there until we were floating up and I got a higher viewpoint."

"Was he armored?"

"Armored and centaured," Jeff said. "Not sure if that's a word. Anyway, he was definitely leading from the rear, as we used to say in the Marines. We didn't say it very kindly."

"I suppose not," Nicole said, frowning. But if the Shipmaster was in centaur armor, that probably meant he was carrying a set of greenfire weapons with him. With that kind of weaponry, why had he been hanging back? Surely he wasn't afraid of two unarmed humans and a Ghorf.

For that matter, if he had greenfire weapons available, why had the Koffren been using spider guns?

"Come on," Jeff said, taking her arm. "Let's get someplace where we can talk."

"Not yet," Nicole said. "First we need to find Kahkitah. Then we can talk."

"You have any idea where he went?"

Nicole nodded. "He said *Bungie den* just before we separated. That's got to be either the pump room where I stashed Bungie after he got shot in the arena or else the ready room he went to afterward to hide out."

"I guess that makes sense," Jeff said, a bit doubtfully. "Would have been nice if he'd made it a little clearer."

"He was probably afraid he'd be overheard and didn't want the Koffren or Shipmasters figuring it out," Nicole said.

"Maybe," Jeff said. "You realize Fievj knows about the ready room, right?"

"Yes, and Kahkitah knows that, too," Nicole said. "I'm hoping he went to the pump room instead."

"And if he didn't and the Shipmasters have him?"

"Then we go take him away from them."

Jeff pursed his lips, his eyes tracking across her face with an intensity that made her uncomfortable. She held his gaze, and after a moment he gave a small shrug. "And then?"

"*Then* we go and talk," she said. "And come up with ideas."

"Good," Jeff said grimly. "Because we sure as hell could use a few."

two

Nicole decided to try the ready room first, hoping that if Kahkitah had been caught there and captured he would have left behind some trace of his presence. But there was nothing. No trace, no Shipmasters, and no Kahkitah.

He wasn't in the pump room, either. But even as she and Jeff sat down to try to come up with their next move the door opened and the big Ghorf slipped inside.

"I'm so sorry to have concerned you," he apologized.

"Don't worry about it," Nicole assured him. "We're just glad you're here. How did you get away?"

"I thought it best to continue with the façade my people have carefully constructed these many years," he said, sitting down beside her. "Instead of running to the first group of Wisps I continued past them as if I had panicked and had no idea what I was doing."

"The Koffren eventually connected with a shot and brought me down."

"They _got_ you?" Jeff asked, frowning. "And then they just let you go?"

"Yes, but not without considerable persuasion," Kahkitah said. "I explained that Nicole had asked me to bring food and water for a meeting you were planning. I told them this was my first trip to this region of the *Fyrantha,* and that I'd only brought a few food bars and water bottles."

"In other words, just what you had on you," Jeff said.

"Yes. I told them you were annoyed that I hadn't brought more. I told them I apologized, that I'd misunderstood. Then, when the Koffren appeared, you told me they were here to kill me for my failure and ordered me to run."

"What about the fact that you helped me get away?" Nicole asked.

"I told them I thought some creature from the *Fyrantha*'s dark underbelly had attacked us," Kahkitah said. "I panicked and pulled you free. I was also startled and confused to learn that you'd left long before the Koffren caught me."

"And they *bought* that?" Jeff asked, frowning.

"The conversation wasn't actually with them," Kahkitah said. "One of the Shipmasters—Fievj, I believe—did the questioning. The Koffren merely stood by and acted angry."

"I doubt they were acting," Nicole said.

"And then he just let you go?" Jeff asked.

"He did better than that," Kahkitah said. "He brought me to the hive himself. Did you know that centaur armor could fly straight up the heat-transfer ducts?"

"No, but it makes sense," Nicole said. "They have to be able to get around somehow, and they still don't control all the Wisps."

"But he just let you *go*?" Jeff persisted. "I can't believe even Fievj is *that* naïve."

"Oh, not at all," Kahkitah said. "He placed a device on the back of my jumpsuit that I assume was a location tracer of some kind." He whistled something untranslatable. "Sadly, there was a lingering odor from the removal chemical that I found distressing, so I left the jumpsuit in my room and changed into another."

"They used a chemical to get the stuff off?" Jeff asked. "I'd assumed they would have to cut it."

"No, it was a far more elegant solution," Kahkitah said. "They had a small bottle with a dropper built into the lid. Two drops on the tangler tendrils dissolved and evaporated them in short order."

"A liquid chemical, huh?" Jeff said with a lopsided smile. "An elegant solution. Nice."

"I don't follow."

"A liquid chemical," Jeff said. "A solution."

Kahkitah looked blankly at him a moment, then turned to Nicole. "I think I must be missing something."

"Oh," Jeff said, the smile disappearing. "Never mind. I forget you're not speaking English. *Solution* probably doesn't have the same double meaning in your language."

"No, not at all," Kahkitah said. "But I'm sure the joke was amusing."

"Like we say, you had to be there," Jeff said dryly. "Forget it."

"I will," Kahkitah said. "Someday, when this is all over, we must discuss wordplay." He gave a short whistle. "But that is the future. This is the present. I presume you've come up with a plan in my absence?"

"We're working on it," Jeff said. "We spent most of the last hour worrying about *you*. I guess we'll know better next time."

"Your concern was indeed unnecessary, but nonetheless greatly appreciated," Kahkitah said, ducking his head. "Hopefully, the information I gleaned during my interrogation will make up for the lost time."

"You reverse-interrogated them?" Jeff asked. "Nice."

"I don't know that term," Kahkitah said. "I asked no questions, but simply observed. First, the entanglement weapons."

"You mean the spider guns?" Nicole asked.

"Yes," Kahkitah said. "Is that what humans call them?"

"I don't know if humans call them anything," Nicole said. "It's what *I* call them. I'm not sure we even have anything like that on Earth."

"We didn't as of a few years ago, anyway," Jeff said. "What about them?"

"They aren't designed for the Koffren," Kahkitah said. "The grip and the placement of trigger and other controls don't fit hands and fingers their size."

"So they're Shipmaster weapons," Jeff said, nodding.

"So I conclude," Kahkitah said. "I furthermore don't believe the Koffren ever shot them before today."

"You getting that from their rotten accuracy?"

"Rotten at the beginning, but much better at the end," Kahkitah agreed. "I furthermore conclude that projectile weapons of that sort aren't completely foreign to them."

"Interesting," Jeff said thoughtfully. "Not just that, but the other implications. Fievj was with them in the lower level, and I can't see him bothering with that centaur section unless it's stocked with those greenguns."

"So why were the Koffren using spider guns?" Nicole murmured.

"Exactly," Jeff said. "Even if they're trying to take us alive, a greenfire bolt is a hell of a lot harder to dodge than a spider glob. And a precision weapon like that would make it a lot easier to disable a target without killing him or her."

"Which means they don't trust them," Nicole said. "Fievj and the Shipmasters. They don't trust the Koffren."

"Not surprising if the Koffren are merely more warriors for the arenas," Kahkitah said.

"Yeah, well, that's where it gets confusing," Nicole said. "One of the Shipmasters—probably Fievj—told me the Koffren had been taken from their homes and were mad about that. But then one of the Koffren said that the one who'd brought them in wasn't Fievj but Nevvis—he's another Shipmaster—and that Nevvis deals with the buyers."

"Could have been a little psych going on," Jeff suggested. "Pretending they were higher up the food chain to put us at a disadvantage."

"I don't think so," Nicole said. "The Koffren also said they were testing us for our value in battle. I can't see the Shipmasters telling just *anyone* what they're up to."

"Well, *somebody's* lying," Jeff said. "Big surprise there."

"Assume for the moment that the Koffren are telling the truth about being buyers," Kahkitah said. "That raises more interesting questions."

"Such as?" Nicole asked.

"Have the Koffren always been aboard?" Kahkitah said, ticking off fingers. "Are they newcomers? If so, were they brought in specifically for you, or were they here for a different purpose? Are there more than just two of them?"

"And why would the Shipmasters give them spider guns instead of greenguns?" Jeff added. "By the way, as to that last one, we don't know for sure that the two in the lower level were the same ones we tangled with in Q1."

"They were," Kahkitah said. "I saw marks on their wrists from the tridents."

"We cut them?" Nicole asked, frowning. "I don't remember seeing any blood."

"There wasn't any," Kahkitah confirmed. "The marks were not so much cuts or scratches as they were indentation marks. Their skin appears to be quite thick and dense, though there's a subtle color variation toward the neck that perhaps suggests the skin of their faces is thinner and less durable."

"Hence the helmets," Jeff said, nodding.

"That was my thought, as well."

Nicole winced, thinking back to that first confrontation. Just as well that she *hadn't* tried to take one of their swords while the Wisps held them frozen. She probably couldn't have cut through their skin even if she'd tried.

"Anyway, good catch," Jeff said. "Though just because we've already met these two it doesn't prove there aren't more of them wandering around the *Fyrantha.*"

"Agreed," Kahkitah said.

Nicole sighed. A lot of questions, not a lot of answers. "So what's their next step? Bring in a whole army of Koffren to hunt us down?"

"That would be the logical escalation," Kahkitah agreed. "Assuming the Wisps are willing to do that."

"If the teleport rooms are in Q1 the Wisps probably wouldn't have a choice," Jeff said. "The Shipmasters have that section pretty well locked down."

"Perhaps," Kahkitah said. "But I'm beginning to suspect the dynamic is considerably more complex."

"I agree," Jeff said. "Let's hear your take and see if it matches mine."

"Very well." Kahkitah paused a moment, steepling his fingers in front of him as if collecting his thoughts. "The Shipmasters are unwilling to face us directly. Not in combat, at least. The Koffren, whether permanent residents or recent arrivals, are therefore pressed into service as surrogates."

"Only they didn't do all that well," Nicole pointed out.

"Exactly," Kahkitah said. "But at this point, the Shipmasters have a dilemma. If they can't stop us quickly, they risk us doing permanent damage to the ship, or at least to their plans. But if they bring in more Koffren to assist them, it underscores the Shipmasters' weakness. Worse, if the Koffren are indeed buyers, they might decide they have sufficient numbers to take the entire *Fyrantha* for themselves by force."

"Cutting out the middleman," Jeff said, nodding.

"Exactly," Kahkitah said. "I daresay that a ship run by Koffren would be worse for us than a ship run by Shipmasters."

"*If* they could really take control," Nicole said. "The Shipmasters might be able to turn the whole ship against them before they were taken down. If they did that, I don't think even Koffren would do very well."

"Perhaps not," Kahkitah said. "But that doesn't mean they wouldn't try." He looked at Jeff. "Did I miss anything?"

"No, I think you covered it pretty well," Jeff said. "Just one more point. I agree that right now the Shipmasters probably don't want to show weakness by bringing in more Koffren. But if and when that resolve breaks, it'll break all at once. In other words, we won't be able to just push them back gradually. The minute they think we might get the upper hand they'll crack, and we'll be up to our armpits in Koffren."

"Ouch," Nicole said, wincing. "How do we know when that's about to happen?"

"Unfortunately, probably not until we're up to our armpits in Koffren."

Nicole snorted. "You're a big help."

"Sadly, he's not wrong," Kahkitah said. "There's seldom any way to anticipate an enemy's desperation level. Worse, when Fievj decides to bring in reinforcements he may not bring Koffren. He might instead bring in someone worse, someone we've never seen and don't know how to fight."

"You think they've got someone worse than Koffren they could call?"

"I wouldn't want to bet they don't," Jeff said. "Of course, the nastier the ally, the bigger the risk that they'll turn on the Shipmasters and we'll get running battles through the *Fyrantha's* passageways."

"Until the Wisps catch up with them," Nicole said. "Near as I can tell, they can immobilize anyone they can get a grip on."

"Which means that if Fievj ever gets control of all of them, in all four quadrants, we're toast," Jeff said, scowling. "You're absolutely sure he can't send any of the Q1 group here?"

"As far as I can tell, the Wisps can't even see any of the *Fyrantha* except the part they work in," Nicole said. "Plus a corridor or so into the next section."

"You realize how bizarre that is, right?" Jeff asked. "What if there's an emergency? Do you have to reprogram all of them before you can send them somewhere else?"

"No idea," Nicole said. "But I've questioned a bunch of them, and that just seems to be the way it works. Trust me, if I could have brought some Q4 Wisps into the Q1 arena, I'd have done so. We'd have taken down the Koffren with a lot less trouble."

"I'm not doubting you," Jeff assured her. "I'm just thinking about going up against a quadrant's worth of Wisps you can't control. Unfortunately, that's where the Shipmasters and the greenguns are, so that's where we have to go."

"You intend to capture some weapons, then?" Kahkitah asked.

"Well, we're sure not going to take out the Koffren with the toy arrows and swords the Ponngs and Thii brought along," Jeff said. "You know, it occurs to me that one other reason the greenguns haven't come out to play might be that the Shipmasters don't want the Koffren to even know they have weapons like that. If that's any part of it, us just having one that we could bring out for show-and-tell might make for a decent bargaining chip."

"I'm not sure what you think we can bargain for," Kahkitah said. "But I agree that better weapons are vital. Have you a suggestion on how to proceed?"

"We get a crew together and head into Q1," Jeff said. "There has to be an armory in there somewhere. We find it, we get in, we get armed, we get out."

"Just like that?" Nicole asked, frowning.

"More or less," Jeff said. "That's the easy-to-remember version, anyway."

"Sort of skips over the part about dodging Wisps, Shipmasters, and Koffren, doesn't it?"

"I didn't say there wouldn't be challenges," Jeff said with a shrug. "But the *Fyrantha*'s a big ship, and there can't be *that* many Shipmasters and Wisps aboard."

"What about Ushkai?" Nicole countered. "If he and the Shipmasters are watching the whole ship, it's going to be pretty hard to keep dodging everyone."

"Only if there are enough of them to watch everywhere at once," Jeff said. "Once we're ready to move on the armory, a couple of nice diversions will hopefully help clear the way."

"Though you first have to find this hoped-for armory."

"Number one on our things-to-do list," Jeff agreed. "You coming?"

"If you think I'll be useful," Kahkitah said.

"Oh, I'm pretty sure I can find something for you to do."

"I'm coming, too," Nicole said.

"Uh-uh," Jeff said firmly. "Sorry, but you're too valuable to risk."

"And you aren't?" Nicole countered. "Besides, I know the ship better than you do."

"*And* you know the Shipmasters, as well," Kahkitah said, his birdsongs suddenly sounding thoughtful. "Interesting."

"What's so interesting about it?" Nicole asked. "I've spent a lot more time with them, that's all. It's no big deal."

"You also understand how to deal with the Thii," Jeff said, eyeing her thoughtfully. "And from what you told me earlier, you did the same thing with the Ejbofs in Q2."

"And the same answer for both of them," Nicole said. "Are we going to go hunt down some weapons, or aren't we?"

"What do you think, Kahkitah?" Jeff asked, making no move to stand up. "The inhaler?"

"She hasn't used it for quite some time."

"Residual effects, maybe?"

"Perhaps," Kahkitah said. "Though you'd then have to explain why none of the other Sibyls could do such things."

"Maybe they can," Jeff suggested. "Maybe they all get these same hints and feelings, but Nicole's the only one who hasn't ignored them."

"Also, none of the others were declared the *Fyrantha*'s Protector."

"Point."

"Okay, just stop it," Nicole cut in. "If you're talking about me, you *do* know I'm right here. Right?"

"We are indeed talking about you," Kahkitah said. "Specifically, we're noting the ease with which you understand the *Fyrantha* and everyone aboard."

"I already told you that's not a big deal," Nicole said. "I had to learn to read people back in Philly. It was how you stayed alive in Trake's gang."

"Reading humans is one thing," Kahkitah said. "Reading Wisps, Shipmasters, and Thii is something else. I believe there's more at work here than just your Earth experience."

"I agree," Jeff said. "I'm thinking you've become more of an ally to the *Fyrantha* than you realize. It's picking up information on everyone aboard and feeding it to you, maybe on a subconscious level. Giving you stuff you otherwise wouldn't know or understand."

A cold chill ran up Nicole's back. She'd known he was going to say that. Somehow, she'd known.

How in hell had she known?

"We know the *Fyrantha's* on our side," Jeff continued. "The fact that it· hasn't blown the whistle on the Ghorfs' secret comm system shows that much. If it wants the Shipmasters kicked out, or at least doesn't want them turning it back into a warship, then it makes sense it would do whatever it could to help you."

"Yeah, interesting," Nicole said, pushing herself up off the floor and standing up. A little too fast; a whisper of light-headedness touched her.

Jeff was up and at her side in an instant. "You okay?" he asked, taking her arm in a steadying grip.

"I'm fine," Nicole said, trying to pull away. For half a second he seemed to resist, then let go. "*You* must be feeling better."

"I'm pretty much healed," he said. "Whatever else the *Fyrantha* might be, it's got a really good medical service. Doesn't mean I ever want to get shot by another greengun, of course."

"Yeah, let's all try to avoid that," Nicole said. "I'm going to Q3 to find Wesowee and Kointos's gray group. Maybe I can talk them into helping us."

Jeff glanced at Kahkitah. "I thought you wanted to help us look for the armory."

"I thought *you* said that was too dangerous," Nicole shot back. "So how do I use these secret Ghorf phones?"

Another look between Jeff and Kahkitah, a longer one this time. "Just find another Ghorf," Kahkitah said. "Seven of the eight Q3 repair teams have one. Any of them will know how to get a message to me."

"Fine," Nicole said. "Send a message to Wesowee when you're ready to head to Q1 so he'll know I'm coming."

"Yeah," Jeff said, sounding distinctly unhappy. "Nicole, I really don't like the idea of you going off alone."

"She won't be," Kahkitah assured him.

"No, you need to go with Jeff," Nicole told him firmly.

"Not me," Kahkitah said. "I was speaking of Moile and Teika."

"What, the Ponngs?" Nicole scoffed. "Sorry, but I'm not waiting for you to go back and get them."

"No need," Kahkitah assured her. "They're already here."

Nicole felt her eyes widen. "They're *what*? Where?"

"In a room a few doors down the corridor," Kahkitah said. "I thought they might be useful, so I brought them with me from the hive."

"And just left them outside?" Jeff asked, frowning. "Why didn't you bring them in?"

"I thought we might discuss matters they would not yet be permitted to hear." Kahkitah looked at Nicole. "You *will* take them with you, won't you?"

Nicole glowered. For a second, Kahkitah had seemed like the earnest, simpleminded creature he'd always pretended to be.

She would never again see him as simpleminded. But maybe the earnest part was real.

She'd hoped to go off on her own for a little while, to work through the stuff Jeff and Kahkitah had just dumped on her. Clearly, that wasn't going to happen. Maybe that was what Kahkitah had planned all along. "Fine," she bit out. "Whatever. Go grab them, and let's get moving."

Moile and Teika were more than willing to accompany Nicole, their pointed but otherwise useless swords held proudly.

Useless swords; and out here in the *Fyrantha*'s hallways, mostly useless Ponngs. But at least they knew how to keep quiet.

They were doing a lot of that now as Nicole led the way up along a nearby stairway, her mind churning. Maybe the idea that she was becoming linked to the *Fyrantha* was something new, something she'd never thought of before. More likely, it was something she'd already known and simply pushed into the back of her mind with all the other thoughts and memories she didn't want to admit were there.

Now, thanks to Jeff and Kahkitah, those suspicions had been dragged out into the open where she could no longer ignore them.

It made a certain amount of sense, really. Ushkai had told her the original Lillilli owners had set up the *Fyrantha* so that only humans could repair it, though he hadn't known why. Maybe that was because they knew that humans could connect to the ship on a level that would let them become true friends and allies. If Nicole thought about it that way, it was like she suddenly had a boyfriend.

Problem was, she didn't *want* a boyfriend.

She'd worked incredibly hard over the years to avoid that exact situation. She'd played Trake's men against each other, favoring one and then another, talking one into giving her crash space—and hopefully nothing else—then making sure to move on to the next before she wore out her welcome. Every time she'd slipped up, every time she'd been forced to endure one of those horrible and thoroughly unwanted couch sessions, it had left another black scar on her mind that needed to be buried away.

It wasn't just that there was no one in the gang she liked enough to be a willing participant in such things. It was that anchoring herself to any one person was incredibly dangerous. With all the jockeying back and forth for position, with Trake ruling over everyone with an iron fist, and with deaths and injuries sometimes a monthly occurrence, picking the wrong partner could be fatal for a woman. If she lost her man to gang violence, she would be fair game for whoever grabbed her first. If she lost him to gang politics, she would be bit by the same backlash.

What would happen to her if the *Fyrantha* lost its battle against the Shipmasters?

Because it might. Probably would, in fact. The Shipmasters had all the cards, all the weapons, and the most critical parts of the ship. They had allies and servants and the teleport rooms and a full quarter of the Wisps. All Nicole had was Jeff, Kahkitah, a handful of humans and Ghorfs—

"Where are we going?" Moile asked from a few steps below her.

Nicole sighed. And two Ponngs and four Thii.

Wonderful.

"Up another couple of levels," she told him. "We'll be heading back down to the arena, but I want to cross the central heat-transfer duct a few levels above it. Less chance of running into a Q3 Wisp that way."

"I thought the Q3 Wisps were under your control," Teika said.

"I haven't really tested that," Nicole said. "Anyway, whatever it was before could have changed in the past few hours. Why, you getting tired?"

"Not at all," Moile assured her. "We will follow the Sibyl wherever she leads."

Nicole hissed silently. Still playing their self-chosen roles as her loyal slaves. The whole thing still set her teeth on edge.

And it got worse. One of Trake's gang getting kicked under the bus usually bounced the same mess to his woman. If the *Fyrantha* lost, and Nicole lost along with it, would that happen to the Ponngs and Thii? The Shipmasters needed the humans to fix their ship, and the Ghorfs to provide the necessary muscle, but she doubted they needed a half dozen aliens who barely came up to Nicole's chin and had no strength or technical expertise to speak of.

Could she persuade Jeff and Carp to take them into the blue group and teach them how to repair the *Fyrantha*'s circuits? Maybe their thinner fingers could get into places that human ones couldn't reach.

Another chill ran through her. What in hell's name was she doing?

She'd spent half her life training herself not to care about other people, because caring never gained anyone anything but a punch or a knife in the gut. She'd started life aboard the *Fyrantha* by playing Carp and the others against each other, making sure to never get close to any of them. Maybe she'd gotten a little too close to Jeff and Kahkitah, but that was purely because they could be useful to her as allies.

But the Ponngs and Thii were of no value to her. None at all. So why did she care what happened to them?

Or was any of this coming from her at all? Was it instead coming from the *Fyrantha*?

Get out of my head! she thought viciously at the ship. *You can tell me what to do, but you can't tell me what to think.*

There was no answer. She hadn't really expected one.

But her concern for the Ponngs and Thii was still there.

Ushkai had declared her to be the *Fyrantha*'s Protector. He hadn't mentioned anything about her also becoming the ship's slave.

three

She led them all the way up to level 22, a full ten levels above the arena. Partly that was to make sure they crossed the centerline at a spot where they would hopefully not be expected. Mostly it was to test the Ponngs' stamina.

To her private annoyance, they handled the climb better than she did.

"We'll now be carried across the gap?" Teika asked as they waited for the Wisps Nicole had called to show up.

"That's how you got to Q4 in the first place," Nicole reminded him. "Why, were you thinking about seeing if you could jump it?"

"No, of course not," Teika said hastily. "I just . . . we don't have good memories of these creatures."

Nicole rolled her eyes. "Sorry," she said.

And immediately felt disgusted with herself. The Wisps had brought all of them aboard the *Fyrantha,* and probably none of them had pleasant thoughts about that experience. Sarcasm on her part wasn't really called for. "I didn't mean to be snippy. I've got a lot on my mind."

"We understand," Moile said. "As the *Fyrantha*'s Protector, all that we do ultimately rests upon your arms. Leadership can be a terrible burden."

"Thanks," Nicole said dryly. Exactly the kind of pep talk she needed right now. "So what's your story? Where were you when the Wisps showed up?"

"I had gone to see Vjoran regarding a business transaction," Moile said. "Do you remember Vjoran?"

Nicole nodded. "He was the one who was so hot to fight the Thii over the food dispenser. I got the feeling he was disappointed when that whole thing ended without a battle."

"Very much so," Moile confirmed. "Teika was the one who opened the door that day and led me to his presence."

"So you were a servant?" Nicole asked, looking at Teika.

"I was a slave," Teika corrected.

"Oh," Nicole said, floundering. A *slave?*

But really, why was she surprised? Both Ponngs had quickly offered to be her slaves in return for Nicole fixing their food supply. That should have told her right there that slavery was something they were familiar with. "So then the Wisps swooped down in the middle of your meeting and took all three of you? What were you, Moile, some kind of businessman?"

"Not at all," the Ponng said, his burning-fire voice oddly wistful. "I had come to Vjoran to negotiate for my own slavery."

Nicole blinked. "*What?*"

"My family's debts were great," Moile said. "My conversion was the only way to solve the problem."

"Oh," Nicole said, for lack of anything better to say. If she'd known from the start that the Ponngs were a slave culture, maybe she wouldn't have been so quick to help them.

A moment later that reflexive thought caught up with her with a second wave of secret shame. What in the world was she thinking? Abandoning the Ponngs would have been like leaving her whole neighborhood to starve just because Trake's gang was a bunch of vicious jerks.

Which, of course, had totally been how she'd seen things back then. As long as she had food and alcohol and a safe place to sleep it off, she really hadn't cared what happened to anyone else. "So when you offered to be my slave, that was just part of your deal?" she asked.

"Not at all," Teika said. "Our slavery was shameful and unpleasant. We'd hoped that our arrival here was a new chance at a better life."

"I'll bet *that* thought disappeared pretty quick."

"Indeed it did," Moile said ruefully. "Our next hope was that serving Vjoran as soldiers would raise our societal value to a point where he would be forced to free us, or at least to renegotiate for our service. When the starvation began, we realized that being soldiers was a double-edged sword." He lifted his sword a few inches. "So to speak."

"Yeah," Nicole said. "I used to think this place was better than my old life, too. Sometimes it doesn't work that way."

"I agree," Moile said. "But here, at least, we have a chance to build something better."

Nicole was still trying to think up something that wouldn't sound completely cynical when she was saved by the appearance of the three Wisps she'd called.

"Relax," she told the two Ponngs as both lifted their swords. "It's under control."

"Are you sure?" Moile countered darkly. "Kahkitah told us about the Wisps in Q1 that tried to kill you."

"We intend to make sure that doesn't happen again," Teika added.

Nicole scowled at the approaching Wisps. A wonderful sentiment, and one she totally agreed with.

The problem was that once they were locked in the Wisps' arms they were helpless to act. Or to move, or to blink, or to do anything else. If the Shipmasters had extended their control into

Q4, all three of them would be tumbling down the heat-transfer duct before they could do anything about it.

Unless . . .

"Okay, here's what we'll do," she said. "You two hang back while I let the first Wisp take me. I'll tell it we want to be taken across to Q3, then tell it to let me go. If it does, that'll prove they're obeying me. If it doesn't—" She felt her lip twitch, thinking about their non-edged swords. "Then you two do whatever you can to get me free."

"Understood," Moile said, his tone grim. "And we *will* free you."

"Just don't jump the gun," Nicole warned. "The last thing we want is the Q4 Wisps keeping away from us because you drew blood."

Bracing herself, she strode toward the Wisps. She waited until she was three steps away, then stopped and turned around, presenting her back to them. She felt the ripple of air as the first Wisp came up behind her; saw the silver-veined arms as it reached around and pulled her to its chest.

Welcome, Protector. How may I serve?

Again, it was physically impossible to heave a sigh of relief. Again, Nicole really wished she could. *Release me for a moment.*

Yes, Protector.

The arms opened, and Nicole was again free to move. "It's okay," she told the Ponngs. "They're obeying me. Come on."

"We obey," Moile said. He still looked unhappy, but he backed obediently into the second Wisp's arms. Teika, looking even less thrilled than his fellow slave, did the same with the third.

Nicole waited until they were settled, then backed up again into the first Wisp's arms. *Take us across to Q3,* she ordered.

Yes, Protector.

She felt the heat as the door opened; and then they were on the move, the Wisps carrying them to the edge of the duct and unfurling their wings into the updraft. A minute of blasting hot air from beneath her as they floated across, and then the door on the opposite side opened and she and the Ponngs were set down onto the deck. The Wisps turned back to the duct—

"Wait," Nicole said.

The creatures paused. Nicole touched one of them on the arm—*Come with us,* she thought the command to it.

Come where? the bemused-sounding answer came.

Through Q3, Nicole said. *Through the corridors and rooms in this part of the* Fyrantha.

I see no corridors and rooms.

Let me lead you. Shifting her touch to a solid grip on its arm, she led the way across the corridor.

The Wisp moved docilely at her side, looking straight ahead, not speaking into Nicole's mind. They walked across the long corridor that paralleled the heat-transfer duct and started into the cross-corridor.

Three steps in, the Wisp abruptly stopped. "No, keep moving," Nicole urged, tugging at its arm.

The creature didn't move. *There is nothing there,* it said.

"Sure there is," Nicole said. "There's a whole quarter of the *Fyrantha.* Here, watch me."

She let go and moved a few steps down the corridor. "See?" she said, turning back to look.

The Wisp hadn't moved. It was still facing her, but its head was slowly moving back and forth. "Can you hear me?" Nicole persisted. "I'm right here. Can you *see* me?"

The Wisp's head continued moving back and forth, as if trying to locate an elusive sound. But it clearly couldn't see her.

It was clearly also unwilling to keep going. With a sigh, Nicole retraced her steps and again touched the Wisp's arm. *Couldn't you see me?* she asked.

I cannot see what is not there, the Wisp replied, sounding confused.

I was there, Nicole insisted.

You were not, the Wisp said. *I could hear you. I could not see you.*

Nicole scowled. That couldn't possibly be the way the *Fyrantha* had been set up, with the Wisps permanently confined to their own quadrants. Clearly, there were parts of the ship that still needed to be fixed.

But until they figured out where that problem was—or, rather, until the *Fyrantha* got around to telling some Sibyl where the problem was—this was how it was going to be. *Fine,* she said. *You and the others wait here for us, all right?*

We will, the Wisp promised.

And you will obey orders these two give you, she added. She'd already given Jeff and Kahkitah control of the Q4 Wisps. She might as well add the Ponngs to that list. *If they come back here without me and ask you to take them across to Q4, you'll do so. Please?*

We understand.

Nicole let go of its arm and turned to the Ponngs. So the Wisps still couldn't see past the inner corridor, but at least they could hear her when she was out of their sight. That was something, anyway. "Okay," she said. "Let's find the stairs and head down."

Just find another Ghorf, Kahkitah had said. *Any of them will know how to get a message to me.* It had sounded so nice and simple.

It wasn't.

The *Fyrantha* had a total of ninety-six levels. The entire ship was around two miles long and half a mile wide, which meant Quadrant 3 was a full mile long and a quarter mile across. That made for a *lot* of territory to cover.

Nicole did her best. She had them stop at every level on their way down toward the arena, walk inward a few hallways from the inner corridor and forward and back another few, all the time listening for the sound of a work crew.

Nothing.

"Are you sure they're here?" Teika asked at their eighth stop. "This section of the ship appears to be deserted."

"Oh, they're here," Nicole said, wincing at the pain jolting through her legs with each step. After all the walking she'd done on the *Fyrantha*, her muscles ought to be used to it by now. "They're here somewhere. I don't know why I was thinking it would be easy to find them."

"We could split up," Moile offered. "That would let us cover more territory."

"Great," Nicole said. "How does whoever finds a Ghorf first tell the others?"

"Oh," Moile said. "Yes, that could be a problem."

"Besides, we need to guard the Protector from Wisps," Teika reminded him.

"The ones here should be safe, shouldn't they?" Moile said. "The Shipmasters can't send theirs from Q1."

"The *Protector* can't send them across lines," Teika countered. "We don't know for sure that the *Shipmasters* can't. I don't mean to imply insult to you, Protector," he added hastily.

"That's okay," Nicole assured him, scowling. That was a good point, actually. Fievj may not have sent any Wisps into Q4, but that didn't mean he couldn't bleed a few over from Q1 into Q3.

But she couldn't spend all day in here hunting for Wesowee, either. The Shipmasters and Koffren were probably already planning their next move, and she and Jeff had to get moving if they were going to get ahead of them.

Which left Nicole really only one option.

Jeff hadn't liked this idea. Nicole hadn't liked it, either. But with all the other lines of communication either getting blocked or taken over, this was the one thing she hadn't yet tried.

"Keep an eye out," she told the Ponngs as she pulled her inhaler from its vest pocket. Squeezing it tightly between her fingers, wondering fleetingly how much of her life this experiment was going to cost her, she put it between her lips and gave herself a jolt of the powder.

The two-one-seven circuit in bahri-*seven-six-nine is broken,* the ship's voice came in her mind. *The electrical locus in* bahri-*three-three-one-two has short circuits in the two-two junction and the nine-one-nine-one rectifier simplex . . .*

She waited while the voice finished its recitation of the *Fyrantha's* current ailments, an odd sense of loss tugging briefly at her. Life had been so much simpler when all she had to do was relay all of this to Carp and Levi and then sit back while they did the repairs.

But that life hadn't been real, any more than the supposed friendships and family in Trake's gang had been real. It was all just a paper illusion, something people decided to believe because it made them feel better.

This—what she was facing right now—*this* was reality. Like it or not.

The voice finished its recitation. *This is the Protector,* Nicole thought, focusing her mind, trying to make the words as clear as she could. It would have been easier if she could also speak the words aloud, but she didn't dare. The Caretaker part of the ship could be listening in, and she couldn't risk the Shipmasters eavesdropping. *I want you to send a message to the Sibyl with Wesowee and Kointos's gray team. Tell them I want them to meet me—*

She hesitated. The arena's number two door would be closest to where she and the Ponngs were right now, as well as the closest to the centerline heat-transfer duct if she needed to beat a hasty retreat back to Q4.

But it was also the farthest from the center of Q3 and the likely areas where the gray group would be working. The farther they had to travel to meet her, the more likely that Kointos would decide that a vague request for a meeting wasn't worth his trouble.

And as Moile had said, she ought to be reasonably safe in here. A quick escape hopefully wouldn't be necessary.

—at the number one door into the Q3 arena, she continued. *That's the door closest to the front and left-hand side of the ship— make sure they know that.*

She repeated the message once more, just to make sure. "Did you speak to it?" Moile asked.

Nicole nodded. "Yes."

"Did it hear you?"

"I don't know," Nicole said, looking at the inhaler in her hand. If she took another whiff, the ship might give her an answer, either to confirm it had gotten the message or to tell her it hadn't.

But then, it might not say anything at all. And either way, it would cost her.

Resolutely, she tucked the inhaler back into its pocket. She hated waiting, but right now there really wasn't much else she could do. "I guess we'll find out," she said. "Let's get down to the arena and see what happens."

They'd made it down to level 32, and Nicole was leading the way toward the arena door she'd specified when she first noticed the odd smell.

She slowed down, sniffing the air. It wasn't like anything she'd ever run across before on the *Fyrantha,* in any of the sections she'd visited. "Moile, Teika, do you smell that?" she asked, keeping her voice low.

"Yes," Moile said.

"It's been there since we left the stairway," Teika added. "I assumed it was another of the many scents aboard that are new to us."

"It's new to me, too," Nicole said, running the possibilities quickly through her mind. It didn't smell like any variation of the ship's list of lubricating, cooling, or transformer oils. It wasn't any of the foods she was familiar with, nor could she attach it to any of the beings she'd run into.

She felt her throat tighten. Foods or beings she'd run into . . . but the *Fyrantha*'s arenas were always playing host to newcomers. Could one of those exotic aromas have escaped from the arena they were walking past right now?

The problem was that all the arena doors she'd used had seemed pretty airtight. It wasn't until she'd opened them up that she'd ever gotten even a whiff of the plants and creatures inside.

The arena's number two door, the one they'd passed on their way from the stairway, had been properly sealed. If the smell was coming from the arena, it must mean that the number one door, the one they were heading toward, had been recently opened.

Or was open right now.

"New plan," she murmured, motioning the Ponngs to stop. "Back to the stairs, up four levels, then across and come back down on the far side." She turned around—

And stopped. Gliding silently toward them along the corridor were a pair of Wisps.

"Back up," Nicole bit out, waving her hands to both sides.

To her surprise, the Ponngs ignored her. Instead of backing up away from the Wisps, both of them stepped around in front of her, holding out their swords defiantly toward the Wisps.

"Go now, Protector," Moile said over his shoulder. "We'll hold them back while you escape."

Nicole hissed between her teeth. So basically they were offering the same tactic she'd used in the Q1 arena, except that in that case Bungie's men hadn't volunteered to be grabbed like Moile and Teika were. But other than that it should work: Wisps with their arms wrapped around Ponngs couldn't then also grab Nicole.

But in Q1 the Wisps—and the Shipmasters controlling them— had had their own plans for the humans and had no intention of hurting them. Here, the Ponngs had no such guarantee. If Nicole ran, the Shipmasters might order the Wisps to dump them into the duct just to be rid of them.

Or to teach Nicole a lesson.

Maybe that was why there were only two Wisps instead of three. Maybe they wanted Nicole to watch the Ponngs get killed to show her the cost of fighting against them.

Nicole squared her shoulders. Whatever the Shipmasters had in mind, there was no way in hell she was going to lose the Ponngs. Not without a fight. "Wisps, stop!" she snapped. "Stop, and move aside."

For a fraction of a second she thought they were going to obey. Both creatures slowed, their smooth movement faltering a little. But then the wavering stopped, and they resumed their forward motion. "Stop and move aside, please," she tried again.

Again, a flicker of hesitation. But they kept coming.

"Okay, we're getting out of here," Nicole said. "Moile, how well can you walk backward?"

"Very well," Moile said. "I'll keep watch on them."

"Good," Nicole said. "Teika, stay with him and make sure he doesn't fall or trip. They get too close, we'll give it up and go with a flat-out run. I'll watch ahead for traps." She turned around—

And once again jerked to a halt. Four beings had emerged from a cross-corridor a hundred yards ahead, somewhere near the arena door she and the Ponngs had been heading toward. They were tall, taller even than Kahkitah, but thin, and with the mixture of chest and hip bulges and thin waists she remembered seeing on a display of hornets back at school. Each of them had a sort of flat tablet in his hands, bigger than the cell-phone-sized notepads Nicole and the rest of the repair crews carried, with a strange set of grips on the sides. Behind them, just visible as he peeked cautiously around the corridor's corner, was an armored Shipmaster.

Hovering silently in the air in front of the aliens were four disks the size of dinner plates, spinning like helicopter blades.

An old saying flashed through Nicole's mind. Only in this case, it seemed she'd brought toy swords to a drone fight.

Four

"Are those attack flyers?" Moile asked from behind her, his voice tense.

"Yeah, I think so," Nicole said. At least the Ponngs didn't need to be brought up to speed on the things. "We call them *drones*."

Moile muttered something Nicole's translator couldn't handle. "We should have brought arrows," he said.

"We have few left, and weren't expecting full combat," Teika reminded him.

"They wouldn't have been much use against those, anyway," Nicole gritted out, trying to figure out what kind of weapons the drones might be carrying. She didn't see any guns or missiles. Were they designed to just ram into people and things?

A second later she got her answer. The drones shifted position, two going high and two going low, each one abruptly seeming to double in size as some kind of string or wire played out from their spinning edges. It reminded her of the weed-whackers she'd seen the landscaping people in the park using.

"Looks like wire or possibly blades," Teika confirmed. "They're designed for slashing attacks."

Killer drones in front of them, paralyzing Wisps coming up behind them. Nicole glanced over her shoulder, wondering how much closer the Wisps had come while she'd been focused on this latest threat. If the drones were just a diversion, the Wisps might be right on top of them by now.

She frowned, taking a second, longer look. Instead of continuing forward, the Wisps had stopped twenty yards behind her and were just standing there. Waiting for her to make a decision on who to attack first?

She muttered a curse. Of course they were. The Shipmasters were still trying to figure out how she —and humans in general— did in combat. This time, the test was probably to see if she would stand aside and throw the Ponngs at the attackers. Or maybe it was whether the Ponngs would willingly let themselves be sacrificed that way, or whether she would have to talk them into it.

Fine. Maybe she could throw them a curve. Turning back to the stick hornets and their drones, she filled her lungs. "Hey!" she shouted. "Weren't you warned about attacking or bothering people wearing jumpsuits?"

One of the aliens opened his mouth and spit out a quick series of singsong sounds, like the kind of talk she sometimes heard coming out of Chinese restaurants. A small wave of air wafted down the corridor along with the words.

At least now she knew where the odd smell was coming from.

"We were told to attack you," the translation came in Nicole's mind. "We were given new orders."

"By who? *Him?*" She pointed past them toward the lurking Shipmaster. "He doesn't make the rules here. The *Fyrantha*—the ship—makes the rules, and the rule is still to leave us alone."

The drones had been inching forward. Now they stopped, resuming their hovering. The stick hornet who'd talked to her took a step backward and began talking to the Shipmaster, his voice too soft for Nicole's translator to pick up. The other three aliens kept watch on Nicole and the Ponngs.

"What's your plan?" Moile murmured.

"She's bought us time," Teika told him.

"Yeah, but probably not much," Nicole warned, glancing around. Stick hornets in front of them, Wisps behind them.

And between the two groups, a single door.

Nicole smiled tightly. So that was it. The Shipmaster was hoping the two threats would drive them into that room for refuge. Once they were inside, he would probably just lock them in and call it a day.

And Jeff and Kahkitah could search for months without ever finding them.

Teika was obviously thinking along the same lines. "Perhaps they've outsmarted themselves," he suggested quietly. "There may be a second door on the room's other side through which we could escape. I've noted that some of the rooms in the hive have two entrances."

"Yeah, but not many of them," Nicole said. "We can't risk it."

"What do you wish us to do?" Moile asked. "Whatever you ask, we will do it."

Nicole eyed the stick hornets. The one was still talking to the Shipmaster, and the other three didn't seem inclined to do anything more until that conversation was over. The question was, what would they do in response if Nicole and the Ponngs made a run for it?

Only one way to find out. "We're going through the Wisps," she decided. "When I give the word, run as fast as you can: Moile along the left-hand wall, Teika along the right. If they reach for you, try to dodge your ways clear. You can maybe bat their hands away with the flat sides of your swords to keep them from grabbing you."

"Just the flat sides?" Moile asked. "You don't wish them injured?"

Nicole hesitated. If she called this one wrong, and the Ponngs got captured as a result, it could cost them their lives.

But somehow, she knew this was the right thing to do, just like she'd somehow known how to bargain with the Thii Maven. "I don't want them injured, yes," she said. "While you go up the sides, I'll go up the middle. If they let you get past them, just—I don't know. Tackle them from behind if you can, or keep going and get back to the Q4 Wisps if you have to. We'll just have to play it by ear."

"Understood," Teika said. "Tell us when to go."

The stick hornet finished his conversation and started to turn back around—"Go," Nicole ordered.

She spun around toward the Wisps and charged toward them as fast as she could. A second later she remembered that the Ponngs had to get there first and slowed down.

She needn't have bothered. Both of the shorter aliens had put on bursts of speed of their own, hugging the walls as they tore down the corridor. So far the Wisps hadn't moved, either outward to catch the Ponngs or inward to double-team Nicole.

What were they waiting for?

Unless those small hesitations she'd seen earlier meant they *weren't* under as much control as the Shipmasters liked?

One way to find out. "Wisps, stand still!" she shouted. "Just stand still. Please."

And to her mild surprise, they did just that. Both stood motionless, their eyes forward, their arms at their sides. The two Ponngs shot past—

A second later Nicole ducked as one of the drones shot over her head, its spinning blades sending a gust of wind through her hair. The disk angled up onto its side, skidded a few feet farther past her—she had no idea whether a drone could actually *skid,* but that was what it looked like—and as it stopped it flattened out again, ready for another try.

Nicole tensed, slowing a little as she watched the drone, wondering if dodging it would send her right into the Wisps' arms. Maybe *that* was the Shipmaster's real plan.

With her full attention focused on the drone she didn't even see Teika doubling back. Not until he slipped between the Wisps and stabbed his sword upward through the drone.

The drone didn't disintegrate completely. But it came pretty damn close. The whole edge seemed to explode outward, sending small pieces of itself spinning across the corridor's walls, ceiling, and floor. One piece sliced past her cheek, scratching a brief flash of pain across the skin, but most of the ones that hit her bounced off her jumpsuit with less jolt than a snowball. As the drone's outer rim scattered itself across the corridor, the central core dropped to the floor like a rock, hitting and spinning around madly like a top that had fallen over.

It was still moving when Teika darted a hand into the machinery, grabbed the core by a piece of bent tubing, and ducked back again. "Come on!" Moile called to Nicole, beckoning urgently from the wall just past the Wisps.

Nicole didn't need any encouragement. She didn't know what exactly the drones would do if one of them hit her, and she wasn't anxious to find out. She dodged between the still-motionless Wisps—

"Wisps! Open your wings," she called over her shoulder. "Please."

She glanced over her shoulder as the Ponngs joined her in her run. The butterfly wings stretched out, filling much of the corridor and blocking the stick hornets' sight. And, hopefully, their drones.

Once again, the Wisps had obeyed her. So had they ever been under Shipmaster control at all?

She scowled. The long corridor at the inner edge of Q3 was still pretty far away, and her leg muscles were already complaining at her. But there was another cross-corridor about fifty yards ahead that they should be able to duck around. Once around the corner, they should be clear of the Shipmaster and stick hornets, especially if the two Wisps continued their blocking action.

But if Nicole left now, she might never see these particular Wisps again. And suddenly she really, really wanted to talk to them.

It was dangerous. It was probably also stupid. But she needed information, and this was the only way she could think of to get it. "Wisps!" she called behind her. "Come with me. Hurry."

"What are you doing?" Teika demanded, half turning to stare at her as he ran.

"I want to talk to them," Nicole said, starting to pant with the exertion.

"What if they're obeying the Shipmasters?"

"They aren't," Nicole said. "Turn right here."

She glanced back as she and Teika rounded the corner. Moile was hanging back, trotting along backward, his attention on the Wisps. With the butterfly wings still extended the stick hornets weren't visible, and Nicole wondered if they were even now charging toward them.

And then she was around the corner and still running. The adrenaline that had fueled the last few minutes was wearing off, and the lead in her legs was starting to be replaced by jolts of pain. "Go back," she panted to Teika. "Make sure Moile is all right."

"He is," Teika assured her. "There haven't been any screams of warning or distress."

"Doesn't mean the Shipmaster isn't about to grab him," Nicole countered. "Or if those drones get to him he might not have time to shout."

"The Dronemasters won't follow," Teika said. "With the Wisps no longer under firm control, the Shipmaster dare not risk losing his servants and weapons to our hands."

Nicole lowered her eyes to the drone piece still clutched in his hand. "*If* we can figure out how to use it."

"This?" Teika hefted the twisted chunk of metal and plastic. "It's a simple gyroscopically stabilized flying device with counter-rotating blades. Not difficult to understand."

Nicole felt her mouth drop open. "It's—*what?*"

"Do I surprise you?" Teika asked quietly. "Just because we were given swords and bows to use, Protector, don't assume that the Ponngs are primitives."

"I guess not," Nicole said, feeling a rush of heat to her face that had nothing to do with her physical exertions. "Sorry."

"That's all right." Teika looked over his shoulder. "They should appear soon."

"Yeah," Nicole said, frowning as a sudden thought struck her. If these were like the drones other gangs sometimes used . . . "Can you tell if it can see us? Or is it just a weapon?"

"Attack flyers would be largely useless if they couldn't also see." Teika slowed to a jog, holding the mechanism up to his eyes. He reached three slender fingers into a half-circle pit at one edge, there was a soft snap—

"It can no longer see," he declared. He peered closely at the little disk he'd pulled from the drone, then tossed it to the side of the corridor. He looked over his shoulder again—"Here they come."

Nicole looked back. The two Wisps had appeared around the corner, gliding along the floor toward her and Teika, their wings still extended and blocking Nicole's view behind them. Between her and them—

She tensed. Between her and them should have been Moile. But he was nowhere in sight. "What happened to Moile?" she asked, stopping. If the Shipmaster had taken him, there was no way she and Teika could rescue him alone.

"Nothing, I hope," Teika said. "He stopped at the corner to observe the Shipmaster and Dronemasters and confirm they weren't following us."

"I didn't hear him say he was going to do that."

"He didn't speak with his voice," Teika said. "But I was watching, and he used hand signals to alert me before letting the Wisps pass him by."

Nicole frowned. "I didn't know you had hand signals."

"Vjoran taught his system to us in the arena," Teika said. "Before he was my master, he was a soldier."

"You're just full of surprises, aren't you?" Nicole said, feeling a fresh wave of cautious hope. She'd always assumed that the Shipmasters mostly grabbed their test subjects at random. Certainly the Micawnwi she'd first met in Q4 seemed to have all been civilians.

Had Fievj narrowed his search when he trolled for Ponngs? Or had it been pure luck that he'd grabbed a trained soldier? Either way, the fact that Teika and Moile had had at least a little training meant she and Jeff had more than just themselves and the Ghorfs to count on.

There was a shadow of movement behind the Wisps, and to Nicole's relief Moile slipped around their outstretched wings. He nodded to her and Teika, and his hand made a quick movement.

"They're not following," Teika translated.

"Good," Nicole said, a little of the tension leaving her. Though she wouldn't put it past the Shipmasters to wait until Moile disappeared before charging after them. "Wisps, fold your wings," she called. "Please."

Again, there was a moment of hesitation. Then the wings collapsed against their backs, unblocking the view behind them. The cross-corridor was indeed empty.

"Come on," she told Teika, and started toward them. Might as well meet the Wisps and Moile halfway. "I want to talk to the Wisps."

"About what?" Teika asked as he fell into step beside her.

"The Shipmasters," Nicole said. "The ship. Pretty much everything they can tell me."

"That might be dangerous."

"So is not knowing everything that's going on," Nicole countered. "Don't worry, they won't grab me."

"Very well," Teika said, clearly reluctant. "But I suggest you speak quickly. More enemies may be on the way."

Nicole winced. "Yeah."

"Are we going back?" Moile asked as they reached him and continued past.

"We're having a talk," Nicole said, stopping and holding out her hand toward the Wisps. "Stop."

They took two more steps, plus one hesitation, then stopped. Nicole walked around the one on the left, making sure to stay well out of easy reach, and stepped up behind it. Making sure she was ready to back away if either of them made any sudden moves, she rested her palm against one of the silver-laced shoulders.

In Q4 the Wisps typically greeted her and asked what she wanted. Not this pair. *Do you know who I am?* she thought at it.

You are the Fyrantha's *Protector.*

So at least it knew that much. *That's right. Tell me what the Shipmasters told you to do.*

There was a short pause.

Wisp? Tell me what the Shipmasters told you to do.

We were to secure you, the Wisp said hesitantly. *We were to hold you until Nevvis came and took you to himself.*

Nicole pursed her lips. So Nevvis himself was in charge of hunting her down now? According to the Koffren, he was the

one who dealt with the buyers. If the Shipmasters followed the
same sort of pattern as Trake's gang, that would make Nevvis
the boss.

Apparently, Nicole had become more important since the days
when Fievj had been sent to deal with her and the rest of the
work crews. *So you followed us when we reached this level and
headed toward the arena,* Nicole said. *But you didn't grab me. Why
not?*

You are the Protector. You ordered us to stop.

You didn't obey that order right away, Nicole reminded it. *You
kept coming.*

*Our orders were . . . conflicted. Incompatible. We could not obey
both.*

So you decided to obey your Protector instead of Nevvis?

Yes. But our orders are still conflicted.

So the Shipmasters were still trying to control the Wisps, but it
wasn't working. *How did you know where to find us?*

You sent a message. It was heard.

Did the Caretaker hear it and tell the Shipmasters?

*Not the Caretaker. The Oracle. The part of the ship that speaks
for the Shipmasters.*

I thought it spoke to the Sibyls and fighters, Nicole said.

It's the part that speaks for the Shipmasters, the Wisp repeated.
Just as the Caretaker speaks for the Fyrantha *itself.*

Who speaks to the Sibyls? Nicole asked.

The Oracle.

*So the Shipmasters are the ones who are telling us how to fix the
ship?*

No. That is the Oracle.

Nicole made a face. Clearly, there was something here she
wasn't getting.

Though with the *Fyrantha* still fragmented, maybe she wasn't the only one who was confused about how things worked. *Are you talking to the Shipmasters now?*

No.

Can you talk to them?

The Wisp hesitated. *Yes.*

All right. Nicole paused, collecting her thoughts. At the moment all she had was the vaguest hint of a plan, and if she couldn't get it to work then provoking the Shipmasters probably would be a bad idea. But this might be her only way to get their attention without having to get within shouting distance of them. It was worth the risk to see if this was a channel they could use somewhere down the line. *You tell them that they can't win. They can't win because I understand them. I understand them, I understand the Wisps, I understand the Koffren. In fact, I understand the whole damn Fyrantha. I know how everything works, and I know how to make it all work against them. You got that?*

Yes, the Wisp said.

Good. One more thing. I understand them. They don't understand me. Not a single bit. They don't, and they never will. Can you make sure they get that message?

Yes.

Good. Then you two can go back to your duties.

She started to pull her hand away, then pressed it again against the Wisp's shoulder. *One more thing. When the Oracle was finished betraying the* Fyrantha's *Protector, did it send my message to the gray group's Sibyl?*

Yes.

Good. Go back to your duties now.

For a moment the two Wisps continued to stand motionless. Then, they turned and headed back the way they'd come.

"Did you get the information you wanted?" Teika asked.

"Some of it," Nicole said. "We had a nice conversation."

"What did you say to them?" Moile asked.

"I told them they can't win."

"Do you think they believed you?" Moile asked.

"If not, we'll just have to prove it to them." Nicole took a deep breath. "Come on."

"Where are we going?" Teika said.

"Back to the arena door," Nicole told him. "Hopefully, by a safer route."

"We're going back to the arena?" Moile said. "Why?"

"Because Wesowee is probably waiting by now," Nicole said. "And I'd rather not make him mad."

By the time they went down the four levels Nicole wanted, walked all the way past the arena, then came back up near the door, Wesowee was indeed waiting.

Luckily, he didn't seem to be mad.

"Nicole!" he called, his birdsong trilling as he trotted down the corridor toward her and the Ponngs with open arms. "I'm so pleased to see you."

"I take it you got my message?" Nicole asked.

"Yes indeed," the Ghorf said, coming to a halt, his neck gills fluttering. "Though at first I thought it wasn't from you at all. I thought our Sibyl was playing a trick on me. Then I thought the ship was playing a trick. Then I thought you must have changed your mind. Then I thought you'd been captured. Then I thought *you* might be playing a trick." He huffed out a breath. "I'm so relieved I was wrong on all of them."

It was a wonderful performance, Nicole decided: the same strong, cheerful, slow-witted role that Kahkitah had pulled off so successfully the whole time the Ghorfs had been aboard the

Fyrantha. Briefly, she wondered what the Ponngs would say when they learned the truth. "I'm sorry I worried you," she said.

"I'm just pleased you're unhurt," Wesowee said. "How may I help you?"

"Well, I started out wanting to talk to Kóintos and the rest of your work team," Nicole said. "There's something we need to do, and the more people on our side, the better."

"Some kind of major work project?"

"You could say that, yes," Nicole said evasively. She didn't know how much Wesowee knew—or for that matter, how much Kahkitah had told the Ponngs—and it would probably be better to keep the details quiet. "But first, there's something else I need your help with. We need to go into the arena, and we might need your muscle."

"Into the arena?" Wesowee echoed. "What for?" He looked at the Ponngs. "Do they need to be rescued again?"

"We didn't *need* to be rescued at all," Moile said stiffly.

"Yes, we did," Teika said. "Now, we return the debt as the Protector's guardians."

"Indeed," Wesowee said, looking pointedly at Moile's toy sword. "I'm certain Nicole feels much safer."

"Anyway, we're not rescuing anyone today," Nicole said. "There's a new batch of fighters in there, and they have these." She pointed to the wrecked drone in Teika's hand.

"It looks damaged," Wesowee said, leaning over for a closer look. "Do you wish to return it to them?"

"No," Nicole said, taking the drone from Teika. It was heavier than she'd expected. "I want to steal another one."

Five

There were a couple of back doors into each of the arenas, entrances that bypassed the main hatches and took the visitor into the side away from the living areas. But getting to one of them would require extra time and, worse, take them dangerously close to the observation balcony where the Shipmasters could watch the fighting. The main hatch they were now standing beside would be faster and easier.

Unfortunately, it would cost Nicole another puff on her inhaler to get the access code. But it was becoming painfully clear that she wasn't likely to die of old age, anyway.

In fact, odds were that she wasn't even going to last long enough for the inhaler to kill her.

"Caretaker, I need to get into the Q3 arena," she called out into the empty corridor. "Have the *Fyrantha* ready to give me the code when I use the inhaler. Please."

She gave it a few seconds, then put the inhaler into her mouth and sent a blast into her lungs.

Enter the arena with the code seven nine two zero nine four seven.

"Got it," she said, putting the inhaler away. She stepped to the door and punched the code into the keypad.

The lock snicked open. Wesowee was ready, his big hands already gripping the handle, and as Nicole stepped back out of the way he swung the door open. Taking a deep breath, motioning to the Ponngs to stay close, she headed inside.

The door on this side of the arena opened up near one of the two hives. Nicole's first fear was that the Shipmaster and stick hornets would be right in front of her, maybe standing around talking about what had just happened in the corridor. To her relief, none of them were anywhere in sight. With the others beside her, she headed in.

She looked closely at the hive entrance as they headed for the tall grass that filled most of the arena, wondering if the Shipmaster might be lurking in there. But again, no one was visible.

She'd taken three more steps and was starting to breathe easier when the grass ahead parted and a pair of wolves stalked out and headed toward them.

Nicole jerked to a halt, her heart seizing up. What the *hell*—?

She was still staring when the wolves lurched up onto their hind paws and continued toward them on two feet, their forelegs now hanging very much like normal human arms at their sides.

"Those are new," Wesowee murmured from beside her.

"Or really old," Nicole murmured back. Now that the creatures were walking upright, she could see that they looked more like really hairy men than wolves. Hairy, hunched-over men with long snouts, rounded shoulders, and short-fingered hands. "We used to have stories about things called *werewolves*."

The two wolfmen stopped, and one said something that had a lot of pops and crackles in it. "Who are you?" the translation came through. "What are you doing with our flyer?"

"What, this?" Nicole asked, hefting the drone a couple of inches. "First off, it was one of the other guys' flyers, not yours. Second, it's not really a flyer anymore. I mean, it doesn't fly."

"The flight doesn't matter," the other wolfman said. "It's still food for our bellies. You will hand it over."

They started forward.

"Explain," Moile said, stepping in front of Nicole and lifting his sword to point at the wolfmen.

They ignored him and kept coming.

Beside Nicole, Wesowee gave a rumbling birdsong warning. "No—stay back," Nicole ordered him quietly. The Shipmasters would be monitoring the arena action, and she didn't want them spotting an aggressive or even a protective Ghorf. "Let's see how the Ponngs handle it."

The wolfmen were still coming.

"He asked you to explain," Teika said, stepping to Moile's side and also raising his sword.

"It's a simple question," Nicole added. "A simple answer, and you can have the flyer."

"We will have it regardless," the first wolfman said.

"*When* we've had our answer," Nicole said firmly. "Really, are you that eager to lose some blood? Especially when it's going to drain out onto all that fur? It must look really gross when it mats up."

The wolfmen stopped. "Are you trying to be funny?" the first demanded.

"What does appearance matter when one is starving?" the second added.

"Not much," Nicole agreed. "And I wasn't trying to be funny. I was trying to get an answer. How are these flyers connected with your food?"

The first wolfman gave a brief scrunch of his snout. "We've been ordered to fight the Skinless. We have been—"

"The Skinless?" Nicole interrupted. "You mean those stick hornet things?"

"*Stick hornet?*" the wolfman echoed, scrunching his snout again.

"The ones we got the flyer from," Nicole said. "That's what we call them."

"Stick hornet," the wolfman said again as if trying out the term. "No. The Skinless."

"Whatever," Nicole said. "So how do you fight?"

"We are twenty," the wolfman said. "The Skinless, too, are twenty. Each group has fifteen flyers."

"Fifteen of us operate the flyers," the second wolfman said. "We search the grasslands for the Skinless operators. When we find one, we use the flyer's flail-tips to briefly paralyze him."

"So the spinning weed-whacker edges are drugged?"

"I don't know what a weed-whacker is," the first wolfman said. "But yes, the edges contain a suppression poison."

Nicole shivered. So that was why the Shipmasters had recruited the stick hornets and their drones. A single touch, and the Shipmaster could have just strolled over and picked her up.

"Those of us who aren't operating flyers then go to him and take his controller," the first wolfman said. "We use it to bring his flyer to us, then bring it to our hive. For each drone we have at the end of the combat period, we receive one ration of food."

Nicole nodded. So each side needed to keep all its own drones intact plus capture five of the other side's, or someone was going to go hungry. That sounded like a Shipmaster scheme, all right. "Don't they try to protect their operators?"

"There are fifteen operators and only five to guard them," the wolfman reminded her.

"And those same five also have to retrieve the enemy operators' controllers," Teika added. "Too many tasks for them to accomplish them all."

"I suppose." Nicole shifted her drone to a two-handed grip and held it up in front of the wolfmen. "So how much of the drone do you need to get food? And do you also need the controller?"

"That much will be sufficient," the first wolfman said. "The Masters understand that damage can happen."

"And the controller?"

"Unnecessary and unneeded. In the morning fifteen flyers and fifteen controllers will await us."

"Great," Nicole said. "Here's the deal. You can have this one— *if*"—she lifted a finger—"*if* you help us steal an intact one and its controller."

"Why would we help you do that?" the second wolfman countered. "We would be helping you steal food from our companions' bellies."

"You wouldn't be any worse off than you are now," Moile said.

"How would you steal it?" the first wolfman asked.

"These are Moile and Teika," Nicole said, gesturing to the Ponngs. "I'm the Sibyl, by the way. And you two are . . . ?"

"Our names are unimportant," the second wolfman said.

"And you two are . . . ?" Nicole repeated pointedly.

"Our names are—"

"I am Worwol," the first wolfman said. "He is Rywoo."

"Thank you," Nicole said. "As to Moile and Teika, their people once fought in this same arena. They may know things about it that you don't."

"Such as?" Rywoo asked, not sounding particularly impressed.

"Moile?" Nicole invited.

"Have you investigated the various types of grasses in the arena?" Moile asked.

Rywoo made a sound that sounded a lot like a dog sneeze. "Grass is grass," he said contemptuously. "Only the bushes matter."

"The bushes?" Nicole asked, frowning.

"The bushes are the favored hiding places for Skinless flyer operators," Worwol told her. "They lie beneath them so that our own flyers cannot see them from above."

"And I suppose you use the bushes on your side the same way?" Nicole asked.

"We do," Worwol said. "Our strategy is to—"

"Are you mad?" Rywoo cut him off, slashing a hand past the other wolfman's snout. "How do we know they're not spies for the Skinless?"

"Let me guess," Nicole said. "Your strategy is to sneak around their side trying to find them."

"Or else hoping your appearance will drive them from hiding," Teika said. "We can help."

"How?" Worwol asked.

"Some of the grasses don't wave very much when passage is made through them," Teika said.

"Particularly when passage is made near the roots," Moile added. "The grasses flare out from a central core, rather like our own species of—"

"Stick to the point, Moile," Nicole murmured.

"My apologies, Protector," Moile said, ducking his head. "The point is that the operator won't hear us coming, and there won't be any disturbance in the tops of the grasses to warn him or the other flyer operators."

"How do we do this?" Worwol asked.

"*You* don't," Teika said firmly. "You're too large. We're the only ones who can do it."

Rywoo gave another dog sneeze. "And once you find him, you'll defeat him?"

"There *are* two of us," Moile said, a little stiffly.

"Who together barely make up a single Skinless," Rywoo shot back. "What if the operator has a guard? Will you defeat both?"

"Who says they have to defeat anyone?" Nicole asked.

"Weren't you paying attention?" Rywoo gritted out. "We need the flyer to earn food."

"Yes, I got that," Nicole said. "Why can't they just grab the controller and run?"

"Because—" Rywoo broke off. For a long moment he and Worwol looked at each other. "Because they would be caught," Rywoo continued at last a little hesitantly. "Wouldn't they?"

"Moile?" Nicole again prompted.

"We would split up," the Ponng said. "The Skinless would have no idea which of us had the controller."

"Furthermore, once we were out of the immediate area we would again go to the ground and travel unseen through the grasses," Teika added.

"What of the river dividing our territories?" Rywoo asked.

Nicole cocked an eyebrow. So the Shipmasters had left the river the way it was after she'd flooded the once-empty channel? Interesting. She'd expected them to drain it again, out of spite if nothing else.

"One of us will swim it while the other remains in hiding," Moile said. "If there's no reaction or attack from the Skinless, the one will reach the shore and the other will throw the controller to him. After that, retrieving the flyer will be easy."

"Why not reach the river and throw it across to one of us?" Worwol suggested.

"And meanwhile, you can let us have that," Rywoo added, holding out a hand and wiggling his fingers at the broken drone as he took half a step forward.

Nicole felt her forehead crease. There'd been something odd in the wolfman's voice just then. Actually, there's been something odd in *both* their voices.

"Yeah, let's hold on a second," she said quickly, taking a step backward. Rywoo started to take another step, stopped as the Ponngs twitched their swords warningly.

"Why do we wait?" Worwol growled. "You take food from our bellies."

"I said hold on," Nicole said. Was this just paranoia? The

uneasiness of someone who'd too often seen the chaos and betrayal that tended to follow a deal where either the sellers or the buyers seemed too easily convinced?

Or was this the *Fyrantha*, doing its brain nudging thing again?

She looked around, trying to see the scene with fresh eyes. Standing near their hive and the exit door, discussing how to get the wolfmen more food. Nowhere near the quiet war going on elsewhere in the arena. Worwol and Rywoo didn't seem to be drone operators, which meant they must be two of the five guards and hunters. So why were they here instead of guarding or hunting?

Were they working with the Shipmasters? Had they been warned Nicole was coming and ordered to retrieve the broken drone the Ponngs had snatched? But then where were the Shipmasters, and why hadn't they already attacked?

And then, she saw it, and all the troublesome pieces fell together. "So what are the Masters offering you to grab your people's flyers and hand them over to the Skinless?" she asked.

"*What?*" Moile asked, half turning to frown at her.

And in that instant of inattention, the wolfmen struck.

Worwol hurled himself at Moile, paws outstretched toward the Ponng's throat. At the same time, Rywoo threw his own long arms up over his own head, probably in hopes of drawing Teika's sword up out of guard position and allowing for a strike at his torso.

But they hadn't reckoned with Nicole.

Rywoo had finished his diversion and was starting to drop his arms for a jab at Teika's head when Nicole hurled the damaged drone with all her strength into his stomach. The impact jerked him to a halt, half folding him over. Worwol's paws were past Moile's sword and nearly to his throat when Teika's sword point jabbed hard into his side.

The wolfman's arms jerked away from Moile and grabbed at his wounded side. He turned snarling jaws toward Teika, just in time to catch the flat of Moile's sword across his face. Even as the two wolfmen staggered away from the attack, the two Ponngs leaped to counterattack, pressing their sword tips against the wolfmen's throats and forcing them to hastily back up.

"How did you know?" Moile asked, his voice cold.

"They were in the wrong place at the wrong time," Nicole said, suddenly weary of all this. "They'd been tipped off that we were coming. But the Shipmasters aren't here, so they didn't get here ahead of us, so they must have had some other way of communicating with them."

"That's not true," Worwol insisted. "We were merely returning to our hive and happened to find you here."

"Really?" Nicole asked, raising her eyebrows. "Why?"

"Ah . . ." Worwol looked at Rywoo as if for help.

"It's not that hard," Nicole said. "Either you came here because the Shipmasters ordered you to, or else you were bringing in a trophy to add to your flyer collection. Which was it?"

Again, Worwol and Rywoo looked at each other.

"We have a flyer," Rywoo said.

"We left it in the grass when we heard you," Worwol added.

"Why?" Nicole asked. "No, don't bother. You left it behind because you *weren't* delivering it to the hive. You were delivering it to the Shipmasters, probably putting it in the corridor outside the door."

"Why would they do that?" Moile asked.

"Because they're traitors," Nicole said bluntly. "They're sneaking up on their own operators, stunning them, and stealing their flyers."

Worwol twitched back as Moile pressed his sword tip a little harder into the wolfman's throat. "Is this true?" the Ponng asked.

"It's a lie," Worwol protested. "The human is trying to sow distrust and bitterness among us." He twitched again, harder this time, as Moile again pressed his sword tip into the wolfman's throat.

"Really," Moile said coldly. "And how did you know her kind is called *human*?"

Nicole had barely met this species, and had no idea of their range of expressions. Just the same, she was pretty sure the hooded eyes and clenched teeth indicated chagrin at his slip.

Not that it mattered. Nicole already had all the proof she needed.

"It's all right, Moile," she said. "It's their own people they're betraying, not us. Anyway, I should have seen this coming. The Shipmasters have already played around with different species fighting each other. Sooner or later they would want to see if they could talk or bribe someone into turning on their own side."

She gestured to the wolfmen. "So what did they promise? That you'd each get a ration for every flyer you delivered to the Skinless?"

For a moment neither wolfman answered. Then, Worwol's jaws separated a couple of centimeters. "Two rations," he said. "Two rations each, and safety from our people if they learned of the deal."

"Traitors," Teika muttered.

"Realists," Worwol countered. "Why should one starve because one's leaders are fools?"

"Maybe *you* should have been the leader," Nicole said.

"I should have," Worwol agreed. "I *would* have. But Owrogor insisted." He bared his teeth again. "Let them starve."

"They certainly made it easy for you," Nicole said. "Once your drones were all over the Skinless side of the arena there was no way for any of your side to see what you were doing. The Shipmasters probably gave you some of the flyer drug, and you just took it to the nearest operator, stunned him, and took his controller and the flyer."

"Easy, and profitable," Moile murmured.

"Unless they got caught," Nicole agreed. "But with everyone working more or less on their own, and with all the grass to hide in, there wasn't much chance of that unless they got sloppy." She smiled tightly. "Or unless they switched to a smarter leader."

Worwol bared his teeth again, but remained silent.

"What do we do with them?" Moile asked.

"I'd love to turn them over to their own people," Nicole said. "But we really don't have the time. So we say good-bye, and send them on their way." She raised her eyebrows questioningly. "Or you stab them and let them bleed out. Their choice."

"Point taken," Worwol said with a touch of humor as he gingerly touched his injured side.

"May we have the flyer?" Rywoo asked, pointing to the one Nicole had thrown at him.

Nicole stared at him. "You're kidding, right? No, you may not have it. And you can't keep the one you were bringing the Shipmasters, either. Just go, both of you. If we see you again, we *will* kill you."

"You may try," Worwol said. "You may not succeed."

"Oh, we will," Nicole said. "Trust me. Now go."

Without another word, the wolfmen backed up. They paused at the edge of the field, then turned and disappeared into the grass.

"Moile, Teika—go find that drone," Nicole ordered. "And watch yourselves—they might try to argue the point."

"They won't succeed," Moile promised grimly. "Come, Teika."

They, too, disappeared into the grass.

"Interesting," Wesowee said quietly, coming up from behind Nicole. "How did you know?"

"The river," Nicole said, walking over to the broken drone she'd thrown at Rywoo and picking it up. "Like I said, the only two reasons for them to be here at this time of day was an order by the Shipmasters or a drone delivery. Either way, their own actions convicted them."

"But if they had a stick hornet drone—ah." Wesowee nodded. "One or both of them would be wet from swimming across the river."

"Exactly," Nicole said. "That, and the fact they were trying to hide the drone they'd brought, made it suspicious. I just had to put the pieces together."

There was a rustling in the grass, and the Ponngs emerged, Moile carrying both swords, Teika carrying an intact flyer with a phone-sized tablet balanced on top of it.

"We found it, Protector," Teika said. "Exactly as you said."

"You can see the markings are different than those on that one," Moile said.

"For the different sides," Nicole said, peering at the drone in her hands. The damage had partially obliterated the markings, but even so she could clearly see what Moile was talking about. "Another good reason for them to hide it until they figured out who we were and whose side we were on."

"Whose side *are* we on?" Wesowee asked, smoothly switching back to his big dumb Ghorf mode.

"Ours," Nicole said. "The *Fyrantha*'s."

"Ah," Wesowee said. "So they betrayed their own people? That doesn't sound like something true soldiers would do."

"It's not," Moile said grimly. "But it's something the Shipmasters would be more than willing to exploit."

Wesowee pondered. "Then the Shipmasters are not true soldiers, either," he concluded.

"No, they're not," Nicole agreed.

"What now, Protector?" Teika asked. "We have the drone you wanted. What do we do next?"

Nicole peered up at the sky. Like a real sky, on a real planet, with a sun, clouds, and everything. Also up there was the Ship-masters' observation balcony.

Had the Shipmasters watched the little drama that had just played out down here? If so, they might already be on their way, possibly with their tame Koffren in tow.

But if for some reason they *hadn't* seen it . . .

"We have one drone, yes," she said. "But as long as we're here—and as long as you and Moile have figured out a system—we might as well go ahead and get another one."

"Are you certain?" Wesowee asked, sounding more confused than his dumb Ghorf role probably needed. "It would put even more pressure on everyone's food supplies."

"I know, and I don't like that part," Nicole admitted. "But there may be something else we can do about that. Anyway, I think it's worth trying. If you're willing, that is."

"We follow the Protector," Moile said firmly. "You may wait in the corridor if you wish."

Wesowee squared his lumpy shoulders. "I will also follow the Protector," he said. "Do we stay here while the Ponngs search out a controller?"

"We've already got the wolfman version," Nicole said, hoping fervently she knew what she was doing. "I was thinking we'd head out the door, circle around to the stick hornet side, and grab one of theirs."

"As you wish," Wesowee said. "Lead us, Protector. We will follow."

six

Nicole had been impressed by the plan the Ponngs had described for the wolfmen.

She was even more impressed when it worked.

Not perfectly, of course. Even Trake's plans had seldom worked perfectly, and Trake was as clever and street-smart as anyone.

In this case, the problem came when the stick hornet drone operator turned out to have a guard. That was followed by a lot more flailing than Nicole had expected as the two Ponngs tried to keep them from alerting the rest of the group.

Fortunately, Nicole had brought the captured wolfman drone along, and was able to get the paralyzing cords far enough out of their sheaths to stun both stick hornets. In the end there was no alarm, and no injuries on either side.

On the plus side, the plan got an unexpected bonus when Wesowee suddenly declared he wanted a quick swim in the river. The presence of a big, lumpy alien in the middle of their war zone brought fighters from both sides of the river to stare, which helped divert their attention from the quiet fight.

Twenty minutes after the Ponngs first led the way into the grass the little group was back at their exit door with the controller. A little experimentation, and they soon had the associated drone flying to them. Three minutes after that, Wesowee having completed his swim and joined them, they were back in the corridor, the Ponngs each with a drone tucked under an arm.

"And now?" Teika asked.

Nicole looked around. The biggest danger had been the chance that the Shipmasters would be waiting for them when they emerged from the arena. But there was no one in sight: no Shipmasters, no Wisps, no Koffren.

Did that mean Nicole had read them correctly and that her vague, hastily thrown-together plan was working? Or were they simply leery of tackling Nicole now that she had a pair of drone weapons? If so, they might be delaying while they gathered a bigger force to take them out.

Or they could be simply playing along, waiting for her to make a mistake that would play right into their hands.

Unfortunately, the only way to find out was to keep going.

"Wesowee was right earlier," she said. "Taking the drones means we're taking food away from both sides. I don't like that any better than he does. Let's see if we can do something about that."

"I have food bars," Wesowee offered eagerly.

"They probably can't eat them," Nicole said. "But there may be another way. Back in the Q4 arena Jeff and I found a place where the Shipmasters had cut into one of the food dispensers from the back so they could more easily control how much came out. They must have something like that here."

"When we fought here, the food conduits fed into the grassland," Moile reminded her.

"Right, but there's clearly another system that goes directly to the hive, since that's where they collect the drones, count them, and dump the right amount into each side's bin," Nicole said. "If we can find where they're tapped in and mess with it, we might be able to give both sides enough food that they won't need to fight."

"Just because they don't *need* to fight doesn't mean they won't," Teika muttered.

"I know," Nicole agreed reluctantly. "But all we can do is offer them the choice."

"That's very sad," Wesowee said, his tone matching his words. "Fighting is terrible."

"Yes, it is," Nicole said. "So here's what we're going to do. Wesowee and I will head around the rear corridor and try to find where they've tapped into the food conduit. But first, Moile, we'll find you and Teika an empty room where you can practice using the drones. Learn how they work, how to trigger the weapon, how to maneuver. That sort of thing."

"Shouldn't we stay together?" Moile asked. "Surely the Shipmasters are even now preparing a new attack."

"We'll be okay," Nicole assured him. "You won't be far away, and I'll shout if we need you. But I don't want you practicing out here in the open where someone might see you. It's possible the Shipmasters haven't figured out we have working drones, and if they haven't I want it to be a surprise."

"Very well," Moile said. He didn't sound convinced, but as usual he was willing to accept Nicole's orders. "Let's go, then."

"Yes," Teika agreed grimly. "Before the Shipmasters deliver a surprise of their own."

The corridor running along the rear of the arena was long and slightly curved. On the arena side, where much of the equipment for the air, food, and water systems was located, there were only a few doors. The other side had a few more, irregularly spaced along the wall. It was a pattern Nicole had seen a lot of on the *Fyrantha*, and on her first try found exactly the sort of room she was looking for.

"Is this another hive?" Wesowee asked, looking around at the orderly rows of cots laid out on one side of the large room and the low storage bins lining the other side.

"Something like that," Nicole said. "I think it's called a *barracks*. It's a place where a lot of people can sleep together."

"It's not very private," Wesowee said doubtfully.

"It's not meant to be," Nicole said. "Okay, this looks good. You can probably start by flying the drones around, figure out what all the controls do—"

"We understand how to approach this task," Moile said.

"Right," Nicole said. "Sorry. We'll come back and get you when we're finished fixing the food supplies."

"But also listen for Nicole to shout," Wesowee added. "If the Shipmasters find us, we'll need your assistance."

"We'll be ready," Teika said. He laid his drone on the nearest bed, peered at the controller, and touched a green spot. The drone lifted a few inches—

"You can go," Moile said. "Unless you feel we need you to watch over us."

"That doesn't sound very polite," Wesowee said, a little uncertainly.

"No, he's right," Nicole said, wincing a little. She'd always hated it when Trake had someone sit on her when she was learning something new, whether it was how to take a gun apart or even just how to pick a good lookout post. Hated and resented it, and she wasn't surprised that the Ponngs felt the same way. "Sorry. We'll be back in a few minutes."

A moment later they were back in the still-deserted corridor. "Adjusting the food supply may take some time," Wesowee warned as Nicole steered them toward one of the doors on the far side. "I also understood that a special code may be required as to the proper mixture."

"I know, and we might have to pass on that part," Nicole said. "The main reason I wanted to get away from the Ponngs is that I want you to send a message to Kahkitah. Can we get to your secret phone system from here?"

"Of course," Wesowee said, craning his neck to peer at the door indicators. "In there," he said, pointing to the second one down.

The room turned out to be a pump room. "Memories," Nicole said under her breath as she looked around.

"Pardon?" Wesowee asked as he worked his way through the cables and racks filling the rear section of the room and reached a pair of thick pipes running horizontally along the far wall.

"It's like the room where I put Bungie after he got shot," she told him. "So how does this work?"

"These are water conduits," Wesowee said, pointing at the two pipes. "*This*"—he tapped a small box running between them— "is a temperature sensor." Shifting the finger to a corner of the box, he flipped open the lid. At the bottom of the box, beneath a rectifier simplex, was a small adjustment screwdriver. Wesowee pulled it out and began tapping one of the rectifier's connection pins.

Nicole watched him, thinking about the old movies and TV shows she'd seen where someone used Morse code to send messages. Wesowee finished tapping and then pressed a finger against one of the other pins. "Could you hear?" he asked, looking back at Nicole.

"I didn't hear anything."

"Understandable," Wesowee said, nodding. "There's a sound, but it's much higher in pitch than most other species can hear."

"But Ghorfs can?"

"Actually, we don't *hear* the sound so much as we *feel* it," Wesowee said. "It creates a sort of tingling in the network of small bones that support our gill structure. It's much clearer underwater than it is here, but this is adequate for our needs. Kahkitah has been called, and we need only wait for him to find an opportunity to—ah." He broke off, shifting his finger and tapping the pin again. "He's here. What's your message?"

"Tell him I need him to send a couple of the Thii over here to me," Nicole said.

Wesowee trilled an acknowledgment and started tapping. Nicole listened to the clicks, running the images of the four aliens through her mind. Insect-thin, narrow heads, thin limbs, four arms each, taller than the Ponngs but thinner. Nise was the leader of the group; Sofkat and Misgk were his two main soldiers, and—"Tell him to make it Nise and Iyulik."

"*Iyulik?*" Wesowee asked, his birdsong voice sounding confused. "He's the youngest and least experienced of all of them."

"I know," Nicole assured him.

"But if we're going to fight the Shipmasters, shouldn't we use the best soldiers we have?"

"Just send the message," Nicole said, waving toward the box.

Wesowee gave the warble that was the Ghorf equivalent of a sigh and resumed tapping. He paused and again held his fingertip to the pin, and a moment later nodded. "Kahkitah acknowledges and promises to send the Thii to you as soon as possible. Is there any place in particular you'd like them to meet us?"

"Let's try the other side of the Q3 arena—the side toward the front of the *Fyrantha*—on level 36."

"That's only four levels below the arena entrance level," Wesowee reminded her. "A coordinated search would quickly locate them."

"It'll be all right," Nicole said. "I know what I'm doing."

For a moment Wesowee eyed her in silence. Then he did the sighing thing again and tapped out the rest of her message. "He acknowledges," he said, returning the screwdriver to the sensor box and replacing the cover. "Have you discussed this plan with Kahkitah or Jeff?"

"No," Nicole said. "Mainly because I didn't come up with it until we found out about the drones."

"They will be useful weapons," Wesowee said. "But good weapons require good soldiers to best use them."

"If this is about Iyulik again, don't worry about it," Nicole said. "Young and inexperienced is sometimes a good thing."

"In what way?"

"There were these two things Jeff was very big on when we were talking about plans," Nicole said. "He called them *assumption* and *misdirection*. The Shipmasters have made some assumptions about us—"

She broke off. "Did you hear something?" she asked, lowering her voice.

"In the corridor," Wesowee said quietly. "Shall I look?"

"I will," Nicole said. "Be ready to run."

She stepped to the door, waiting while Wesowee disentangled himself from the machinery. She spotted a small bucket on the floor beside the door and picked it up. It wasn't much of a weapon—small, light, and awkward to hold—but it was all she had.

Wesowee was standing behind her now, waiting for her to make her move. Bracing herself, she opened the door and stepped out.

And nearly walked straight into an armored Shipmaster.

"*Yeeeough!*" she shrieked.

Luckily, he seemed as startled by the near collision as she was. He jerked back, jerking a second time as he reacted to her unexpected scream.

Fortunately, he wasn't carrying a weapon. Unfortunately, the same couldn't be said of the two Koffren five steps behind him.

Even as Wesowee popped into the corridor behind Nicole the big aliens grabbed for the spider guns holstered beside their swords and started lifting them into firing position.

"Run!" Nicole shouted, and hurled her bucket as hard as she could toward the Koffren.

Useless as a weapon, as she'd already noted. But the Koffren hadn't had time to focus on what was in her hand. Reflexively, they dodged sideways to get clear of the unidentified object arrowing toward them.

A second later, Nicole was snatched off her feet as Wesowee wrapped his lumpy arms around her, turned his back to the Shipmaster and Koffren, and took off at a dead run.

"What's the danger?" he asked in a bewildered tone as he raced down the corridor, his voice just loud enough for the Shipmaster to hear. Even in the midst of a potential battle—maybe especially in the midst of a battle—he needed to continue playing the role the Ghorfs had set for themselves. "Nicole? What's the danger? Why are we running?"

"There are bad people back there," she said, trying for the same volume level. She didn't know whether or not the Shipmasters were still buying this act, but she owed it to the Ghorfs to do whatever she could to maintain it.

"Stop!" a Shipmaster voice demanded from behind them. "I order you to stop."

"Let me down," Nicole murmured to Wesowee. "We can run faster that way."

"Not yet," Wesowee said. "I need to shield you from the spider guns. If I fall, go on without me."

"But—"

"Have no fear, Protector," he said. "I know how to pretend foolishness."

"That wasn't what I meant—"

An instant later a spider shot flashed past to slap into the ceiling. Nicole frowned, wondering how on Earth the Koffren could have missed—

And as a second shot plastered against the wall ahead to her right a drone shot past overhead. It tilted up sharply on the back edge, the air blast from the rotating blades killing its forward momentum, then headed back, its poisoned whipcords snapping out into attack mode.

Apparently, the Ponngs were fast learners.

"Let me see," Nicole whispered.

Wesowee hesitated, then loosened his grip a bit, just enough for Nicole to twist around in his arms and look over his shoulder.

The two Koffren had been taken completely by surprise by the sudden attack from behind. One of them was staggering along, barely maintaining his balance, his spider gun forgotten as he pressed both hands against the right side of his head where the drone must have tagged him. The other Koffren seemed unhurt, but he was also clearly off balance, his gun spitting spider shots uselessly into floor, ceiling, and walls as he tried to take down the zigzagging drone now coming back toward him. The Shipmaster, his armor presumably protecting him from both the drug and direct physical impact, had nevertheless ducked to the side of the corridor as far out of the way as he could get. He was pressed against the wall, half-turned as if trying to hide his face from the drone.

And then, Nicole's brain caught up with her. The Shipmaster wasn't trying to hide.

He was going for a greenfire weapon.

She twisted back around, cursing under her breath, mentally urging Wesowee to run faster, knowing full well that all the wishing and urging and running in the universe wouldn't save them now. The end of the corridor was still a good ten seconds away.

The Shipmaster would have his weapon out of storage and ready in half that time.

Wesowee's massive body could protect her from a spider gun shot. With the bolt from a greenfire weapon, they would simply die together.

Maybe the Ponngs could do something. Maybe they could keep the drones flying through the spider gun barrage long enough to distract the Shipmaster, or ruin his aim, or maybe even knock the weapon from his hand.

But only one drone was in the air, and even if the second emerged from the barracks right now, it would be too late to affect anything. Wesowee would die, and Nicole would die; and then the Ponngs, too, would die.

And Jeff would never even know what had happened to her.

And then, to her amazement, a hidden panel in the corridor wall ten feet in front of them popped open, one of the hidden staircases that even a lot of the *Fyrantha's* long-term workers didn't know about. "In here!" a hoarse voice came from the opening. "Come on! In *here!*"

"Do it," Nicole said, her thudding heart suddenly in her throat. The voice was strained, but it sure sounded like—

Wesowee barreled through the open door, nearly flattening the person holding it open for them . . . and with Nicole's first glance her suspicions became certainty.

It was Bungie.

"What the *hell?*" she breathed as he slammed the door shut behind them.

"Yeah, later," Bungie shot back, pointing up the staircase. "Right now, run. It won't take them long to find the door and figure out how to get through it."

"If they don't just blast it open," Nicole warned. "Wesowee, put me down."

"How are they going to—? Oh, *hell*. Has he got a greenfire weapon?"

"He's got a whole buttload of them," Nicole bit out as Wesowee set her down on the stairs. "Where to?"

"Five floors up," Bungie said. "I've scoped out a room where they shouldn't find us."

"No, let's go down," Nicole said, brushing past him to the down part of the staircase.

"What are you doing?" he snarled. "I already have a place."

"So do I," Nicole said. "And it'll be harder for the Shipmasters to track us there."

"I know this ship, damn it."

"So do I, and better than you."

She kept going down, Wesowee clomping along beside her. She was making the first turn when Bungie caught up with them. "Fine," he snarled. "How far are we going?"

"Not far," Nicole said. "Level 36."

With adrenaline still pumping through her blood, Nicole did the four flights in record time and without a single ache in her leg muscles. She opened the hidden door, checked both directions, and slipped into the corridor.

"Where now?" Bungie asked tightly.

"This way," Nicole said, turning to the right.

"You'd better sure as hell know what you're doing," Bungie warned as he hurried along behind her.

"I do," Nicole said. For a moment her thoughts flicked to the Ponngs, wondering if she'd just left them to die. Hopefully, the Shipmaster and Koffren would concentrate on Nicole and let the small aliens escape back to Q4. If the Wisps Nicole had left on the Q3 side of the central heat-transfer duct were still there, they should be able and willing to ferry the Ponngs back to safety.

But whether they were or not, there was nothing else Nicole could do for the Ponngs now. Nothing but make sure that whatever suffering they might have to go through wouldn't be for nothing.

seven

Bungie was not impressed by the room Nicole found for them.

"You've got to be kidding," he grumbled, looking around. "What the hell is this place, an army barracks?"

"It's got room, it's got beds, and there's a water dispenser in the corner," Nicole said. She walked to one of the nearby beds and sat down at one end.

"So did my place," Bungie said sourly, coming over and sitting on the bed facing hers. "*And* food, *and* places to hide if the Shipmasters got too close. *And* it had some leftover tubing from when they were parking fighters here that we could have used for weapons."

"Tubing against greenfire weapons?" Nicole scoffed. "Right. No, thanks."

"That's why I wanted hiding places," Bungie said with exaggerated patience.

"You can hide under the beds."

"I stopped doing that when I was three."

"Excuse me," Wesowee said hesitantly. The Ghorf was still standing, looking uncertain, but Nicole noticed that he'd picked a spot where he could watch the door but also get to Bungie in a hurry if he had to. "You say the tubing was from fighters? What did the people do with the tubing? Wrap it around themselves for protection?"

"What? Oh." Bungie rolled his eyes. "Not *fighters,* like people that shoot at each other. *Fighters* like airplanes that shoot at each other."

Wesowee gave a startled-sounding birdsong. "There were *airplanes* aboard the *Fyrantha?*"

Bungie snorted and looked at Nicole. "You always knew how to pick 'em, didn't you?"

"I'd put his loyalty up against your street smarts any day," Nicole said stiffly. "Speaking of loyalty, you won't mind if I ask what the hell you're doing, right? Starting with how you knew we'd be down there, and why you got us out."

"*How I knew* is because I'm still in with Fievj and the other Shipmasters," Bungie said. "They think I'm their best chance of talking you down, or whatever the hell they want to do with you."

"What *do* they want with me?"

"They want you to just go away, I guess," Bungie said. "You're messing things up, and it's gonna come back and bite you. And Jeff and the rest of your buddies, too."

"But I don't want to be bitten," Wesowee said plaintively. "Being bitten *hurts.*"

"Yeah, you want to shut up and let us talk?" Bungie growled, glaring at the Ghorf. "Pretend you're not here or something."

"Oh—*pretend* games!" Wesowee said, his birdsong voice brightening. "I like those."

"Good." Bungie rolled his eyes again and turned back to Nicole. "Anyway, they spotted you in the Q3 arena but weren't able to get down there before you left."

"More likely couldn't get the Koffren to come with them," Nicole said. "Or they were worried about the drones."

"Yeah, they said you had drones now," Bungie said, nodding. "They're worried about *that,* too, I can tell you."

"Why?" Nicole asked. "The poison can't get through those centaur suits."

"I think they're more worried about you using the drones to spy on them," Bungie said. "There are cameras inside that feed pictures to the controller."

"Yeah, the wolfmen said something about that," Nicole said. "I don't know if Moile and Teika have figured that part out yet. Did they get away, do you know?"

"How could I?" Bungie retorted. "I've been with you the whole time."

"Right," Nicole said. "Right. Sorry. So Fievj couldn't get down to the arena, but you figured you could?"

"They want you to quit messing with the ship, but they're not doing a hell of a good job of stopping you," Bungie said. "I figured that while they were scrambling to get the Koffren into place I'd give it a shot. If anyone can talk some sense into you it'll be me."

"Yeah," Nicole said, passing over the extreme unlikelihood of *that* happening. "How did you know where I'd be?"

He snorted. "What, after all that grandstanding in Q4 and Q3 to get food to the poor helpless aliens? Of course you'd be trying to do that with this bunch."

"Okay, that answers the *how,*" Nicole said. "Now, let's hear the *why.* Why did you get us away from them?"

"Like I said, I wanted to talk."

"About what? And don't tell me to quit, because I'm not going to."

"I'm not." Bungie lowered his eyes. "I'm here because I decided you were right."

"I was *right*?" Offhand, Nicole couldn't remember him ever actually saying those words. "About what?"

"About that they're not going to send us home." He looked back up at her face for a second, then again lowered his gaze. "They're just using us. Using *me*. We could all have been killed in the arena when they sent in the Koffren." He sent a hooded look at Wesowee. "Me, anyway. That other Ghorf—Kahkitah—sure as hell wanted to break me in half."

"I can't believe that," Wesowee said, sounding both confused and nervous. "I remember meeting Kahkitah. He would never do such a thing. Especially not to a fellow worker."

"Well, if he didn't, Jeff sure did." Bungie waved a hand. "Never mind. The point is that the Shipmasters aren't going to do anything for us. If we want to get home, we have to do it ourselves."

"You think that's a good idea?"

"What, go home instead of hanging out here? Damn right. Why, do *you* want to stay?"

"Not the way things are," Nicole admitted. "So what do you think we can do about it?"

"We need to join forces," Bungie said. "I know a lot about Fievj and the other Shipmasters. They've taken me around Q1 a lot, and I know where all the good stuff is."

"What sort of stuff?"

"The room we landed in when they brought us from Philly, for starters," he said. "They call it the teleport room. I also know where they keep their guns."

"Really," Nicole murmured, sitting up a little straighter. "That could be *very* useful."

"Yeah, but not so much for me," Bungie said. "They usually have me on a pretty short leash." He shot another look at Wesowee. "But you have friends. You could use some weapons."

"I suppose." Nicole took a deep breath, let it out in a long sigh. "Though Jeff might not want to change his plans at the last minute."

Bungie snorted. "What plans can he have that can't use a few guns?"

"I meant change his plans so that we're working with you," Nicole said. "I mean . . . he doesn't really trust you."

"In that case he's screwed," Bungie said bluntly. "He'll never get to the guns without me, and he'll never get anywhere against the Shipmasters without guns."

"I know," Nicole said. "But you know Jeff. I don't know—maybe his plan doesn't need guns."

"I'd sure like to hear what kind of plan doesn't need guns."

"Me, too," Nicole said. "I really don't know much about it." She screwed up her face. "I don't think he trusts me, either."

"Yeah," Bungie said contemptuously. "Hell. You hook up with *him*"—he hooked a thumb toward Wesowee—"and you hook up with Jeff. You should have stuck with me from the start. At least I'd have treated you right. Did he tell you *anything*?"

"Just that he thinks it'll work," Nicole said. "He's pretty proud of it. And now that we've got drones . . ." She trailed off.

"Now that we've got drones what?" Bungie pressed.

"I don't know," Nicole said, hunching her shoulders. "I was just wondering . . . you said there were cameras on them, right? If we can get them into Q1, maybe we can find the guns."

"What for? I already told you *I* know where they are."

"But you can't show us the way," Nicole pointed out. "If the Shipmasters catch you, they'll never trust you again."

Bungie snorted. "Don't worry, I can talk my way around *them*. It's Jeff who'll be a problem. You think you can find out his plans? Come on to him or something?"

"He probably knows that trick," Nicole said. "But maybe *you* can get to him."

"What, *me*?"

"Why not?" Nicole asked. "You've got the guns. He's got the plan."

"And he wants to kill me." Bungie shook his head. "I don't think so. Anyway, I can't go to Q4. If Fievj catches me there, I'm done."

"So I'll get him to come here." Nicole looked up at Wesowee. "Wesowee, can you go to Q4 and ask Jeff if he's got time to come talk to me?"

"You want me to bring someone *here*?" Wesowee asked. On the surface his tone was eager and willing, but Nicole could hear the sudden uneasiness underneath it.

"Yes, please," Nicole said, pretending she hadn't heard the doubt. "His name's Jeff, and he'll be wearing a blue jumpsuit like mine. Just ask anyone you see—they'll be able to take you to him."

"Wait a second," Bungie protested. "I haven't even said yes yet."

"Oh, and if you run into Nise and the other Thii, tell them I'm sorry I haven't been back to see them," Nicole added casually. "I know they don't like it if I ignore them too long."

"You have *Thii* with you?" Wesowee asked, eyeing Nicole closely. "I thought they all went home."

"A few got stuck behind," Nicole said. "My fault, really. Now they think I'm—well, I don't know what they think. Just tell them I'll see them soon. If you see them."

"I understand," Wesowee said, and in the subtle tones of his birdsong Nicole could tell that he genuinely did. "I'll be back with Jeff as soon as I can."

"Only if he's willing to come," Nicole said. "He doesn't like me sounding like I'm ordering him around," she added to Bungie.

"I understand," Wesowee said, some doubt creeping back into his voice. "Are you sure . . . ?" He pointed a big finger at Bungie.

"I'll be fine," Nicole assured him. "He's not going to hurt me. Are you, Bungie?"

"Course not," Bungie said. He snorted. "Hey, you can call Wisps and make them do what you want. I'm sure as hell not going to start something with them around."

Except that the Wisps in Q3 weren't under her full authority, and Nicole was pretty sure Bungie knew that. But it was a gamble she had to take.

Besides, she wasn't the same helpless girl who'd been snatched from the streets of Philadelphia all those months ago. Presumably, Bungie knew that, too.

"All right," Wesowee said, giving Bungie a long, cool stare. The Ghorf equivalent, maybe, of the look Trake used to give people who'd made what he called his *crapadoodle list*.

Or what he'd called it to her, anyway. He'd liked to pretend she was hopelessly naïve.

"I'll be back as soon as I can," Wesowee said. He left the room, pausing first for a careful look in the corridor outside, and then for one final look at Bungie.

The door closed behind him. "He doesn't like me any better than Kahkitah does," Bungie grumbled.

"Do you blame him?" Nicole asked. "All he knows about you is what he might have heard from his work crew or some of the other Ghorfs. And all *they* know about you has come from Kahkitah."

"Or you."

Nicole shrugged. "I may have mentioned that you and I don't always get along."

"Yeah," Bungie said, standing up. "No, this is a bad idea. Tell you what: *you* talk to Jeff and get back to me."

"No, wait," Nicole said quickly, standing up and touching his forearm. "Please don't go."

"Why not?" Bungie retorted. "Jeff's just gonna pick a fight when he gets here. You know that."

"But this is our best chance," Nicole said, hearing the pleading in her voice. The intensity of the emotion startled her a little. "If you go, we'll never be able to stop the Shipmasters."

"Lover boy doesn't think he needs me," Bungie bit out. "Neither do you."

"That's not true," Nicole protested. "I—*we* need you. Please. Just stay and talk this out. If it goes south, you can always leave."

For a long moment he stared at her. Then, slowly, he sat back down.

But not before Nicole caught a hint of a brief smile, quickly smoothed out. Bungie, in full manipulation mode.

She'd always hated when he did that. Usually it didn't work.

Sometimes it did.

"So what do we talk about?" he asked as she also sat back down. For a moment he reached toward her as she withdrew her touch, apparently decided he didn't need to push it. "You know *anything* about this plan of his?"

"I was . . ." Nicole lowered her eyes. "I was thinking we could talk about . . . I've been thinking a lot about Philly lately. The first time I met Trake. You were there, weren't you?"

"Yeah," Bungie said, studying her face. "You were with Clinks then, weren't you?"

"Sort of," Nicole hedged. "I was never really *with* anyone. Or, you know . . . tried not to be. Sometimes . . ." She shook her head. "It was kind of funny. I'd been to a couple of parties with Clinks, but it wasn't until the fourth one that Trake actually noticed me."

"Not sure *any* of us noticed you," Bungie said. "You were pretty invisible."

"I think that's why Trake let me start working as a lookout," she said. "I think he figured that if I was that invisible to him I'd be just as invisible to everyone else."

"That wasn't the only reason," Bungie said. "It was that thing with Brook and Piddle. Remember?"

Nicole frowned. "Brook and Piddle?"

"Yeah," Bungie said. "They were doing a deal with old Wolf Face when a couple of cops wandered in. You got them out without the cops ever seeing a thing."

"Oh. Right." Nicole had forgotten all about that. "Yeah, I saw them getting close and walked straight up to them. They asked me what I was doing out so late, and I told them my cat had gotten out and I was looking for her."

"And they helped you look?"

"Was *that* the story Brook told everyone?" Nicole shook her head. "It was even better than that. I'd seen posters out for a missing boy cat and asked the cops if they might be hiding together. One of them said he didn't think they would be *hiding,* exactly. So I asked what he meant."

"And he told you?"

"No, he really didn't want to." Nicole shrugged. "I always looked young for my age, you know, and he figured I was . . . well, you know. A kid. He sort of fumbled around the question while I just looked at him wide-eyed and kept asking."

"I'll bet his partner was dying."

"Yes, she was," Nicole said, smiling as the images from that night came back to mind. "She sort of hustled him out of there, trying not to laugh out loud. I trailed after them for another half block, still trying to get him to answer, just to make sure they were gone."

"And next thing you knew you were Trake's chief lookout."

Nicole frowned. "*Chief* lookout? He never told me that."

"He wasn't much for patting people on the head," Bungie said. He smiled slyly. "Least, not the girls. He liked patting *them* other places."

"What about you?" Nicole asked. Definitely time to change the subject. "How did *you* join up? You were there a year before I was, right?"

"Year and a half." Bungie shrugged. "Trake was having some trouble with a guy. I was having the same trouble with the same guy, and I made the trouble go away. Trake was grateful, invited me in, and that was that."

"Sounds pretty straightforward," Nicole said, a shiver running through her. It wasn't hard to guess what *made the trouble go away* meant.

"*Straightforward?* Whoa," Bungie said. "Pretty big word for a street rat. This place is getting to you."

"I suppose," Nicole said. "Do you know how Trake got Packer to join the group?"

"Packer?" Bungie echoed, frowning. "Who cares how Packer got in?"

"I was always curious," Nicole said. "He must have had some medical training to do the stuff he did."

"You just liked him because he always had booze on hand when you brought someone in to get fixed up," Bungie scoffed.

"Well, that, too," Nicole admitted. "But I still always wondered—" She broke off as the door opened.

Bungie was on his feet in an instant, his hands balling into fists. "Excuse me," Wesowee said, shying back at the snarl on Bungie's face. "I'm sorry, Nicole. I'm afraid—"

"What are you doing back here?" Bungie demanded. "You can't have gotten to Q4 already."

"I know," Wesowee said. "I didn't." He turned to Nicole and lowered his eyes. "I'm afraid I got lost."

Bungie rolled his eyes as he dropped back onto the bed. "Oh, for—"

"It's okay," Nicole said quickly. "It's okay, Wesowee. I shouldn't have . . . Here. Come over here and I'll write you out some directions. You have your notepad?"

"Yes." Wesowee walked over to Nicole, sidling nervously past the still glowering Bungie. "I'm sorry."

"Not your fault," Nicole assured him, taking the notepad and stylus from him. "Okay. Here's what you need to do."

And as he leaned down to peer over her shoulder, she began to write.

I assume you found Nise and Iyulik? "You got this far, right?" she asked.

"Oh, yes," Wesowee said eagerly.

I need them to follow Bungie when he leaves here. There's a main horizontal air vent between this level and the one below us. There should be a way in from either the corridor or one of the air pump rooms. "This could be a little tricky," she warned.

"Oh, no, I can do that," Wesowee assured her.

I was in one of the main vents, and there are others that travel up and down. They should hopefully be able to fit through those. They need to follow Bungie and see where he goes.

"You don't need to write him your life history," Bungie said impatiently. "Just point him in the right direction and boot him."

"I'm almost done," Nicole promised.

I'll try to eliminate the Q1 communications system so he has to go to the Shipmasters directly. If they find the armory or the teleport room, one of them can bring back news. Tell them I'll meet him here in this room, the one we're in right now.

"Is that clear now?" she asked, handing him the notepad.

"Yes, I can do that," Wesowee said.

"Good," Nicole said. "Good luck."

Wesowee whistled a Ghorf farewell and hurried back to the door. Again he checked outside for trouble, then headed out.

"Idiot," Bungie muttered.

"Not their fault," Nicole said. "Anyway, Trake had some idiots in the group, too, and we got by okay. Hmm."

"What?" Bungie asked.

"I was just thinking," Nicole said slowly. "If we *do* get home, I wonder if Trake will even take us back. I mean, we've been gone a long time. Maybe he'll think we ducked out on him, or went to the cops or something."

"Not when we show him the guns we'll be bringing back," Bungie said.

"I thought you said you couldn't get any guns."

"Not to wave around *here,* no," Bungie said. "But I'm betting we could pick up a few on our way out."

"*If* we can get to the teleport room."

"I already told you I know where it is," Bungie reminded her. "But you're thinking too small. We get a couple of tangler guns and we won't need Trake anymore. We can start our own gang."

"I don't think the Shipmasters are stupid enough to leave the gun room unlocked," Nicole warned. "But the Koffren are both walking around with them. We could probably take those."

Bungie snorted. "If you've got a death wish."

"Don't be silly," Nicole scoffed. "I understand the Koffren and how to fight them. I took them down once, you know. I can do it again if I have to."

"You sucker-punched them last time," Bungie countered. "You try it again, and they'll be ready for you."

"I'm not worried." Nicole wrinkled her nose thoughtfully. "Sure wouldn't hurt to have a few more allies. Someone like the Ghorfs, only smarter, would be perfect."

"You know where to go hunting?" Bungie asked. "Because like I said, I can get you to the teleport room."

"Not yet," Nicole said. "But it's something to think about. Anyway, right now Jeff's the one with the plan. We'll see how it works, and keep this in mind if it goes south."

"If it goes south, we're probably dead," Bungie warned.

"I hope not," Nicole said. She took a deep breath. "You know, maybe you're right about not waiting for Jeff. If the Shipmasters are still looking for us—"

"Oh, you *think*?"

"—then I don't want to be caught," Nicole continued, standing up. "And *you* don't want to be caught with me. Is there any way I can get hold of you if Jeff wants to talk?"

"Don't worry about that," Bungie said, standing up with her. "You go anywhere out of Q4 and there'll be Shipmasters and Wisps and Koffren on your butt the whole time. I'll be around them somewhere. Just whistle if you want me. If you haven't already been caught."

"I won't be caught," Nicole said. "I understand the Shipmasters and the Wisps, too. Matter of fact, I understand everyone and everything aboard. Comes from being the *Fyrantha*'s Protector."

"Yeah, well, you didn't do so well back there by the arena."

Nicole shrugged. "I understood what they were doing just fine. Doesn't mean I can't get outnumbered. Anyway, thanks for getting us out of there. I hope this is where we can start working together like a team."

"Me, too," Bungie said.

And before Nicole could react, he threw his arms around her, pulled her close, and kissed her.

Her first instinct was to try to push him away. But the stakes were too high. She held her pose, enduring his touch, trying not to go so stiff that he'd become suspicious.

Finally, it was over, and he pulled back. "Yeah, I should have done that a long time ago," he said, that small smirk on his face again. "See you, babe."

Nicole waited until the door closed behind him, then wiped her mouth on her sleeve. She was still trying to purge her lips and mind of his touch when Wesowee slipped back into the room. "Are you all right?" he asked anxiously.

"I'm fine," she assured him, still wincing at the memory. "Did you get Nise and Iyulik into the air vent?"

"Yes, we found the access and they're inside," Wesowee said. "I see now why you wanted Iyulik for this mission. As the youngest Thii, he's also the smallest."

"Exactly," Nicole said. "Hopefully, neither will get stuck, but if they wind up in narrower vents Iyulik's got the best chance of getting through."

And now came the part she most dreaded. She pulled out her inhaler—

"Wait," Wesowee said, hurrying toward her, his hand outstretched as if to snatch the inhaler from her hand. "You mustn't do that. The Sibyl drug is a poison."

"I know," Nicole said with a sigh. "But I need information, and this is the only way to get it." She squared her shoulders and focused on the ceiling. "Caretaker, I need to know if there's a way to shut down the Q1 communications system—the radio boosters or whatever—from somewhere in Q3," she called. "Please have the *Fyrantha* ready to give me the instructions when I use the inhaler."

"Are you sure there *is* a booster system?" Wesowee asked.

"Jeff and Kahkitah think there is," Nicole said. "The point is that Bungie's going to want to tell the Shipmasters about our meeting. I need him to go to them himself, instead of just calling it in, so that the Thii can follow him."

"To the armory or teleport room?"

"If we're lucky," Nicole agreed. "If we're *very* lucky." Bracing herself, she put the inhaler into her mouth and sent a blast of powder into her lungs.

The system you request is not properly part of the Fyrantha's

*original equipment. It was added by the Lillilli after their acquisi-
tion from the—*

I don't care about the history, Nicole interrupted. *Is there a system like that, or isn't there?*

There is.

Then tell me how to shut it down in Q1.

The four junction box . . . The voice faded away.

Cursing, Nicole gave herself another inhaler puff.

The four junction box in bahri-*one-one-two-eight has two rectifiers connected by a modulator and twin simplex ellie sixes,* the voice
resumed. *Apply four seconds of three-hundred volt and fifteen-amp
current to the rectifiers to destabilize the communications relay system in Q1 and Q3.*

The voice went silent. This time, it was clear that it had finished. "*Thank* you," Nicole growled, scribbling the instructions on
her notepad. "Okay. We need to find *bahri*-one-one-two-eight."

"I can do that," Wesowee said. "What do we need to do?"

"This," Nicole said, holding up her notepad.

"I see," Wesowee said. "Interesting."

"Interesting how?"

"For the entire time I've been aboard, the *Fyrantha* has focused
exclusively on repairing itself," he said. "If it's now willing to create
new damage at your request, it must truly be on your side."

"Maybe," Nicole said. "Or maybe it just doesn't want to be a
warship again."

"Which I would argue is essentially the same thing. Come."
Wesowee gave an amused-sounding trill. "Let us turn a small bit
of order back into chaos."

eight

The room the *Fyrantha* had specified turned out to be a three-minute walk away. Inside were a dozen junction boxes neatly arranged along the back wall. "Can you find me some high-voltage current?" she asked, stepping to the array and popping the lid on the fourth box in line.

"No problem," Wesowee said, crossing to the side wall and a pair of power cubes.

"Thanks." Nicole frowned into the junction box. "Okay, something's wrong."

"What is it?" Wesowee asked.

"This isn't the box the ship described," Nicole said. "Not even close."

"Perhaps the box numbering system doesn't follow the same pattern as the rooms," Wesowee suggested.

"Or else the *Fyrantha's* not being as cooperative as we'd thought," Nicole said as she started opening the rest of the boxes.

"Interesting problem," Wesowee said, turning back to his power cube. "Tell me, has the *Fyrantha* ever specified a specific junction box to your team? I don't recall my team being so directed."

"I don't remember anything like that, either," Nicole said. "But most of our jobs were in places where there was only one box, so there was never—ah; here it is," she interrupted herself as she popped the seventh box lid. "Looks like it, anyway. I guess four now equals seven?"

Wesowee glanced over. "It's the fourth-largest box," he said.

Nicole peered at the boxes. He was right. "I'll have to remember that one. You ready?"

"Yes." He'd attached a coil of cable to one of the cube's output slots and now walked over to her, uncoiling the cable as he walked. "You might want to step back a bit and shade your eyes."

"Just watch yourself," Nicole warned, stepping back out of his way.

"I will."

He touched the end of the cable to the rectifiers, and the room came alive with blue-white light and a hissing sizzle. Wesowee held the pose for four seconds, and Nicole grimaced as the stench of burnt electronics curled her nostrils.

The Ghorf lifted the cable, and the light and sizzling stopped. "If the *Fyrantha* is correct, easy communication with Q1 should now cease," the Ghorf said as he coiled the cable and returned it to the power box. "I wonder . . ."

"What?" Nicole prompted.

"You've said the *Fyrantha* is somewhat at odds with itself," Wesowee said. "I wonder if the next instruction our team's Sibyl receives will be to come here and make repairs."

"Huh," Nicole said, frowning at the scorched circuit box. "I hadn't thought about that. Or worse. If the Shipmasters can figure out where the problem is, they might be able to fix it themselves."

"I thought only humans could make repairs."

"That's what I was told," Nicole said. "But that could be mostly because only humans can be Sibyls and hear the Oracle's instructions, and the Oracle told me this system was added by the Lillilli after they took over the ship."

"The Shipmasters are the Lillilli?"

"Or maybe just a special group of them," Nicole said. "Though, you know . . . once when the *Fyrantha* was being shot at and needed me to fix something at the top of the ship I was nearly caught by a couple of Shipmasters who came charging in after me."

"Did they think they could fix it?"

"I don't know why else they would have been there," she said. "Maybe this isn't the only thing they added." She nodded toward the box. "And in this case, it's pretty obvious what we did and how to fix it. All you need to do is read the numbers off the rectifiers and swap them out for new ones."

"Perhaps it's not as obvious to the Shipmasters as it is to you."

"I'd hate to bet on that," Nicole said. "Maybe we ought to stick around for a while just to make sure."

"Perhaps," Wesowee said doubtfully. "But not in here."

"You're right," Nicole said, shivering. Earlier, she'd considered the catastrophe of getting trapped in one of the *Fyrantha*'s smaller rooms. That situation didn't sound any better now than it had then. "Let's see if there's someplace across the hall we can watch from."

"There should be several choices," Wesowee said, opening the door and looking back and forth. "Stay here while I go look."

"Okay, but make it quick," Nicole said, an odd feeling tingling itself up her back. With the door open, something suddenly felt wrong. She moved forward quickly, catching the door before it could close behind Wesowee, and leaned up to the opening.

She was right. There was some kind of whining sound coming from down the corridor, still too soft to identify, but somehow ominous.

And it was getting louder.

"Wesowee!" she whispered, easing an eye around the doorjamb. The sound was still too soft to identify, but she knew she'd heard it somewhere before. Out of the corner of her eye she saw Wesowee step back toward her, and could sense him bracing for trouble . . .

And then, even as the sound abruptly clicked in Nicole's mind, the drone appeared around the distant corner.

Nicole froze, hardly daring to breathe. Had it spotted her at the same time she'd spotted it? She was still mostly hidden inside the room, but if the drone operator was looking closely he was bound to see the small piece of human face looking back at him.

If he spotted her . . .

She clenched her teeth. If he spotted her, she would have to make sure she was the last thing the operator saw. The minute the drone started toward them she would duck back into the room, assuming her sudden movement would catch his attention. She would have maybe fifteen seconds to make her preparations before the drone reached her; and the second the device was in range she would try to zap it with the same power surge Wesowee had just used to blast the rectifiers. With luck, it would be enough of a jolt to destroy it.

At which point, of course, she and Wesowee would have to run. But they were going to have to run, anyway, and at least this way they could run without someone staring over their shoulders.

And then, even as she mentally unwound the cable Wesowee had used, filling in the details of her plan in her mind, a second drone floated around the corner to join the first.

Nicole hissed. *Damn.* Because the operators would have to be idiots to send *both* drones into range of the enemy. Now she and Wesowee would need something he could throw—maybe two or three somethings, if they weren't very big or heavy—to take out both machines. Two figures stepped around the corner—

Nicole huffed out a relieved sigh. It was Moile and Teika, drone controllers gripped in their hands. "Protector?" Moile called softly.

"Here," Nicole said, stepping out into the hallway. "Are you all right?"

"Quite all right," Moile confirmed.

"They're fine," a new voice called.

And to her surprise Jeff stepped around the corner. "The question is," he continued as Levi and Tomas appeared behind him, "are *you* all right?"

"I'm fine," Nicole assured them, hurrying forward to meet them halfway. All three men were wearing large boxes on their backs, and were carrying what looked like a strap-pack of ceiling vents in each hand. From the way they were all walking, she guessed all of it added up to a lot of weight. "What are you doing here?"

"Kahkitah passed on Wesowee's message that you wanted Nise and Iyulik to meet you here," Jeff said. They reached each other—

And Nicole paused, suddenly uncertain. She was the *Fyrantha's* Protector, after all. Did that position allow her to show affection, or even relief?

Jeff wasn't bound by any such restrictions. Even as Nicole hesitated, he set his strap-packs on the deck and gave her a quick but intense hug. "I figured that whatever you were planning you could probably use some extra hands," he finished as he pulled away.

"Probably," Nicole said, taking a deep breath. So different from Bungie. "Hey, Levi, Tomas."

"Good to see you," Levi said, making no move to come in for a hug of his own.

"This had better be good," Tomas warned grimly, also keeping his distance.

"It will be," Jeff promised. He looked past Nicole at Wesowee, and she saw his eyes flick back and forth across the corridor. "Where are they?"

"Nise and Iyulik? I sent them on a job," Nicole said evasively, eyeing Tomas. He had a look that she'd seen a lot of back in Philadelphia. There was a simmering anger beneath the surface, along with a thirst for revenge.

Hardly a surprise. He'd been nursing a quiet but intense bitterness ever since the Koffren killed his friend Bennett, and that bitterness was showing no signs of fading away.

Nicole could sympathize, and had more than enough reasons herself to want the Koffren taken down. But she'd also seen enough with Trake to know how bloodlust could affect judgment and brains and mouths. If Tomas got into a rant with the Koffren or Shipmasters and said too much, he could ruin everything. Best to keep the Thii mission quiet for now.

Unfortunately, Levi didn't have Nicole's experience in such things. "What sort of job?" he asked.

"I sent them to check out the Q2 arena," Nicole said, thinking quickly. "I thought we might be able to pick up some allies or weapons." She nodded at the box on his back. "Speaking of weapons, it looks like you're pretty loaded, too. Or is all of that just supplies?"

"We *think* it's weapons," Jeff said. "We won't know how effective they are until we get a real field test."

"Which had better be soon," Tomas warned.

"Don't worry, it will," Jeff promised, picking up his strap-packs again. Now, up close, Nicole could see that they were indeed a set of rectangular ceiling vent covers. "Moile, Teika: I want you to run the drones as far as you can in all directions without losing them. Make sure there's nothing nearby that could jump out at us. Levi, Tomas, stay with them in case of trouble."

"What about you?" Tomas asked suspiciously.

"I need to show him something Wesowee and I found," Nicole spoke up. "We'll be back in a second."

She led the way back toward the room with the sabotaged booster junction. "Glad to see the Wisps are obeying you like I told them to," she commented. "I assume you ran into the Ponngs on their way back to Q4?"

"Basically," Jeff said. "Interesting fact. Did you know the Wisps can tell you where someone is?"

Nicole felt her stomach tighten. "No, I didn't," she said as casually as she could.

"Only if you're in their quadrant, though," Jeff amended. "The Q4 Wisps couldn't see into Q3 and tell me exactly where you were. But they were able to tell me the Ponngs were getting ready to come across from the edge of Q3. Good thing, too, or we might have crossed opposite directions on different levels and missed each other completely."

"Ah," Nicole said. She could see where Jeff was going with this. "And that's how you know I didn't send the Thii to Q2?"

"Basically," Jeff said. He was trying to be casual about it, but Nicole could hear the edge beneath the words. "I should mention that lies in the middle of an operation always make me nervous."

"I was going to tell you," Nicole said. "I just didn't want the others to know yet. In case . . . look, I'm not saying—"

"In case Tomas goes full Rambo, gets caught, and spills the details?"

Nicole winced. "Something like that. Sorry."

"No apology needed," Jeff assured her. "I figured it was something like that, which is why I didn't call you on it in front of him. Just between us, I'm a little worried about him myself. I would have left him behind, but he and Levi were the only ones willing to come with me."

Nicole frowned. "The others don't want revenge for Bennett?"

"Oh, they want revenge," Jeff said reluctantly. "It's just that they kind of blame you and your tactics for getting him killed. *I* don't," he hastened to add, "because I saw everything and know there wasn't anything you could have done to stop it."

"But the others still blame me."

"Yeah," Jeff conceded. "Anyway, like I said, Levi and Tomas were the only ones willing to come with us to hit the Shipmasters' armory."

"Uh-huh," Nicole said, wrinkling her nose. She'd been pretty sure that was where this was going. "So this *is* an armory raid?"

"That's all they would agree to," Jeff said. "They want to kill someone, and for that they need weapons."

"And the whole thing about not tipping off the Shipmasters that humans can fight?"

"They don't care," Jeff said. "And I'm pretty sure we're way beyond that point anyway."

"Maybe," Nicole said. "But we're not ready for the armory. For starters, we don't even know where it is."

"Preaching to the choir here, sister," Jeff said ruefully. "But it was that or I was going to be hoofing it alone. So what exactly are the Thii up to?"

Nicole braced herself. This could get awkward. "They're following Bungie into Q1. Hopefully to the armory or the teleport room, but we won't know which one they found—if either of them—until they get back."

"Bungie, huh?"

"Yeah."

For another couple of steps Jeff remained silent. Nicole braced herself, waiting for the inevitable question about how exactly the Thii had been able to connect with Bungie in the first place. "Okay," he said at last. "In that case, running a little sortie into Q1 might be exactly what we want. It would help draw the Shipmasters' attention outward."

"Toward us?"

"You got it," Jeff said. "You remember talking about setting up diversions while we hit the armory? Same thing."

"Except that we're not hitting the armory yet. Are we?"

"No, but you can also use diversions on recon missions."

"I was just wondering if they might catch on if we do that too often."

"Maybe," Jeff said. "But not likely. It's not like this is going to be a long campaign. We don't have the time or the troops for that. Moile said you swiped the drones from the Q3 arena?"

"Yes," Nicole said. "He told you about the cameras and weapons?"

"Both very useful things," Jeff agreed. "So they're what inspired you to this new plan?"

Nicole nodded. "I hope you don't mind me taking charge this way."

"You're the Protector," Jeff said. "You've got knowledge and resources the rest of us don't."

Nicole winced. "I don't know about *that*."

"I do," Jeff said. "Besides, as a wise man once said, no battle plan survives contact with the enemy. You get new stuff—troops, weapons, or just a better field position—you run with it. So. You have a plan for the drones?"

"I think so. At least, part of a plan."

"Great," Jeff said. "Fill me in."

Jeff was impressed by the sabotage Nicole and Wesowee had used on the radio booster. Levi, from the look on his face, was probably automatically thinking what it would take to fix it.

Tomas was mostly intrigued by the high-power port.

"So are there plugs like this in all the work spaces?" he asked, fingering the cable Wesowee had used.

"I don't know if they're in *all* the work spaces," Wesowee said, sounding a little confused. "I've seen them in some of the places where my team's worked."

"The *Fyrantha* told me to apply high voltage to the rectifiers, so I assumed there would be a source somewhere in the compartment," Nicole added. "Once I knew that, I told Wesowee to look around until he found something that looked promising."

"And when I saw this port I remembered Kointos—he's our team leader—telling us all to stand back when he used one just like it," Wesowee added with a childlike eagerness. "And then there were sparks and noise. And a smell that hurt my nose," he added ruefully.

"Ozone," Tomas said. "Hadn't seen any high-voltage outlets like this before. Could be useful."

"We'll think about how to use it the next time," Jeff said. "Right now, let's stick with the stuff we know works."

"What next time?" Tomas countered, frowning. "I thought we were hitting the armory. Not going to need any of this junk-heap stuff once we have some real weapons."

"We will if we can't find the armory or can't get inside," Jeff said. "Don't worry, our stuff will work."

"Yeah, you keep saying that," Tomas said sourly. He tapped the cable one last time and then backed out of the compartment. "Fine. We going, or what?"

"We're going," Jeff confirmed. "Nicole, is there any spot that would be better than anywhere else to cross into Q1?"

"I doubt it," Nicole said. "The big question is whether I'll have enough control of the Wisps to get us across the duct. As far as I can tell, that doesn't depend on where we are."

"Except which quadrant we're in," Levi said.

"Right," Nicole said. "Obviously."

"Don't get snappy," Tomas said tartly. "Fine. If Q3 is iffy, why don't we cross from Q2? Jeff said you had better control there."

"I don't know if it's better or just the same as here," Nicole said. "Sometimes I can control them, sometimes I can't. Sometimes it's like I'm taking control away from the Shipmasters. I did that here once, anyway. Don't know if I can always do it."

"Well, if it's going to be potluck no matter where we start, we might as well save ourselves some time and walking," Jeff said. "We'll head straight to the heat-transfer duct, you can call some Wisps, and we'll see what happens."

"What about them?" Tomas asked, jerking a thumb at Moile and Teika. "Those drones could be handy."

"We'll come with you," Moile announced, his voice firm.

"Not so fast," Jeff said. "Nicole, did you have a different plan for the drones and the Ponngs?"

"Why do we care what *she* wants?" Tomas cut in before Nicole could answer. "We've got a plan, and we're ready now."

Nicole hesitated. The last thing she wanted was to take the drones into Q1 right now.

But looking at the others' faces, she knew she didn't really have a choice. Levi and Tomas already blamed her for Bennett's death. If she tried to take control from them and Jeff, she would risk having them turn their backs on her for good.

And she would need them before this was over. She would need all of them.

"He's right," she said, trying to sound calm and controlled. "Being able to see ahead could make all the difference."

"And him?" Tomas asked, nodding at Wesowee.

"He should stay here," Nicole said, watching Wesowee's face. He wasn't happy about letting her go off with Jeff and the others—that much was clear. But unlike Tomas, he trusted her.

"That's right," the Ghorf said, whistling a little nervously. "I have to get back. Kointos will be wondering where I went. I don't want him to think I got lost again."

"No, we can't have *that,* can we?" Tomas said sarcastically. "So: two Ponngs, three men, and no Ghorfs. Works for me."

"Plus Nicole," Jeff reminded him firmly.

"Yeah. Nicole." Tomas shot her a look, then turned deliberately back to Jeff. "So what are we waiting for? Let's do it."

"What about your weapons?" Nicole asked. "Shouldn't I at least have some idea what they are and how they work?"

"I'll give you the full rundown when we get to the duct," Jeff promised. "We'll put everything together while we wait for the Wisps to show up. Marching order: Nicole and I will take point, Levi and Tomas at the rear, Ponngs in the middle with the drones flying about fifty meters ahead and behind. Clear? Good. Nicole?"

Nicole nodded. "This way."

She headed down the corridors, the others falling into place according to Jeff's orders. The drones likewise took up their positions, floating sentries for their little army.

Nicole listened to her heart pounding in her chest, trying to suppress her misgivings. This wasn't the way she'd planned this. Not at all. But this was what she had.

She could only hope she hadn't been lying when she'd told Bungie that Jeff had a really good plan.

nine

They didn't see anyone as they wove their way through the passageways. As far as they could tell, and as far as the roving drones could see, the whole quadrant might be deserted.

That didn't stop Nicole from tensing up at every closed door. The drone thing was what her grandmother always called a *two-edged sword*: the Ponngs could see anyone who might be around, but the drones' very presence could also alert the Shipmasters that there were intruders nearby.

But the Shipmasters seemed to have missed out on that one. Ten minutes of walking, and the group reached the blank wall that marked the Q1/Q3 heat-transfer duct. Nicole called for Wisps, and while they waited the others began assembling their weapons.

It was intriguing to see what Jeff had come up with. It was also just a bit disappointing.

Jeff's backpack contained a small pump, a battery pack to run it, and a tank of the plastic sealer the work crews sometimes sprayed over new electronics. Levi's pack held another pump and battery pack plus a tank of lubricating oil. Tomas's pack held an extra tank each of the sealer and the oil.

"I know it's not much," Jeff said in response to Nicole's expression. "But this is what you get when you have to improvise everything."

"Yeah." Nicole looked over at Levi and Tomas, busily assembling the pumps a few yards away, and lowered her voice. "What about the Q4 arena observation gallery?" she asked. "Did you ever send Kahkitah to look up there?"

"Yeah, he and another Ghorf did some recon," Jeff said. "The place was deserted. No Shipmasters, no recording equipment, no weapons. They seem to have pulled out completely."

"What about the arena floor?"

"No one down there, either," Jeff said. "And we haven't seen any Shipmasters anywhere else in Q4. They seem to have ceded us the whole quadrant. I guess that makes sense, given that they can control the ship from Q1."

Nicole nodded. "So how's this supposed to work?"

"We use the plastic spray to hopefully slow down the Shipmasters and Koffren a little," Jeff said. "The oil is for their eyes."

"Or maybe to gum up those tangler guns," Levi said.

"If we're lucky," Jeff said.

"Right," Nicole said, eyeing the plastic-film tanks. She knew how long it took the plastic to set, and she'd seen how fast the Koffren could move. It wasn't a race she was willing to bet on. "What's with all the ceiling vents?"

"Oh, these are the best part." Jeff hooked one of the stacks of gratings with his toe and slid it across the floor to her. "Take a look."

Frowning, Nicole picked up the stack. The vents were like the thousands she'd seen all over the ship: each one about two and a half feet long, a foot and a half wide, and about half an inch thick. Each was covered with a pattern of small holes, like a pizza pan she'd seen once at a friend's house.

The stack was also a lot lighter than she'd expected. "Okay," she said, unhooking the strap that was holding them together.

Only even with the strap gone the vents stayed stuck together.

Frowning, she took a closer look, to find that they were fastened together by a long bolt set a little ways up one edge and running through all of them. Near the bolt was a stiff U-loop handle like the ones she'd seen on shields once at a museum.

She blinked. *Shields?*

She looked up again, to find Jeff smiling tightly. "Yep," he said. "Grab the handle and give the outer vent a spin."

Nicole got a grip on the handle with her left hand and pushed the edge of the vent farthest out. The whole mass spun around the central point, each vent catching partway around the circle as the outer vent completed its rotation.

And she found herself holding a bumpy-edged shield

"Nice, huh?" Jeff said. "You can thank Carp and Duncan for this one—they came up with the design and the mechanics."

"Uh-huh," Nicole said, looking more closely. The whole shield had a slight outward bulge in the middle, and all the holes made it easy to look through while still protecting herself.

On the other hand, the faceplates of the Koffren helmets had openings like this, too, and that had come back to bite them.

"We're pretty sure the spider gun rounds won't get through, but will just splatter on the surface," Jeff continued. "Or, if we're lucky, bounce off to the side completely—that's why they made them a little bit convex. And if a spider round splatters across one set of holes, you can just rotate the shield to bring another set up so you can still see out. There's a clasp there between the last two—push it to the side and you can collapse the whole thing back down again."

Nicole found the clasp and swiveled the vents back around into their original stack form. "Yeah, I see," Nicole said, running her eyes over the other stacks. Six of them, one for each member of the party. "Kind of big for the Ponngs, aren't they?"

"Probably," Jeff conceded. "But this is the only size we've got. If we get into a fight, I'm thinking they can just hunker down behind them while the rest of us do whatever charging we need to."

"While they also run the drones," Levi added.

"If they haven't already been shot out of the air," Tomas said.

"There's that," Levi conceded. "Ready here."

"Me, too," Tomas said. "Where are the damn Wisps?"

"I'm sure they're coming," Nicole said, filling her lungs. "Wisps!" she called, her shout echoing off the metal walls and ceiling. "The Protector needs six of you. Come here, please."

For another moment nothing happened. Then, from the distant corner to their left, six Wisps appeared and glided toward them.

"Finally," Tomas said under his breath.

"Yeah, great," Jeff muttered. "I don't suppose there's any way to tell whether or not they're on our side."

"No problem," Nicole said, stepping toward the Wisps. "Moile, Teika? Same as before."

"Same what?" Jeff asked.

"You'll see," Moile called back over his shoulder as he and Teika moved up to flank Nicole, their swords held ready.

The Wisps were five steps away now. "Stop," Nicole ordered.

They obeyed. Taking a careful breath, Nicole stepped to the closest one and backed toward it. The silver-veined arms wrapped around her, paralyzing her—

Welcome, Protector. How may I serve?

Nicole felt a surge of relief. *Release me for a moment.*

Yes, Protector.

The arms opened, and Nicole was again free to move. "It's okay—they're on our side," she called to Jeff and the others. "Come on."

Jeff gestured to the rest of the group, and they started toward her. Nicole waited until they were nearly there, then backed again into the Wisp's arms. *Welcome, Protector. How may I serve?*

We need to cross the heat-transfer duct to Q1. Can you take us all across?

Yes, Protector.

Out of the corner of her eye she saw the other Wisps glide past her, heading toward the others. Jeff turned around, presenting his back; after a second's hesitation Levi and Tomas did likewise. The Ponngs were last, Teika in particular still looking uncomfortable with this arrangement.

It wasn't until the Wisps were carrying them through the blast of heat toward the open vent door that it belatedly occurred to Nicole that while *her* Wisp might be obeying her there was no guarantee that the others weren't under Shipmaster control. If they were, then this might be the last time she would ever see the other five alive.

Do you wish to cross to this same level?

No, take us down to level 25, she ordered. The Q1 arena entrance was on level 32, and the majority of her activities lately had been at that level or above. Crossing Q1 *beneath* the arena was something a little different, and might throw the Shipmasters off.

Her Wisp spread its butterfly wings, stepped into the open vent, and began drifting downward. A minute later, another door opened on the far side, and with a final burst of air at her back, Nicole and the Wisp settled onto the deck.

Have you any further orders, Protector?

Yes, Nicole said, wishing she could turn her head and see if Jeff and the others had also made it across safely. But she couldn't do that until the Wisp released her, and she had one more order to give first. *I need you and the other Wisps to remain here until we return and then take us back to Q3. Will you do that?*

Yes, Protector. It opened its arms. Nicole turned around.

To find that her fears had been for nothing. All five of the others were beside her, alive and well, though Levi and Tomas looked a little shaken. "Everyone okay?" she asked.

"I'm fine," Jeff said, eyeing the other two men. "I'm guessing you forgot what it was like."

"Didn't forget," Levi said tartly. "Hated it the first time, too."

"Talking about it doesn't make it any better, either," Tomas said.

"Point taken," Jeff said. "Subject closed. Any ideas, Nicole?"

"Not really," she said. "Might as well just head forward and see if we can find the inhabited sections."

"Hopefully, before the inhabited sections find us," Levi said.

They set off again. As they reached the midpoint of the corridor, Jeff casually moved closer to Nicole's side. "I assume you told the Wisps to wait for us?" he asked quietly.

"Of course."

"Good. What happens if they don't?"

"Then we go with plan B."

"Which is?"

Nicole braced herself. "It starts with me calling new Wisps . . ."

Tomas wanted to head forward in a straight shot, under the theory that the Shipmasters' lair would be as close to the *Fyrantha*'s front as possible. Nicole wanted instead to run a kind of zigzag pattern, a section of straight followed by a turn right or left for a section or two before turning straight again.

Tomas objected to that plan. Levi didn't care one way or the other. Jeff and the Ponngs sided with Nicole. That ended the discussion.

Or rather, it meant that Tomas had to brood quietly to himself instead of out loud to everyone else.

Which was fine with Nicole. A lot of Trake's group discussions had ended the same way, and she'd learned how to deal with it.

Everywhere else that Nicole had been on the ship she'd seen work crews, or heard them in the distance, or at least seen evidence of their presence. Not here. Here in Q1 the Shipmasters held all the cards, and either had had everything already fixed or had learned to live without it.

Nicole also wasn't surprised that they weren't seeing any Koffren. There were only the two of them aboard, as far as she knew, and they had a lot of territory to cover if they were going to patrol even just Q1. More ominous to her was the complete absence of Wisps.

Jeff noticed that, too. "Awfully quiet in here," he murmured to Nicole as they approached yet another corner. "You'd think they'd have figured out a decent trap by now."

"Maybe they want us to get farther in," Nicole suggested. "Make it harder for us to escape."

"That's one strategic philosophy," Jeff agreed. "The other is that the farther in they let us get, the closer we are to critical areas where they don't want us at all."

"Except that we don't know where any of those are."

"Which *they* don't know," Jeff said. "They may be able to tap into the Oracle and Ushkai *now,* but they have no idea what the *Fyrantha* might have told you before they got their fingers into those parts of the ship."

"Maybe," Nicole said doubtfully.

"Trust me," Jeff said with a hint of a malicious smile. "There's nothing like uncertainty to spook an enemy."

Ahead, Moile's drone reappeared around the corner where it had been checking out the next cross-corridor. "All appears clear," Moile reported softly.

"Right, left, or straight?" Jeff asked.

Nicole felt a tingle on the back of her neck. Had that been a slight change in air pressure, the faintest whisper of additional breeze across her forehead? Like a door had opened or closed nearby?

"Back," she breathed. "Fall back. *Now.*"

"What?" Tomas demanded. "The hell—"

And around the corner ahead, striding behind the drone where he was just out of view of its camera, one of the Koffren appeared. He raised his spider gun, pointed it at Nicole, and fired. Nicole jerked backward—

The shot exploded into a sticky black splotch across Jeff's shield as he thrust it in front of her. The Koffren fired again as Jeff squeezed close beside Nicole, hiding both of them behind his shield. There was another jerk and splash, and another section of vent holes was now blocked.

"Got it!" Nicole snapped, belatedly getting her own shield up into position and stepping away from Jeff. A spider round slapped into her shield, harder than she'd expected, and she spun the shield around in her hand to bring a section of unclogged holes up in front of her. The Koffren was walking toward them, not particularly hurrying. He shifted his aim to fire a couple of rounds behind her, and she heard the slaps as one of the other shields took the impacts.

"Here!" Jeff snapped, thrusting his shield at her. She caught it, fumbling the grip a moment as she tried to handle both shields, keeping one in front of each of them. Jeff slapped the pump control with his elbow.

And as another spider round hit Nicole's shield he leaned around the edge of his and sent a burst of oil at the Koffren.

The big alien was ready. Even before the stream exploded from Jeff's hose he had his left forearm in front of his helmet faceplate, protecting his eyes.

He was still moving forward when Levi suddenly appeared at Nicole's side and sent a spray of liquid plastic at his arms, torso, and legs.

Nicole clenched her teeth as she peered through her shield's holes, counting the seconds. If the plastic didn't dry fast enough . . .

It didn't. The Koffren broke stride for a second, but the sheer momentum of his swinging legs broke the film of plastic before it could properly set. Levi fired another burst, this time focusing on his legs—

And without warning Tomas sprinted past him, his shield held in front of him like a battering ram, charging straight at the Koffren.

With his vision partially blocked by his own arm, the Koffren didn't have a chance. Tomas slammed full speed into him, knocking aside the big alien's gun arm and continuing on to slam into his chest. The impact sent the Koffren to a staggering halt—

And as Tomas danced aside out of the way, Levi sent a final burst of plastic into the Koffren's legs.

The Koffren roared something Nicole's translator couldn't decipher and fired toward Tomas and Levi. He lowered his arm a bit for better aim, only to catch another burst of oil from Jeff squarely in his faceplate.

This time the roar came out more of a gurgle. Apparently, Jeff had hit him in the mouth as well as the eyes.

"Fall back!" Jeff shouted. "Drones?"

"Area behind is clear," Moile reported tightly.

"That won't last long," Nicole warned. The half-blind Koffren was still squeezing the spider gun's trigger, but nothing was coming out. He'd run the weapon dry.

But he'd already done plenty. Nicole's and Jeff's shields were almost completely covered, and Levi's and Tomas's weren't far behind. Even the Ponng shields had taken a round or two each from the Koffren's random shots.

"Same order for retreat," Jeff said as he and Nicole ran past the Ponngs. "Here—trade you," he added, taking the partially covered shield from Teika and handing him his own more completely blacked-out one. "Nicole?"

"Right," Nicole said, swapping shields with Moile. She and Jeff, at the front of the group, needed to be able to spot incoming threats more urgently than the Ponngs marching in the middle. "Anything?"

"Nothing," Moile said with an edge of bitterness and shame. "But then, we also failed to see our last attacker."

"Not your fault," Nicole said. "He was hiding in one of the rooms while you made your sweep and only came out after the drones had turned away from him." She glanced over her shoulder, making sure that Levi and Tomas were back in formation behind the Ponngs. "I think the plan was for him to pop out and surprise us once we passed."

"Only your zigzags kept him out of position to do that," Jeff said. "You think the other one's pulling the same trick?"

"I'm guessing he's a level above or below us," Nicole said. "Trying to parallel us where he could get in position to box us in while the other one held our attention."

"Which means he could show up anytime," Levi said. "Jeff, how's your supply?"

"Down to about half a tank," Jeff said. "You?"

"One canister drained, the other in place."

Nicole hissed out a breath. So they'd spent a full half their resources on a single Koffren.

"That's okay," Tomas gritted out. "It just takes one per Koffren."

"*If* he gives you the chance to use it," Levi warned.

"And if the Shipmasters don't show up," Nicole murmured.

"We'll do whatever it takes," Jeff said. "Now save your breath for running."

———

They were half a corridor from the heat-transfer duct wall and within sight of the six Wisps Nicole had left there when their luck ran out.

But this time, at least, they had a little warning.

"Left side!" Teika warned as his drone flashed past the last cross-corridor before the duct wall and the long corridor running alongside it. "Coming in from a stairway."

"Got it," Jeff said. "Nicole, with me."

He angled off to the left, shield held ready, Nicole beside him. They ran into the intersection and braked to a simultaneous stop.

The Koffren was there, all right, lumbering toward them from halfway down the corridor, spider gun in one hand and sword in the other. As Jeff and Nicole came within his sight he opened up with the gun, blasting their shields. "Levi?" Jeff shouted as he again handed off his shield to Nicole and unlimbered his hose.

The Koffren got three more steps before Jeff and Levi opened fire, spraying him with oil and liquid plastic. The big alien snapped his forearm up to protect his helmet and face from the oil, just as the other one had done.

Only where the other Koffren had kept charging, this one slowed in response, perhaps cautious at his sudden inability to see exactly where his enemies were.

That was a mistake. With his pumping legs slowed down, the plastic spray had more time to congeal. He jerked with a slight pause, tried to keep going, jerked again at Levi's second shot—

And with a furious roar he toppled forward, his spider gun still spitting wildly.

"I'm empty," Levi warned.

"Go!" Jeff snapped, snatching back his now completely covered shield. "Yeah, me, too," he said under his breath. "Time to move 'em out, Nicole."

"On it," Nicole said. Peering watchfully around the side of her shield at the entangled Koffren, she sidled around behind Jeff, then turned and sprinted toward the wall. The Ponngs were running ahead of her, their drones now hovering over the line of waiting Wisps, watching down the long crosswise corridor for any last-minute move by the Shipmasters. Tomas was running beside the shorter creatures, ready to throw the depleted plastic canister at any other attackers who might show up. Nicole kept running, peering closely at the Wisps . . .

And felt her stomach tighten. Six Wisps, waiting just like she'd told them, right where she'd told them.

Only they weren't the same Wisps.

"Well?" Jeff panted as he drew alongside her.

She shook her head. "Plan B."

"Damn," he muttered.

"Nothing for it," Nicole told him. "At least the Koffren helped us out a little." She raised her voice. "Everyone—hold back!" she called. "Let me go first."

She slowed to a trot, passing Tomas and the Ponngs, and stepped up to the nearest Wisp. This was it. Getting a firm grip on her shield, she turned and backed into its arms.

And as the arms closed around her, she knew she'd been right.

No *Welcome, Protector. How may I serve?* No greetings, or communications of any sort.

But she should at least try. *Open the wall and take me across to Q2,* she thought at it.

There was no response. This was a Q1 Wisp, one of the Shipmasters' slaves.

And it was here to kill her.

From behind her came a blast of heat as the Wisp opened the door into the duct. All of the others were within Nicole's line of sight: Levi and Tomas starting the emotional wind-down she'd seen so often in Trake's men after a job or a fight; Jeff standing between and behind them, whispering urgently as he explained what was about to happen; Moile and Teika still on alert, their attention slightly unfocused as they summoned their drones back to their arms. The Wisp swiveled around and glided to the opening . . .

"Go!" Jeff snapped.

An instant later Nicole was jolted forward into the shaft as Jeff slammed his shield hard into the Wisp's back. The Wisp's grip loosened slightly with the impact, and out of the corner of Nicole's eye she saw the upper tips of its wings as they unfurled. She and the Wisp floated together in the flood of hot air whipping past from beneath them, and for a second she thought the Wisp might defy its masters, breaking the order they'd given it so that it might keep the ship's Protector alive. That first heartbeat turned into another, and then a third.

Then, suddenly, the Wisp seemed to notice it was holding Nicole over the opening it had been ordered to take her into. The slender arms opened, and with a single reflexive yelp Nicole tumbled into the fiery air.

And as she fell, with her body released from its paralysis, she got a two-handed grip on her shield's handle and raised it high above her head.

The jolt as the aluminum caught the updraft nearly wrenched it from her hands. She clenched her teeth hard, snarling curses as she squeezed the handle with all her strength. Above her she could hear the clamor of voices and movement as Jeff, taking advantage of the open door, got the others into the shaft and then jumped in behind them.

The fall seemed to take forever. Nicole's hands and arms began to tremble from the strain, the air flowing past her seemed even hotter than usual, and with her shield blocking the view above her there was no way to see whether or not the rest of her team had made it into the duct and were doing their own controlled falls to safety.

For that matter, even now the hoped-for safety was hardly guaranteed. If the Shipmasters were fast enough, they might be able to order the Wisps to close their own wings, drop down the shaft to somewhere below Nicole and the others, and reacquire a grip on their victims. This had been Nicole's only trick, and if Fievj found a way to counter it she had nothing else in reserve.

She was still thinking those thoughts, still waiting in the darkness for Wisp arms to once again wrap around her, when she spotted a faint haze of light beneath her. She barely had time to bend her knees in anticipation before her feet hit the grating at the bottom of the ship and she sprawled off balance onto the floor.

She was still lying there, shaking with reaction, when the others began landing around her.

For a long moment the only sounds were the soft clatter of metal on metal as everyone set down their shields or other equipment, mixed in with the softer mutterings of relief or aching muscles or sheer disbelief. Nicole tried to set down her own shield, but her fingers were locked so tightly around the handle that she couldn't let go.

"Here, let me help," Jeff said, kneeling beside her. He got his fingers on hers and started massaging them. "Seen this happen before, usually with a rifle. You okay?"

"Yeah, I'm fine," Nicole said, her voice shaking. "Anyone hurt? Anyone hurt?" she asked more loudly.

"That," Levi said with a hint of humor in his voice, "has *got* to be the craziest thing I've ever done. Tomas?"

"Yeah," Tomas muttered. "Crazy. Stupid. And damn wasteful."

Nicole looked up at Jeff, saw her same puzzlement reflected in his own expression. "What do you mean?" she asked.

"He was there," Tomas said, and in the dim light Nicole could see that he'd turned a vicious and powerless glare on her. "He was right *there*. *And* with his sword. We could have grabbed it and cut his damn freaking head off. But no. Our great leader and Protector couldn't wait *one more damn freaking minute* before hustling us out of there and into this damn pit."

"Tomas—" Jeff began warningly.

"No, that's all right," Nicole said, a wave of weariness washing over her. "We've just proved to them that we can fight. Why *not* show them that we can kill?"

"Yeah," Tomas bit out. "Why the hell not?" He stood up, looked at his blackened shield a moment, then tossed it aside. "Which way's back?"

"That way," Nicole said, pointing in the direction of Q4. "But it's easy to get lost, so we should—"

"Take your time," Tomas cut her off as he headed that direction at a brisk walk. "I'm going home. Let me know when you get your next big idea. Better yet, call me when you've got the bastards lined up against the wall."

"You can't get up from here without a Wisp," Jeff called after him.

"Watch me!" Tomas shouted back over his shoulder. "I fell down the crap hole by myself. I can figure out how to get back up."

Jeff looked at Nicole. "Can he?"

"I doubt it," Nicole said with a sigh. "I never found a stairway out of here. Neither did Wesowee when he was hunting for me." She held up a hand. "Don't worry. Once we're in Q4 I'll call a Wisp and have it meet up with him."

"He might not trust it."

"Then he can just wait for us to catch up with him."

They watched Tomas as he walked between the support pillars, coming occasionally under one of the dim ceiling lights before disappearing for good into the darkness.

"Well," Jeff said. "At least we know that your radio relay sabotage worked."

"We do?" Nicole asked, her eyes and thoughts still on Tomas.

"Sure," Jeff said. "If they'd been able to warn the second Koffren how we took down the first he'd have tried a different sort of attack."

"Unless they're incapable of such thought or improvisation," Moile suggested. "Sometimes great strength in a person is accompanied by less intelligence and ingenuity."

"Sometimes," Levi said. "Wouldn't want to bet on that in general. So what now?"

"Nicole?" Jeff prompted quietly.

Nicole sighed. "Like Tomas said," she said. "We go home."

ten

The walk back to Q4 felt longer than usual. Part of that was Nicole's fatigue, she knew, and an even bigger part of it was the draining away of the adrenaline that had fueled their short but intense battle with the Koffren.

But most of it was heartache. Some of it was heartache for herself, but most of it was for Tomas. He'd come along with her to Q1 looking for revenge on the Koffren for Bennett's murder, and Nicole had denied him that small bit of comfort.

The real question was *why*.

Because Tomas was right on all counts. The Koffren was there, the weapon to kill him was there, and the act couldn't possibly have made any difference as to the Shipmasters' view of Earth's value to them. Humans as leaders or humans as soldiers—either one made Earth a prized property that would bring a good price in their war slave market.

Had the possibility of dealing with the Koffren simply not occurred to her in the heat of the battle? Certainly her mind had been elsewhere, focused on the Wisps and the Shipmasters' own plan for dealing with Nicole and their Protector problem. If Tomas had pointed out the opportunity that had been staring them in the face, would she have given him the time he needed to do the job?

Because here and now, thinking back on the scene, she was pretty sure she wouldn't.

And that bothered her. Not because she was squeamish about watching someone cut off someone else's head. She'd seen far worse during her time with Trake's gang. Certainly not because the Koffren didn't deserve it, because they absolutely did.

So why did she still think that wouldn't have been the right thing to do?

She didn't have an answer. And until she did, she was pretty sure Tomas wouldn't be getting in line to help her out with any new plans.

And if Tomas was out, there was a fair chance Levi would be, too. He hadn't yelled at her like Tomas had, but he'd been awfully quiet on the walk back from Q1. He'd also never been the type to jump into a knee-jerk decision, preferring instead to think things through carefully. In a couple of days, Nicole and Jeff might find themselves pretty much alone.

Alone except for the four Thii and two Ponngs, anyway. The Ghorfs, too, might be willing to break their long cover and help her, but only if they saw some real chance of victory in her plan. Otherwise, they would probably also sit this one out.

Trake used to brag that he'd started out with only two others when he first started building his gang. If he could start out mostly alone and survive the Philly streets, maybe she and Jeff could do it, too.

Though both of the friends Trake claimed had been with him in those days were long gone, so there was really no way to know if the story was true or more of his usual BS.

Finally, after a wearying trudge through the *Fyrantha*'s basement and the usual ride through the heat-exchange ducts with the Wisps, they were there.

Levi left immediately with a mechanical good-bye and headed

to his own room. The two Ponngs also left for their new quarters for rest and additional drone practice.

Leaving Nicole and Jeff alone.

"Want to get something to eat?" Jeff asked as they walked toward the center of the hive, where the dining room and medical center were located.

She shook her head. "Not really hungry."

"You really should eat something."

"Who are you, my grandmother?" Nicole said sourly. "I said I'm not hungry."

"Maybe," Jeff said. "Or maybe you don't want to risk running into Tomas or the others."

Nicole glared at him. But the glare didn't have much power behind it.

Because he was right. The idea of facing Tomas so soon after he'd stormed off made her heart ache a little harder. As for the others in her work team . . . well, the fact that none of them had shown up to help with the Q1 sortie said it all.

Plus the fact that Tomas had probably already given them his version of what had happened. She'd be lucky if any of them ever even spoke to her again.

"Come on," Jeff pressed. "I doubt any of them are there right now, anyway. And if they don't want to talk to us, they're free to leave."

"Fine," Nicole said with a sigh. She really *was* hungry. "But if someone's there, I'm taking it back to my room."

"Fair enough, I suppose," Jeff said. They reached the dining room, and the door slid open.

And Nicole came to a sudden, jerky stop. There was a man in there, all right, seated at one of the tables as if waiting for a waitress to show up.

But it wasn't any of the blue group. This man was wearing a green jumpsuit, marking him as a member of the green work team.

The team the Shipmasters had just tried to get the blue team to kill. And vice versa.

"Nicole," the man said gravely, nodding his head in greeting.

Belatedly, Nicole focused on his face. Normally, the green and blue work teams didn't mix much, and until they'd been pitted against each other in the Q1 arena Nicole hadn't talked to any of them more than a few times. In fact, up to that point she'd have been hard-pressed to put names to any of their faces.

Now, after all that, she knew all those names and faces painfully well.

"Miron," she replied, nodding back. And not just a green team member, but their leader.

As the work leader, he should logically have also been running their side of the battle the Shipmasters had forced on the two work crews. Instead, the Shipmasters had dumped Bungie on them and put him in charge of the team. Nicole hadn't really heard what Miron had thought about that, but she couldn't imagine him being very happy about it.

So what was he doing here?

"Hey, Miron," Jeff spoke up, matching Miron's tone. "Something we can do for you?"

"I don't know," Miron said. "Let me say right up front that I don't particularly want to be here. I never really thought much of your crew—except Levi; I always sort of respected him. And after the business back in the big beachfront room thing—"

"The Q1 arena," Jeff supplied.

Miron's eyes narrowed slightly in a small glower. His lip twitched and he turned back to Nicole. "Whatever. I'm just saying that getting dragged into that whole thing didn't exactly endear you to us."

"None of that was our doing," Nicole said carefully. "It was the Shipmasters who forced all of us into that mess."

"Yeah, that's what Iosif figured," Miron said. "Not what they said, but it's what he figured." He looked back at Jeff. "He also said you probably had military experience. Soldier?"

"Marine," Jeff said. "I'm guessing he did, too?"

"Navy," Miron said. His lip twitched with a somewhat reluctant smile. "I'm guessing that's enough extra reason right there for him to look down his nose at you."

"Nice to see someone maintaining traditional Earth customs," Jeff said dryly. "Is there a point to all this? Or is this just a *this means war* visit?"

"Actually, it *is* kind of that," Miron said. "Though probably not against you. *Something* aboard the *Fyrantha* has changed, and we don't know what the hell it is. You and Bungie seem to be the only ones who know anything, so we voted to send someone down here to ask you about it."

"And you drew the short straw?" Jeff suggested.

Miron straightened up in his chair. "I'm the green team leader," he said stiffly. "Leaders don't foist unpleasant duty on someone else."

Jeff inclined his head. "My apologies."

"Actually, you're the right person to hear all this, anyway," Nicole said, wondering how much the greens disliked her team that just having a conversation with them was considered unpleasant duty. "When you were made group leader, I assume Plato or someone told you to keep everyone in your team from fighting with each other?"

"It was a guy named Van Damme, actually," Miron said. "But yeah, he told me that. Figured it was a rule the Shipmasters dropped on us to make sure we didn't suck up sick days healing up from bar fights."

"The Shipmasters had nothing to do with it," Nicole said. "Okay. Here's what's going on."

She laid out the whole thing: the Shipmasters' plan to turn the *Fyrantha* back into a warship, their scheme of raising the necessary money by pitting different groups of aliens against each other and selling off their races as war slaves, and the sudden realization that their human workers could do far more than just make repairs.

Midway through the explanation she wondered briefly if she should confess that it was her own actions and stubbornness that had put Earth in this horrible danger in the first place. But at this point it didn't really matter how it had started. What mattered was how they were going to end it.

Or so she told herself.

She finished, and for a long moment Miron stared at her in silence. Then, he stirred in his chair. "I think," he said, "that we need to open up this chat a little." Putting his fingers to his lips, he blew a piercing whistle.

And with a suddenness that sent a violent jerk through Nicole's body, the door slid open and six other men in green jumpsuits boiled into the room, with Iosif in the lead.

"You okay?" Iosif asked tensely, his eyes flicking back and forth between Miron, Jeff, and Nicole.

"Of course I'm okay," Miron said. "Hey, *you* were the one who set up this cockamamie system. Whistle if everything's okay—"

"And girlish scream if it isn't," Iosif finished for him, eyeing Nicole.

"It was a shout, not a girlish scream," Miron said stiffly.

"Whatever," Iosif said. "And, yeah—*I* remember. I just never trust anyone else to."

"Wait a minute," Jeff put in, frowning at him. "You aren't serious. Did you think we were actually going to attack him or something?"

"Why not?" Iosif replied. "Most of the jarheads I've known have been a little unstable. Besides, Bungie warned us that you were a little crazy and couldn't be trusted."

"And you *believed* him?" Jeff scoffed.

"I don't know who to believe anymore," Iosif said. "Oh, and he said that the *Fyrantha* had taken you over, too."

"But *Bungie*?"

"At least that explains Miron," Nicole said.

The budding argument paused as everyone frowned at her. "What?" Iosif asked.

"Why Miron came down to talk to me instead of sending one of you," Nicole explained. "He thought there might be danger and so he took the risk himself. Makes him a good leader."

To her relief, she could sense the relaxing of some of the tension. "Yeah," Jeff said. "Unlike Bungie, who I noticed always leads from the rear."

"I noticed that, too." Iosif huffed out a breath. "Sorry."

"No apology needed," Nicole assured him. "Bungie can be pretty persuasive sometimes."

"Like when he told us we could go home if we whipped your tails in the arena?" Miron suggested.

Nicole winced. "Like I said: persuasive."

"Forget Bungie," Jeff said. "He's never been more than wharf slime. We've got way bigger problems than him."

"Yeah, that." Iosif turned to Miron. "So what the hell is going on?"

"Everyone grab a seat," Miron said, his voice darkening. "You're not going to believe this."

Considering they were getting all of it cold and for the first time, Nicole decided, they took it remarkably well. Though it probably helped that Miron was doing all the explaining instead of her.

"So basically, unless we do something, everything we know is screwed," the green leader concluded.

"*If* this is all for real," Iosif said.

"You think we're lying?" Jeff asked, an edge of challenge in his tone.

"Not necessarily," Iosif said. "But you could be wrong. Your story makes sense, but the Shipmasters are aliens. Their logic may not be our logic."

"Most of this came straight from the *Fyrantha*," Nicole reminded him. "The ship really ought to know what it's talking about."

"Maybe," Iosif said. "But then, it's also alien. So who knows?"

"Well, if it's just some kind of fever dream, then we've got nothing to worry about, anyway," one of the others—Fauke, Nicole vaguely remembered his name—offered. "So let's pretend it's real and hope we all get to laugh about it later." He gestured at Nicole and Jeff. "*My* question is whether these two have the chops to run this thing or whether we ought to put Iosif in charge."

Jeff snorted. "Why? Because he was Navy?"

"No, because he was a Navy SEAL," Fauke countered.

"Whoa," Iosif said, holding up a hand. "I washed out of SEAL training, remember?"

"You were still in the program," Fauke said stubbornly.

"For about two weeks." Iosif looked at Nicole. "Let's try this. Which of you came up with the trick Nicole used to gas all of us just before the Koffren showed up?"

Nicole braced herself. "I did."

"Figured as much," Iosif said. "Good strategy and perfect execution. If you want to run the show, I'm good with it."

A small murmur went through the others. "Wait a minute," Fauke said, frowning. "Because of one trick?"

"Because no battle plan survives contact with the enemy," Iosif said. "The people you want in charge are the ones who can improvise new tactics on the fly." He looked at Nicole. "Right now, that means you." He looked at Jeff, a small lopsided smile tugging at one corner of his lip. "And you can bring him along if you want."

"Thank you," Nicole said, surprised in spite of herself. In Trake's group, women weren't exactly welcomed into the decision-making process. But then, this was hardly Trake's group. "But while I'm happy to give suggestions and ideas, you two"—she pointed at Jeff and Iosif—"are the ones with experience and training. I think that means you should be the real planners and directors."

Jeff looked at Iosif. "You want to be my second-in-command?"

"Or you can be mine," Iosif said. "Never mind. We can work out the chain of command once we've got a plan."

"Thank you," Nicole said again, feeling another trickle of relief. The last thing they needed was their two most experienced fighters arguing about who was in charge.

Maybe that would come later. She would try her best to make sure that it didn't.

"My question is how much time we're going to have," she continued. "We need to get moving on this, but you still need to get your quota of work done. If you don't, the Shipmasters will figure out pretty quick that you're working with me."

"I don't think that's going to be a problem," Miron said grimly. "When we got back from the arena we found out that they'd taken our Sibyl."

"Ours, too," Jeff said, frowning. "That's weird."

"Where did they take them?" Nicole asked.

"No idea," Jeff said. "Fievj just came by and said we weren't going to be working on the ship for a while."

"Maybe it's supposed to be our punishment for not beating each other's brains out like they wanted?" Iosif suggested.

"What, a vacation is punishment now?" Jeff asked.

Iosif shrugged. "Like I said: aliens."

"What about the tool cabinets?" Nicole asked. Maybe Fievj was worried that the blue and green teams would try to damage the ship. "Are they all locked up?"

"Cole?" Miron invited.

"Not as of an hour ago," Cole said. "I needed a wrench, and just grabbed one from the nearest cabinet. No locks or guards or anything."

Nicole wrinkled her nose. So they weren't worried about her and Jeff having tools. Could Fievj be planning to set up another fight between the two groups?

"Well, then—" Iosif broke off as the door opened.

Nicole tensed. But it was only Kahkitah. "Nicole!" he bird-whistled excitedly. "You're back! Tomas said you were. Or he said you were coming back. But you weren't in your room, and Dr. Sam said you hadn't been to the medical center, but he was hoping you'd come see him, and then I came here"—he swept his arm around, taking in the whole dining room—"and here you were. Oh. Hello," he added as if only then noticing all the green jump-suits. "I remember you. You were in the ocean room, weren't you?"

"Yes, we were," Miron said, a little dryly. "Didn't see you help-ing very much."

"Helping?" Kahkitah's whistle sounded confused. "Was I sup-posed to help? Did you need me to help?"

"Don't worry about it, Kahkitah," Jeff said, his tone a mixture of soothing amusement and strained patience. In his own way, Nicole mused, he was as good an actor as Kahkitah and the rest of the Ghorfs. "What was that about Sam?"

"Sam? Oh—yes." Kahkitah turned back to Nicole. "He said he wanted to see you. Were you hurt? You didn't tell me you were hurt."

"I'm fine," Nicole assured him, standing up. Her stomach rum-bled, reminding her that she'd never gotten the meal that had been the reason she and Jeff had come to the dining room in the first place. "I'll go see what he wants."

"Shall I come with you?" Kahkitah asked. "You haven't forgotten the way, have you?"

"No, I'll be fine," she assured him. "But if you want to come along, you're welcome to do so."

"Thank you," Kahkitah said eagerly. "That would be wonderful." He paused, looking back at Iosif and the others. "You won't think me rude if I leave so soon, will you?" he asked, his eagerness turning to anxiety. "I don't want you to think I was rude."

"That's okay," Miron said. "We have some stuff to talk about, anyway."

"Human stuff," Iosif added.

"Oh." Kahkitah brightened. "Can I help? I like to help."

"You know anything about strategy and tactics?" Iosif asked.

Kahkitah looked at Nicole and gave out a soft, confused-sounding whistle. "I don't think so. I don't remember those words."

"Then you can't help," Iosif said.

"That's all right," Nicole said. "Come on, let's go see what Sam wants."

"All right," Kahkitah said, still sounding confused. "I'm sorry. Good-bye. It was nice to see you all again. Oh, and the yellow-swirled redcake here is wonderful if you'd like to try some."

"Thank you," Jeff said. "Good-bye, Kahkitah."

A minute later Nicole and Kahkitah were back in the corridor heading for the medical center. "You never cease to amaze me," Nicole said quietly as they walked.

"I'm sure you played just as convincingly on Earth against Bungie and the group you were with," Kahkitah said. "It's not hard to present a childlike mind to others, especially when their expectations are already low."

"I suppose so," Nicole said. "Must get tiring, though."

"If there were no point to it, it would be tiring and frustrating both," Kahkitah said. "But we travel a long-term strategy. Victory and freedom are goals well worth a small sacrifice of personal pride." He whistled a shrug. "Plus it encourages people to underestimate you. That's always useful."

"Unless you want them to *over*estimate you," Nicole said. "Sometimes that's the direction you need to go."

"True, though that's far more difficult to achieve."

Nicole winced. "Yeah. Tell me about it."

eleven

Sam was waiting in the medical center when they arrived, paging through one of the displays. He looked up as the door opened, his expression settling into something wooden. "Nicole," he greeted her, his voice neutral.

"Hello to you, too, Sam," Nicole said, matching his tone. "Kahkitah said you wanted to see me."

"Yes." His eyes flicked to Kahkitah. "Just leave him outside."

"But I want to help," Kahkitah protested before Nicole could answer. "You said I could help."

"You already did," Sam said. "You found Nicole and brought her here. That was what I needed, and you did it very well. Thank you. You can go away now."

"But—" Kahkitah broke off, looking helplessly at Nicole.

"It's all right, Kahkitah," Nicole soothed. "Don't worry, I'll go eat with you like I promised just as soon as Sam and I are done. Wait outside—I'll just be a few minutes."

"Well . . . okay. I guess." Hunching his shoulders in clear protest, Kahkitah shambled back out into the hall.

The door closed behind him. "A little paranoid, are we?" Sam asked, a bit acidly. "So one scream from you and he's supposed to come charging to the rescue?"

"You blame me?" Nicole countered.

Sam's lip twitched. "No, I suppose not," he conceded.

"Yeah," Nicole said. "Okay, I'm here. What do you want?"

"Tomas was in here a while ago," Sam said, his voice a little too casual. "Strained muscles and some odd abrasions. He had this crazy story about you and those little Ponng things charging into Q1, mixing it up with those big round-helmet guys, and then falling down an air vent. Any of that true?"

Nicole shrugged. "He caught the highlights."

"Uh-huh." Sam fixed her with a hard stare. "So what's the deal? You got an actual plan, or just seeing how pissed off you can make everyone?"

"Why does that matter to you?"

"Because I work here, too," Sam shot back. "That means I'm going to be one of the ones they dump out the airlock if you push them too far."

"Oh, relax," Nicole scoffed. "No one's coming after you. If they dump anyone, it'll be me."

"And Jeff?" Sam countered. "And Levi, and Tomas, and whoever else you're able to talk into this?"

"Maybe," Nicole said, feeling her stomach tighten. "Still not you."

"I'm a doctor," Sam said stiffly. "I'm supposed to care about all my patients. So again: Is there an actual plan?"

Nicole hesitated, studying his face. Whenever she'd talked to him before, she'd never seen anything except smoldering anger and resentment at the Wisps and Shipmasters—and Nicole—for dragging him away from Earth. But now, almost buried in the glower, she could see a new earnestness. An interest, maybe, in what was happening outside the strict boundaries he'd built around his life here.

Interest, awareness . . . and maybe, just maybe, a whisper of hope.

"Yes, there's a plan," she told him.

"Good," Sam said with a curt nod. "I want in."

Nicole blinked. "Excuse me?"

"What, was that too complicated?" Sam growled.

"No, just too far out of left field," Nicole said. "Since when have you cared about anything on the *Fyrantha* except yourself?"

"Don't flatter yourself, *Protector*," Sam said sourly. "I don't care a rat's sphincter about the ship or your charity cases."

"Yeah, that really makes me want to open up to you."

Sam clenched his teeth and hissed out a breath. "Okay. Look. When we all got hauled off to the Q1 arena Fievj told the green team that if they won the fight they would be sent home."

"And they lied."

"Did they?" Sam countered. "Yeah, I know no one went back. My question is, *could* they have sent the greens back if they'd wanted to?"

Nicole hesitated. What should she say? "Fievj says they send the aliens from the arenas back to their home planets when they're done with them."

"Do we know that for a fact?"

"Not really," Nicole admitted. "But if it *is* true, then yes, they can probably send us back to Earth if they want to."

"But they probably don't?"

"Oh, absolutely they don't," Nicole said grimly. "We're the only people who can finish fixing the ship, and they're desperate to get that done."

"But they can always bring in new people, can't they?"

Briefly, Nicole thought about what Miron had said about their Sibyls being taken away. Was that what the Shipmasters were doing? Preparing to bring in fresh blood who hadn't interacted with the *Fyrantha*'s Protector? "Sure they *can*," she said. "But anyone new would have to be trained before they'd be useful. They'd have—what's that thing called?"

"You mean a learning curve?"

"Right—a learning curve," Nicole said. "But we're already trained, so right off the curb we're better workers for them. That means they're not going to kill off anyone they don't absolutely have to."

"But they're also not going to let anyone go."

"No."

"Okay," Sam said, his eyes narrowing a little. "So here's the question. If your plan succeeds, can you get us home? Maybe a better question: *Will* you get us home?"

"*If* it succeeds, I'll certainly try."

"All right." Sam seemed to brace himself. "All right. Like I said, I'm in."

"Great," Nicole said carefully.

But only great if he was sincere about wanting to join up. If this was another game he or Bungie or the Shipmasters had come up with, his grand gesture was useless.

The only slightly smaller question was even if he *was* sincere whether there was anything he could do that would be useful.

"Yeah, you're welcome," Sam said. "So what do you want me to do? I mean, besides being there to patch up your army after the dust settles."

"Right," Nicole said, thinking fast. She needed something that would keep him out of the way but still make him feel useful. "Okay. You saw the Koffren. Big and nasty, and they've got swords and spider guns. We're not going to win against them without some advantage of our own. Is there some kind of drug you can whip up that would give us more strength or speed?"

"You mean amphetamines?" Sam asked, frowning. "I don't know. Those can be dangerous."

"So is facing off against someone who's three hundred pounds of muscle."

"Actually, I doubt they weigh more than two hun—"

"Whatever," Nicole cut him off. "Can you make us up something, or should I go ask Allyce instead?"

"No, I can do it," Sam said with strained patience. "Lucky for you, because Allyce isn't here."

Nicole frowned. "What do you mean, not here? Where did she go?"

"No idea," he said. "She came in after we got back from the fight, collected a bunch of stuff, and left."

"That seems odd."

"Yeah, nice of you to notice," Sam said sarcastically. "Sometimes you seem to pay attention to everything on this ship except us."

"Trust me," Nicole said. "*Everything* is part of my job."

"I had a supervisor once who thought that way," Sam said. "Took charge of everything, and screwed all of it up. So. Amphetamines or something like it. You want me to let you know when I've got it together?"

Nicole shook her head. "Easier for me to touch base with you when I get the chance. I'll be moving around a lot and probably be hard for you to find."

"Fine," Sam said. "Just don't forget about us."

"I won't," Nicole promised. "I'll see you later."

Kahkitah was waiting just outside when she opened the door, in a posture that suggested he'd had his ear pressed against the panel a few seconds earlier. "Are you all right?" he asked as the door slid shut behind her.

"I'm fine," she assured him. "Did you know that Allyce has left?"

"Permanently?"

"I don't know. Did you know anything about that?"

"There was a report that she was out of her usual area," Kaḥ-kitah said thoughtfully. "Ten or eleven levels above us, in the red work crew area. But not every team has a full-time doctor—blue team was very unusual in having two—and we assumed she was simply answering a medical call. Was she not?"

"Doesn't sound like it," Nicole said. "At least, if she was, she didn't tell Sam."

"Unless Sam is lying."

"Yeah, there's that," Nicole admitted. "Let's try something." She turned toward the front of the ship and picked up her pace.

"Where are we going?" Kahkitah asked.

"For starters, away from here," Nicole said. "I want to talk to a Wisp, and don't want anyone else watching me do it."

They went another four cross-corridors before she decided they were far enough away from the hive that they wouldn't stumble across any of their work team. "Wisp?" she called. "Wisp? Come here. Please."

"I didn't think you needed to say *please* to the Q4 Wisps," Kah-kitah said.

Nicole shrugged uncomfortably. "One of the things my grand-mother tried to make me do that I didn't want to," she admitted. "Politeness."

"It *does* aid in interpersonal relationships."

"Yeah, some of them," Nicole said, thinking back to Trake's gang. There, politeness got you nothing but ridicule. "Most of them, prob-ably." She waved a hand. "I suppose better late than never, like she also used to say."

"Indeed." Kahkitah pointed down the corridor to their right. "There."

Nicole turned to see a Wisp gliding toward them. "Come on," she said, and headed toward it.

They met the creature halfway. The Wisp stopped, and Nicole reached out and closed her hand around its arm.

Welcome, Protector, the voice came in her mind. *How may I serve?*

I want to locate Allyce from the blue work team, Nicole thought back at it. *Can you tell me where she is?*

She is on level 10 in bahri-*four-four-six.*

Nicole frowned. *Bahri* was the farthest forward section of Q3 and Q4, right behind the crosswise heat-transfer duct that separated the front half of the *Fyrantha* from the rear half. Level 10 put her only nine levels below the top of the ship.

What in the world was she doing up there? *What's in that room?*

It is a supply room for animal treatment.

Do you know why she's there?

No.

Is there anything up there that we don't have in the medical center?

Many things. Do you wish a list?

Nicole hesitated. Would she even know what she was looking for?

Probably not. But Sam was a doctor, too. He might be able to spot something Nicole wouldn't. *Not right now,* she told the Wisp. *If I want one later I'll ask for it.*

Very well. Do you need anything else?

Not right now, Nicole said again. *I'll need a ride across into Q3, but I can call another Wisp once I'm closer to the heat duct. Thank you.*

She released her grip on the Wisp's arm, and the creature glided away.

"Did it know where she was?" Kahkitah asked.

"Level 10, *bahri* section, in one of the supply rooms," Nicole told him. "It didn't have any idea why she was there. Neither do I."

"The specific room may not be significant," Kahkitah said. "If she's looking for a particular item, or for that matter merely studying the ship and its contents, she may simply be passing through."

"I know," Nicole said. "And I don't have time to go find her now. I need to get over to Q3 and see if Nise or Iyulik is back from their recon yet."

"Do you want me to come with you?"

"That shouldn't be necessary," Nicole said. "The Thii know where to meet me on level 36, and I won't be traveling far in Q3 before I'm out of sight. Anyway, you and the other Ghorfs should probably start figuring out some strategies of your own in case Jeff and I can't come up with something else." She winced. "Or if we do and it blows up in our faces."

"I'll do all I can to ensure that doesn't happen," Kahkitah said quietly. "But you're right. We do need to think and plan for the future."

"Good," Nicole said. "Better get to it, then."

"We will," Kahkitah said. "But first I'll walk you to the heat-exchange duct."

"I'll be all right," Nicole insisted, feeling some irritation. She didn't need to be babied here. "The Shipmasters are smart enough not to come to Q4, where I control the Wisps."

"The Shipmasters may be," Kahkitah agreed. "Bungie may not."

He had a point. "Fine," she said with a sigh.

They found a stairway and climbed the four flights down to level 36. From there Nicole led the way to the centerline and called a Wisp. A few minutes later, as Kahkitah watched silently, she was carried across to Q3.

What do you see? Nicole asked as the panel closed behind them and the Wisp folded its wings. *Do you see the Q3 part of the ship?*

I see a corridor, the Wisp replied. *There is no more.*

Nicole sighed. Still unable to see anything beyond their own sectors.

On the other hand, that blindness might prove to be a useful marker. If and when the *Fyrantha* got the Caretaker connected again to the part of the computer that talked to the Wisps, the creatures should suddenly be able to see everything.

Of course, that might also happen if the Shipmasters got control of all the Wisps, too, either through the Caretaker or Oracle or some other way.

What Nicole could do about that if it happened she had no idea. But at least it might give her some advance warning that something had changed. Best to keep asking the Wisps that question.

The barracks room where she'd had Wesowee tell the Thii to meet her was deserted. Hopefully, that just meant that the Thii hadn't yet returned, not that they'd gotten back and given up waiting for her.

Even more hopefully, it didn't mean they'd come back and been captured.

That was an unpleasant thought. Still, it was unlikely the Thii had been taken without putting up a fight, and she couldn't see any evidence of a struggle. She would just have to trust in their abilities, and hope for the best.

She should also get some rest. That was what she needed most right now. Not sleep, of course—she didn't have time for sleep. But some rest, and some time to think.

She got a drink of water from the room's dispenser, then chose a cot against the wall with the door but nearly to the corner. From there, she would be able to instantly see anyone who came in, while they would have to turn their heads to spot her. It wasn't much of an advantage, but it was all she had.

She lay down on her chosen cot, grabbed two extra pillows and wedged them beneath her head so that the door was directly in her line of sight, and settled down to rest and think.

Two minutes later, she was asleep.

twelve

She was alone in a silent room, aware that there were walls all around her but unable to see them. She tried to cry out, but couldn't speak.

Then, abruptly, the room became one of Trake's parties, with a DJ scratching violently on his turntable in the corner. Nicole wanted to tell him to stop making so much noise, that she was trying to think, but once again she couldn't find her voice—

"Protector?" the translation came in her mind. "Protector, wake up. Please."

Abruptly, the dream vanished. With an effort, Nicole pried open her eyes, to find Nise standing over her, his short sword gripped in one of his two right hands. "Nise," she managed through a mouth that was surprisingly dry. But at least she had a voice again. "Sorry. I must have fallen asleep."

Some of the stiffness seemed to leave his posture. More DJ turntable scratching—"No apology needed," the translation came, the words this time sounding relieved. "I apologize in turn if I shouted unreasonably loudly. I was concerned that the Shipmasters had harmed you."

"No, I was just overtired," Nicole said, blinking a couple of times to clear her vision. "Are *you* all right? And is Iyulik here?"

"I'm unharmed and in good health," Nise assured her. "Iyulik did not return with me, but remains in position above the teleport room."

The last bit of sleep fog abruptly evaporated from Nicole's mind. "You found the *teleport room?*" she asked, pushing herself up into a sitting position.

"Indeed," Nise said. "Bungie led us to one of the Shipmasters, and we then followed them both to the room."

"That's great," Nicole said. If she'd had a choice, she probably would have preferred the armory. But the teleport room was a perfectly good second target. "Where is it?"

"The precise location is a bit uncertain," Nise said. "The markings in and around the air ducts are not as clear as in the normal passageways. But we believe it to be in the *korvuli* section of the ship, on level 52."

"Do you know which teleport room it was? From the descriptions I've heard, I think there are at least two of them."

"We found only one control room," Nise said. "But a bit of exploration showed that it has two different sections, the one to starboard considerably larger than the one to portside."

"So two rooms where people come and go, but both operated by a single control room between them," Nicole said, pursing her lips. Actually, now that she thought about it, that made more sense for technology that the owners wanted to keep centralized and controlled. "Okay. So. *Korvuli* 52?"

"Yes," Nise said.

Nicole nodded, visualizing the *Fyrantha's* layout. So it was in the third section back from the ship's bow, and just beneath one of the networks of horizontal air ducts. "How close was the room to one of the air ducts?"

"As I said, the rooms are directly beneath one of them," Nise said. "Iyulik is able to watch through the various vents as the Wisps and Shipmasters conduct their business."

"Yes, you did say that, didn't you?" Nicole said, her momentary irritation at herself for having missed that point disappearing into sudden dread at the more important revelation. "You said they're doing business in there? What kind? Are they bringing in new people?"

"Indeed," Nise said. "Not aliens this time, but other humans."

Nicole mouthed a curse. So the Shipmasters were indeed starting new work crews. "Did you hear anything about what the new people were here for? Like if they were new work crews or fighters or something else?"

"Nothing was said in my hearing about their purpose," Nise said. "Though as each was brought aboard he was quickly moved from the room, so there was little opportunity for such discussion." He made an extra-scratchy sound that Nicole's translator ignored. "I will say that their choice of language left much to be desired."

"Yeah, we humans can get that way," Nicole said, wincing a little. "Sorry. I hope it wasn't *too* bad."

Nise waved away the apology. "It's of no importance. I've merely never heard so many uses of *excrement* repeated so closely together."

"Sounds like the group I used to hang out with," Nicole said. "They probably thought it made them sound macho. Mostly it just got real tired real fast. Could you tell how many they were bringing in?"

"No," Nise said. "I saw three arrive, but the process was going slowly and I thought it best that I return to report. Iyulik will have gathered more complete information by the time I return to him."

"Yeah," Nicole said, frowning as she tried to force these new facts into her thoughts and plans. Bringing new humans aboard was a worrisome development. On the other hand, knowing where the teleport room was counted as a good thing.

Complications . . . but for the moment, at least, she had a more pressing problem to deal with. "Okay, thanks," she told Nise. "I suppose you might as well go back to Iyulik and see if he has anything new to report. You *can* find your way back to him, right?"

"Yes, of course," Nise said.

"Oh, and you should take more water, too," Nicole added. Now, too late, she realized she should have brought a fresh supply of their granola mix from the hive.

"That's all right," Nise said. "We made sure to bring several water bottles when we were first summoned to your side."

"What about food?"

"Again, no concern needed. We brought some with us, and I gave Iyulik the rest of mine in anticipation of my return to the hive for more. It should suffice until you no longer need us there."

"Okay," Nicole said, hoping that was true. The whole thrust of the arena testing was for the Shipmasters to keep the opposite sides close enough to the edge of starvation that they were forced to fight. She had no idea how long Thii could go without food, and she didn't want to be the one who made everyone find out. "Do you want to go back first and get some more food?"

"If you are returning, I would be pleased to escort you back," Nise said. "Or are you going elsewhere?"

"I'm actually going to Q1," Nicole said. "Just before you woke me up I had a dream that I think might have been the ship talking to me."

"I was unaware the *Fyrantha* did such things."

"So was I," Nicole said. "And I might be wrong. But either way, I need to check it out. See, while you and Iyulik were following Bungie, some of us made a trip into Q1 to try to find the armory. But we ran into the Koffren and had to pull back."

"Did all of you survive?"

"Yes," Nicole said. "Though looking back I'm now thinking that the Shipmasters let us go, just driving us back, so that we'd run back to their tame Wisps and get dropped down the heat duct."

"*What?*" Nise demanded, his grip visibly tightening on his sword hilt.

"It's okay," Nicole said quickly. "I spotted the trap in time and we got around it. The point is, by the time we got back to the duct the six Wisps I'd brought over from Q3 had disappeared and had been replaced by the Shipmasters' Q1 group."

"Where did the Q3 Wisps go?"

"That's what I think the dream—the *Fyrantha*—was trying to tell me. I hadn't really thought about it before, but I'm wondering if the Shipmasters took them farther into Q1, where they can't see anything, and locked them in one of the rooms."

"There are many things there that I don't understand," Nise said slowly. "What I *do* understand is that you are going to a place where you may need protection. May I accompany you?"

Nicole hesitated. It was probably more important that he get more food and then go back to Iyulik while she and Jeff started figuring out the best way to hit the teleport room.

But she also knew that Nise wouldn't be happy if he knew she was wandering around Q1 by herself, and distracted people often got careless. "Sure," she said. "Come on, let's find us a couple of Wisps."

They reached the heat-transfer duct wall without seeing anyone, either Wisps, Shipmasters, or Koffren. Two Wisps came at Nicole's call, and after confirming they weren't under Shipmaster control she had them take her and Nise across.

Wait here for us, please, she ordered as the closing door shut off the blast of heat behind them. *And if my companion returns alone, obey his orders. Please.*

I obey.

The Wisps opened their arms, and once again she and Nise were able to move. "Where do we begin?" the Thii asked, looking around.

Nicole reached back and got a grip on her Wisp's arm. *Do you know if any of your fellow Q3 Wisps are in here?* she asked. *Or if any are missing? Or can you see or hear or sense any of them?*

There is no in here, Protector, the Wisp replied. *There is nothing beyond the passageway where we now stand.*

Nicole grimaced. *Understood,* she said. *Please wait here.*

I obey.

Nicole started to let go—*One more question,* she said. *Can one Wisp paralyze another Wisp by holding it or picking it up?*

Yes. Injured Wisps are often transported that way.

Nicole felt her eyebrows go up. *Injured* Wisps? She hadn't heard about Wisps getting injured.

But now that she thought about it, maybe that was how the Shipmasters had convinced the Q1 Wisps to lock away the Q3 group she'd brought over. If they'd convinced the Q1 Wisps that the Q3 group was injured or sick, that might have done it. *Could I order you to pick up or neutralize another Wisp?*

Is the Wisp injured?

Not necessarily. I'm asking as the Fyrantha's *Protector. Could I order you to pick up or neutralize another Wisp?*

As the Protector, you may order me to do whatever you wish.

Nicole wrinkled her nose. At least until the Wisp was back under Shipmaster control. *Thank you,* she said, and let go of its arm. "They don't know where the other Wisps are," she told Nise. "We're on our own."

"As expected," Nise said. "Where do we begin?"

Nicole chewed at the inside of her cheek. Injured Wisps . . . "It won't be too far," she said, thinking out loud. "It won't be some-

thing small, either, like a pump room or storage closet. Something
with beds, probably."

"Do Wisps lie down?" Nise asked. "I've never seen one that
wasn't moving."

"Neither have I," Nicole conceded. "Except the ones Wesowee
threw into some of the others. They went down flat."

"One of the Ghorfs *threw* a Wisp?"

"Yeah, they're pretty strong," Nicole said. "And the Wisps he hit
fell over, too. But they all got up by themselves just fine, so I guess
that tells us they *can* lie down."

"I believe, then, that we're seeking a barracks room," Nise said,
looking around. "Do you know how this part of the ship is laid
out?"

"Not really," Nicole said. "But barracks rooms are large, which
means extra space between their doors and the doors next to
them. That gives us something to look for."

"That makes sense," Nise said. "Lead, and I will follow."

There were three rooms they could see from their position that
had the kind of door arrangement that Nicole was looking for. In
the second of the three, they found five of the six missing Wisps.

The creatures were lying on the five cots closest to the door,
their bodies stiff, their eyes wide open and staring blankly at the
ceiling.

"Are they dead?" Nise asked, an edge of uneasiness in his voice.
"And you said there were six. Where is the other?"

"I don't know," Nicole said. "Maybe they took it somewhere
else. Maybe it was injured."

"Or was able to return to Q3," Nise suggested. "Do you want
me to go look for it?"

"No, we'd better stay together," Nicole said, walking over to the
nearest of the five. Steeling herself, she gingerly laid her hand on
its arm. *Wisp?* she called.

There was no answer. *Wisp?* she tried again.

Nothing. She moved on to the others, trying with each to spark a reaction.

Still nothing. For all she could tell, they were indeed dead.

"Their flesh is warm."

Nicole turned. Nise was standing beside one of the Wisps, his sword tucked into his belt, each of his four hands resting lightly on a different place on the Wisp's arms, torso, or neck. "Are these creatures living beings, or are they mechanical constructs?"

"I don't know," Nicole said, touching her Wisp's arm again. Nise was right—the skin was definitely warmer than room temperature. "Maybe some sort of mix? A living robot or something?"

"That's possible," Nise said. "Thii science has nothing like that, but we've often speculated on such things. I believe I can feel a faint pulse, as well, either a living heartbeat or else a mechanical rhythm."

"I can't feel anything," Nicole said. "But your fingers may be more sensitive than mine."

"Perhaps," Nise said. "Are you certain these are the same Wisps that you brought across earlier?"

"Yes," Nicole said, looking down at them. "And no, I don't know how I know that, either. But I do."

"I don't doubt your word," Nise said. "What shall we do?"

Nicole touched the nearest Wisp's cheek. *Wisp?*

Still no answer. "Well, we can't leave them here," she said. "Maybe taking them back to Q3 will help them. The Wisps over there might be able to do something."

"Very well." Leaning forward, Nise forced his arms under the Wisp's torso and legs and lifted.

He got the creature maybe two inches above the cot before abruptly dropping it back down.

"You okay?" Nicole asked.

"They're heavier than they look," Nise said ruefully. "We may need to do this together."

"Yeah," Nicole said, making a face. They weren't very far from the heat-exchange duct, but doing the back-and-forth trip five times was begging for trouble from the Shipmasters, especially with both of them encumbered with a Wisp's worth of baggage. But if the Wisps were that heavy, the only option would be to go hunt down a cart.

Impulsively, she leaned over, slipped her arms under the Wisp's shoulders and thighs, and lifted. *Come on, Wisp,* she growled mentally at it. *Wake up and smell the coffee.*

I smell no coffee.

Nicole jerked back, yanking her hands out from under it, the echo of that unexpected thought tingling through her mind.

"What is it?" Nise snapped, and out of the corner of Nicole's eye she saw him snatch his sword from his belt.

"It's okay," she assured him hastily, staring down at the Wisp. Its eyes were still open, but instead of just staring blankly at the ceiling it seemed to be studying it.

Nicole caught her breath. *Studying* it?

She stepped back and touched its arm. *Do you know who I am?*

You are the Protector.

That's right. Can you see me?

The Wisp's eyes turned toward her face. *Yes.*

Can you see the room you're in?

Its eyes shifted sideways. *Yes.*

Describe it.

It is a group sleeping room.

"What is it?" Nise asked.

"It can see the room," Nicole said, hearing a slight trembling in her voice. "It can see me *and* the room."

"Did you think it was blind?"

"You don't understand," Nicole said. "Up to now, none of the Wisps I've talked to could see more than a corridor or two past their own section of the ship. This one has somehow been— I don't know. Enlightened? Unblinded?"

"Perhaps reprogrammed," Nise suggested.

Nicole looked down at the Wisp. If Nise was right, and if *all* the Wisps could be reprogrammed . . .

She touched the Wisp's arm. *What section of the ship do you belong to?*

I have no designated section. I belong with the Protector.

Nicole felt a tingle run through her. Did that mean it could go wherever she did, and do whatever she wanted? *If I give you orders, you'll obey them?*

Yes.

More importantly, did it mean it *wouldn't* do what Fievj and the other Shipmasters wanted? *If the Shipmasters give you orders, will you obey them?*

If you order me to do so, I will obey them.

I don't want you to do so. I want you to never obey the Shipmasters.

Then I shall not do so.

Not ever?

Not ever.

Nicole pursed her lips. Obeying her; not obeying Fievj. Good. Now, how much further could she take this? *Do you remember Jeff? He came across with me earlier from Q3.*

Yes. I remember him.

If I order you to obey him, will you do so?

Yes.

Then I order that. You'll obey his orders, and mine. No one else's. Unless I tell you to do so later.

Understood. I will obey you and Jeff only.

Nicole lifted her hand away, her mind spinning. Even having just one Wisp fully under her and Jeff's control could be a big game changer.

But if all five of them were the same way . . .

She touched the Wisp again. *Do you know what happened to the sixth Wisp who came over with us?*

It was confused. Unable to function. It was taken to a room of reserve to recover its senses.

Do you know where this room is?

No.

Nicole nodded. So; just these five.

Still, five Wisps under her direct control was way more than she'd had any right to expect. *All right. Wait here for further orders.*

I obey the Protector.

Nicole stepped to the next cot and laid her hand on the Wisp's arm. *Wake up,* she ordered. *The Protector wishes you to wake up. Please.*

I obey the Protector, the Wisp said.

Can you see me?

Yes.

Can you see the room we're in?

Yes.

I order you to obey me and Jeff and no one else.

Understood. I will obey only you and Jeff.

Two minutes later, all five Wisps were awake and had promised their obedience. "Wisps: stand up," Nicole said aloud, moving to the door.

Silently, all five stood. "If they're to be your personal servants, perhaps you should name them," Nise suggested.

"I'm thinking they're more allies than servants," Nicole said. "But that's a good idea." She lifted a hand, leveled a finger at the leftmost Wisp. "I'm going to give you names," she announced. "You will answer to *Cambria.*" She moved the finger one Wisp to the right. "You will answer to *Firth.*

"*Hagert.*

"*Jessup.*

"*Lehigh.*"

She ran the Wisps through the names a second time, just to make sure they'd all gotten them. "Any other suggestions?" she asked Nise.

"Not at this time," Nise said. "Interesting names. Is there a significance to them?"

"Those are some of the streets from where I used to live," Nicole said, a stream of dark memories running through her. "Streets I never want to see again."

Nise seemed to ponder that. "If the names don't inspire you, why do you use them?"

"Oh, they inspire me, all right," Nicole said grimly. "They inspire me to never let anything like that ever happen to me again. Or to anyone else I know."

"Good," Nise said, and Nicole could hear a hint of approval in his voice. "What now?"

"First, we head back to the hive and get you more food and water," Nicole said. "Then we find Jeff and he or I will escort you back here so you can return to Iyulik to see if there's any further news."

"And after that?" Nise asked, gesturing toward the Wisps. "What will you do with them?"

"Not sure," Nicole said. "But I can tell you one thing. Whatever it is, the Shipmasters will never see it coming." She lifted a hand and beckoned. "Wisps? Come with us."

thirteen

"Well," Jeff said, scratching his cheek as he eyed the five silent Wisps. "*That's* new."

"I know," Nicole said around a mouthful of green-paste flatbread. It was the first chance she'd had to eat in a long time, and she was determined to make the most of it. "The question is, how are we going to use them?"

"Oh, I can think of a dozen possibilities right off the top of my head." Jeff jerked a thumb at Kahkitah, sitting on the other side of the dining room table. "I'm guessing the Ghorfs could come up with a dozen more."

"Indeed," Kahkitah said, his bird whistles quiet and thoughtful. "Tell me, do you know if the Shipmasters can tell one Wisp from another?"

"No idea," Nicole said. "I don't even know how *I* can tell them apart."

"An effect of your connection to the *Fyrantha,* no doubt," Kahkitah said. "Have you experimented with how many orders you can give a specific Wisp at the same time?"

Nicole frowned. "What do you mean?"

"He means," Jeff said, "can you tell a Wisp to go to one of the tool lockers"—he paused, leaning over to look at the underside of the table—"pick out a number-four tri-wrench, bring it back here, and take one of the table legs off?"

"Why would I—? Oh," Nicole interrupted herself, nodding as she understood.

"Exactly," Jeff said. "If they can remember strings of instructions, we can use them for complicated jobs. If they can't, we can't."

"Shall we try an experiment?" Kahkitah suggested.

"It's as good a time as any." Jeff gestured to Nicole. "Over to you, Nicole."

"Okay," Nicole said, eyeing the Wisps. "Cambria, come here, please."

The Wisp glided to the table and stopped, and Nicole touched its arm. *Cambria, I want you to go to the nearest tool cabinet. Get a number-four tri-wrench and bring it back here to me. Please.*

What is a number-four tri-wrench?

It's the fourth-smallest triangle-shaped wrench, Nicole said. *It takes off triangle-shaped nuts. Do you know what wrenches and nuts are?*

No.

Nicole made a face. Whatever the Wisps' purpose was aboard the *Fyrantha*, apparently it didn't involve the ship's tools. *This is a nut,* she said. Taking its hand and guiding it under the table, she closed its fingers around the nut. *This is a nut. Can you find a wrench that will wrap around it and bring it to me?*

I will try, the Wisp answered.

Good. Go and get it now. Please.

The Wisp turned and left the room. "Trouble?" Jeff asked.

"It doesn't know what wrenches or nuts are," Nicole told him. "I tried letting it touch one, but I don't know if that'll be good enough."

"It apparently believed it was," Kahkitah said. "Otherwise, I

doubt it would have left without obtaining additional clarification."

"Good point," Jeff said. "But it could easily just *think* it has
enough clarification. Let's see what it brings back."

The door opened. Nicole looked over to see Levi glance in, his
expression tense. He started to turn away, spotted Nicole, and
stopped. "*There* you are," he said. "You've got a visitor. Fievj is
coming down the hall."

Nicole felt her eyes widen. "Fievj is *here?*"

"And looking for you," Levi said. "I told him I hadn't seen you
in a while—"

"Is he armored?" Jeff cut in.

"You mean in that centaur suit?" Levi said, jerking a little as he
belatedly noticed the four motionless Wisps. "Yeah. You want me
to tell him you're here?"

"Is Fievj one of the Shipmasters?" Kahkitah asked nervously.
"Oh, please—not in here. They frighten me."

"It's okay, Kahkitah," Nicole soothed, standing up. Back to his
stupid-Ghorf persona; but his message was clear. Letting Fievj
see a group of Wisps hanging around the blue team's dining room
would probably be a bad idea. "Thanks, Levi. I'll go meet him out
there and find out what he wants."

"I'll come with you," Jeff volunteered, standing up beside Nicole.
"Levi, you want to wait here with Kahkitah?"

"I think I'll come watch," Levi said, giving the Wisps one more
look before stepping aside out of the doorway. "From a distance, if
you don't mind."

"No, actually that's a good idea," Jeff said. "I doubt we'll need a
witness, but you never know."

"Yeah," Levi said under his breath as Nicole passed him.
"Terrific."

They found Fievj three corridors away, walking with a mea-
sured, almost hesitant stride. He spotted Nicole and Jeff coming
toward him, and it seemed to Nicole that he picked up his pace a
little. "Remember that he has to turn around to get to his weapons," Jeff murmured. "If he makes any kind of move, you duck
down the nearest cross-corridor and run like hell."

"What about you?" she murmured back.

"If we're close enough, I'll try to beat him to the punch," Jeff
said. "If not, I'll be right behind you."

Nicole swallowed hard. And right here, with the two of them
midway between the nearest escape routes, was Fievj's best opportunity to kill them both.

But to her nervous surprise, he made no effort to get to the
weapons stash, but merely kept walking toward them. Another
dozen steps, and they all came to a halt a couple of yards apart.

"Protector," the Shipmaster's voice came through Nicole's translator. "I'm Fievj. I speak for the Shipmasters."

"I know," Nicole said. "And I speak for the *Fyrantha*."

Fievj might have twitched at that. Probably her imagination.

"What do you want?" she continued.

"We're facing a crisis," Fievj said. "I've been sent to ask for your
help."

"Interesting," Jeff said. "What's the crisis this time?"

"The Koffren." Fievj hesitated. "You must first understand that
the Koffren are not like the aliens we bring to the testing arenas.
They're . . . clients, shall we say. Clients with a strong interest in
the *Fyrantha* and our operation."

"Yeah, we'd kind of guessed that," Nicole said. "So you're scared
of them?"

"You're scared of *two* of them?" Jeff added pointedly.

"They're formidable opponents," Fievj said. "You know that—
you've faced them."

"Twice, actually," Jeff said. "And we've beaten them both times."

"Well, the first time, anyway," Nicole corrected him. "You told them to let us win the second time, didn't you?"

This time there was a definite twitch. "We made no such stipulation."

"Sure," Nicole said. "There's still only two of them."

"Not for long," Fievj warned. "Not unless we can come to an agreement."

"What are you talking about?" Jeff asked, frowning. "What are they going to do, breed a bunch of little Koffren on you?"

"Of course not," Fievj bit out. "They're going to bring in more of their kind. More warriors, and almost certainly better armed."

"How?" Nicole said. "Don't you and the Wisps control the teleport rooms?"

"If they choose to take them over, we cannot stop them," Fievj said. "They are warriors."

Jeff snorted. "They're warriors with swords and spider guns," he said. "You're warriors with greenfire weapons. Two clear shots, and it's over."

"It's not that simple," Fievj said. "We aren't—" He broke off. "We're not warriors," he said softly. "We don't fight. Not like you do."

"We don't fight, either," Nicole said. Not that he was going to believe her, but it was still worth a try.

"But you are leaders," Fievj said. "You're leaders, planners, and encouragers. You're right, there are only two Koffren at present. But we cannot face them without you."

And then, maybe fifty yards behind Fievj, a Wisp came into view from a cross-corridor and glided toward them.

Not just any Wisp. Cambria.

And in its hand, the wrench Nicole had asked for.

Nicole went rigid. If Fievj saw it . . .

"So what do you want us to do?" Jeff asked, easing a half step to his right away from Nicole, clearly hoping to draw Fievj's attention away from the Wisp as it came up to Nicole.

It was a good plan. But not good enough, Nicole realized. Cambria would stop in front of Nicole and hand her the wrench, and even in that armored helmet Fievj's peripheral vision was bound to be good enough to let him see the interaction.

And if the Wisps didn't even know what a tri-wrench was, there was no reason for one of them to be walking around with one, let alone bringing one to a Sibyl. The last thing they needed was for Fievj to start wondering just how much control she had over the Wisps.

For that matter, even just a Wisp appearing here without orders or without Nicole calling for it might spark some of the same curiosity and suspicion. Her only chance was to pretend she was summoning it and hope Fievj didn't have any rearview mirrors in there. She opened her mouth.

"Not yet," Jeff said under his breath, his hand touching hers warningly. Nicole turned to him, frowning—

"We need you to meet with us," Fievj said.

Cambria was still coming. It was thirty yards away now—

"More specifically, to meet with Nevvis," Fievj continued.

—twenty yards—

"He's our leader, and the only one who can command our full loyalty."

—ten yards—

"Now," Jeff murmured.

"Wisp!" Nicole called. "Come here."

Fievj half turned to his left to look behind him—

And like a striking rattlesnake Jeff leaped forward, grabbing

Fievj's right arm with his left hand. "Hold it!" he snapped, taking another step and catching the Shipmaster's left arm in his right hand. "No weapons! You hear me?"

"I wasn't reaching for a weapon," Fievj snapped back. He jerked his arms upward, breaking Jeff's double grip.

And with his torso half turned to the side and his full attention on Jeff, Cambria glided past him on his other side and handed the wrench to Nicole. She nodded thanks and quickly slid the wrench up her jumpsuit sleeve.

"Yeah, you'd better not be," Jeff said, some of the starch gone out of his voice as he stepped back beside Nicole.

"I didn't come here to fight," Fievj said. He turned back, too, twitching again as he belatedly spotted the Wisp that had come up on his blind side and was now standing motionless beside Nicole. "I came for help."

"We'll see what we can do," Nicole said. "Tell Nevvis to come by whenever he wants and we'll talk."

"He won't come here," Fievj said. "He fears for his safety in the center of your stronghold."

"I hope he's not suggesting Nicole come to Q1," Jeff warned. "Because that's a nonstarter from our end."

"Understood," Fievj said. "He suggests the more neutral territory of Q3. The Protector can choose any place within that quadrant for the meeting."

"I'm not sure it's all *that* neutral," Nicole countered. "You control a lot of the Wisps there."

"At times, yes, we do," Fievj said. "But at other times, the control falls to you. The *Fyrantha* is as it is. If you can suggest a better location, I'm willing to listen."

Nicole scowled. But he was right. "Fine," she said. "When, and where?"

"Whenever and wherever you choose," Fievj said. "If you'd like, Nevvis and I can wait across the crosswise duct in Q1 until you send a Wisp to give us your precise location. Would that make you feel safer?"

Nicole smiled tightly. *Would that make you feel safer?* Trake had used lines like that on her and the others all the time to try to put them on the defensive. The idea was to make the other person feel bad about making unreasonable demands and get them to back off.

Unfortunately for Fievj, Nicole had had plenty of experience with this particular game. "Yes, that should work," she said. "You can wait on level 37, directly forward of the level 32 entrance to the Q3 arena."

"And five levels down from it, of course," Fievj said.

"Of course," Nicole said. "Will that work for you?"

"Yes," Fievj said. "When?"

"How long will it take you to get back to Q1 and get Nevvis to the meeting point?"

"No more than an hour," Fievj said. "Perhaps sooner."

"An hour, then," Nicole said. "I'll pick a spot and send a Wisp to bring you to me."

Fievj turned his head slightly toward Cambria. Maybe he figured that was the Wisp she would be sending. Maybe he was just wondering why it was still standing there. "Very well," he said. "We shall see you then." He started to turn away—

"I assume she doesn't have to come alone?" Jeff spoke up.

Fievj was silent a moment, and Nicole had the feeling he was studying Jeff through his helmet. "If you speak of guards, they're unnecessary. Neither Nevvis nor I intend any harm to you."

"That still leaves the Koffren," Jeff said.

"The Koffren will not be there," Fievj said. "But if you fear for the Protector's safety, you may of course accompany her."

"Great," Jeff said. "One more thing. I want a bottle of the stuff that dissolves the tangler rounds."

Fievj looked at Nicole, then back at Jeff. "You've spoken to the Ghorf."

"You mean Kahkitah?" Nicole shrugged. "Of course. He was pretty upset about what happened and blamed me for lying to him."

"As well he should," Fievj said severely.

"Yeah, maybe," Jeff said. "It's not like you can always tell them the truth or expect them to keep secrets. They get confused about what they can tell other people and what they can't."

"Yes, we've noticed," Fievj said. "Still, an easygoing populace makes for a quiet civilization. In some ways, they're lucky."

"Yeah, giving up brains for extra muscle is always a good idea," Jeff said. "So what about that magic paint thinner of yours?"

Fievj half turned around to the horse section of his armor. Nicole tensed; but the hinged cover opened to reveal only a frame holding twelve short black boxes and an equal number of small eyedropper bottles like the ones Kahkitah had described. "Here," Fievj said, selecting one of the bottles and turning back to hand it to Jeff.

"Let's make it two," Jeff said. "And throw in a few tangler rounds so we can make sure the stuff works. I'm guessing those other things are magazines?"

"It's the correct solvent," Fievj said. "You can take my word for it."

"Well, actually, no, we can't," Jeff said. "Come on—you've got a dozen bottles and mags back there. You can spare me one of them."

Fievj hesitated. Then, with clear reluctance, he turned back and picked out one of the boxes and another fluid bottle. "Will there be more demands?" he asked stiffly as he handed Jeff the box with one hand and closed the storage cover with the other.

"No, this should do," Jeff said, peering at the box a moment before lowering his hands to his sides. "Still means you're the only ones with guns, but this stuff will at least lower the odds a little."

"If I'd wished to shoot you or the Protector, I could have brought a weapon with me," Fievj reminded him.

"Except that you need me alive and well," Nicole reminded him.

"I will return to Q1 and await your message," Fievj said, letting her comment pass without response. With a final pointed look at Cambria, he turned and walked away, his rear legs matching his front legs in their slightly off-rhythm way.

"What do you think?" Jeff asked quietly.

"Look like he's falling right into line," Nicole murmured back.

"You mean playing it the way you thought?"

"Yeah." Nicole turned to Cambria and took its arm. *Thank you for the wrench,* she said, sliding it back out of her sleeve. It was a number four, just like she'd asked for. *You may return to the others in the dining room.*

I obey the Protector.

Nicole let go of its arm, and the Wisp turned and glided away. Midway to the next cross-corridor it passed Levi, who'd emerged from the same cross-corridor where he'd been lurking and was now walking toward Nicole and Jeff. He gave the Wisp a quick speculative look as they passed each other, then continued forward. "So what did he want?" he asked as he came up to them. "I couldn't hear the conversation from back there."

"His boss wants to talk to Nicole," Jeff said. "They're meeting in an hour over in Q3."

"Are they, now," Levi said darkly. "I hope you're not trusting him."

"Oh, no, not at all," Nicole assured him. "We're pretty sure he's planning something."

"That's a start, I guess," Levi said. "I don't suppose you happen to know what that something might be?"

Nicole hesitated. She trusted Levi as much as she trusted any of them. But there was still the question of how much the Caretaker could see and hear of what went on inside the ship. And, more to the point, how much of what he heard the Shipmasters were also hearing. "Well, it's a trap," she said. "That much is for sure."

"We're getting an escort together for her," Jeff added. "You interested?"

Levi snorted. "After last time? I don't think you'll find anyone willing to go through that again."

"We've been told the Koffren won't be involved," Jeff said.

"Yeah," Levi said dryly. "*I've* been told unicorns will be serving dinner tonight."

"That's okay," Nicole said. "Actually, I was thinking Moile, Teika, and I would handle it by ourselves."

"Yeah, I don't think so," Jeff said. "We need to make sure you're safe."

"I'll be safe," Nicole said. "The thing is to make sure *you're* safe."

"That *he's* safe?" Levi echoed, frowning. "What's he got to be worried about?"

"Never mind," Nicole said, glaring warningly at Jeff. "The point is that he needs to be ready to move if and when I make a deal with Nevvis." She raised her eyebrows at Jeff. "Right?"

Jeff's face and body language were a mess of silent protest. But he gave a reluctant nod. "Right."

"And now I need to get ready," Nicole said. "We'll go to the dining room first and make sure Cambria and the other Wisps will obey you. Then I'll go find the Ponngs."

"What do you want me to do?" Levi asked.

"Just be ready, I guess," Nicole said.

"Be ready for what?"

Nicole grimaced. "For anything."

Nicole had told Fievj to wait for her message on level 37. She'd also spent a fair amount of time on level 36 after Bungie had gotten her away from the Shipmaster and Koffren ambush, which suggested she might not want to hang around that level.

But there was another level she'd spent even more time on, and which she knew better than any of the others. Leading Moile and Teika to the *Fyrantha's* centerline, she summoned the Wisps she needed, and a few minutes later they all crossed the heat duct to Q3. Leaving the Wisps waiting behind them in the long corridor, she and the Ponngs headed farther into the quadrant.

"This is level 32, is it not?" Moile asked, looking around as they walked.

"It is," Nicole confirmed. "That way"—she pointed to the left—"is the arena where you and the Thii fought."

"And now we and the Thii battle side by side under your leadership," Teika murmured.

"Indeed," Moile said. "We will strive always to be worthy of your trust."

"I know you will," Nicole assured him. Whether or not she would remain worthy of *their* trust, unfortunately, was another question entirely.

"How far are we going?" Moile asked.

"Not much farther," Nicole said, looking back over her shoulder. They were five corridors in, far enough from the centerline to make it all look like good faith but close enough that a solid sprint would get them back to where they'd left the Wisps before any of them ran out of wind. "In fact, this looks good right here."

She stopped and filled her lungs. "Wisps! I need one of you."

She counted out twenty seconds. Then, from one of the main corridors ahead a Wisp appeared and started toward them. "That's far enough," Nicole called as Moile and Teika stepped in front of her and took up guard positions, their swords held ready. "I just have a message for you to deliver."

The Wisp stopped. "I want you to go across to Q1 and down to level 37," Nicole told it. "Fievj and another Shipmaster should be waiting there across from the Q3 arena. Tell them I'm waiting for them here on level 32. Please."

For a moment the Wisp stood there, as if thinking about it. Then, it turned and headed forward down the corridor it had first appeared from.

"Heading to the crosswise heat duct, probably," she commented. "I wonder if they always use the ducts to go up and down or if they ever use the stairs."

"I have no knowledge of that," Moile said. "Do you think it communicates with the Shipmasters the way it does with you?"

"You mean by telepathic touch?" Nicole shrugged. "I assume so. Though if there's a problem, it can probably just lead them up here."

"Yes." Moile hesitated. "I must confess to you, Protector, that I agree with Jeff. I think this plan is highly dangerous. And not just to you personally."

"I know Jeff thinks that," Nicole said.

"And you don't?"

"Well . . . yes, I suppose so," she conceded. "But if I've read the Shipmasters right, this should work. Anyway, I don't see us having any better choices right now."

Moile was silent a moment. "You understand so many things," he said thoughtfully. "Is that because of who you are? Or is it who you are plus the *Fyrantha* speaking and acting through you?"

"I honestly don't know, Moile," Nicole said, wincing. The thought that the ship might be influencing her without her knowledge still gave her the creeps. "As to how much I understand, let's wait on that one until we see what happens in the next hour or so."

"Yes." Another pause. "Perhaps we should at least back up one corridor," he suggested. "If the Wisp tells them exactly where you are, they'll be able to flank us."

"Good point," Nicole said, looking behind her. "Right. Matter of fact, let's back up two corridors."

"We'll still be in sight for a long degree of time," Teika pointed out.

"Yes." Nicole took a deep breath. "But then, we kind of have to be, don't we?"

Nicole had guessed that it would be at least twenty minutes before anyone arrived.

Apparently, the Shipmasters were more anxious and eager than she'd thought.

Two armored centaurs appeared first, clumping into view around the same corner the messenger Wisp had disappeared down. They spotted Nicole and stopped. "Protector?" one of them called. "I am Fievj. This is Nevvis."

"Hello, Nevvis," Nicole called back. "Nice to finally meet you."

"This hardly qualifies as meeting," a darker voice rumbled at her. "Come closer, that we may speak as equals. Or do you fear me?"

"Of course I fear you," Nicole called. "That's the whole point of the armor, isn't it? To scare people?"

"Come closer," Nevvis insisted.

"You want to talk closer?" Nicole retorted. "Then *you* come closer."

"Insolence," Nevvis bit out. "I offered you mercy. Now I offer only defeat and destruction."

Moile made a sound in the back of his throat and lifted his sword a little higher.

"Is that a threat?" Nicole asked calmly. "I thought you wanted to make a deal."

"We will make a deal," Nevvis said. "But you perhaps will not survive to see it."

And from the corridor twenty yards in front of Nicole, Bungie stepped into view.

But for that first moment his back was to her, his face and the spider gun in his hand pointed toward the two Shipmasters.

"No, I'm back here," Nicole called.

He spun around, a confused look momentarily on his face before it was replaced with his trademark smirk. "Thought you were going to wait back there," he said, nodding his head over his shoulder to where Nicole and the Ponngs had originally been waiting.

"*I* thought you weren't going to attack me," Nicole said, ignoring him and addressing her comment to the Shipmasters.

"We shall not," Fievj said. "But you are a danger to us and to all who dwell aboard this vessel. Only if we can contain and neutralize you will the Koffren rescind their challenge to our command of the *Fyrantha*."

"So *this* is your big idea?" Nicole scoffed, waving at Bungie. "*Him?*"

"You're so clever, aren't you?" Bungie said, the smirk growing wider. "Oh, yeah—you understand me, and Fievj, and everyone else. But there's one person you never figured out. Ever."

"Hello, Nicole," a familiar voice came from behind her.

Nicole turned, her stomach tightening into a knot. Standing in a line across the cross-corridor were five men. Big men; brutal-looking men. Dressed in the all-too-familiar gang colors of Philadelphia, spider guns held loosely at their sides.

And standing in the center of the group, looking as always like he owned everything and everyone he could see, including Nicole—

"Hey, Nicole," Trake leered. "How you been?"

Fourteen

There was no time to answer. There was certainly no time to gape. Snatching the sword out of Teika's hand, Nicole spun around and hurled it as hard as she could toward Bungie.

He was still diving for the floor to get clear of the spinning weapon, his spider gun flying from his hand, when she charged. "Come on!" she shouted over her shoulder.

The order was unnecessary. The two Ponngs were already on the move, skittering behind her on their shorter legs.

Nicole eyed Bungie's bouncing spider gun longingly as she ran, wondering briefly if she had time to grab it. But the weapon was too far out of reach, and she didn't dare waste the pair of seconds it would take to go after it. The instant Trake and his gang recovered from their surprise at her abrupt move they would undoubtedly open fire, and the only thing that stood between her and their own spider guns were the two Ponngs. Focusing on pumping her legs as hard as she could—wincing as Ficvj and Nevvis twisted at the waist, turning around to get to their horse-body weapon caches—she reached the corridor Bungie had appeared from—

But instead of turning right, the direction that led forward to Q1, she banked to her left and sprinted off in the opposite direction, toward the arena and the rear of the ship.

As she rounded the corner, she glanced to her left to see Trake and the other four break their stunned paralysis and charge after her.

"Do you want us to delay them?" Moile asked from behind her.

"Not now," Nicole called back, pushing herself as hard as she could. They were still way too close to the Shipmasters, and she didn't know what they would do if they rounded the corner in pursuit to find a webbed and helpless Ponng lying at their feet.

The next cross-corridor was about twenty feet ahead. If she and the Ponngs could get around the corner and out of sight before Trake and the others could reach the intersection they'd just left, she might be able to give them the slip. Or at least get out of spider gun range for another few seconds.

They were three steps away from safety when a spider round shot past her left shoulder and splattered itself on the wall right at the corner.

Reflexively, Nicole dodged to the right. A second round arrowed past, this one passing the cross-corridor and exploding into black goo, again on the far-left corner.

Even using an unfamiliar weapon, Trake should be better with the spider gun than to unload two clean misses. Warning shots, then. Apparently, he didn't want her and the Ponngs turning left toward the heat duct and a possible escape back to Q4.

But he also didn't just want to bring her down like a lion killing its prey. First, he wanted to play with her a little.

Nicole had seen that cruel streak in him many times. Usually it worked exactly the way he wanted, giving him the fun of turning his victim into jelly before he ended the game. Having to watch Trake toy with people this way had been one of the things she'd hated the most about life in his gang. Being the one who was being toyed with was a hundred times worse.

But in this case, making it look like she was dancing to his strings would buy her some time.

And with luck, a little extra time would be all she needed.

"Go right!" she snapped, angling away from the spider gun tendrils dangling on her left and dodging to the right into the cross-corridor.

Once again, they were out of sight. But that breathing space wouldn't last for long. The next main corridor was about sixty feet away, and their pursuers were likely to get around the corner behind her before she and the Ponngs could reach it.

Still, she doubted Trake was tired of the game yet. It would be another corridor, probably a second, possibly a third, before he decided he'd piled enough panic down her throat. Then, a single shot to her legs to bring her down, a leisurely stroll to where she was lying helpless, and he could deliver her to Fievj and Nevvis and claim whatever promise they'd made to him.

What he would say when he found out they'd almost certainly lied to him would be highly interesting. On the other hand, there wouldn't be much satisfaction in it for Nicole if she was already their prisoner.

They were nearly to the corridor when another spider shot splattered against the leftmost corner. Trake was still playing games, and on top of that had apparently decided to herd them in a big circle back to where the Shipmasters were waiting. Probably hoping he could drop her right at their feet. That would be just like him.

At the last junction she'd played along. Time to shake things up a little. "Start to angle right," she muttered behind her to the Ponngs. "But be ready to go left."

A second gooey mass slapped into the wall to her left, followed by a third. Either the Shipmasters had plenty of rounds for the spider guns, or else Trake simply didn't care if he wasted ammo. Knowing Trake, probably the latter. Nicole drifted toward the right, as if she were again letting herself be pushed in the direction he wanted her to go—

And then, at the last second, she pushed off the soft flooring and angled left into the corridor. If Trake were fast enough, and his spider gun was still pointed this direction, the chase could very well end sooner than either of them wanted.

It didn't, but it was a near thing. Trake fired one final shot, the round slashing through the air close enough behind Nicole's head that she could feel the burst of wind as it passed. Trake's startled curse and the impact of the round against the wall came simultaneously—

And then Nicole was safely out of sight in the corridor, the Ponngs right behind her.

Though not quite as safely. Teika yelped something untranslatable as the edge of that last shot caught just the top of his head. But as Nicole braked to a halt and started back toward him he did a sort of corkscrew twist of his head and shoulders and wrenched himself clear.

"You all right?" Nicole asked as Moile grabbed his arm and pulled him the rest of the way around the corner.

"I'm unharmed," Teika said.

"Good," Nicole said. But the bright red spot on his head where some of the green, moss-like hair had been torn away—along with the pale liquid oozing from the wound—were in stark contradiction to his assurances. She needed to wrap this thing up as fast as she could and get him back to the hive for medical treatment.

Right now, though, what he needed most was to get to the next corridor before Trake and his thugs caught up and pinned him to the wall or floor for good. "Come on," she said, grabbing Teika's other arm and hurrying both him and Moile along. Her back tingled as they approached the corner, waiting for the slap against her skin that would end her lonely act of rebellion forever—

They were just rounding the corner when a spider round slapped into Moile's back, knocking him two feet forward past Nicole. He flailed briefly for balance, lost his fight, and pitched forward onto the deck.

"Moile!" Nicole snapped, again braking hard and spinning around.

"Go!" he snapped back, shoving his sword along the floor toward Teika as best he could with his upper arm pinioned to the flooring.

Before Nicole could protest, she was yanked nearly off her feet as Teika grabbed her arm and pulled her away from the corner. "Come," he said sharply, scooping up the sword with his other hand. "We must go."

Nicole knew that. But it didn't make it any easier. "Moile—"

"Go!" Moile cut her off.

Clenching her teeth, Nicole turned and sprinted down the corridor, swapping grips with Teika so that she, and not the injured Ponng, would be doing all the pulling. Unless she'd gotten turned around, the door she was looking for should be only a few feet away . . .

There. She skidded to a halt and popped open the hidden stairway door.

But instead of heading in, she turned and crossed the corridor to an electrical room. She got the door open and shoved Teika inside, following him in and pulling the door closed behind them.

Just in time. As she pressed her ear to the door, she heard the unmistakable sound of muffled voices and the not-quite-muffled sound of Trake swearing. "The freaking *hell*? Where'd the freaking bitch go?"

"Here," Bungie's voice came faintly. "Hold it, Trake—right *here*."

Nicole tensed, her hands forming into useless fists. Out of the corner of her eye she saw Teika bring his two swords up a little to point at the door . . .

"I'll be freaking damned," Trake said. "What the hell is *this*?"

"It's a stairway," Bungie said. "It goes—"

"I know it's a freaking stairway, you freaking idiot," Trake snapped. "Which freaking way did she go?"

"Probably up," Bungie said. "She likes to go up. Figures who-ever's chasing her will get too tired to keep going."

"Yeah, like that's freaking gonna happen," Trake growled. "Come on."

There was a muffled sound of footsteps and voices. The stair-way door closed.

"Now?" Teika murmured.

"Almost," Nicole whispered back, counting out the seconds. Bungie had said to go up, and that was what it had sounded like. But if Trake was still running true to form . . .

She reached her mental countdown. "*Now.*" Leaning her full weight on the door, she popped the latch and charged out.

The thug Trake had left as a guard outside the stairway door had just enough time to drop his mouth open—and not nearly enough time to bring up his spider gun—as Nicole and Teika slammed bodily into him.

Nicole had hoped that, if Trake had left a sentry, her hope-fully unexpected appearance and the sheer energy of their attack would take him out of the fight. Unfortunately, he was bigger than she was and shrugged off the impact with a single grunt. Half a second later, Nicole was sent sprawling as a jerking sweep of his arm sent her tumbling away into the center of the corridor. She rolled half over, trying to make it back to her feet before he could get his spider gun up—

And watched the thug stagger in turn as Teika slapped the flat of his sword hard against the side of the man's head. His knees buckled, and for a second Nicole hoped he might go down.

But even as she scrambled back to her feet his knees steadied, and he shook his head a couple of times to clear it. His eyes came back into focus, locking onto Nicole, his slightly unsteady hand once again bringing his spider gun up toward her.

There was only one chance. Grabbing the end of his weapon, praying that his muscles still weren't fully recovered from Teika's attack, she shoved on the gun, twisting his wrist inward to point back at himself. Before he could do more than gape in surprise, her fumbling finger found the trigger and squeezed it.

The gun kicked back against her hand as it spat out a black glob. The round slammed into the thug's chest and shoulder, and he staggered a second time as it burst into the familiar black tentacles. Most of them wrapped around his arms and torso, but a couple splashed backward into the door behind him, pinning him in place.

Unfortunately, one of the threads also splashed forward toward his bent wrist and the spider gun still gripped in his hand. Nicole barely got her own hand out of the way before the tendril effectively glued the gun to him.

"*Damn*," she bit out. She'd hoped to neutralize Trake's spotter; she'd hoped just as hard that she could get his spider gun away from him.

With one of Jeff's eyedropper bottles of neutralizing liquid she might have been able to free the gun without freeing its owner. But Jeff wasn't here, and neither were his bottles. Even if they had been, Trake had undoubtedly heard the sound of Nicole and Teika slamming the thug into the door. She had to get out of here before the rest of the gang made it back down the stairs.

Teika had lifted his sword for another shot at knocking the thug unconscious. "Come on," Nicole said, touching his arm and turning back toward the cross-corridor they'd turned off of a minute ago. She glanced both directions, confirmed that no Shipmasters or Wisps were in sight. She sent a single, helpless look at Moile as he lay pinned to the floor, then turned to the right, heading as fast as she could toward the central heat-transfer duct three corridors away.

She and Teika had passed the first corridor and were midway to the second when a spider round from behind them slammed into Teika's back, wrapping its tendrils around him and throwing him forward. "Go!" he shouted, the word changing to a strangled gasp as the impact with the deck knocked the breath out of him.

Nicole had already veered sharply to her left, a reflexive movement that saved her as a second shot whizzed past her shoulder and arced to the deck far ahead. She started to veer right, veered left instead, and had the satisfaction of watching another round shoot past instead of connecting.

But she couldn't keep this up forever, especially not if Trake gave up his attempts to take her down personally and ordered the other four to also open fire. The centerline corridor was just ahead now, with the Wisps she'd left there a short ways to her left. If she could just get to them before Trake nailed her . . .

She was three steps from that final corner when her luck ran out.

It was the first time she'd actually been hit by one of the spider shots, and she gasped at the sheer bludgeoning strength of the impact as it sent a sharp stab of agony through the skin and muscle just below the shoulder blade. But watching the Ponngs succumb to Trake's attack had given her at least partial warning of the weapon's effects, and even as the tendrils wrapped around her she fought to keep her feet under her. One tendril stretched down and latched itself to her left thigh, but it remained mostly loose and didn't interfere with her running. Another round hit her right shoulder, this one expending most of its energy and tendrils straight ahead or bouncing back against her chest. She reached the corner, and with a burst of speed dodged to her left into the centerline corridor.

And immediately stumbled into a fast but uncontrolled drunkard's stagger as her lack of proper arm assistance threw her completely off balance.

She managed to get the rest of the way across the corridor without falling, but she was going way too fast to stop. At the last second she managed to spin halfway around so she could at least slam into the wall back-first. The pain of the impact elicited another gasp. As she blinked away the sudden light-headedness she saw Trake and the others trot triumphantly around the corner, Trake with his spider gun still pointed at her. She tried to drop to the floor to make herself less of a target, but discovered she was now glued to the wall. Trake's smarmy smile widened.

And with their full attention on her—

She filled her lungs. "Wisps!" she shouted. "Grab them!"

Trake swore, his leer of victory vanishing as he belatedly focused on the line of fifteen Wisps that Nicole had brought over from Q4. Wisps that had been lined up along the wall out of his sight but were now spreading out to fill the whole corridor as they glided toward him and his thugs. "*Get them!*" he yelped, his voice on the edge of panic as he jerked up his spider gun and opened fire on the creatures coming at him. The air was suddenly filled with projectiles, and the nearest Wisps jerked and wobbled as their torsos, arms, and folded wings erupted in black wrappings. Trake continued to swear, his initial surprise changing to anger and then malicious glee as he saw the helplessness of the Wisps to withstand his attack.

He was still snarling happily when the two drones came swooping in from behind him, their whine masked by Trake's swearing and the sound of the thugs' own fire.

Bungie and Trake were the first to get hit by the drones' para-lyzing cords: Trake, because Jeff had probably picked him out as the group's leader; Bungie, because Levi at the second drone's controls, really, *really* hated him.

The remaining three thugs belatedly caught sight of their at-tackers as the drones' momentum took them past the group before they swung back for their second pass. Two of the men likewise fell to the cords before they could do anything to fight back. The last thug spun around, trying frantically to hit one of the flyers with a shot as it overcorrected and continued on toward Jeff and Levi.

He got off two rounds, missing with both of them, before freez-ing in mid-aim as one of the Wisps came up behind him and wrapped its arms around him.

A moment later, Jeff was at Nicole's side, his eyedropper bottle ready. "Are you all right?" he asked as he carefully squeezed a drop of the liquid onto the center of the black goo wrapped around her chest.

"I'm fine," Nicole assured him, watching in fascination as the goo began to burn away from the drop in all directions, disinte-grating like tissue paper that had had a lighted match dropped on it. "Moile and Teika both got shot, too."

"I know—we spotted them down the cross-corridor as we passed." Jeff looked over his shoulder as Levi and Miron joined the group, scooping up the spider guns now scattered across the deck and handing them out to some of the other six green-jumpsuited men who'd come up behind them. "Shipmasters?"

"Five corridors to portside and one forward," Nicole said. "At least, that's where I left them. Oh, and one of Trake's men is webbed up around the corner a couple of corridors in, too, near where Moile got hit. Afraid his gun got webbed up with him."

"No problem," Jeff grunted. "We'll make sure to knock him out before we get it. Iosif? You get all that?"

"Yeah," Iosif said, coming up beside him. "What do you want us to do?"

"Head up the corridor, check on the Ponngs, and make sure the Shipmasters aren't headed this way," Jeff said. "If you have to shoot, remember that that armor of theirs is damn slippery—not sure this stuff will even stick. Aim at their helmets or legs, try to get the goo to wrap around and stick to itself. As soon as Nicole's able to move, we'll join you and I'll unweb the Ponngs."

"Don't dawdle," Iosif warned. He turned, pointed down the cross-corridor in silent command, and he and his men headed out.

"You got *all* of the green team to come along?" Nicole asked.

"*I* didn't," Jeff said. "Iosif did. Natural leader, and they trust him." He eyed the disintegrating goo another moment, then put the eyedropper back into its bottle. "I guess a single drop *does* do the trick. Kahkitah might have mentioned that it's not exactly instantaneous." He scowled at the goo, then gestured behind him. "Levi?"

"Here," Levi said, coming up to them, his drone floating along in front of him. "Ready for me to do recon?"

"New plan," Jeff said. "Bench the drone and stay with Nicole until she's free."

"What about my recon pass down the centerline?" Levi objected, hefting the drone control for emphasis.

"Canceled," Jeff said, pointing at the drone and then at the deck. "This stuff takes longer than I expected, I need to get started on the Ponngs, and we can't leave Nicole alone."

"Since when is she alone?" Levi asked, nodding at the Wisps as he nevertheless lowered the drone to the floor. "What about them?"

"They don't move all that fast," Jeff reminded him. "Not exactly great guards. On top of that, we don't know how fast Bungie and his buddies will recover. They may need another zap or two to keep them quiet."

"That's okay," Nicole said. "Wisps? Please pick up the men on the floor and hold them until Jeff or I tell you to let them go."

The five nearest Wisps stepped out of the line still stretched across the corridor and glided forward, two of them limping a bit with the spider goo interfering with their waists and hips. They leaned over, picked up Trake and Bungie and the others, then straightened up, the thugs frozen stiff in their arms. "Now you can both go," Nicole said to Jeff and Levi.

"Or you can go and I can do my recon," Levi suggested.

"I don't—" Jeff broke off, his lip twisting. "Fine," he said. "Just be careful. We can't afford to lose the drones."

"Yeah, yeah, I know," Levi said. "You want to get moving before the Shipmasters figure out they lost and run back home?"

"I'm going," Jeff said. He nodded at Nicole, then took off down the cross-corridor.

"That guy worries too much," Levi grumbled as he set his spider gun on the deck and took the drone controller in both hands. "Okay. Let's see what's at the other end of this corridor."

The drone lifted off the floor, hovering at waist height as Levi fiddled with its leveling. The webbing pinning Nicole's left arm dissolved, and with a grunt of relief she reached up with that hand and rubbed away the nose itch that had been bugging her ever since she'd first hit the wall. Levi got the drone leveled and started it moving down the corridor.

It was barely past the line of Wisps when the two Shipmasters stepped into view around the next corner.

Each of them now carrying a long black greenfire tube.

"Oh, *crap!*" Levi gasped. "Nicole—!"

"Get down!" Nicole snapped back, bending her knee to put her left foot against the wall behind her and pushing as hard as she could. No good—she was still pinned to the wall. "You hear me? Get *down*."

There was no response. Levi was still frozen to the spot, his eyes wide, the drone control clutched in his hands.

Cursing under her breath, Nicole lunged forward as far as she could with her free hand and managed to slap the control out of his grip. "Damn it, Levi—get *down*," she snarled.

"What are you doing?" Levi barked, her action finally snapping him out of his paralysis. He hunched over and dived to the floor, aiming for the drone control. "The drone's our only chance."

"Leave it," Nicole ordered, throwing a quick look to her right. The Shipmasters were standing side by side in the middle of the corridor, their greenfire weapons pointed at the drone that was now drifting to the deck in response to the sudden lack of a controller. Possibly deciding whether or not the flyer was a threat, and if so whether or not to shoot it.

But their interest in the machine wouldn't last long, Nicole knew. The minute they focused past the Wisps and saw her stuck to the wall, she would be dead.

The drone might be a chance to save her. Luckily for her, it wasn't the only one. "Wisps, open your wings!" she ordered tersely. "Quickly!"

She was about to add a belated *please* when the Wisps' wings unfurled, stretching out and filling the corridor with butterfly colors.

And, more importantly, blocking the Shipmasters' view.

Again, Nicole shoved at the wall behind her, and this time managed to wrench herself free. She was tumbling toward the deck, her left arm stretched out to break her fall, her right arm still partially webbed, when a flash of brilliant green sliced through the wall of Wisps and slashed a burn mark into the wall right where she'd been standing.

Levi had reached the drone controller and scooped it up. "No," Nicole ordered, grabbing his arm with her left hand and finally managing to pull her right arm free of the remaining goo. "We need the drone."

"We need to not die!" Levi retorted.

"Yeah, I'm on it," Nicole said. She swiveled around on her hip just as a second greenfire blast cut through another of the Wisps, this shot going wild, and snatched up Levi's spider gun.

She was peering at the line of Wisps in front of her, trying to figure out how she was going to shoot with them blocking her line of sight, when out of the corner of her eye she saw a figure suddenly loom behind her.

Reflexively, she flinched away, letting go of Levi's arm. The figure dove past her, landing on the floor right at the Wisps' feet. Even as Nicole's brain registered that it was Jeff, he stuck his spider gun between a pair of Wisp legs and opened fire.

A third greenfire bolt slashed through the Wisp line, this one slicing through the air just over Jeff's head. He ignored it and continued to fire. The hiss of the shots kept going—Nicole wondered if he could even see his targets or whether he was just shooting blindly—a fourth greenfire shot cut through the line and burned into the ceiling—

And then, silence.

Nicole counted out twenty seconds. No sounds, no spider gun shots, no greenfire blasts. "Jeff?" she whispered.

"Stay there," he whispered back. Easing forward, he pressed his face up against the filmy Wisp robes and carefully moved them aside to look between the Wisps' legs. He nodded and got to his feet. "They're gone," he said.

Nicole swallowed. Gone, or maybe just waiting for a better shot? "Wisps, lower your wings," she ordered.

The wings folded back out of the way, revealing an empty corridor with a dozen black spider globs scattered around the walls, ceiling, and floor. Nicole braced herself, ready to order the wings back up if the Shipmasters reappeared. But the corridor remained empty.

The battle was over.

And then, even as she started to breathe again, she belatedly realized that four of the Wisps hadn't furled their wings. She frowned, shifting her gaze from the wings to their faces.

And felt a horrified chill run through her.

Wisp faces were always somewhat blank. These faces were blanker. Wisps were always quiet. These four were quieter. Wisp skin was clean and pure, white with an overlay of silvery threads. The skin of these four were marred by ugly black greenfire burn marks.

Nicole didn't know how it was she could tell one Wisp from another. But somehow she knew such things. It was the same way she knew what she was looking at now.

"Nicole?" Jeff asked softly.

"Yes," she said, the ache in her throat settling into an ache in her heart.

"They're dead."

FiFteen

"It was half a victory," Jeff insisted quietly from across the dining room table. "That's what you have to hang on to. Half a victory."

Nicole didn't answer. The plate in front of her was loaded with food, and before she'd headed out to meet Fievj and Nevvis she'd promised herself a good meal when it was over.

Now, even with her stomach rumbling, she had no appetite.

What had she done?

"This is the part when you tell me I'm right," Jeff said into the silence. "You can also add that I'm usually right if you want. I'll wait."

He was trying to cheer her up, Nicole knew. Trying to ease some of the pain choking her heart and mind.

In some ways his attempt at humor was an insult, as if he were brushing aside her failure and ignoring the terrible consequences of her actions. But she was too weary and heartsick to even feel offended.

"Nicole, you have to snap out of it," he said. "You can yell if you want, or cry if you want, or even call me a coldhearted bastard if that helps. But you have to come back."

"How?" Nicole asked, feeling fresh tears welling up in her eyes. "I killed them, Jeff. All of them."

"You didn't kill anyone," he said firmly. "It was all Fievj and Nevvis."

"Was it?" Nicole countered. "What if I'd let Levi throw the drone at them like he'd wanted to? You were right there, ready to fight back. Maybe if they'd had to take a moment to dodge the drone you'd have gotten there before they had a chance to shoot the Wisps."

"First: You didn't know I'd heard the ruckus and was on my way," Jeff said. "Second: You don't know that they'd even have bothered with the drone. They came to the meeting wanting to eliminate you, and there's a 90-plus-percent chance they'd have ignored anything that got in the way of that."

"You don't know that."

"Trust me. I do." Jeff hesitated. "And third: We need those drones. Both of them. If they'd taken the time to shoot it, okay, maybe they would only have had enough time to take out two or three Wisps instead of all four. But it would have cost us."

"So you're saying that our plans and our gadgets are more important than people's lives?" she snarled.

He held her gaze without flinching. "Our plans are for freeing the *Fyrantha* and saving the lives of everyone aboard," he said. "There are certain things we need for that plan. You had to make a choice between something we absolutely need and some lives that the plan could manage without."

Nicole shivered. "You make me sound like a monster."

"No," Jeff said quietly. "I make you sound like a general."

The tears filling Nicole's eyes flowed over and down her cheeks. "I don't want to be a general."

"I don't blame you," Jeff said. "Being the leader in a war is a huge burden. But it's the job—and the burden—that the *Fyrantha's* given you. And whether you like it or not, you're pretty damn good at it."

Nicole huffed a half laugh, half sob. "Really? I was supposed to trap Trake's men, get their spider guns, then hit the Shipmasters hard enough to get their greenfire weapons. The whole World War II Liberator gun thing—remember?"

"I remember," Jeff said. "So we only got the spider guns and not the greenguns. Like I said, half a victory."

Nicole wiped at her tears. "So if we'd gotten the greenfire guns, we could have paid another four Wisp lives for them?"

"It doesn't work that way, and you know it," Jeff said, the first hint of annoyance creeping into his voice. "Forget about the guns and the Wisps for a minute. You played the Shipmasters, Nicole— played them perfectly. You convinced them that you understood them and could anticipate their moves, and that they needed something new to throw at you. You guessed they'd go to Bungie for advice, and you knew he'd tell them that Trake was the one person you never understood. You had them, Nicole, all the way down the line."

"Then why didn't it work?" Nicole demanded. "Why are four Wisps dead?"

"You're missing the big picture," Jeff said. "Remember what Iosif said? *No battle plan survives contact with the enemy?* Well, yours did a lot better than most. That fact gives me a great deal of confidence that you'll be able to pull off the rest of the campaign."

He reached over the table and touched the back of her hand. "I know you're hurting about the Wisps. So am I. But we're in a war, and war requires choices. No general worth an honest salute likes making the decisions that will cost people their lives. But they keep making the choices, and the sacrifices that go with them, because if they don't a lot more people will die. Understand?"

"I suppose," she said, turning her hand over and getting a grip on his. "Did you ever have to make that kind of decision?"

"Me personally?" Jeff shook his head. "I never got anywhere near that kind of rank. But I knew people who did, and almost all of them came back feeling the same way you are right now. Especially the first time they had to send someone to their death."

"*Almost* all of them?" Nicole asked. "What about those who *didn't* come back feeling that way? Were they handling it better?"

"No, they were handling it like bastards," Jeff said. "Probably why we called them that."

"You didn't."

Jeff shrugged. "Well, not to their faces."

The dining room door slid open, and Nicole looked over to see Levi and Iosif come in, followed by Moile and Teika.

"Well, they're here," Iosif announced as he headed toward the food dispenser. "Not exactly happy campers."

"Not surprised," Nicole said. "One of the empty rooms, right?"

"Six of them, actually," Jeff corrected. "Figured we didn't want them talking and plotting together. Did the Wisps take up guard positions like I'd ordered them to?"

"Yep, two on each room," Levi said. "Don't worry, they're well buttoned up."

"Good," Jeff said. "You checked for hidden weapons, right?"

"Oh, yeah," Iosif said. "We got three shiny new knives out of the deal."

"Any good?"

Iosif shrugged as he punched in his food order. "If we want to cause mayhem we've got better things in our tool lockers."

"Figured." Jeff looked at the two Ponngs. "You two all right?"

"We're fine," Moile said, holding up a red-blotched arm. "The reaction seems to be largely superficial."

Nicole winced. The chemical that dissolved the spider webbing had unexpectedly turned out to be an irritant to Ponng skin. Just one more small glitch in her great plan.

"So what are we going to do with them?" Iosif asked.

Nicole started, belatedly realizing that the question had been to her. "I thought we'd put them in the arena," she said. "The Shipmasters have all pulled out of Q4, and we've checked the place for weapons. If we program the dispenser for human food, they should be okay until we figure out something more permanent."

"Bungie eating dog kibble," Jeff said with an evilly satisfied smile. "I like it."

"It's more trail mix than dog kibble," Iosif pointed out.

"I'll still tell him it's kibble," Jeff said, turning again to the Ponngs. "Speaking of which, are you two hungry? We've got the dispenser here programmed with your stuff if you want to give it a try. Real food, too, not just your version of trail mix."

"Really?" Teika asked. "How did you learn Ponng recipes?"

"We didn't, really," Jeff conceded. "But Joaquim fiddled around and combined a couple of our food varieties with your nutritional needs. He claims it will be good, but none of us really knows."

"Then we should address your uncertainties," Moile said. "Only yesterday we were discussing some of our favorite foods from home."

"I'm afraid this probably won't be anything close," Jeff said.

"Perhaps it will become one of our favorites," Moile said. "Show us this food, that we may examine it."

"I like your sense of adventure," Jeff said, standing up. "I'll show you how to program it."

He headed between the tables to the food dispenser, the Ponngs close behind.

"Can I talk to you a minute?" Levi asked quietly as he sat down beside Nicole.

"Sure," she said, eyeing him. Levi was never exactly outgoing or flamboyant, but even for him this seemed unusually subdued. "What's up?"

His eyes flicked to Jeff and the Ponngs at the dispenser, then to Iosif eating his meal alone at a table halfway across the room. "That thing back in the corridor," he said, looking back at Nicole. "When you tried to take the control away from me. You didn't have to do that."

Nicole frowned. "What?"

"I know I froze," he went on hurriedly. "But I was coming out of it. I just hadn't expected them to surprise us that way. But I was all set to ram the drone down their throats."

"Of course," Nicole said. *That* was what he thought she'd been trying to do? To take over the drone from him?

"Really, I was," he insisted. "It would have worked better than the tangle gun you tried."

"It's all right," Nicole said. "We were all improvising there." She swallowed hard. "And it didn't come out as clean as I would have liked. But we're all okay, and we got the spider guns, and that's what's important."

"I suppose," he said. "I just wanted to say you won't have to do that again."

"I'm sure I won't," Nicole said. "You should probably get something to eat."

He looked over at Jeff and the Ponngs. "Yeah, I think I'll wait until they're finished. Not really interested in sampling old-style Ponng cooking. I'll be in my room if anyone needs me."

"Okay," Nicole said. "And, you know . . . thanks for everything. I know you weren't enthusiastic about this plan."

Levi shrugged. "Like you said, we got some weapons out of the deal. That's better than I was expecting."

"And we'll do even better next time," Nicole promised.

"Yeah, let's not get ahead of ourselves," Levi said, standing up. "See you later."

"Right. Rest well."

With a nod, Levi headed back out into the corridor. Nicole

watched until the door closed behind him, then turned back to the mostly untouched food sitting in front of her. She still wasn't hungry, but starving herself wouldn't bring back the dead Wisps. She scooped up a bite and forced herself to eat it.

She was halfway through the meal when Jeff and the Ponngs returned, the latter with trays piled high with different-colored variants of the food Nicole had been eating since she first arrived on the *Fyrantha.* "You're certainly confident," she commented, eyeing the masses of food.

"I pulled up a sample tray first," Jeff said, waving at their trays. "These are the variants they liked the best."

"Not precisely like the food of home," Teika said. "But the taste is that of the ground food we had in the arena, and it and the texture are quite satisfying."

"At least that's one thing we got right today," Nicole said.

"Come on," Jeff chided gently. "Half a victory, remember? Okay, so what's next?"

"We need to get Bungie and Trake locked in the arena," Nicole said, dragging her mind back to the problems of the present.

"We'll need a code to unlock the door," Jeff reminded her.

"I can get it for you," Nicole said. "While you do that, I should go over to Q3 and check in on the Thii."

"When's Nise due to check in?"

"Not really sure," Nicole said. "He has to gauge his movements to what the Shipmasters are doing. But it should be soon, and I don't want him having to wait. I should probably take them more food and water, too."

"Tell you what," Jeff offered. "How about *you* go take a nap, and *I* go find Nise?"

"He'll be expecting *me.*"

"He'll be expecting someone with fresh supplies," Jeff said. "And all things considered, it might be better if it's someone the

Shipmasters aren't desperately trying to kill. Besides, you need to get some rest."

"I'm okay," Nicole said. He was right on both counts, but her depression had suddenly sparked an unexpected surge of stubbornness. "I'm the reason everyone's having to run around like crazies. I need to at least pull my own weight."

"Right," Jeff said. He looked at the Ponngs. "I'm heading over to Q3 to check on the Thii. You two want to come along?"

"We would be honored," Moile said.

"Unless the Protector needs us," Teika put in. "Our first duty is to her."

"No, go ahead," Nicole said, the stubbornness fading back into common sense. She *was* pretty tired, and Jeff could certainly handle the rendezvous with Nise. "I've got Cambria and the others if there's trouble, and Kahkitah's wandering around somewhere, too."

"If you're sure," Teika said, sounding a little doubtful.

"I'm sure," Nicole said. "But thank you."

"Good," Jeff said briskly. "And when I say *take a nap*, I don't mean *go stuff Bungie in a padded cell*. They'll be fine right where they are for now. I'll wake you when we're back, and we'll move them together."

"Fine," Nicole said tiredly. Actually, the thought of getting Trake's gang to their permanent prison hadn't even occurred to her. "Be sure to take a couple of spider guns with you."

"First on my list of things to do," Jeff said. "Eat up, gentlemen, and let's get this show on the road."

"This will keep until later," Moile said, taking a last bite and then pushing his tray a few inches away.

"Yes," Teika said. He took two hasty bites, and Nicole noted that he seemed more reluctant when he also pushed away his tray.

"You really don't—" she began.

"Yes, we do," Jeff cut her off as he stood up. "Any new instructions for Nise?"

Nicole sighed. "Just that they're to keep watching and listening. And tell him we'll be there to relieve them as soon as we can."

"Got it," Jeff said. "Sleep well."

"And wake me if anything changes."

"Of course," Jeff said. Ushering the Ponngs in front of him, he left the room.

"He's not a very good liar, is he?" Iosif commented from his table.

"Excuse me?" Nicole asked.

"He has no intention of waking you up for anything short of the Second Coming," Iosif said. "He worries about you."

"I'm fine," Nicole groused.

"You look like something the cat dragged in," Iosif said. "Who's Cambria?"

"One of my five special Wisps."

"Special how?"

Nicole hesitated. Those special Wisps were supposed to be a secret, but she was too tired to play games. Besides, as far as she was concerned, Iosif's and his team's actions in the Q3 battle had more than proven their commitment. "We told you how the Wisps seem anchored to their own specific quadrants, right? Well, these five are apparently anchored to me."

"Really," Iosif said thoughtfully. "Interesting. That could be useful."

"So we hope," Nicole said. "Thank you for your help in Q3, by the way. We couldn't have done it without you."

"Glad we could help," Iosif said. "Actually, if the Shipmasters are that easy to outmaneuver, this may be easier than I'd expected."

"Well, don't get overconfident," Nicole warned. "They may not be terrific at fighting, but they've got resources and weapons that we don't."

"Maybe," Iosif said. "But wars are won by men, not weapons. Men *and* women," he added, inclining his head to her. "But you're right about the overconfidence. Never a good idea." He looked over at the door as it slid open and a Wisp glided in.

Not just any Wisp, but one of her special five. But up to now, they'd always stayed put unless she gave them orders to the contrary. "Hagert?" she asked. "Is something wrong?"

The Wisp came over to her and stopped beside the table. Nicole reached out and laid a hand on its arm. *Is something wrong?* she thought at it.

The Caretaker speaks to me, Hagert said into her mind. *Allyce is with him in the animal treatment room on level 6. She wishes to see you.*

All right. Go and bring her here, please.

She wishes to see you there.

Nicole frowned. *In the treatment room?*

Yes. She asks that you come alone.

"What is it?" Iosif asked. "Trouble?"

"Allyce is upstairs and wants to see me," Nicole said. "She's one of our doctors."

"Yeah, I know who she is. You want me to go with you?"

"She wants me to come alone."

Iosif straightened up a little, his eyes narrowing. "*That* doesn't sound suspicious or anything."

"It does, doesn't it?" Nicole agreed, a bad feeling settling into the pit of her stomach. *Ask the Caretaker if there is danger there.*

He says there is not.

Which meant not a single damned thing, Nicole knew. With the Caretaker partially under Shipmaster control, or at least under Shipmaster influence, his assurances were worthless.

"Thanks for the offer," she told Iosif as she stood up. "But the Caretaker says it's safe."

"You believe him?"

"It's okay," Nicole said. Which wasn't actually an answer to his question, but he probably wouldn't notice. "Allyce has been . . . a little touchy lately. She may just need a woman-to-woman talk."

Iosif grunted. "Yeah, I remember woman-to-woman talks. I never saw any of them end well."

"Well, then, this can be a first," she said, standing up. "But thanks for the offer."

"You sure?" he persisted.

"I'm sure." Nicole pointed to his tray. "Besides, I haven't finished eating, and Jeff hauled the Ponngs away from their trays. We really should let *someone* finish a meal in peace today."

"Now you're just reaching."

"Fine," Nicole said. "Joking aside, I want someone competent here in case of trouble with Bungie and Trake."

"Better," Iosif said, gazing hard at her. "You and Jeff still need to work on this deception stuff."

Nicole sighed. "I'll be fine," she said. "This is Q4, remember? One shout, and every Wisp in earshot will be there."

"Fine," Iosif said, waving his fork. "It's not like you couldn't lose me if I tried to follow you, anyway. What about that one?" He nodded toward Hagert.

"I'll send him back to my room with the other four," Nicole said. "If Fievj or Nevvis drops by, I don't want them wondering why a bunch of Wisps are just hanging around doing nothing."

"Yeah," Iosif said. "Well. Be careful, okay?"

"Don't worry," Nicole said. "If I die, I'll be sure to leave a note for Jeff not to blame you."

Iosif grunted. "Not funny."

"Sorry. Back as soon as I can."

"You're at least taking a spider gun, right?"

"Sure," Nicole lied. "I'll grab one on my way."

Which she wouldn't, of course. She and Jeff could summon Wisps, but no one else here could do that. The spider guns were all they had to protect themselves, and she had no intention of unnecessarily reducing their odds.

Besides which, she thought darkly as she headed down the corridor, if this was a trap of some sort, anything she was carrying would be permanently lost. She had no intention of risking herself *and* one of their weapons. This day had been too costly as it was.

The last two times she'd entered the treatment room she'd come from the aft part of the room. This time, mindful of the oddness of the situation, she decided to try a door she'd noticed closer to the area where the hologram of Ushkai typically waited for her.

The hologram wasn't visible as she slipped through the door and into the high-ceilinged room with its rows of cages. But Allyce was. The doctor was sitting cross-legged on the floor near Ushkai's usual spot, about fifty yards away, gazing down at the floor in front of her as if in a yoga meditation. She had some kind of handmade scarf wrapped loosely around her neck, the ends dangling down over her chest. Nicole thought about calling to her, decided she'd wait until she was closer, and headed in.

She was halfway to Allyce when a quiet alarm bell went off in the back of her head.

Something was different.

She stopped short, holding as still as she could, her eyes darting everywhere within view as she tried to figure it out. She couldn't see anyone besides Allyce. There were no sounds other than the background noises she'd always heard when she was here.

Was the oddness the reason Ushkai's hologram hadn't appeared?

He'd always been there waiting for her. Had Allyce somehow blocked him, or sent him away? Or could it have something to do with the Shipmasters' control?

"Thank you for coming," Allyce said into Nicole's sudden fears. There was an odd tension in her voice as it echoed through the room. "I hoped you would. I prayed you would."

Nicole swallowed hard. "I'm here," she said, wincing at the unnecessary words. Allyce already knew she was here. "What do you need from me?"

"I need to set things right," Allyce said. "I need to put things right. You're the only one who can help me do that."

Nicole caught her breath as it suddenly clicked. The sights of the room, and its sounds—all of those were normal.

But not the smell. The smell was different. Just a hint, but it was there.

The smell of Koffren.

"I'm sorry," Allyce said. "But it was the only way."

And as Nicole broke her paralysis and started toward her, she heard a faint scuffling behind her. She spun around—

To see a Koffren striding toward her, his short sword gripped ready in his hand.

sixteen

"Wisps! To me!" Nicole shouted desperately, spinning back around and sprinting toward Allyce. There was another door beyond her at the other side of the room, as well as the one past the treatment cages to her right. If she could stay ahead of her attacker long enough to reach one of those, she would hopefully be able to find some Wisps to assist her. She picked up her speed, not knowing how much closer the Koffren behind her might have come and not daring to slow down long enough to find out.

She was a couple of steps from the end of the cages now. Flipping a mental coin, she decided to turn right and try for the door at that end. It was farther away, but she knew the layout better at that end. She reached the end of the cage and started to turn right.

"No—*left*," Allyce said, so quietly that Nicole barely heard her over the clump of her own footsteps.

She hesitated, uncertainty braking her rhythm and slowing her down. Allyce's face was rigid with stress and resolve, but there was pain and something that looked almost like pleading in her eyes. Nicole hesitated another step, slowing even further. Then, somewhat to her own surprise, she shifted direction, turning to her left as Allyce had ordered and trying to pick up her speed again. Out of the corner of her eye she saw the Koffren looming behind her, much closer than he'd been, his sword raised toward her. She turned her attention forward again—

And saw to her horror that, barely fifty yards away, the path was blocked by a line of crates, stacked two high, laid across the entire width of the room. A single gap remained, all the way to the left, beckoning invitingly.

Except that it was just more of the trap. Even as she continued running toward it, she could see that it was too narrow to allow her to slip through. She would make it probably halfway before getting stuck, leaving her helpless to get hacked to death by the Koffren behind her.

Unless . . .

She eyed the top level of crates. Allyce was the only one she knew had been up here, and the other woman had never struck her as being all that strong. On top of that, this was a treatment area for animals that had long since disappeared from the *Fyrantha*. There was no reason for any supplies to still be here, and anyway Allyce could hardly have lifted that many packed crates up there by herself.

And if they were indeed empty, there was a chance Nicole could slip into the gap, reach through to the far side of the barrier and get her hand on the back side of one of the second-tier crates, and push it past her to slam into the Koffren.

It was a huge gamble, possibly the last gamble she would ever make. But at this point it was her only chance. It was too late to veer around toward one of the other doors without crossing the Koffren's path, and the barrier was too tall for her to jump over.

She was bracing herself, eyeing the gap and mentally running through the procedure, when the second Koffren leaped into view from behind the barrier, soaring effortlessly over the top of the crates and landing with a thud almost directly in Nicole's path.

He straightened up, his sword gleaming in his hand. His face was invisible behind the perforated helmet, but Nicole could imagine the look of triumph and anticipation that must be plastered across his face.

And suddenly Nicole had no chances left. None.

She slowed down her mad dash, coming to a halt a few yards from the Koffren. With her own footsteps silent, she could hear the thuds of the Koffren coming up behind her. Her comment to Iosif about leaving a note for Jeff flashed to mind, together with all the heavy weight of irony that now wrapped around it.

"I'm sorry," Allyce said quietly.

Nicole turned her head. Allyce had left her seat on the floor and was walking toward her, her arms wrapped around her midsection as if she had a stomachache, the dangling ends of her scarf bouncing gently against her chest in rhythm with her walk. "Yeah," Nicole said. "Me, too."

"It was the only way," Allyce said. She straightened up. "Watch her," she warned in a louder voice. "She may be booby-trapped. Hold her arms away from her sides and let me check."

Nicole frowned as the two Koffren wrapped their hands around her wrists and twisted the arms to point straight up over her head. She could feel their breath on her cheeks and the top of her head: a soft, leisurely flow from the one who'd jumped the barrier; faster, heavier puffs from the one who'd had to chase her. Allyce walked up to them, and once again Nicole saw her brace herself as she reached up to the ends of her scarf.

But instead of taking hold of the scarf itself, Allyce's hands reached up behind the scarf and pulled out two objects that had been pinned there out of sight. Her fingers wrapped around them; and as Nicole's eyes and brain belatedly identified them as hypodermics with extraordinarily long needles Allyce thrust them up at the Koffren's faces. The needles slipped through the holes in their masks—there were simultaneous jolts as the needle tips jabbed into the hidden flesh behind them—Allyce's thumbs squeezed the plungers—

An instant later one of the Koffren let go of Nicole and slapped his arm against Allyce's chest, the impact sending her flying backward into the side of one of the cages. She gasped with pain as she bounced off the bars and dropped to the deck, rolling half over as both Koffren yanked the hypos from their faces and helmets and threw them aside. The one who'd hit Allyce strode toward her, lifting his sword for a killing blow. Nicole tried to pull away from the other Koffren, but could only gasp as he tightened his grip still further. Allyce pushed herself weakly up onto one elbow, her face twisted in pain as she watched her death approaching.

Then, to Nicole's astonishment, the grip on her arm loosened. At the same time the other Koffren broke stride, his sword drooping, his body swaying. Nicole frowned, wondering what was happening.

And as she watched in stunned disbelief, both aliens collapsed to the deck and lay still.

For a long moment she just stared at them. Then, she raised her eyes to Allyce, still half lying on the deck.

Allyce nodded wearily at Nicole's silent question. "Cyanide," she said, the word coming out with difficulty and a spasm of pain. "It blocks oxygen absorption into the blood. Figured it would kill anything that breathes the ship's air."

"The animal treatment room," Nicole murmured. "You had plenty of hypos in the medical center, but you needed to find longer needles."

Allyce nodded. "Sorry." Another spasm of pain. "The only way to get them close enough together was to convince them I was on their side and use you as bait. Can you give me a hand?"

"Sure," Nicole said, hurrying over. "How bad is it?"

"At a guess, a couple of bruised or fractured ribs, possibly a broken collarbone"—she broke off for a stifled gasp as Nicole knelt down beside her—"and maybe some internal injuries. No—don't touch me. You can call Wisps, right? Can you get some of them to carry me back to Sam and the hive?"

"Sure," Nicole said, frowning. Now that Allyce mentioned it . . .

She looked around. She *had* called for the Wisps, hadn't she, just before the big chase started? Yes, of course she had. But that had been a good couple of minutes ago, and not a single Wisp was in sight.

"I had to do it," Allyce said, her voice twisted with pain and pleading. "You know that, don't you? It was my fault they killed Bennett. My drug. My stupid damn—" She broke off in a gasping sob as fresh pain stabbed through her. "I was so focused on going home I didn't think."

"It's okay," Nicole soothed, still looking around. Had the Wisps not heard her? Were they afraid to respond?

"I messed it up for everyone," Allyce went on.

"You didn't know what they were going to do," Nicole said. "None of us did."

Or were they simply not able to come into the Caretaker's stronghold?

Nicole hissed under her breath. Fine. If they weren't coming on their own, she would just have to go get them.

"I'll be right back," she told Allyce, straightening up. She would head through her usual door, she decided, and the route she knew best. "Stay here."

She headed off, hurrying down the wide lane between the cages. If she couldn't get any of the regular Q4 Wisps to come, then she'd have to go back to the hive and grab Cambria and the others. Whatever was keeping the Wisps away, her personal group would hopefully not be so squeamish.

Still, as she jogged along, she kept her eyes open for a gurney

or cart or something else she could use to get the injured woman
out of here. But there was nothing. It was going to be Wisps, or
Nicole's own arms and back.

She reached the door and touched the release. It slid open and
she stepped out into the dimly lit corridor. A couple of corridors
over, she knew, would be one that connected to the crosswise vent
between her and Q3. There were bound to be Wisps there. She
rounded a corner—

And jerked to a sudden, horrified halt. Ten feet in front of her
was an armored Shipmaster.

Only he wasn't standing facing her. He was lying sprawled on
the deck, his front legs twisted around each other, his neck tilted
backward at a strange and painful-looking angle. The tilt had
opened a space between two of the neck plates, and there was
a pale pink liquid oozing slowly from the gap, adding to a puddle
staining the deck.

He wasn't moving. He wasn't breathing. He was dead.

Murdered.

For maybe ten seconds Nicole just stood there staring at the armored corpse. It shouldn't have been as bad as the human bodies
she'd seen sometimes after a shoot-out or one-on-one killing, she
told herself numbly. But somehow, it was.

Maybe it was even worse. The Shipmasters always seemed so
proud and invulnerable in their shiny armor and fake centaur bodies. Seeing one dead was somehow even more shocking than seeing one of the far more fragile Wisps dead.

Something cold settled around her heart. *Fake centaur bodies . . .*

Breaking her paralysis, she forced herself to walk over to the dead
Shipmaster. Forced herself to roll him over onto his right side so she
could get at the storage compartment. Forced herself to probe at the
slippery metal until she found the catch. Forced herself to open it.

The storage compartment was empty.

She swallowed hard. Back in Q4, Fievj had been carrying spider gun magazines and dissolving liquid. But the rack holding them had been different than the one she was looking at here. This rack was like the one she'd first seen in Fievj's storage compartment, designed to hold the four-foot-long tubes of greenfire weapons.

That rack had enough slots to hold six of the weapons. If this one had been full, and if the Koffren murderers had gotten all six of them . . .

And then, an even more horrifying piece of the puzzle dropped into place.

She was panting heavily when she reached Allyce. "Come on," she said between breaths as she crouched down beside Allyce and got her arm around the injured woman's shoulders. "We've got to go."

"What's wrong?" Allyce asked, her face contorting with pain as Nicole levered her to her feet. "Where are the Wisps?"

"I don't know, but we can't wait for them," Nicole said. Easing Allyce around, trying to give her support without further damaging her ribs, she started her toward the door. "There's a dead Shipmaster back there, and we need to get out of here."

"A dead—? *What?*"

"*And* he had greenfire weapons with him," Nicole went on, hurrying her along as quickly as she dared. "Maybe as many as six of them. They're all gone."

"But—" Allyce turned her head to look at the dead Koffren behind them. "They why didn't they . . . ?" Her voice and the question faded into horrified silence.

"Yeah, you got it," Nicole said grimly. "He was killed by a Koffren, all right—the sword mark in his throat shows that much. Only these two weren't carrying the weapons. Which can only mean one thing.

"There are more of the damn aliens aboard."

Nicole had been afraid she would have to carry Allyce the whole
way, probably aggravating her injuries in the process. To her relief,
they'd only gone a couple of corridors before Nicole's periodic call
for Wisps finally brought a pair of them out from wherever they'd
been hiding. She ordered them to bring Allyce along behind her
and hurried on ahead to the hive, wishing now that she'd listened
to Iosif and brought a spider gun with her. They weren't a lot of
use against greenfire weapons, but it would have been better than
nothing.

She'd been afraid she would find chaos, with dead bodies scattered in the corridors, dining room, and medical center. But to her
relief, she found no evidence of a battle.

On the other hand, as she walked quietly through the corridors and checked the public rooms, she also found no evidence
that anyone was there at all, alive *or* dead. The greenfire weapon
she'd used in the big Q4 battle hadn't disintegrated people, but
just poked holes through them. Could there be a setting she didn't
know about?

For that matter, it was only a guess that the dead Shipmaster
had been carrying that particular weapon. If he'd had something
even worse, they were all probably dead.

It was with a painful mix of relief and horror when she reached
the cluster of rooms farthest toward the rear of the *Fyrantha* that
she found the nine dead Wisps, scattered across the deck with
the familiar greenfire weapon burns scarring their delicate bodies.

"It was your Ghorf—Kahkitah—who came and warned us," Iosif
said, gazing into the coffee cup he'd barely touched. "He barreled
in, babbling about a bunch of Koffren being on their way and

carrying greenfire weapons. We first thought he was hysterical, but there was something about his face and voice that finally convinced me. Damn good thing I listened."

Nicole nodded silently, feeling as hollow inside as Iosif looked.

Nine Wisps dead, killed by a single greenfire shot each. A tenth dead from multiple spider gun rounds, which Sam said had suffocated it by constricting its chest and lungs. Two other Wisps still alive, but hit with so many spider shots that their wings might never function properly again.

And Travis and Bungie and the other four gang members gone. Apparently, the Koffren had decided they wanted some prisoners.

"We tried to warn the Wisps," Iosif went on, a fresh edge of bitterness creeping into his voice. "We didn't just run and hide. But Jeff had ordered them to guard the prisoners, and we didn't know where you'd gone, and they wouldn't listen to any of us. We didn't have enough people to carry them all away, and even if we had they'd probably have gone back. We didn't have a choice but to leave them."

"I know," Nicole murmured, the faces of dead Wisps floating accusingly in front of her face. Ten more lives to add to the growing guilt crushing down on her heart and mind.

"So what now?" Iosif asked.

What now? That was the question, all right.

In theory, the plan she and Jeff had concocted could still work. The crucial problem, though, was that it had been designed for only two Koffren. Now, even with Allyce's small victory they had a bunch more to deal with. Could the plan be adjusted to take account of that number?

Especially since she didn't even know how many of them there were. However they'd come aboard—whether through the Wisps and the *Fyrantha*'s teleport or from a ship or something else—there was no way to know what that number was. They had six greenfire weapons; but whether there were six Koffren, or six hundred, or six thousand was completely up in the air.

For that matter, did the Koffren really only have six weapons? All she knew was that they'd killed the Shipmaster up on level 6. If they could kill one, why not more? Why not even all of them?

"Fievj said he and the other Shipmasters were worried that the Koffren might take over the ship," she said slowly, trying to think it through.

"Jeff told me that was just a line to sucker you into walking into that trap in Q3."

"It was certainly a line," Nicole agreed. "Doesn't mean there couldn't have also been a grain of truth. What if they really *are* worried about the Koffren and don't know what to do about them?"

"I hope you're not suggesting we ask Fievj for another meeting."

"Hardly," Nicole said. "Though if a panicked Nevvis walked in here without armor or weapons, I'd probably listen to him. No, I was thinking more along the lines of finding a way to take out the Koffren before we present our terms to the Shipmasters."

"Interesting," Iosif said. "Any idea how we would do that?"

"Not yet," Nicole said, looking at her five Wisps, gathered in defensive positions by the dining room door. At least they'd been out of the Koffren line of fire. "Jeff will be back soon. Hopefully, the three of us can come up with something."

"Yeah," Iosif said. He didn't sound all that enthusiastic. "Well, until then you'd better get some rest. Before, you looked like something the cat dragged in. Now, you look like the dog's breakfast."

"I suppose," Nicole said, too weary to know whether he was being insulting or just trying to be funny and not caring either way. "I need to check on Allyce first."

"You want me along?"

"No, thanks." Nicole stood up. "Cambria? Come on. Time to go."

Allyce was lying on one of the medical center beds when Nicole arrived, her eyes closed, her breathing slow and a bit labored. "How is she?" Nicole asked.

"Not too bad, all things considered," Sam said, sounding unusually subdued. He'd never really warmed up to anyone aboard the *Fyrantha*, as far as Nicole knew, but he'd at least respected Allyce on a professional level. "One cracked rib, two more bruised, a wrenched shoulder, and a mild concussion. Her spine was undamaged, and she even got away without breaking either collarbone. Pretty lucky, really, for someone who got thrown against a wall."

"Yeah," Nicole said. "Real lucky."

Sam's lip twitched. "You know what I mean. What the hell happened, anyway?"

"She laid a trap for the Koffren," Nicole said. "Hypos with cyanide and long needles to get through the holes in their masks. One of them lived long enough to throw her against a cage."

"So they both died?"

"Yes," Nicole said. "And no, that doesn't mean Kahkitah lied about Koffren with greenfire weapons on the hunt. There's a new group of them aboard the ship. I don't know how they got here."

"Great," Sam muttered. "Like things weren't bad enough already."

"Yeah," Nicole agreed soberly. "And they're probably going to get worse before they get better."

"Maybe." He eyed her closely. "There *is* an easy solution, you know."

"That I die?"

"Funny," he said. "I was thinking more that you turn yourself in."

"Same difference."

"I don't think so," Sam said, his voice low and earnest. "They don't want you dead. They just want you to stop making trouble."

Nicole snorted. "Haven't you heard a single thing Jeff and I have been saying since the Q1 arena? Earth is on the line, Sam. They want fighters—whole planets' worth of battle slaves—and they know now that humans can fight. The only way to save our world is to stop them here on the *Fyrantha*."

"You don't know that," Sam insisted. "Besides, you also said that humans are the only ones who can do maintenance on the ship. If they take everyone off Earth and throw them into battles, who's going to fix things when they break down?"

"Do you even *hear* yourself?" Nicole demanded. "How many of us are aboard the *Fyrantha* right now? A couple of hundred? A thousand? Fine—let's say the Shipmasters keep a million of us around to fix things. That leaves—what? Six billion they can send off to get slaughtered?"

"More like seven and a half," Sam corrected coolly. "And the million they kept out would be the best of the best. Frankly, I think humanity could do with a little thinning."

Nicole stared at him. He returned her gaze without flinching, his expression set in stone. "You mean people like me?" she asked.

He shrugged slightly. "You and your boyfriend kidnapped me. He said—"

"Bungie isn't my boyfriend."

"He said he'd shot a man," Sam continued, ignoring her protest. "So yes, actually, I think civilization would get along just fine with fewer people like you."

Nicole took a deep breath. This wasn't the time to have this discussion. Especially since, speaking of Bungie and Trake, she could almost agree with him. "I'd prefer to eliminate bad people by encouraging them to become better people," she said. "The

Fyrantha's resources and science might help that happen. But they won't if everyone's lying dead on some alien battlefield."

Sam shrugged again. "You first have to be willing to change. Not sure how many of them want to. But I suppose that's not the issue here."

"No, it's not," Nicole said, feeling her brief surge of passion fade again into her tiredness. "What's important right now is that Allyce is going to get well."

"She'll be fine," Sam said. "She's patched up and started on the fast-track to healing. She'll be functional in a few days and fully healed in a couple of weeks."

"Does she need someone to stay with her tonight?"

Sam shook his head. "I gave her a sedative to help her sleep, and I'll keep an eye on the monitors in my room. I'm not expecting any problems, but if there are the alarms will signal me and I'll be on it."

"Okay," Nicole said. "Thank you." She turned to leave.

"You aren't going to ask about the drug?"

"What—? Oh, right," Nicole interrupted herself. She'd almost forgotten that she'd asked if he could whip up a drug that would enhance human combat capabilities. "Did you come up with something?"

"I think so," he said. "I've been playing with a mix that would have most of the amphetamine pluses and none of the minuses. Another day or two and I should be ready to give it a test." He cocked his head. "I trust you'll be able to find me a volunteer?"

"I'm sure I will," Nicole assured him. "Good night. And if you need any help with Allyce please come get me."

"Of course," Sam said. "Sleep well, Nicole." He gave her a brittle smile. "Pleasant dreams."

———

Nine hours later, still not feeling fully rested, she dragged herself out of bed. She spent the next hour eating while she, Jeff, and Iosif discussed possible ways of dealing with the unexpected influx of Koffren.

And somehow, despite Nicole's best efforts, her thoughts and plans kept coming back to Sam and the drug she'd asked him to make.

It was an unexpected and unsettling development, especially since the reason Nicole had suggested the project in the first place was simply to give him something to do that would keep him busy and out of everyone's hair. The thought that it might actually have become a vital piece of the campaign was strange in the extreme.

It was strange to Jeff and Iosif, too, and just as unpleasant to them as it was to Nicole. They weren't any happier with the plan that emerged from the discussion, Iosif in particular pointing out the huge risks, the small chance of success, and—in his mind—the unnecessary complications.

But it was the best they had, and Nicole hung on to it grimly. In the end, with nothing else that offered a better chance, the others reluctantly agreed.

Later that night she slipped into the medical center. Luckily, Allyce was awake, and Nicole was able to have a long, private talk with her. The injured woman wasn't any happier with the plan than Jeff and Iosif, but her anger at the Koffren and her still lingering guilt over her supposed complicity in Bennett's death were more than enough to bring her on board. Leaving her to her task, Nicole slipped out of the room, not wanting to be there if Sam checked his monitors, saw that Allyce was awake, and decided to look in on her.

One more night's sleep, this one much shorter than the last and even less restful, and it was time. She sent Jeff and Iosif to their appointed tasks; and then, feeling a little like a lamb going to the slaughter, she returned to the medical center.

This time, she found Allyce asleep. "How is she?" Nicole whispered to Sam.

"Better," he said. "Don't worry, you're not going to wake her up."

"More painkillers?"

"No, just the *Fyrantha's* healing enhancements," Sam corrected. "Kicking the metabolism to full repair mode tends to put people to sleep. You just drop by to check on her?"

"No," Nicole said, watching Allyce another moment. The other woman's breathing was definitely smoother and easier than the last time. That was a good sign. "No, I came to see if your drug was ready to go."

"Really," Sam said. "Well, you're in luck—I finished the last non-bio test this morning. What I need now is a human subject for the final test."

"Good," Nicole said. "Here I am."

Sam's eyes narrowed. "*You?* I assumed Jeff would insist on playing guinea pig."

"He's busy with other things," Nicole said. "Besides, if something goes wrong, you said yourself that I was one of the expendable ones. Remember?"

For a moment his face went blank. Then his lip twisted as that part of their previous conversation, apparently forgotten, came back to him. "Fine," he growled. "Sit down—that chair by the door—and roll up your left sleeve."

Nicole did so, watching as he walked over to one of the workstations and picked up a bottle and a hypo. "How long until the drug takes effect?" she asked.

"Not long," he told her as he filled the hypo about halfway. "A few minutes."

"And I'll have enhanced speed and strength?"

"That's what you asked for, wasn't it?" he countered. He set down the bottle, did the little tap-and-squeeze thing Nicole always saw doctors do on TV, and then walked back to her. He tapped twice on the skin just above the inside of the elbow, then slipped the tip of the needle into the flesh just over the vein. "Okay," he said as he pulled it out and set the hypo aside. "Give me a rundown on how you feel so we can get an idea of the timing."

"Right," Nicole said. "Nothing yet—"

She broke off, gasping, her arm suddenly feeling like it was on fire. Reflexively, she grabbed it, pressing hard against the skin.

The pressure seemed to help. The heat faded . . .

A strange dimness seemed to wash across her eyes and mind, like the sun going down and leaving everything looking flat and dim, all the colors washed out. The sun had gone down on her brain, too, leaving it hard to think or comprehend what was happening. "Sam," she breathed, her voice sounding strange and distant. "Sam, what's happening?"

"You're saving the ship," he said, his voice as distant as hers. "That's what you wanted, right? Well, you're saving it. You're saving it in the only way you ever could." He stood up and took her arm. "Come on. We're leaving."

Nicole tried to fight it. But somehow it was impossible to disobey his voice. She stood up at his urging and turned toward the door. "Where are you taking me?" she asked.

"The place you've been heading since you first got here," he said. "The place you've been trying to take all the rest of us.

"I'm taking you to hell."

seventeen

The hallway outside was deserted. Sam led the way, walking fast, gripping Nicole's upper arm as if afraid she was going to fall over. The corridors were as empty as the one outside the medical center had been. Not really surprising, Nicole decided, though it took her a couple of minutes to work her way through to that awareness. Jeff, Iosif, and the Ponngs were long gone, and in the aftermath of the Koffren raid it was likely that everyone else was trying to lie low.

At the first stairway Sam took them down four levels, then turned and continued forward. A few more deserted corridors later, they reached the crosswise heat transfer duct separating them from Q2.

A Shipmaster in full armor was waiting for them there. "Was there trouble?" he asked as the two humans approached. "Were you seen?"

"No, and no," Sam said. "Who are you?"

"I am Ryit," the Shipmaster said. "I serve directly under Fievj."

"Fievj told you about the deal?"

"I serve directly under Fievj," Ryit repeated.

"So that's a yes?"

"I said already," Ryit said. "I'll take her now."

"No," Nicole said. Her voice still sounded distant, and she could now hear some slurring in it, as well. "Don't give me. He'll drop me down shaft. Kill me."

"Well, that'll still save the ship," Sam said. "That's what you wanted, right?"

"Not save," Nicole said. "If he kills me, then wrath of God. No." She paused, trying to find the right word. "No. Wrath of Caretaker. Wrath of *Fyrantha*."

"I'll take her now," Ryit said, taking a step toward them.

"Back off," Sam warned, pulling Nicole back a step of his own. "What does she mean, the wrath of the Caretaker and the *Fyrantha*? What happens with the ship if you kill her?"

"We aren't going to kill her," Ryit said, taking another step.

"I said back *off*," Sam snapped. "And that's not what I asked. She's the *Fyrantha*'s Protector. Does the ship do something bad if you kill her?"

"We aren't going to kill her," Ryit repeated.

"Liar," Nicole muttered. "Kill me. Bad to be aboard when that happens. Bad, bad, bad." She pawed weakly at Sam's arm with her free hand. "'f I were you, I'd get off. Right now."

"Yeah, that's the plan, sweetheart," Sam said. But even in Nicole's glazed vision and fogged mind he seemed uncertain. "That *is* still the plan, right?" he added to Ryit.

"Of course," Ryit assured him. "Your deal with Fievj. Your return to Earth in exchange for the Protector."

"Don't trust him," Nicole insisted. "Kill me. You smart, you get off first."

"Actually, that's not a bad idea," Sam said. "Yeah, okay. We'll do it that way."

"Impossible," Ryit said. "The deal was for you to—"

"I know what the deal was," Sam interrupted him. "And I don't recall any mention of which part came first."

"She's babbling," Ryit protested. "I've given you my word, as has Shipmaster Fievj."

Nicole snorted. "Word. Right."

"Yeah, I'm inclined to agree," Sam said. He dug into his pocket and pulled out a small, round capsule. "Okay, pay attention. This is the antidote for the drug. One whiff of this, and she'll be alive, well, and screaming for the nearest Wisps. I'm pretty sure you don't want that."

Ryit was standing very stiffly. "What do you want?"

"You'll take us to the teleport room," Sam said. "Once you've set the coordinates and the Wisp has me ready to go, you can have her. Not until then."

Ryit's face wasn't visible behind his armored helmet. But Nicole nevertheless had some fun imagining what it might look like right now.

"Very well," the Shipmaster said, his voice low and very reluctant. "I'll take you there."

"Good," Sam said. "Now—"

He put the antidote capsule back in his pocket and pulled out a square one. "*This* is a dose of the drug I just gave her. If I break this under her nose, she'll be in an instant overdose state. That means she'll die. Remember what she said about the ship reacting badly if that happens?"

"I don't believe her," Ryit said stiffly.

"I don't necessarily believe it, either," Sam said. "But I also don't believe in taking unnecessary chances. I'm going to the teleport room and leaving. After that, if you still don't believe her, you're welcome to gamble with your own lives if you want."

"I've already said we don't intend—"

"And if you screw with me, we all find out the hard way," Sam again interrupted. He started to put the square capsule back in his pocket, then raised it up again. "No, I think I'll keep this handy. So. How exactly do we do this?"

How they did it was by riding on Ryit's back like a horse.

Really. Just like in the movies. At Ryit's instruction, Nicole climbed up and sat on the centaur part, right behind his real body. Once she was settled, Sam got up and squeezed in close behind her.

It was cozy. Way cozier than Nicole normally would have been comfortable with. Shot full of Sam's drug, though, she could recognize the unpleasantness but not really feel any of it. In front of her legs and behind Sam's, two sets of wings extruded from the centaur body, ending up with something that reminded Nicole of how dragonflies looked. Except with a horse instead of a dragonfly body, of course.

Shipmasters as dragonflies. Wisps as butterflies. Idly, Nicole wondered if that was just because wings like that worked best and most efficiently, or whether it was because the *Fyrantha's* designers had had a weird sense of humor.

Wisps could open the access doors to the heat ducts telepathically. Ryit, though, had to use a small flat box, pressed against the wall, to open the panel. He also flew a lot less smoothly than the Wisps, bucking and bouncing back and forth and at one point coming close to losing both of his passengers. But Nicole had her arms wrapped around the slippery metal encasing the Shipmaster's chest, and Sam had an even more uncomfortable grip around hers, and they made it across.

Though not *straight* across, the way Nicole usually did when she was traveling by Wisp. Instead, he angled them downward, dropping eight levels during the short crossing. Whether it was deliberate or whether Ryit just wasn't very good at this, Nicole couldn't tell.

She'd never ridden a horse before, but despite the jolts it was kind of fun. She hoped Ryit would let her ride the rest of the way to the teleport room, or at least until they got across Q3 and through the next heat duct into Q1.

Sadly, the door behind them had barely cut off the flow of hot air before he pulled the wings back in and ordered both her and Sam to get off.

She was pretty sure the full comment was actually *get the freaking hell off.* But her translator didn't get that one particular word.

They saw two Wisps along the way through Q3, and Nicole hoped Ryit would call on them to carry them across the heat duct instead of doing it himself. But he didn't. Her next thought was that she could call them herself. Surely they would obey her, provided she remembered to say *please.*

But Ryit was striding along like his butt was on fire, and Sam was tugging on her arm, and before she could make up her mind the three of them were past, and the Wisps were gone, and it was too late.

She probably would have forgotten to say *please,* anyway.

The second heat duct passage was as bouncy as the first one. Sam still held on to her way too tightly, but she realized now he was just afraid he was going to fall off. He'd be better once they were across and back on a solid deck. Again, Ryit dropped them eight levels before reaching the door on the far side of the duct.

And then they were in Q1.

The last time Nicole had been here she'd been worried about Shipmasters and Koffren and Wisps and everything else that she might run into. This time, with the dreamy clouds from Sam's injection drifting across her mind, she had no worries of any sort.

At one point along their twisty way she realized she should probably have been memorizing the route, just in case she needed to find her way back. But the quadrant was confusing, and she couldn't remember all the sector names on the room plaques, and by the time she thought about it, it was probably too late, anyway.

A pair of Wisps wandered into view, and she thought about calling to them, just to see if they would listen. But Ryit led the way around a corner before she could decide, and they probably wouldn't have, anyway. She sent one final look at them as she and Sam turned the corner.

She turned back to find a Koffren standing in the center of the corridor ahead, blocking their path.

Sam came to a sudden stop. Ryit took another step before he, too, halted. "What are you doing here?" the Shipmaster asked cautiously.

"Waiting for you," the Koffren said. "Is this her?"

"You're supposed to be ten levels up," Ryit said stiffly, ignoring the question. "The humans are invading. You're supposed to be up there to aid in their capture."

The Koffren gave out a snort. "We don't capture humans anymore. We kill them."

"We don't want them dead," Ryit insisted. "The *Fyrantha* still needs many repairs, and they're the only ones who can do the job."

"There are many more where these came from," the Koffren countered. "Perhaps even ones that are not so abysmally stupid."

"We're not stupid," Nicole objected. "We're actually pretty bright, some of us."

"You are as stupid as you are useless," the Koffren said bluntly. "Did you truly not realize that the monitor cameras on your stolen drones could be accessed by the Shipmasters? The pitiful attack force moving through Q1 has been tracked since it left Q3. We'll let them get another few corridors, and once we've determined they don't have even the smallest chance of escape, we'll destroy them."

"*Capture* them," Ryit insisted. "We only want to capture them."

"We know what you want," the Koffren said.

"You agreed to our plan."

"And perhaps we shall comply with it. Perhaps not." The Koffren pointed at Nicole. "I ask again. Is this her?"

"We cannot linger," Ryit said. "We're expected elsewhere."

"Perhaps *you* are," the Koffren said. "This one is not. Not any longer. She killed two Koffren. Her life is forfeit."

"I haven't killed anyone," Nicole protested. The Koffren's sword was still in its sheath, she noticed idly, and he wasn't carrying any of the stolen greenfire weapons, either. Maybe he wanted to kill her with his bare hands?

"She's the *Fyrantha's* Protector," Ryit said. "Do you know what the ship will do if she's murdered in cold blood?"

"I don't care what it does."

"Well, you should," Sam spoke up. "You're stuck aboard it along with the rest of us. If we get screwed, you get screwed."

The Koffren seemed to think about that. "I don't fear the ship," he said. "But speak on. What will it do?"

"We don't know," Ryit said. "That's the point. None of us does. What we *do* know is that the *Fyrantha* is very protective of itself and the people and things it considers important. You'll have your justice—Nevvis has already promised you that. But not now."

"Justice is me dead, right?" Nicole asked.

"Quiet," Sam muttered, squeezing her arm harder.

"Just asking," Nicole murmured, feeling a little annoyed. "Don't think it's *that* hard a question."

"*I* am Justice," the Koffren said. "I am Revenge and I am Fire."

"Wow," Nicole said. "I'm just Nicole. Your name's a lot cooler. Can I call you *Justice* for short? Lot easier."

For a long moment the Koffren's helmet continued to be pointed at her. Presumably he was staring or glaring or something. Then, the helmet turned slightly back toward Ryit. "You say you're expected," the Koffren said. "Where?"

"The teleport room," Ryit said, pointing down the corridor. "In return for delivering the Protector to us, we've agreed to send this other human home."

"So *that* you can do?" the Koffren snarled. "You can send humans wherever you wish? Yet you cannot bring warriors from Shikoffra as we've ordered?"

"Nevvis has already explained the difficulties," Ryit said, his voice starting to sound strained. "The teleport parameters for Earth were programmed into the ship long before the Lillilli ever found it lying derelict in space."

"So they could build and repair," the Koffren said contemptuously. "So Nevvis has said." He snorted. "Primitive creatures with little strength and less intelligence. The builders were fools."

"The builders had their reasons," Ryit said, though to Nicole's foggy ears he didn't sound like he really believed that. "The point is that Earth is a known system and thus easy to transport people to and from. Shikoffra's parameters are far less established—which is *your* doing, I may add—and small perturbations can create severe difficulties in creating a clear pathway for the Wisps to follow."

"That lie falls glibly from your mouth," the Koffren said, his voice dark and menacing. "The same lie, and many of the same words, that Nevvis has tried to gull us with. But we're not fooled. We may accept your excuses now, but we won't accept them forever."

"I'm certain the procedure will grow clearer and easier with each attempt," Ryit assured him. "We just need time."

"And, of course, your precious humans," the Koffren said. He eyed them another moment, then stepped unhurriedly out of their path. "But you have a killer to deliver to your master, as well as a traitor to send home. Continue."

"Thank you," Ryit said, taking a hesitant step forward.

"And I'll go with you," the Koffren added.

For a second Nicole thought Ryit was going to object, maybe to tell the Koffren that his presence wasn't needed or wanted. But he said nothing, and merely continued walking. The Koffren watched as he went by, continued to watch as Sam somewhat gingerly edged past, his hand still on Nicole's arm, and then fell in silently behind them. Nicole thought about turning to see if he'd drawn his sword, decided it wasn't worth the effort.

Anyway, more important to her right now was how long before they reached the teleport room. If there was going to be much more walking she was going to ask Ryit if he could give her another piggyback ride.

Ten steps later, they were there.

Nicole blinked, mildly surprised, as Ryit stopped in front of a door to their right and once again pressed his handy door-opening box against it. Though maybe it shouldn't have been that surprising— the door was the only opening on that side of the corridor, which should have been a clue that there was a big room behind it. The door slid open—an extra-thick door, sliding into an extra-thick wall, Nicole noticed—and together they walked through.

It was a big room, all right, but not as big as Nicole had expected. Not much bigger than the dining room in their hive, really, though it didn't look anything like that one. This room was round with a high ceiling, bright overhead lighting, and lots of colored lights laid out along the walls. Between the lights the walls were white with the same silvery threads as on Wisp skin.

It was, in short, just as she remembered from that terrifying day when she'd been kidnapped from Philly and brought here. It was the teleport room, all right.

The last time she'd been here, though, she'd missed the fact that on the far side of the room was another tall rectangular section where there weren't any lights.

Another door? She turned her head around as the door they'd come in through closed behind the Koffren. No lights there, either. The gap in front of them was indeed probably another door, then.

"We're here," Ryit called.

Nicole turned back toward him. Sure enough, the empty panel now slid open to reveal a second room.

She craned her neck, trying to see. The room ahead was also round, a little bigger than the one they were currently standing in, with its curved walls lined with consoles. The control room, probably. On the far side was another vertical rectangle, most likely the door into the other, larger teleport room that Nise had told her about.

She focused again on the walls where she was currently standing. For sheer number of glowing and flashing lights, she decided, the control room had this one beat.

A movement caught her eye, and she looked into the control room again as a Wisp appeared around the edge of the doorway. "Hey!" she called, her voice still sounding slurred. "Are you the one in charge?"

"The Wisp has its orders," Ryit said, gesturing to Sam. "It just has to double-check the coordinates and it'll be ready to take you home."

"Good," Sam said, eyeing the Koffren still standing behind them by the door. "How long?"

"Two minutes," Ryit said. "No more."

"Okay," Sam said, his eyes still on the Koffren. He looked at Nicole, letting go of her arm and letting his hand fall to his side. "Well—"

"Can I have that pill?" Nicole interrupted, taking a step back.

Sam frowned at her. "What?"

"The pill," Nicole said, pointing at his pocket. "Or the capsule, or whatever it was. The one that'll make me all better again."

"Not yet," Ryit said before Sam could answer. "Not until we have you safely locked away. Speaking of which . . . ?"

"Yeah," Sam said, digging out the round capsule and handing it to the Shipmaster. "Sorry, Nicole."

"That's okay," Nicole assured him, slipping her hand into her jumpsuit pocket and pulling out a square capsule. "I've got my own."

Sam's eyes went wide. "No! Wait—that's *poison!*"

Holding the capsule under her nose, Nicole squeezed and took a deep breath.

Ryit shouted something and lunged toward her. Sam was a hair behind him, reaching desperately for Nicole's arm, surely knowing he'd never make it. Beside the door, the Koffren gave off a deep laugh.

And as the antidote Allyce had mixed up for her blew away the fog and confusion from her mind, Nicole saw that every eye in the room was fixed on her. Which meant no one was paying the slightest attention to the control room.

Which meant none of them saw the two Thii drop silently to the control room deck from the ventilation grate above.

Nise's first spider gunshot slapped across Ryit's helmet, blinding him. His second wrapped around the Shipmaster's legs, pinning them together and sending him crashing to the deck. Iyulik's shots were an exact mirror, except aimed at the Koffren's helmet and legs. One more shot from both Thii, and their enemies' arms were similarly pinioned.

"Are you harmed?" Nise asked as they stepped into the teleport room. Sam had frozen with the first shot; now, at a warning motion from Nise, he stepped away from Nicole, his hands held in front of him, palms outward.

"I'm fine," Nicole assured the Thii. "Excellent work, both of you." She pointed at the door. "Iyulik, seal that door—as many shots as you think it needs. Nise, come with me and we'll do the other one."

"What the *hell*?" Sam breathed.

"Later," Nicole said. "Come on, Nise."

She led the way through the control room, past the Wisp standing motionlessly—"I'll be with you in a minute," Nicole called to it as they passed—and to the door on the far side. If they could block the door into the other teleport room before the alarm was given, they would have full control over the entire teleport setup, with all the possibilities that would give them. She found the control—it wasn't as obvious or simple as the *Fyrantha*'s usual door controls—and keyed it.

The thick door slid open and they stepped through into another, much larger teleport room, this one more the size of one of the barracks rooms Nicole had been in. Probably the one they used to bring in twenty aliens at a time for their damn testing arenas, she realized. With Nise beside her, she headed toward the far end.

They'd gotten three steps when the door opened and a Koffren charged into the room.

eighteen

Instantly, Nise opened fire. But it was too late. The Koffren that Iyulik had immobilized behind them had been standing still. This one was alerted and on the move, running and zigzagging, and Nicole knew there was no way Nise could take it down in time. "Back!" she snapped, skidding to a halt and reversing direction. "Into the control room!"

And even as they backed hurriedly through the door, the Koffren swiveled a black tube Nicole hadn't noticed off his shoulder and into firing position.

A greenfire weapon.

And then the door slid shut in front of her, cutting off her view. "Seal it!" she snapped, stepping back out of the way.

Five seconds and eight spider gun shots later, the door was sealed. For now, anyway. Touching Nise on the arm, Nicole turned and hurried back to the smaller teleport room.

"So what now?" Sam bit out. "We saw it all. There's a Koffren with a greenfire weapon out there."

"Yeah, thanks for the tip," Nicole said. "So much for all of them being eight decks up waiting to jump on Jeff's team."

"We knew the Shipmasters were preparing the teleport room," the Koffren who'd called himself Justice said, his voice mocking. "We didn't know which entry point would be chosen, so we guarded both."

"Yes, you're all so smart," Nicole said, looking around. The Thii could escape back the way they'd come, but from Nise's description the air ducts were way too narrow for her and Sam.

But if the Wisp in there would follow her orders . . .

She hurried back into the control room. "Wisp, can you send a message to another Wisp?" she asked, taking its arm. "It should be nearby, close to the teleport room."

There was a moment of silence. *No,* the Wisp said.

Nicole hissed out a curse. One of the Q1 Wisps, still under Shipmaster control.

Still, if she could get Ryit to cooperate, maybe she could still pull this off. Cambria was out there nearby, sent ahead by Jeff to escort her back to Q4 whenever she was ready to retreat. If Cambria could get into the big teleport room and immobilize the Koffren, she could still get away.

But it was already too late. There was a terrific crash against the control room door, as if someone had thrown himself bodily against it, and as the boom faded away she could hear two or three different voices. The Koffren planning to ambush Jeff had made it down here way faster than she'd expected, and were clearly determined to get to her.

Cursing again, she hurried back to the smaller teleport room. "Ryit, how many charges are there in those greenfire guns?"

"Don't tell her," Justice bit out. "Let her fear they will soon cut their way inside and deliver her destruction."

Nicole clenched her teeth. She didn't have time for this crap. "Ryit—"

"You don't have to say," Iyulik spoke up. "Just hold up the appropriate number of fingers."

Nicole looked at Justice, belatedly remembering that the spider shot on his helmet had effectively blinded him. Iyulik was right: it was time for a bluff. "Three?" she said. "Good—that's what I thought."

"Shipmaster, your life is forfeit!" the Koffren thundered, straining uselessly against the spider goo. "Aiding and consorting with the enemy—"

"Oh, stuff it," Nicole said scornfully. "He didn't say anything. But thanks for confirming my guess."

Justice made a final lunge and subsided. "You are *dead*," he snarled.

"Yeah, and you can stuff that, too," Nicole said, running the numbers quickly through her head. The Koffren had stolen six greenfire weapons, which at three shots each meant they'd started with eighteen total. They'd spent nine of them killing the Wisps that had been guarding Trake and Bungie, leaving another nine. Back in Q3 she'd seen how relatively little damage the Shipmaster's shot had done to the corridor wall, and the walls and doors around the teleport section looked a lot thicker and tougher than that.

Bottom line: the Koffren weren't getting in here any time soon.

On the other hand, the door wouldn't last forever, either. The tool lockers scattered all over the ship held a variety of cutting tools, and even if the Koffren couldn't figure out how to use them the Shipmasters probably could. She'd bought them some breathing space, but it was hardly time to kick back and relax.

"You have a plan," Nise said quietly. It was a statement, not a question.

Nicole looked around. The *Fyrantha*'s teleport room . . .

"Actually, I do," she said over her shoulder as she headed back into the control room. "Watch them. I'll be right back."

The Wisp was standing where she'd left it. She stepped up to it and took its arm. *Can you teleport me from here to some other point inside the* Fyrantha? she thought toward it. *To our hive in Q4, or even into the Q4 arena?*

No.

Why not? You teleport people billions of miles away, don't you?

The teleport system can send and receive from distant places. It cannot teleport objects or beings within the Fyrantha *itself.*

Nicole chewed at her lip. Her whole escape plan from this little trip depended on the Wisps being able to send her back to Q4. If they couldn't, this day was going to end very badly.

Unless . . .

You were ordered to send Sam back to Earth? she asked.

Yes.

Good. On my command, you'll teleport him to Philadelphia, to the same spot where he was when he was taken.

I cannot guarantee the same spot.

Nicole rolled her eyes. *Then just somewhere in Philadelphia,* she said. *Once you've left him there, you'll immediately come back. Can you do that?*

Yes.

Good. Get ready to do so.

She stepped into the doorway. "Sam? Get in the middle of the room. You're going home."

"What?" Sam asked, frowning.

"You heard me. The Wisp here is going to take you back to Philly."

"But—"

"It's what you always wanted, right?" Nicole cut him off. "Fine. So get your butt to the middle of the room and get ready. Wisp? Come here."

"But I assumed—I mean—"

"You assumed you were going to be screwed again," Nicole said as the Wisp glided past her. "Yeah, I know. Wisp? Pick him up and take him back to Earth."

Obediently, the Wisp glided past her. Sam watched it approach, a mass of conflicting emotions chasing each other across his face. "I never—"

"I'll say good-bye for you," Nicole promised, backing up into the doorway between the teleport and control rooms and throwing a quick look at the consoles. The pattern of lights seemed mostly stationary at the moment. Presumably, that was about to change. She looked back to see the Wisp step behind Sam and wrap its arms around him. "Go," she said, watching them out of the corner of her eye as she turned her main attention back to the consoles.

She wondered if there would be a flash. There wasn't. She wondered if there would be a bang or hiss or sizzle. Nothing. No light, no sound. The Wisp spread its butterfly wings, and the two of them simply vanished.

The monitor lights on the consoles, on the other hand, went crazy.

Really crazy. Suddenly everything seemed to be in motion: lights flicking on and off, lines of lights forming patterns, then dissolving and reforming into new patterns, numerical displays sweeping through numbers faster than she could keep track of them.

Mentally, she counted out the seconds, wondering how long it would take. Her hazy memory of her trip from Philly to the *Fyrantha* would suggest that it had taken several minutes.

"Your companions will still die," Justice snarled into the silence. "The Koffren will attack, and they will die. Then you will be alone."

"How many Koffren would that be, exactly?" Nicole asked absently, her eyes and mind still on the teleport controls.

Justice snorted. "You wish to know our numbers."

Nicole shrugged. "Don't see why that's a problem. We're all dead, anyway, remember? I figure there's maybe six of you. Sorry— *four* of you. Forgot we killed two."

Out of the corner of her eye she saw him once again furiously strain at the spider goo. A corner of it seemed on the edge of coming loose—

And was again sealed as Iyulik casually fired another spider shot across the Koffren's chest. He spat out a word that Nicole's translator ignored, and then subsided. "There are more than enough of us for your companions," he said.

"They attack now," Ryit murmured.

Abruptly, the light show again froze in place. Twenty-eight seconds, by Nicole's count. A lot less than she'd thought it would be. "I hope they have fun," she said, restarting her count. She reached five; then, the skittering light pattern resumed. "Well, I've got you, plus the three Koffren—maybe four by now?—in the other teleport room. That and the number Jeff's seeing right now should give us a good count of your total numbers."

"How many last breaths do you expect us to give him, that he'll be able to whisper that number to you?"

"Lots of last breaths, probably," Nicole said. "Jeff and the others aren't there."

"*What?*" Ryit demanded. "Of course they are. We watched them enter Q1."

"Sure," Nicole agreed. "You saw the whole force gather just inside the crosswise heat-transfer duct from Q3, get their equipment organized, then head in behind the drones. Probably also heard them talking to each other as they moved."

"Shipmaster?" Justice prompted, a dark threat to his voice. "*Shipmaster?*"

Ryit made a strange sound, half throat-clearing, half whimper. "They aren't there," he said. "The drones . . . the human intruders are no longer following them."

Again, Justice tried to break free of his restraints. Again, all it bought him was another spider shot from Iyulik. Nicole's mental count reached twenty-nine—

As quietly as he'd disappeared, the Wisp was back.

Nicole nodded to herself as the Wisp's wings folded back in place. So each trip to Earth took about half a minute. It would still be tricky, but it should work.

She hoped.

"I imagine Jeff's having a good laugh right now," she said, beckoning the Wisp and the two Thii toward the control room. The aliens moved obediently toward her, stepping past and continuing on into the control room. Nise paused at the entrance, keeping his eyes and spider gun watchfully on Ryit and the Koffren.

The Wisp didn't follow. Nicole gestured again, got the same nonresponse, and walked over to it. She took its arm—*I need you to take me to Earth,* she thought toward it. *Can you do that?*

I have been given no such instructions.

You just took another human there, she reminded it. *This is just an extension of that same order.*

The Wisp was silent a moment. *You are the* Fyrantha's *Protector?*

I am.

You can give orders to the Fyrantha?

Nicole considered. She hadn't exactly told the ship where to go, or what to do when it got there. On the other hand, she *had* given orders to open doors and turn off the water flow in the Q1 arena. Close enough. *Yes.*

Then I will accept your request as part of my orders.

Good, Nicole said. *Here's what you're going to do. You'll take me to Earth. Then you'll bring me back; but you'll bring me back to the other teleport receiver room, the one on the other side of the control room. Can you do that?*

You wish to leave the Fyrantha, travel to Earth, then immediately return?

Yes, but I want to return to the other teleport receiver room.

I understand.

Good, Nicole said. *Can you do that?*

I can. Are you ready to proceed?

In a moment, Nicole said. *I first need a moment to instruct my allies.*

She released its arm and stepped into the control room. "Do you have a plan for your escape?" Nise asked, sounding a little anxious. "We can leave through the air duct, but you won't fit in there."

"I know," Nicole said, keeping her voice down. The last thing she could afford was Ryit and the Koffren eavesdropping. "Here's what we're going to do." She pointed out at the Wisp. "The Wisp is going to take me back to Earth, then bring me right back here, only to the other teleport room. Now, the indicator lights in here will go crazy during—"

"A moment," Iyulik interrupted, his voice suddenly stiff. "You wish to go in *there*? The place where even now our enemies try to break into this room?"

"Right, except that they'll be so focused on the door they're trying to break into that they won't even notice I'm there," Nicole told him. At least she hoped that was how it would play out. "Anyway. The lights in here will go crazy twice, once while we're heading to Earth, the other time when we're on our way back. Understand? Lights mostly stationary, then flashing like crazy, stationary, flashing, stationary."

"What if they see you?" Iyulik persisted.

"Don't worry, we'll have a little insurance," Nicole said. "Or *you* will, anyway."

She stepped over to the nearest console and crouched down in front of it. Four twists of quick-release bolts later she had the protective screen off, exposing the maze of electronics behind it. "As soon as the second flashing part is over—and make sure it's *really* over—get into each of these consoles and pull out one or two of these small blocks." She touched a rectifier simplex and pantomimed pulling it out. "Dump all of them in one of your empty food bags, climb back into the vent, and then get back to Jeff in Q4 as fast as you can."

"This is a dangerous plan," Nise said. "Not just for you personally, but for the entire war effort."

War effort. The words sent a shiver up Nicole's back. But he was right. They really *were* engaged in a war here.

"Protector?" Ryit called from the teleport room. "Where are you? What are you doing?"

"I can't say I'm thrilled by it myself," Nicole admitted. "But unless you have a better plan for getting me out of here, I think we're stuck with this one." She jabbed a finger toward the teleport room. "Let's get to it."

"Very well," Nise said, still sounding unhappy.

"Protector?" Ryit called again.

"What?" Nicole called back. "No—never mind. I'm not talking to you right now." She raised her eyebrows. "You two ready?"

Nise and Iyulik exchanged looks. "Yes," Nise said.

"Good." Nicole beckoned to the Wisp. "It's time. Come with me."

She led the way back into the teleport room. Silently, she pointed the Wisp to the center of the room. It glided into position, and she backed into its arms. She felt the familiar paralysis, saw peripherally that it had opened its wings . . .

The teleport room vanished into a complete and utter blackness.

On her first trip, Nicole had been screaming-crazy terrified. The fact that she'd been paralyzed and unable to give voice to that scream had only made it worse.

This time, with the Wisps and their characteristics far more familiar, she could almost enjoy the ride. There was a certain peace inherent in the blackness, especially in contrast to the violence and strife aboard the *Fyrantha*. Automatically, she found herself counting off the seconds again, wondering if she would reach the same number as before or if the fact that she was doing the traveling would change her perception of the time any. She vaguely remembered one of her teachers talking about that, with someone called Einstein.

And then, suddenly, the blackness lifted.

She was back.

It was nighttime, the Philadelphia streets quiet and mostly deserted, the streetlights blazing. A thin layer of snow lay along the sides of the pavement, and with a shock she realized that while she'd been on the *Fyrantha* she'd completely lost track of the seasons back home. The air was cold, and she knew that if she could breathe properly she'd be able to see her breath.

She'd always hated the cold of winter. The cold, the short days, the misery of standing watch for one of Trake's schemes. Now, though, it was almost with nostalgia that she took in the muted sounds of the city she'd grown up with.

She'd never really understood Sam's and Bungie's passion for getting back here. Now, in this single moment, she could almost sympathize. For all its faults and dangers and frustrations, Philly and Earth were still home.

Then, as suddenly as it had disappeared, the blackness returned.

Philly was gone. Earth was gone. She was on her way back to the *Fyrantha*.

And if she'd been wrong about the Koffren in the larger teleport room, she was going to be in serious trouble. She counted out the seconds—twenty-seven of them this time—and the black again lifted and she was back.

She'd expected to find herself looking at two or more Koffren, grouped angrily around the control room door as they tried to break in. But the door in front of her was intact, and there was no one standing there. Had they given up and gone away?

Belatedly, her brain caught up with her. She and the Wisp had arrived facing the exit door. The control room door, and any associated Koffren, were on the other side of the room.

The Wisp opened its arms. Holding her breath, Nicole turned around and peeked gingerly around the Wisp's side as it refolded its wings.

They were there, all right. Not the two or three Koffren she'd expected, but five of the massive aliens. They were hunched over a cutting torch one of them had taken from an equipment closet, poking and prodding and trying to figure out how it worked.

Nicole let out her breath in a silent sigh. It had worked. She was back, and the Koffren had completely missed her return.

But the moment of grace wouldn't last long. With the ambush of Jeff's supposed invasion now over and done with, the rest of the Koffren could be charging through the door in front of her at any time.

She touched the Wisp's arm. *Thank you.*

You're welcome. Protector.

With a final careful look at the Koffren, Nicole crossed the room and slipped out the door.

The corridor outside the teleport room was deserted. If she hurried, she should have a clear path back to Q3 and then to safety in Q4.

Only with all the confusion that Sam's drug had pumped into her, she had no idea how to get there.

She hurried to the next cross-corridor, painfully aware that she also didn't know which direction the incoming Koffren would be coming from. Fortunately, the cross-corridor was also deserted. "Cambria?" she called softly. "Cambria? Come here, please. I need you. Cambria?"

No answer. She stood still, her heart thudding, trying to listen for ominous footsteps. She'd looked over Q1's section layout a little back when she was learning everything she could about the ship, but most of that knowledge had gone vague in her mind. If she mixed up the sector names, she could end up going the completely wrong direction. Worse, without Cambria she would have no safe way of crossing either of the heat-transfer ducts, whether to Q3 or Q2.

She'd been lucky with the teleport room Wisp, talking it out of the Shipmasters' control. But she couldn't count on pulling that off a second time.

That was a problem she needed to deal with.

Out of the corner of her eye she caught movement as a figure came around the corner. She tensed, then relaxed as she recognized Cambria. "Come here," she ordered, beckoning.

The Wisp was already on its way. It reached Nicole, and Nicole took its arm. *We need to get back to Q4,* she told it. *You know the way, right?*

Of course, Cambria replied. *Come. I will guide you.*

The approaching Koffren footsteps were audible as Nicole and the Wisp headed toward Q3 and safety.

nineteen

"So that's it?" Allyce asked. "He's gone?"

"He's gone," Nicole confirmed. "Back to Philly. I hope he's happy there."

"I'm sure he is," Allyce murmured. Lying on the medical center bed, her latest batch of meds on a tray beside her, she looked ten years older than she had even a few days ago. "I wish I could have said good-bye. He wasn't a bad man, you know. No worse than some of the rest of us, anyway."

"I know," Nicole said. Dr. Sam McNair. The man who'd once hoped to sidetrack Nicole's humanitarian efforts in the Q4 arena by trying to get her drunk. The man who, when that didn't work, had tried to poison her.

But of course Allyce didn't know any of that. "I'm sorry, but there was no other way," Nicole said. "I needed to see how much noise or light the teleport system made, and he was the only one around to try it with."

"You could have sent one of the Thii and then had the Wisp bring him back," Allyce said.

"And then what?" Nicole countered. Allyce was weak and hurting, and down deep Nicole knew it was a waste of effort to argue with her. But she was tired, too, and right now her tolerance and self-control levels weren't very high. "There was only one Wisp in the room, and they can only teleport one at a time. I was barely able to get to the other teleport room and out the door without being seen. There was no way we could have done it with two of us and two trips."

"How do you know they can't carry more than one at a time?"

"Because when they brought me here from Earth they had to send two more Wisps for Bungie and Sam," Nicole said. "Would you rather I ran off and left Sam with Ryit and the Koffren?"

"Why not? He wouldn't have gotten in trouble. Everything he did was according to Shipmaster instructions."

"Except the part about letting me break free and get them spider gunned."

"That was you, not him."

"*You* know that," Nicole said. "But they don't. Do you think Ryit would believe Sam hadn't betrayed them? Or the Koffren?"

Allyce closed her eyes. "No, I suppose not," she said, her antagonism disappearing. "I'm sorry."

"It's okay," Nicole said, her own brief flicker of fatigue-driven stubbornness fading as well.

The first thing she had done once she and Cambria returned from Q1 was to locate Jeff and confirm that he and the rest of his diversion squad had also made it back safely. After that had been a long, hot shower in her room, followed by a quick snack. Only then did she think to come to Allyce to tell her how things had worked out, and to thank her for her help in creating an antidote to Sam's drug.

In retrospect, her brain probably would have done better with a nap than a shower and food. "I am sorry I couldn't bring him back."

"I know," Allyce opened her eyes again and smiled tiredly. "Maybe I should have let the Shipmasters bribe *me* into betraying you instead."

"You'd never have made it past that first Koffren," Nicole said, a shiver running through her as she thought back to his voice and murderous stance at that encounter. "The one who calls himself Justice. He's furious about what you did up in the treatment room. Deal or no deal, if you'd been there he would have killed you." She reached over and gently touched Allyce's hand. "Don't worry. We'll get you home."

"That's okay," she said, closing her eyes again. "Maybe it's not even worth thinking about. After twelve years . . . Tad's probably decided I'm dead or run away and moved on by now. How soon after you disappear can they declare you dead?"

"I don't know," Nicole said, wincing. That thought hadn't even occurred to her. Could everyone aboard already have been declared dead?

That would be bad. Very bad. Going home had to be the main motivation for most of the people who'd accepted her leadership in this war. If she couldn't deliver on that implied promise, what else could she possibly offer them?

"But at least we're in charge of the teleport room now, not them," Allyce said, visibly dragging herself away from the depressing thoughts of home and the husband the Wisps had snatched her away from. "I'm glad it worked."

"It worked perfectly," Nicole assured her. "Oh, and this will give you a laugh. Remember that you put the antidote in a square capsule? Turns out Sam used one of those for a second dose, telling Ryit and the Koffren it would kill me."

"Not sure he was right," Allyce said doubtfully, frowning into space. "The design profile he put together when he designed the drug was *very* specific about the dosage parameters. Doesn't mean a second dose would have been exactly good for you, though." Her face twitched with sudden understanding. "Oh! You're saying that when you brought it out, they all thought you were about to kill yourself?"

"Exactly," Nicole said, smiling tightly. "I couldn't have asked for a better way to keep their attention on me if I'd tried. It was perfect."

"Well, I *did* have a fifty-fifty chance with the capsule choice," Allyce pointed out. "But if you want to credit me with extra insight or brilliance, I don't mind."

"You deserve every bit of credit we can give you," Nicole assured her.

The door slid open and Jeff walked in. "*There* you are," he said, nodding to Nicole and then Allyce. "Firth thought you were still in the dining room."

"No, I'm here," Nicole said. "I wanted to bring Allyce up to date on everything. So have you figured out yet how many Koffren we're dealing with?"

Jeff wrinkled his nose. "It's a work in process," he said. "*I* think there were eight of the beasts visible before they got to the drones and smashed them. Levi thinks there were only seven; Iosif is pretty sure there were nine or ten."

"So with the two in the teleport rooms, we're talking ten to twelve total?"

"Right," Jeff said. "Unfortunately, that assumes they didn't have another battalion or two in the corridors who didn't have time to show themselves before the vanguard got to the drones. So it could be ten or twelve or a whole lot more."

"I don't think so," Nicole said. "I got the impression that the Koffren *really* wanted to intercept Sam and me before we got to the teleport room. If they had a bigger group to draw from, you'd think they'd have put more than just two of them on that job."

"Good point," Jeff said. "Still, even just twelve makes for a pretty hefty stack of enemies."

"And no more drones to hunt them down with," Allyce said.

"Not a problem," Jeff assured her. "We always assumed the

Shipmasters could monitor their cameras. We just needed to come up with a situation where we could use that against them. And we'd already drained the paralyzing drug out of the drone's whips for possible future use, so I'd say we got our money's worth."

"Good," Nicole said. "I'm thinking the Ponng and Thii arrows might be the place to use that. Though we'll need to do some tests and make sure the stuff adheres well enough to stay there until it's delivered."

"It will," Jeff said. "I took a good look at those arrowheads, and they're made of an odd kind of porous material. I'm thinking the Shipmasters might have designed them with an eye toward adding poison for some future test."

Nicole shivered. "Lovely."

"Agreed," Jeff said sourly.

"Speaking of drugs and poisons," Allyce said, "did the Ponngs get back yet with my cyanide mix?"

Nicole frowned. "What cyanide mix?"

"They heard about what I did to the Koffren and asked if I could make them another batch," Allyce said. "I told them some of my original mixture was still upstairs in the animal treatment supply room—tenth level, *bahri* something."

"And you sent them up there *alone*?" Jeff asked.

"*I* didn't send them anywhere," Allyce said, a bit crossly. "It was their idea. And they're not alone. Nicole's Wisp—Cambria—went with them."

"Wait a second," Nicole said. "The Ponngs asked Cambria to go with them, and it *obeyed* them?"

"I don't think they ever asked it anything," Allyce said. "They left, and it left with them. My point is that the mix is very dangerous, and I need them to bring the container here right away before someone mishandles it."

"Yeah," Nicole said, frowning as she crossed to the door. Her five Wisps were supposed to be attached to her and Jeff, and only because she'd specifically added Jeff to the list. What in the world was Cambria doing, wandering off without orders?

Could the whole anchoring thing be starting to unravel? Cambria and the others had been Q3 Wisps before Nicole woke them from their trance, or whatever the hell it was she'd done. Could they be reverting back to that orientation?

But in that case, how was Cambria even able to move around in Q4? As far as she could tell, the only reason her Wisps could see Q1 and Q4 was because of her. Maybe it had followed the Ponngs because they were all it could see?

Whatever the reason, she needed to figure it out before all five suddenly walked out on her.

"Trouble?" Jeff asked, moving aside as she reached the door.

"Maybe," Nicole said. The door slid open and she looked out. Jessup was a few feet down the corridor, standing guard over Allyce and the medical center as Nicole had ordered it to. "Jessup? Come here, please."

The Wisp glided over, and Nicole took its arm. *Where is Cambria?* she thought at it.

I don't know, Jessup replied.

Nicole frowned. *What do you mean, you don't know? I thought you could see Wisps and other people anywhere aboard the* Fyrantha.

I can see only Q4.

You can't see Q3? But you all came from Q3.

You are here. While you are in Q4, we can only see Q4.

So if I were in Q1, you could only see Q1?

Yes.

Nicole glowered down the corridor. A damn good thing, then, that she'd arranged to have Cambria come across from Q3 *after* she and Sam went over instead of before. *You still obey Jeff, right?*

Yes.

If Jeff were in Q3 and I were in Q4, could you see both quadrants?
Yes.

Okay, so that was a *little* better. Still, it was a limitation she needed to remember.

She half turned to see Jeff watching them, his eyes wary. "I asked it where Cambria was," she relayed, letting go of Jessup's arm. "Turns out it can only see the quadrants where either you or I are."

"Interesting," Jeff said. "So Cambria's not in Q4 anymore?"

"Oh," Nicole said, wincing. She'd been so busy tracking through this latest twist of Wisp logic that she'd completely missed that point. "No, I guess not." She took Jessup's arm again. *What about Moile and Teika? Can you see them?*

I can. They are on level 10 in bahri-four-four-six.

Nicole frowned. Wasn't that the storage room where Allyce had concocted her cyanide mixture? She was pretty sure it was. *What are they doing?*

They are doing nothing. They are motionless.

Something cold ran up Nicole's back. *How long since they last moved?*

Thirty-five minutes.

"Damn," Nicole muttered, again letting go. "The Ponngs are in trouble."

"The cyanide?" Allyce asked, her voice dark with dread.

"I don't know," Nicole said, pushing past Jessup. "I'm going to check."

"Hold it," Jeff said, catching her arm as she started down the corridor. "Let's get a party together—you, me, Iosif, and a few more."

"There's no time," Nicole insisted. "They may still be alive."

"Then at least grab a couple of your Wisps," Jeff said. "We'll leave Jessup here to watch over Allyce and call Lehigh and Hagert."

Nicole clenched her teeth. Finding the two Wisps would take time they might not have.

But he was right. After the Koffren humiliation in the teleport room, the big aliens would absolutely be looking for her head. "All right," she said. "But make it fast."

"Two minutes," Jeff promised, squeezing her arm and setting off at a fast jog. "Pretty sure I know where they are."

Two minutes later, as promised, they were off. Five minutes after that, with the two Wisps having carried them up twenty-two levels with their usual speed and efficiency, they reached Allyce's supply room.

Where they found the two Ponngs.

"Oh, God," Nicole muttered under her breath over and over, staring at the unmoving figures as Jeff crouched down beside them. She knew she should be doing the same—checking for life, examining injuries, doing *something*—but the sight of her two beaten and bloody companions somehow had frozen her to the deck. "Oh, God."

"The good news: they're both alive," Jeff reported. If he was bothered by her lack of usefulness, he at least wasn't saying anything about it. "The bad news: they're in pretty bad shape. We need to get them to Allyce right away."

"Right," Nicole said, breaking free of her paralysis. "Lehigh? Hagert?" She beckoned to the two Wisps, standing just inside the door. "Come help."

"We need to keep them as flat as possible," Jeff warned. "There may be broken bones or internal injuries."

"I know," Nicole said as the Wisps joined her. "Wisps: stand side by side and stretch your arms out in front of you, waist high."

They did so. Nicole motioned to Jeff, and together they care-fully lifted Moile from the floor and set him across their arms. "You and I will be carrying Teika?" Jeff asked.

"For now," Nicole said. "As soon as we're out in the corridor I'll call for more Wisps. Hopefully, enough of them will show up that we can hand him off to them."

For once, one of her plans worked as she'd hoped. They'd made it to the next cross-corridor when six Wisps appeared in answer to her call. She and Jeff handed off their burden, the Wisps con-firmed that they understood her order to take the injured Ponngs to Allyce, and the whole crowd glided their way toward the heat duct.

"What's the plan?" Jeff asked quietly as he and Nicole watched the others go.

Nicole gazed at the injured Ponngs, her throat tight and aching. *If you will provide for my people,* Moile had said when she first met them back in the Q3 arena, *I will be your slave. So will Teika, if you wish it.*

Nicole hadn't wanted slaves. She still didn't. Whatever the Ponngs called themselves, she'd never used that word, even in her own mind. She'd always thought of them instead as allies, maybe even friends.

And allies and friends were supposed to look out for each other.

"We're going to find out what happened," she said. "And we're going to rain hell on whoever did this."

"Agreed," Jeff said darkly. "Where do we start?"

"Where everything always seems to end up," Nicole said. The procession of Wisps disappeared around a corner, and she turned toward the animal treatment room. "We're going to have a little chat with Caretaker Ushkai."

———

They found the familiar hologram waiting as they made their way between the rows of treatment cages. "About time," Nicole called as they approached. "Where the hell were you the last time I was here?"

"I was told to not speak with you," Ushkai said.

"Really," Nicole said. "Told by who? The Shipmasters?"

There was a brief hesitation. "I was told by the Oracle."

"So who told the Oracle? The Shipmasters?"

"No one told the Oracle," Ushkai said. "The Oracle spoke for itself."

"Why?"

"I don't know. You would have to ask the Oracle itself."

"Yeah, if I could find it I would," Nicole growled. "Never mind. What happened to the Ponngs back in that supply room? And don't tell me you don't know."

"Of course I know," Ushkai said. "Your fellow humans found them and beat them."

Nicole felt her mouth drop open. What in the *world*? "That's crazy. None of us would attack them. They're our helpers. Our friends."

"They're not friends to all of them."

"But—"

"Oh, *damn* it," Jeff bit out. "He's talking about Bungie."

Nicole bit down hard on the curse that wanted to come out. Of course it was Bungie. Bungie, and Trake, and all the rest of the Trake's worthless gang. "Which means it was the Koffren," she said.

"Well, they're the ones who sprung them," Jeff said. "So, yeah, probably."

"I guess we'll just have to find them, won't we?" Nicole said. "Where are they, Ushkai?"

Ushkai paused again. Thinking? Listening? "They await you on level 36 near Q3 heat-transfer duct access door four," Ushkai said. "They will speak with you there."

"Will they, now?" Nicole said. "And what the hell makes them think I'll show up?"

"They have one you care about," Ushkai said hesitantly.

Nicole frowned. "Who?"

"They don't understand—"

"*Who?*" Nicole screamed. A sudden, horrible premonition of what he was going to say . . .

"The Wisp," Ushkai said. "The one you call Cambria."

No! Nicole filled her lungs to scream again.

The scream never came. Suddenly, unexpectedly, the blazing anger and rage and helplessness swirling like storm clouds inside her vanished.

And in its place was a dark, hard, frozen resolve.

"I see," she said, almost wincing at the complete lack of emotion in her voice. "Well. I guess I'm going to Q3. You coming, Jeff?"

"Of course," Jeff said. "We'll just stop by the hive first and check on the Ponngs, okay?"

Nicole smiled. Yes; they should check on the Ponngs. They should probably check on Allyce, too. And then they could go and make sure Trake and Bungie knew exactly what it was they were facing here.

Before she killed them all.

twenty

Nicole hadn't given numbers to the access doors into the various heat-exchange ducts. She hadn't even counted them, for that matter. But she knew approximately where they were, and she certainly knew how to get to them.

As it happened, she didn't even need that much information. The moment the duct door closed behind her and Jeff, dropping them onto Q3 level 36, they could feel the flow of warm air coming steadily down the corridor from the front of the ship.

"Looks like they figured out a way to get the access door open," Jeff murmured.

"Yes," Nicole agreed, frowning. Shipmasters and Wisps could open the doors, and of course the Q1 Wisps obeyed the Shipmasters. No real mystery as to how Trake could get here.

But every other time she'd crossed the ducts the doors had closed again as soon as she and her party were across. The flow of warm air here, though, suggested the door was sitting open. "And to *keep* it open."

"I gather that's something new?"

"I haven't seen anyone else do it," Nicole said. "Though on a ship this size, that doesn't mean much."

"I suppose," Jeff said. "This could be easier than I'd thought it would be."

"Maybe," Nicole agreed cautiously. The hot air was still flowing across them, meaning the door was still open . . .

"We doing this?" Jeff prompted.

Nicole squared her shoulders. "Absolutely." She turned to the two Wisps she'd commandeered to ferry them across from Q4. "Wait for us here, please. Jeff?"

"Ready," he said, hefting his spider gun. "Unless you've changed your mind about carrying this yourself?"

She shook her head. "Thanks, but I'm good."

It would be best if Jeff carried the weapon. Trake always assumed unarmed people were helpless, and she really wanted him to think of her that way right now.

Besides, the only thing that he would hate more than losing to a woman would be losing to an unarmed woman. "Let's go."

They were standing in front of an open vent door as Jeff and Nicole came around the corner: four figures, no more than a couple of feet from the edge of the vent, their bodies swaying a little with the gusts of hot air jostling them from behind.

Nicole had guessed that Bungie and Trake would be there. She'd also assumed Cambria would be with them, since in Trake's mind there was no point in taking a prisoner if you couldn't terrorize him.

What she *hadn't* expected was that a Shipmaster would also be standing among them.

Or rather, *kneeling* among them.

She felt her stomach tighten as she and Jeff walked toward the little group. She'd seen a couple of Shipmasters without their armor once before, and even then, tense and terrified, she'd noticed how small and frail and helpless they looked. But this one had gone way past even that assessment. He was slumped forward, his face turned toward the deck, his kimono-style robe torn and wrinkled. Bungie was gripping his right arm at the elbow, and Nicole had the feeling that if he opened his hand the Shipmaster would collapse flat on his face.

A second later Trake spotted them. "About time," he called, the smugness in his voice matching the smugness in his expression as he gave Nicole half a wave with his spider gun. "I was starting to think you didn't think as highly of this thing as everyone said you did."

"I care about everyone aboard the *Fyrantha*," Nicole said as she and Jeff continued toward them. "That's what it means to be the ship's Protector." At least Cambria was standing tall and straight, unlike the Shipmaster, and apparently unharmed.

Or so Nicole thought until Trake turned toward her and she saw that Cambria's wings were pinned to its back by multiple spider shots. "You didn't need to do that," she said.

"Probably," Trake said with a casual shrug. "But it was fun. You remember fun, don't you, Nicole? You used to be so *good* at it."

Nicole felt a flush of anger and embarrassment rise into her cheeks. Jeff was standing right there beside her, and she could guess what he probably thought Trake was talking about. For a second she froze, wondering if she should defend herself, or deny it, or just let it pass—

"We're not talking about Nicole," Jeff put in calmly. "We're talking about you. Most people where I come from would think it's pretty damn cowardly to pick on someone who can't fight back."

"Don't really care what you think," Trake said, flashing Jeff the kind of look Nicole had usually seen him reserve for rival gang leaders.

"Fine with me," Jeff said. "More interested in seeing what people do than what they think. So what's this current farce supposed to prove?"

"And you can shut your freaking mouth anytime," Trake snarled.

"Yeah, about that," Jeff said casually. "You could come over here and try to make me." He hefted his spider gun. "Course, I'm pretty sure I'm a better shot with this thing than you are."

"You want to try it?" Trake challenged, his eyes narrowed, his forefinger tapping on the side of his weapon. "Any time you want. Of course"—he half turned and peered down into the shaft behind them—"if you miss, you're going to send someone a freaking long way down."

"I've got 50 percent chance that it's you or Bungie," Jeff pointed out.

"Enough," Nicole said, gesturing Jeff back. His awareness of her mental state and his verbal sparring had given her the minute she needed to regain control of herself. "You've got Cambria. Fine. You didn't ask us here just to gloat. What do you want?"

"Pretty boy said this wasn't about you," Trake said. "He's wrong. We're here to find out what kind of person you are, Nicole."

"Not the kind who has fun, we know," Bungie put in.

"Shut it," Trake said. His voice was calm, and he didn't even look at Bungie. Just the same, Bungie flinched as if Trake had hauled back to hit him. "Here's the thing. Our new friends think you're a sweetheart who'd never hurt a fly. I told them they were wrong, that you could be just as nasty as they are."

"So I'm wrong, and they're wrong," Jeff said. "Going to be your turn to be wrong next."

"I am going to shut you up, you freaking butt wipe," Trake grated out.

"We're back to you making me," Jeff pointed out. "I don't see that happening anytime soon."

Nicole felt her breath catch in her throat. Trake absolutely hated *anyone* picking at him this way, especially in front of any of his gang.

And yet, he wasn't doing anything. He wasn't shooting at Jeff, or coming at him, or even sending Bungie to take a swing at him.

Whatever he was planning, apparently he and Bungie needed to stay right where they were. "Yeah, this reminds me of all the fun you say we used to have," she said. Time to get him to show whatever cards he was carrying. "Tell me what you want, or we're leaving."

"You're going to make a decision," Trake said. "One of these helpless butt wipes is going over the edge today. You get to pick which one."

"You mean, pick which one dies? And why would I do that?"

"Because if you don't, all of them die," Trake said, his voice suddenly low and deadly. "And I mean all three."

Beside him, Bungie twisted his head around to stare at his boss, his mouth dropping open. "Trake—?"

"Shut it," Trake bit out.

Again, Bungie jerked back. A sudden image flashed across Nicole's face, that of a dog she'd once seen flinching from its owner's suddenly clenched fist.

"Why do you think we'd care if Bungie took the long step?" Jeff asked.

Bungie turned suddenly furious eyes toward Jeff. "You rat-ass bastard—"

"I said shut it," Trake said. "I won't say it again."

"Sure, Trake," Bungie muttered. "Sure."

"But hey, if he's the one you want to drop, come on over and do it," Trake said, gesturing to Nicole.

Nicole clenched her teeth. Trake had always liked playing with his victims. The more terrified he could make them, the better. Threatening Bungie with instant death played right into that pattern.

But what did he intend to accomplish by dragging in Cambria and the Shipmaster?

"And we haven't got all day," Trake added. "Come on. Let's get it over with."

Could he be setting her up for an ambush? But there wasn't much of anything between her and Jeff and the open vent; no room doors that she'd be conveniently putting her back to as she approached them, and no concealing walls or other hiding places where the rest of his gang could be lurking.

In fact, if that was the direction he was going, the perfect move would have been for his gang to come up behind her from the corridor they'd just left. Surreptitiously, she glanced over her shoulder.

But there was nothing. None of his gang, none of the Koffren.

So they weren't trying to capture her? Were they trying to kill her, then? Hoping she'd let Trake lure her close enough for him to grab her and throw her down the shaft?

And then, suddenly, she understood.

"Wait here," she murmured to Jeff, and started forward.

"Nicole—" Jeff warned, taking a long step to her side.

"No, it's okay," she said, gesturing him to stop. "They're not going to hurt me. They don't dare."

Jeff came to a reluctant halt. Nicole continued forward, watching Trake closely. He seemed surprised at first, but as she steadily closed the distance between them his expression changed to confusion, then suspicion, then gloating anticipation.

She came to a halt a couple of steps in front of the group, half closing her eyes to protect them against the blast of hot air still streaming into her face. The force of the wind required her to lean slightly forward to keep from being pushed backward, bringing her a couple of extra inches toward Trake. "So," she said. "One of you needs to die?"

"Or all of them do," Trake said. "That's the deal."

"What if the one I pick is you?"

Trake shook his head. "I'm not part of the bet."

"Yes, but I don't know all the rules," she reminded him. "I might break them without knowing it."

"Let's make it clear," he said, waving his spider gun across the three lined up beside him. "One of *them* has to die. You get to choose which."

"And then, what, you'll push them down the shaft?"

He smiled thinly. "The Koffren already know I'm a nasty-ass killer. They want to know if you are, too."

"So *I'm* supposed to push them?"

"You push one, or I push all three," Trake said. "And now you're just stalling."

"Not really," Nicole said. "I just wanted to make sure I'd figured it out right."

Trake's eyes narrowed a little. "You mean about the one or the three?"

"No, I mean about the real reason for this little game," Nicole said. Almost . . .

"I already told you—"

"The Koffren want me out of the way," she said. "But they're worried about what Sam said about killing the *Fyrantha*'s Protector. So they're thinking now that if they can get me to not be Protector anymore, maybe they'll have a shot at me without the *Fyrantha* making trouble for them."

Trake's expression had gone rigid. Either the Koffren had told him, or he'd figured it out on his own.

"The Protector is supposed to defend the ship and everything aboard it," she continued. "So I guess the idea is that if I kill someone—not just let someone get killed because I can't stop it, but actually and deliberately make someone dead—the Caretaker and *Fyrantha* will decide I'm not worthy of the title. Once that happens, they figure they'll be free to do whatever they want with me."

Trake shook his head. "Bungie said you'd gotten smarter. Thought maybe he was just getting dumber. But he was right. Only you're missing the big point."

Abruptly, he reached to his side and put his arm across Cambria's chest. "And I figure that if you could stop a death and didn't, that might be enough."

"I doubt it," Nicole said. "But anyway, it's already too late." She lifted her arm and pointed back toward the corridor she and Jeff had come from a few minutes ago. "Firth! Hagert! Now!"

Trake and Bungie both looked toward the corner, Trake lifting his spider gun and tracking in that direction—

And as they did so, in the shaft behind them the two Wisps Nicole had called floated down into view, their wings curving as they angled toward the group at the edge.

"The two humans," Nicole ordered.

Either Trake had a sudden premonition about what was happening, or else he saw something in Nicole's eyes. He spun around, his body jerking as he saw the Wisp moving toward him, trying to bring his spider gun around.

But there was no time. He was facing Firth, his gun arm stuck out to the side, when the Wisp wrapped its arms around him and froze him.

Bungie, without any of Trake's insight or reflexes, was caught flat-footed right where he stood.

Nicole huffed out a breath. "Jessup, Lehigh, you can come down now, too," she called up into the shaft. She moved over to Cambria and took its hand, leading it away from the shaft edge.

Thank you, the Wisp said into her mind.

You're welcome, Nicole thought back. *What were you doing there, anyway?*

I was captured when the human Trake attacked the Ponngs.

What I meant was why were you there in the first place? Did Moile or Teika ask you to go with them?

I was summoned by the Caretaker.

Nicole stared at it. *You're saying* Ushkai *called you? What did he want?*

I don't know. There was no time to speak before the attack.

Nicole felt her lips curl back from her teeth. No time to speak, because the ambush was all primed and ready. How very, very convenient for someone.

And she was pretty sure she knew who.

She pulled Cambria a couple more steps into the corridor and then let go of its hand. Stepping back to the shaft, she grabbed the Shipmaster's arm, the one not still being held in Bungie's frozen grip. "You and I need to talk—what the *hell?*" she broke off as she finally spotted the thin plastic strap binding the Shipmaster's wrist to Bungie's.

"The Koffren could not deduce whether you hated us more than you hated the human called Bungie," the Shipmaster said, an odd almost sadness in his chattering alien language. "So they decided that whichever of us you chose for death, the other would follow."

"A two-for-one deal," Jeff commented as he came up behind Nicole. "Not sure whether to be impressed or disgusted."

"You can have both," Nicole told him. "Call it another two-for-one. Which one are you?"

The alien lifted its head, its eyes boring into hers. "I am Nevvis."

Nicole felt her eyes go a little wider. "You're *Nevvis?* Master of the masters?"

"Hardly," Nevvis said. "I'm now merely one among many prisoners."

Nicole exchanged looks with Jeff. "So the Koffren are running the *Fyrantha* now?" she asked.

"We still control the *Fyrantha*," Nevvis said. "But they control us."

"Hostages," Jeff murmured.

"Yes."

"I guess that explains where Trake's other four goons are, too," Jeff said.

"Also hostages," Nicole said, nodding. "I guess the Koffren don't trust anyone."

"With their track record, that's not really surprising."

"I suppose not," Nicole said.

"And now they come," Nevvis added softly.

Nicole felt her stomach tense. *Damn* it. "It's an ambush, all right," she said, throwing quick looks both ways down the corridor. No Koffren yet, but that wouldn't last. "Only they were waiting to spring it until I'd lost my Protector status."

"Time to fall back?" Jeff asked, pulling out a knife and getting to work on the strap tying Nevvis to Bungie.

"Time to fall back," Nicole confirmed. She went over to Trake, worked the spider gun out of his frozen hand, and took a couple of steps back. "Firth, Hagert: let them go."

The two Wisps opened their arms. Trake started to lunge toward Nicole, stopped as she raised the spider gun warningly. "You think you're smart, don't you," he said coldly. "Well, it doesn't matter how smart you are. There are twenty of them, and only one of you, and they're desperate. Sooner or later they'll get you."

And then, out of the corner of her eye, Nicole saw a group of Koffren charge around the far corner. "Firth, take me," she ordered, turning and backing into its arms. "Hagert, take Jeff; Lehigh, take Cambria. Into the sha—"

The word was cut off as Firth's embracing arms paralyzed her. But none of them needed to be told what to do. Even as the Koffren raised their spider guns and opened fire the Wisps carried the three of them into the shaft and rose swiftly on the updraft.

Below them, the faint corridor light vanished as the shaft door finally slid closed.

Where do you wish to go? Firth asked.

Bring all of us to Q4, Nicole told it, scowling inside. Too late, now, she wished she'd had Jessup grab Nevvis and bring him along. But the Koffren had been on the move, and her first instinct had been for her own people.

Still, it sounded like the Koffren needed Nevvis. Anyway, the Shipmasters hadn't been part of this particular scheme. Trake and Bungie should be the ones to get the sharp end of the stick.

But there were things she needed to know that Nevvis probably could have told her.

Never mind. She was starting to learn that there were always other ways of doing things.

Besides, the Ghorfs had sat on their hands long enough. Time to bring them into the game.

twenty-one

"They're in pretty bad shape," Allyce said as she carefully straightened up from the twin beds where the Wisps had laid the injured Ponngs, wincing as she strained her own injuries. "No broken bones—which wasn't from lack of effort on their attackers' part—multiple epidermal bruises, lacerations, and muscle bruising. Teika has some internal bleeding, and both of them may have some organ damage, but I don't know enough about their physiology to be sure."

"So how do you intend to learn?" Nicole asked.

Allyce seemed taken aback. "How do I intend to learn what?"

"They're hurt," Nicole said with strained patience. "You're their doctor. Figure out how to heal them."

"Nicole, they're *aliens*," Allyce protested. "I don't have the slightest idea how to treat creatures like this."

"We could ask the Caretaker," Jeff suggested.

Allyce frowned. "What does the Caretaker have to do with anything?"

"No, he's right," Nicole said, embarrassed that she hadn't thought of it first. "The *Fyrantha* used to be a zoo. It must have health data from all sorts of creatures. If we're lucky, they may have something on Ponngs."

"I thought we didn't trust the Caretaker," Allyce said. "Wasn't he the one who lured Cambria into the ambush?"

"Yes, but that was probably at the Shipmasters' instructions," Nicole said.

"Or the Koffrens'," Jeff said. "If Nevvis wasn't lying, they're the ones calling the shots now."

"And they may not have the same control of the Caretaker that the Shipmasters had," Nicole said slowly. Thinking about the Caretaker's connection with the Shipmasters had started her on an entirely new train of thought. "Even if they do, they may be too busy to notice a request for alien medical information."

"It's still risky," Jeff warned. "We'll want a team with us."

"I think you, me, and the four Wisps should do," Nicole said. "Besides, there's a little experiment I want to try, and if it doesn't work we might need a quick exit."

"We could still bring Iosif," Jeff suggested. "He seemed hurt that he didn't get to join into our last outing."

"Really?" Nicole asked, frowning. "Is this one of those Navy/Marine things?"

"Probably," Jeff said with a grin. "I'll go find him. You should probably go see how Levi and Carp are doing with Cambria, anyway."

Nicole winced. "Yeah. But make it fast. If Ushkai has Ponng medical information, I want Allyce to have it as soon as possible."

Levi and Carp had set up in the dining room, pushing two of the tables together to make a workstation they could lay Cambria on while they got the spider goo off it. "How's it going?" Nicole asked as she walked in.

"Slowly," Levi said. "They slapped it with a lot more shots than they needed just to immobilize it."

"Yeah, that sounds like Trake," Nicole said sourly. "If you like doing something, do it as many times as you can. Especially if it makes someone else hurt."

"I don't know if it hurts, but it's got to be damn uncomfortable," Levi said. He held up the bottle of dissolving liquid. "Speaking of uncomfortable, we're getting uncomfortably low on this stuff."

"It's okay—Jeff's got another bottle stashed away," Nicole said. "Do you have enough there to finish with Cambria?"

"I think so," Levi said, leaning over the Wisp and peering at the remaining goo. "Carp?"

"Yeah, we'll be fine," Carp seconded. "But this one will be pretty much dry at that point."

"We'll just have to try to limit the number of times we get shot, then," Nicole said. "Thanks."

She laid a hand on Cambria's arm. *They'll have you free soon,* she told it. *Are you doing all right?*

I'm fine, Protector, it replied. *The Oracle wishes to speak with you.*

Nicole frowned. *The Oracle?*

Yes.

She looked at Levi, who was carefully squeezing another drop onto the spider goo. If the Caretaker was to be believed, the Oracle was the part of the *Fyrantha* that spoke for the Shipmasters.

Except when it was speaking for itself to the Sibyls. Nicole still hadn't figured out how that worked.

She'd heard the Oracle speak before, giving orders and instructions to the combatants in the *Fyrantha's* various arenas. But this was the first time it had asked to speak to Nicole personally. *Did it say why?*

No.

Where can I talk to it? One of the arena hives?

The Oracle will speak to you on level 10 in bahri-*four-four-six.*

That's where the Caretaker hangs out.

Yes.

Are the Oracle and Caretaker the same?

No.

Nicole made a face. Back to that again.

Still, she'd been planning to go talk to the Caretaker, anyway. If the Oracle was able to join the party, it would save her a trip. *Fine. Tell it I'll meet it there.*

I'll do so. Thank you.

The door opened behind her. "Ah—Protector," Kahkitah said as he lumbered into the room. "I thought I'd find you here."

"I was just checking on—wait a second," Nicole said, frowning at him as the implications of that sank in. "Are you saying I'm always eating?"

"No, of course not," the Ghorf said with a mix of earnestness and shyness. "Besides, Jeff said you're our leader, and a leader has to keep up her strength."

"Yeah, and I've got the pink slip on Independence Hall," Nicole growled.

Kahkitah gave a confused whistle. "What's a pink slip, and why is a building wearing one?"

Levi snorted. "*Jeopardy!* really missed its chance with him, didn't it?"

Kahkitah's next whistle sounded plaintive. "I don't understand," he said. "I wish you wouldn't say things I can't understand."

"It's all right, Kahkitah," Nicole soothed. "Just ignore him. Did you finish that job I asked you to do?"

"Oh, yes," Kahkitah said, brightening again. "That was what I came to tell you."

"Great," Nicole said, looking back at Levi and Carp. "You two all right here?"

"We're fine," Carp said. "Go ahead."

"And, Kahkitah?" Levi added. "Sorry. We were only kidding."

"Oh," Kahkitah said cheerfully. "That's all right, then. I like it when people kid each other. It's good to be happy."

"Yes, it is," Nicole said, gesturing him back toward the door. "Show me."

They left the room. "I'm really looking forward to seeing their faces when you're finally able to drop the act," Nicole murmured as they walked.

"As am I," Kahkitah said ruefully. "But I'm afraid that will be some time yet."

"It may happen sooner than you think," Nicole said. "What does the magic Ghorf network tell you?"

"That you were right," Kahkitah said. "All the Sibyls have disappeared. Not just the ones with the blue and green work teams, but every Sibyl from every crew aboard the *Fyrantha*."

"You're sure? *All* of them?"

"Certainly from all the groups with one of my people on the crew. There are a few groups that don't, but the local Ghorfs say there are strong suggestions that their Sibyls are gone as well." He cocked his head toward her. "Do you know what it means?"

"Not yet," Nicole said. "But at least it answers the question of why the Koffren want me back so badly. If all the other Sibyls are gone, I'm the only one who can fix the teleport for them."

"Assuming they want to bring in more of their kind," Kahkitah said. "Which of course makes sense if they're trying to take command of the *Fyrantha*."

"Yeah, we're not going to let that happen," Nicole said firmly. "Cambria tells me the Oracle wants to talk to me, and it sounds like the Oracle is the section of the *Fyrantha*'s mind that the Shipmasters have most under their control. Maybe Nevvis is trying to open communication."

"The last time one of the Shipmasters suggested a communication it was to betray you."

"Yeah, but things have changed a lot since then," Nicole reminded him. "The Koffren have basically made them working prisoners, I've proven to be a harder nut than anyone expected, and I've started collecting Wisps under my personal control."

"Five Wisps hardly constitutes an army."

Nicole shrugged. "Okay, so right now it's not much more than a commando team. But I know how to make more."

"Pour a mixture of Q2 and Q3 Wisps into Q4, allow them to marinate for a while, then spoon onto the Protector and serve."

Nicole had to smile at that one. "You remind me of my grandmother trying to teach me how to cook."

"Really, Nicole," he admonished her, his neck gills flapping with suppressed chuckling. "Did you think Ghorfs didn't cook?"

"No, of course not," Nicole assured him with a straight face. "Actually, I was planning to put you in charge of the big victory feast when this is all over. So did anyone have any idea where the Sibyls might have gone?"

"There was one thought," Kahkitah said hesitantly. "But it seemed to make so little sense that I hesitate to mention it. One of the Q2 Ghorfs said his team had been brought in to convert the Q1 arena dispensers to distribute human food."

"Why is that so outrageous?" Nicole said. "If the Shipmasters are trying to hide them from the Koffren, it's a perfect place."

"From the *Koffren*, yes," Kahkitah said. "But hardly from us. We've already shown our ability to get in and out of the arena whenever we want."

"Maybe that's the point," Nicole said thoughtfully. "The Shipmasters know you got me out through the ocean half of the arena and the *Fyrantha*'s water system. Maybe Nevvis is counting on us to sneak the Sibyls out of there before the Koffren figure out where they are."

"To what end?"

"To hide them someplace where *we're* in control," Nicole said. "The Shipmasters don't dare traipse over here to Q4 to stash the Sibyls, so they do the next best thing and put them someplace where we can grab them. If we do that, even if the Koffren find out they've been stashed in the arena it won't do them any good. They can beat at the doors all they want and still not get anywhere near the Sibyls."

Kahkitah pondered that for a few steps. "You realize your analysis presumes that the Shipmasters are now acting as our allies," he said. "I was unaware they'd made any such offers to you."

"They haven't," Nicole conceded. "On the other hand, maybe this is their way of doing that. This, plus their request to talk to me via the Oracle."

"Or perhaps it's another trap."

"I don't think so," Nicole said. "Remember what I said about being a hard nut to crack? Well, that raises my value as both an enemy *and* an ally."

"One would think the Koffren would come to that same conclusion."

"I'm sure they have," Nicole said, grimacing with memory. "Only they know there's not a chance in hell I'll come to their side. Not after Bennett's murder right in front of me."

"Yet the Shipmasters have also killed many Sibyls."

"It's different," Nicole said. "I mean, maybe it's not. But it is. I'm sure they didn't set out to deliberately poison us with the chemical in our inhalers—they needed the *Fyrantha* fixed, and that was the only way they had to do that."

"They've sent many from other races to their deaths in alien wars," Kahkitah continued doggedly. "They've also kidnapped everyone aboard the ship to serve as their slaves."

"What are you trying to do, Kahkitah?" Nicole asked, glaring at him. "We may have a chance here to pick up some allies. Are you saying we should just ignore that?"

"There's a human saying we've heard during our years aboard the *Fyrantha*," Kahkitah said. "*The enemy of my enemy is my friend.*"

"Yeah, I've heard that one," Nicole said. "What's your point?"

"My point is it's untrue," Kahkitah said. "The enemy of my enemy is merely the enemy of my enemy. The bits of Earth history we've been able to glean show that with distressing regularity."

"So you're saying what?" Nicole asked. "That we go it alone and fight both the Koffren *and* the Shipmasters?"

"I don't believe the Shipmasters are truly fighters," Kahkitah said. "But yes, I believe the price for their assistance and their weapons would be higher than you would wish to pay." His birdsong trill went dark and bitter. "It is certainly higher than the Ghorfs wish to pay."

"Okay," Nicole said. "Noted. So. Bottom line. If I enlist the Shipmasters to my side, does that mean the Ghorfs will abandon us?"

"Of course not," Kahkitah said firmly. "You're the *Fyrantha*'s Protector, and you're also our friend. No matter what else you do or don't do, whatever you need from us we'll do. I just wanted to make our thoughts known."

"I appreciate that," Nicole said.

She meant it, too. The Ghorfs had been good allies, and their secret communication system was a resource that could make a crucial difference in any future action against the Koffren. The last thing she wanted to do was drive them away. But she might not have a choice.

Because without the Shipmasters and their greenfire weapons, they didn't have a chance. Not against the Koffren. Especially not if the Koffren had gotten more greenfire weapons of their own.

Not a chance. Not a chance in hell.

Surreptitiously, she looked at Kahkitah as he walked stolidly beside her. The Ghorfs were warriors, or at least had trained themselves to be warriors. They would surely understand.

But did Nicole herself understand?

Kahkitah had a good point. The Shipmasters had caused all sorts of misery and death and destruction. Could she really in good conscience cooperate with them?

Even more importantly, would the *Fyrantha* understand? Would it approve?

She frowned suddenly. No. It didn't matter if the *Fyrantha* didn't approve. It didn't really even matter if the Ghorfs approved.

She was the *Fyrantha's* Protector. All that mattered was whether *she* approved.

And she didn't. Suddenly, she realized that down deep she didn't.

"All right, then," she said. "We'll do it ourselves."

Kahkitah turned his head, his bird whistle taking on a surprised tone. "You really don't need to decide so quickly, Nicole," he said.

"Too bad, because I have," Nicole said.

"You have a plan?"

"Maybe," she said. "First, I need to grab Jeff and Iosif and go see what the Shipmasters want to talk about."

"Shall I come along?"

"No, I think the three of us and my Wisps can handle it," she said. "Besides, I want you to talk to the other Ghorfs. I need to see if a crazy idea I've just come up with is even possible."

"It will be," Kahkitah promised. "For the Protector, we'll make it possible."

"I'll hold you to that," Nicole warned. "Okay. Here's what I'm thinking . . ."

Ushkai was waiting when Nicole, Jeff, Iosif, and their three-Wisp escort arrived in the animal treatment room.

But this time he wasn't alone. A tall, heavyset creature stood beside him, towering over him by probably eight inches, with long, braided hair and a face that reminded Nicole of a koala she'd seen once on TV. Its arms were ape-long, and its legs were like horse's legs, complete with hooves and horseshoes that flickered with colored lights. It wore a triangle-shaped piece of dark red cloth that started at its shoulders and angled down to a spot between the knees, with an edge that flickered like the horseshoes. "I am the Oracle," it announced as they came closer.

Or rather, *she* announced. The voice coming from that v-shaped mouth was high and female and surprisingly gentle.

"I am Nicole," Nicole called back. "The Protector. Do you speak for the Shipmasters, Oracle?"

"Welcome, Protector," the creature said. "You may address me as R'taas, just as you may address the Caretaker as Ushkai. I speak for the Shipmasters when it serves the purposes of the *Fyrantha*. But I prefer to speak to the sisterhood of the Sibyls."

"You're the one telling them how to fix the ship?" Jeff asked.

"I am," R'taas said.

"And killing them?" Jeff added pointedly.

The big alien seemed to slump. "That was never our intent. We did not so design this vessel. But circumstances were changed, and the ship altered—"

"Wait a second," Nicole cut in. "*You* designed the *Fyrantha*?"

"We designed *Leviathan*," R'taas corrected. "We designed it, and in conjunction with the humans of Earth we flew it to the stars."

"Yeah, about that," Jeff said. "Why humans? Why us? We must have been pretty damn primitive when you found us."

"Primitiveness is a state of knowledge," Ushkai spoke up. "Knowledge may be added and instilled and nurtured."

"Not so spirit and inward talent," R'taas said. "You had both. You still do."

"This is all really fascinating," Iosif put in. "But we have a war to fight. You got something useful to say, or did you just call us up here to say hi and shoot the breeze?"

"The Core," Ushkai said solemnly.

"The Core," R'taas agreed.

"I hope that's not what they consider useful," Iosif muttered.

"Yes, tell us about the Core," Nicole said. If this was the part of the *Fyrantha* that spoke to the Sibyls, then this could be about fixing something important. "Where is it, and what do we need to do about it?"

"It centers the four quadrants," R'taas said. "It nests at the crossness of the heat ducts."

"Very poetic," Iosif said sarcastically. "You—Caretaker—you want to put it in plain English?"

"I don't speak English," Ushkai said. "But the Oracle is correct. The Core rests at the intersection of the four quadrants on level 51."

"How big is it?" Jeff asked.

"Each section fills a space four *pess* by two *pess*," R'taas said.

"You've got to be kidding me," Jeff muttered. "*English, Care-taker?*"

"Approximately the size of two of the animal treatment cages behind you," Ushkai said. "They're densely packed, but there are narrow access corridors through the lines of consoles."

"The Core needs to be repaired," R'taas said. "Until then, I—we—I—will be fragmented."

"If it's that important, why isn't it already fixed?" Iosif demanded. "It's not like we haven't been aboard for the last jillion years."

"It *has* been fixed, hasn't it?" Nicole asked as she suddenly understood. "All except the part in Q1." She turned to Jeff and Iosif. "Don't you see? The Shipmasters have kept everyone out of that quadrant, probably ever since they started kidnapping people."

"Paranoid that we'll rise up against them," Jeff said, nodding.

"Pretty good assumption, if you ask me," Iosif said. "So how do we get into the Q1 part?"

"There's a horizontal air duct between level 51 and level 52," Ushkai said. "Perhaps you can move through it to the entrance, then move in quickly before the guards can block you."

"Guards?" Nicole asked. "You mean Q1 Wisps?"

"Yes."

Jeff looked at Nicole. "Well, you were talking earlier about having your Wisps convert a bunch of their fellows. Sounds like this would be a good time to give that a try."

"That'll take too long," Nicole said. "No, I've got a better idea." She turned back to R'taas. "Are you in contact with the Shipmasters?"

"I am."

"Send them this message," Nicole ordered. "This is the Protector. I have a way to free you from Koffren domination. But to do so, you need to release all the Wisps to my control. And I mean *all* of them, including the ones in Q1."

"What if they refuse?" R'taas asked.

"Then I'll just have to take over the ship without them," Nicole said, trying to project a confidence she absolutely didn't feel. Her plan was only half-formed, and relied completely on whether or not the Ghorfs could pull off the engineering feat she'd set for them. "Of course, if I don't get their help now, they won't get my help after it's all over. Fair is fair."

For a moment R'taas and Ushkai stood silently. Neither looked at the other, but Nicole had the eerie feeling that they were communicating. "The message is sent," R'taas said at last. "How do they acknowledge?"

"When the Q1 Wisps come under my control, I'll know it," Nicole said.

"You will?" Jeff asked, frowning.

"I think so," Nicole said. "If not, giving one of them an order should do it."

"Which requires you to be in Q1 at the time."

"He's got a point," Iosif said. "*My* question is, how are the Shipmasters going to hand them over with the Koffren sitting on top of them?"

"I don't think that'll be a problem," Nicole told him. "The Koffren may be watching them, but I doubt they really understand everything that's going on. Should be easy enough to slip in a quiet order in the right place. Anyway, that's their problem. If they want my help kicking the Koffren out of their lives, they'll figure it out." She turned back to the two holograms. "Next question: How many Koffren are aboard?"

Another silent consultation. "Thirty-eight," Ushkai said.

Jeff swore under his breath. "Thirty-*eight*? Trake said there were only twenty."

"Yeah, well, he would, wouldn't he?" Nicole said grimly. Still trying to build favor with the Koffren or at least prove himself useful, Trake would certainly downplay their numbers. "Are you sure about that?"

"I'm sure," Ushkai said.

"I'm sure," R'taas repeated.

Jeff looked at Nicole. "So. Do you still have a plan?"

"Don't be snide," Nicole reproved him. "*Yes,* I still have a plan. Okay, just one more question. How can I get a message to the Koffren?"

"We could send a Wisp with a note," Iosif suggested.

"You think these work with reading material?" Jeff asked pointedly, touching the side of his head where the hair covered his implanted translator.

Iosif reddened. "Right. Damn. I'm so used to this crazy setup I sometimes forget. Sorry."

"It's okay," Nicole said. "What about the recorder that—what's his name? Ezana—that Ezana built? I know the one you used to fake your voices with the drone diversion got smashed, but does he have another one we could use?"

"No, that was it," Iosif said. "And it took him two years to figure out how to make that one."

"Only one answer, then," Jeff said. "Oracle, where's the nearest Koffren?"

"*Scrinthu* section, level 51," R'taas said.

"Don't think I know *scrinthu*," Jeff said, looking at Nicole. "Which one is that?"

"It's the farthest aft part of Q1," Nicole said, wincing a little. "Right in front of the crosswise heat-exchange duct."

"Ah," Jeff said, nodding as he got it, too. "And level 51. In other words, he's helping the Wisps guard the Q1 section of the Core."

"Sounds like it," Nicole said. "Oracle, where's the *next* nearest Koffren?"

"No, no, this is fine," Jeff assured her. "Might as well walk into a stronghold section where they feel all safe and confident. Less likely to spook someone into thinking I'm the lead unit of an attack."

"Is *that* how they teach you to do things in the Marines?" Iosif asked.

"Mostly they taught us to improvise," Jeff said. "Nicole, if you can lend me one of your Wisps for transport, I'll head on over. What's the message?"

"Hold it," Iosif objected. "I'm not done yet. Who says *you're* the one going?"

"Who says I'm not?" Jeff countered. "Face it—it has to be one of Nicole's closest allies for the Koffren to take him seriously."

"Who says I'm not a close ally?" Iosif shot back. "And who says that they won't see that close ally as a potential hostage?"

"Better they take me hostage than they figure it's someone Nicole doesn't care about and flat-out kill him."

"Enough," Nicole cut in harshly. The minute she'd seen where this was going she'd known Jeff would volunteer and suspected Iosif would do likewise.

Unfortunately, just because Jeff was the best choice didn't make the decision any easier.

"Jeff's right, Iosif," she said. "Okay, here's the message. Tell them I'll fix the teleport for them if they'll all come to the Q1 arena and let me talk to them."

"The Q1 arena?" Jeff asked carefully.

"The Q1 arena," Nicole confirmed.

Jeff looked sideways at Iosif. "You realize that the Sibyls—"

"Yes, that they're all stashed away in there," Nicole said. "But it's the only arena that has the landscaping I need."

"Okay," Jeff said, his tone only slightly less concerned. "If you're sure. I only ask because your memory hasn't always been the best lately."

Nicole's first impulse was to deny it. Her second was to wonder if maybe he was right.

The inhalers the Sibyls used to hear the *Fyrantha's* telepathic work instructions contained a slow poison that ate away at the user's life span. Who was to say it didn't also have other, equally horrendous effects? Effects on health, perception, reflexes?

Memory?

"My memory's doing just fine, thank you," she said tartly. "Tell them I want all of them there because I have a proposition to pitch and I want to make sure it gets to whoever's in charge. I mean, *really* in charge."

"Play them off against each other," Jeff said, nodding. "Got it. Anything else?"

"They need to bring the Shipmasters with them," Nicole said. "Again, *all* of them. What I have to say is about everyone, and they all need to hear it."

"That's going to be quite a crowd," Iosif warned. "You sure you don't want to do something more of the hit-and-run attrition variety?"

"Nope," Nicole said. "Time's getting short. We might as well have it out all at once." She looked at Jeff. "Can you remember that long enough to spit it out to the Koffren?"

"I think so," Jeff said, still eyeing her closely. "When do you want this grand assemblage to take place?"

"Let's make it this time tomorrow," she said. If the Ghorfs could pull off her plan at all, that should give them enough time. "The Shipmasters can get them in. Tell them I'll meet them where the river meets the ocean."

"Tomorrow; Q1 arena; oceanside; everybody," Jeff said. "Got it."

"Good." Nicole half turned and beckoned. "Jessup, Lehigh: you're going with Jeff. Remember you're to obey his orders the same as you'd obey mine."

The two Wisps glided forward. She touched an arm on each one as they came to a halt, repeating the order telepathically and confirming their acceptance of Jeff as their master. "Go quickly," she said, trying to hide her misgivings.

"Don't worry, I'll be fine," Jeff said. Giving her a reassuring smile, he headed back toward the door they'd entered by, the two Wisps gliding along at his sides.

Nicole watched him go, a hollow feeling in her stomach. Up to now she'd been pretty good about guessing what the *Fyrantha* and the various groups aboard it were thinking and planning. But that depth of insight wasn't exactly guaranteed.

And with Jeff heading off for a confrontation with the Koffren this would be the worst possible time for her instincts and hunches to fall on their faces.

"I could go with him," Iosif offered quietly as they watched him go. "Better yet, I could grab a couple of my guys and some spider guns and ease in behind him. Take up backup position in case the Koffren decide to be cute."

For a long moment Nicole was tempted. She and Jeff had been together a long time, they'd gone through hell together, and she'd become a lot closer to him than she'd probably been to anyone in her life. She desperately wanted him to be safe.

More than that, she *needed* him to be safe. There were more battles yet to fight, more decisions to make, more conversations and confrontations to prepare for. She needed his insights and his steadying presence through all that.

She needed *him*.

That was a new thought. A scary thought. She'd never needed anyone before. Not since she was ten. Not like this. She'd *pretended* to need Trake or Bungie or some of the others through her years with the gang. But that had all been an act, a calculated play to their egos or desires or whatever she needed to do to survive.

She'd seldom been in control of her life or the people or events around her. But she'd always been in control of her feelings, deadening them as needed to get through whatever crisis dropped onto her. Now, unbidden and unwanted, emotions and feelings she'd thought were in check were suddenly bursting out of their crypt.

And that was terrifying. Needing people was the fastest way to become vulnerable to anyone who wanted to hurt you.

Iosif was still waiting for an answer. "No," she said. "Thanks, but no. They need something from me, and killing Jeff is the surest way for them to never ever get it."

"They could still take him hostage," Iosif warned darkly. "Like we said earlier. *And* they could hurt him. As long as he's alive, they've still got leverage on you."

"They might take him," Nicole conceded. "But I don't think they'll risk hurting him. Not yet."

"And if they take him?" Iosif persisted.

Nicole gazed at the door Jeff had disappeared to. "Actually, I almost hope they do," she said. "Come on, let's get back to the hive. I need to talk to Kahkitah."

twenty-two

For Nicole, each of the *Fyrantha*'s four arenas held their own particular collection of memories.

The Q4 arena was where she'd first learned the Shipmasters' true purpose for the huge onetime warship they'd taken over. She'd also learned to her surprise that she could actually make a difference in the lives of other people, a *real* difference, even with alien people who a few months ago she would never even have believed could exist.

In Q3 she'd first awakened the Shipmasters' notice and animosity. There, she'd not only made a difference, but made friends and allies among both the Ponngs and the Thii, allies who'd more than proved their worth and their loyalty.

The Q2 arena had tested her problem-solving skills, and taught her that she could sometimes talk people out of fighting and find more peaceful solutions.

And the Q1 arena, with its rolling ocean, pleasant beachfront sand, and tropical-looking trees, was where all those people and diplomatic skills came to nothing as she watched the Koffren casually murder one of her own. It was also where she'd first learned that she, too, could be a planner and a fighter, a realization that had been forced on her by the Shipmasters and the Koffren.

In the next twenty-four hours, if things went well, she would make them regret having dropped that lesson on her.

The first step, even before Jeff finished his journey across the *Fyrantha* to confront the Koffren, was to get the rest of the Sibyls out of harm's way. Kahkitah had suggested that they'd been stashed in the Q1 arena, so that was where she would start. With Iosif and two of her Wisps she sneaked across the crosswise heat duct and made her way to the arena.

The Ghorfs had been right. The Sibyls, forty-seven of them, had taken up residence in and around one of the hive sections at the end of the arena farthest from the ocean. Their forced isolation and leisure were starting to freak them out, and Nicole spent a few minutes reassuring them that everything was all right, and that they would be free soon. Warning them that they would soon have unwelcome company, she gently herded all of them inside the hive itself and slid the door closed.

Then, calling on Iosif's mechanical expertise with the *Fyrantha's* electronics, she locked it.

"They don't sound very happy," Iosif said, pressing his ear against the door. "You sure you wouldn't rather get them out of here and stash them in one of the barracks rooms down the hall?"

"I don't know if those doors can be locked," Nicole said, wincing a little. Even without her ear against the panel she could hear the fists pounding and the faint sound of raised voices. One voice in particular stood out among them, high and shrill and extremely angry. That one was going to be trouble down the road. "If any of the Sibyls wander out—or even if they stay inside and make this much noise—the Koffren would have to be deaf *and* stupid not to find them."

"I suppose," Iosif said. "Hey, they've got food, water, and bathrooms in there. They'll live."

"It's a lot better than some places I've been," Nicole said.

"Me, too," Iosif said, stepping away from the door. "Okay, Sibyls secured. What's next?"

Nicole peered up the slope toward the aft end of the arena. "We check out the river flow valves," she said. "We need to make sure they can deliver the volume I'm going to need." She beckoned to the two Wisps standing motionlessly beside the hive. "Firth, Hagert, you two wait here. We'll be back in a little while."

The climb up the rocky slope was every bit as difficult this time as it had been the last few times Nicole had tried it. Fortunately, she knew now how to use the trees and larger bushes for balance and to help pull her along as the slope became ever steeper.

"You said there was a way in through an air duct from the other end?" Iosif asked, his breathing sounding a little strained as they worked their way through a particularly tricky section.

"Yes," Nicole said. Unlike him, she was panting openly. "But I'm pretty sure the Shipmasters know how I got in that one time, and if they know, the Koffren might, too. It's narrow and tricky, and we don't want to get caught in there."

"Okay," Iosif said. "Just asking."

A few minutes later, they were there.

"Nice view," Iosif commented. He still wasn't panting, exactly, but his chest was definitely heaving.

Nicole nodded, too winded herself to answer aloud.

It *was* a nice view, she realized as she gazed out across the arena. The river ran down the slope, churning with fake white water, flowing between the two tall rock bluffs at the end of the riverbed. Once past the bluffs it flowed out onto the sand, eventually meeting up with the roiling ocean. The ocean itself was in the process of receding from high tide, she saw, the white-water breakers fading into foam fifty feet from the mouth of the river, leaving a wide strip of wet sand. By the time of tomorrow's confrontation with the Koffren and Shipmasters, she estimated, the strip of sand should be a little narrower, probably between thirty and forty feet. On either side of where she and Iosif stood the low trees growing near the hive gradually gave way to bushes, and then reeds, and then dry sand before reaching the wet sand and the ocean.

She nodded to herself. Yes, this would do.

"So how much volume exactly were you looking for?"

Nicole turned around. Iosif was standing beside the rock wall at the end of the arena, leaning precariously out over the racing water and holding back some weeping willow–type branches that had been hanging down beside the river duct.

In the rock behind the branches were two more pipes, one above the other, equal in size to the one out of which the river water was flowing. "Whoa," she said.

"Yep," Iosif agreed. "They're dry right now, but they look like the same kind of pipe that's feeding the river." He nodded across the churning water. "And I'm guessing there are two more pipes on the other side."

"Probably," Nicole said, shifting her gaze to the similar group of hanging branches on that side. "I think we can take that one on faith."

"I was hoping you'd say that." For a moment Iosif poised, then shoved back from the wall and branches and regained his balance on the slope. "The river must have run deeper and wilder back in the old days."

"There's certainly enough room for more flow," Nicole agreed, eyeing the height of the riverbed relative to the water level. "Or else those extra pipes were used when they wanted to clean the trees and bushes and everything else around the channel."

"With this kind of pressure?" Iosif asked doubtfully. "You're more likely to strip off the bark than wash them."

"Maybe these trees need that," Nicole suggested. "Aren't there trees on Earth that need a forest fire to come through so they can drop their seeds? I thought one of my teachers said something about that once."

"Could be," Iosif said. "Not something we needed to worry about in the Navy. So will this do it?"

"It should be perfect," Nicole confirmed. "Now all we have to do is figure out how to get the *Fyrantha* to open up all the spigots."

"Lucky for me, that's *your* job," Iosif said. "All I have to do is run the gauntlet of Q1 Wisps and get you back to Q4. Any idea whether the local Wisps are listening to you yet?"

"How would I know that?"

"You said you would," Iosif reminded her, a frown creasing his forehead. "You said you'd know when they were obeying you."

"Sure," Nicole said. "If I give them an order and they obey, they're obeying me."

Iosif rolled his eyes. "That's helpful."

"Oh, don't worry," Nicole chided. "We'll have Firth and Hagert with us. Come on, let's—"

She broke off as Iosif took a quick step forward, grabbed her arm, and pulled her down. "What—?" she gasped as he dropped into a low crouch beside her.

"Company," he said tersely, nodding down the slope.

She turned her head. Walking the strip of wet sand between the river and the ocean was a Shipmaster, dressed in a kimono instead of the centaur armor.

Behind him, their big feet kicking up sand as they walked, were two Koffren.

"Where'd they come from?" Nicole asked tensely.

"Must have come in from the right," Iosif said into her ear, his voice barely audible above the roar of the water. "Sorry—I was too busy with the pipes to keep an eye out."

"Not your fault," Nicole said. "The question is whether or not they saw us."

"If they did, they're playing it damn cool," he said. "Haven't looked up here even once since we've been watching. Anyway, they'd have come in under the trees."

"Not necessarily," Nicole said. "There's a hidden door in the far right-hand side wall, just inside the tree line. If they came through there, they'd have been on sand most of the time."

"With nothing to block their view," Iosif muttered. "Terrific."

"Still not looking up, though," Nicole said. "That's a good sign."

"Yeah, I'll tell you what *isn't* a good sign." Iosif pointed past her shoulder. "They're just carrying swords. No spider guns."

Nicole frowned, wondering how he knew. The spider guns would be strapped to their right sides, which weren't visible as the group walked toward the left side of the arena.

And then she got it. The guns themselves might not be visible, but the holster straps would be.

So. No spider guns. If they needed to fight, for any reason, they were planning to kill.

"Oh, hell," Iosif said suddenly. "The Sibyls. The Shipmasters gave up the Sibyls."

Nicole felt her heart seize up. No—that couldn't be. Her scheme depended on her being the only one who could fix the teleport. If the Koffren got hold of the rest of the Sibyls, the entire plan was ruined.

"And your Wisps are down there, too," Iosif added. "Come on— we've got to get them and get out of here."

Nicole tore her eyes away from the distant Koffren and peered down the slope she and Iosif had just climbed. Going down would be a lot faster.

And at the speed he was suggesting it would also be lot more dangerous. *And* a lot noisier.

The rushing water would mask a lot of that noise. But would it be enough?

Worse, there were areas along their route with no trees and just the low bushes. As soon as the Shipmaster and Koffren came around that leftmost stone bluff, all it would take would be a single look upslope and she and Iosif would be dead.

Her two Wisps could immobilize the two Koffren, assuming Nicole could figure out a way to sneak them behind the enemy without being spotted. But they would have to let go eventually, and when they did she would have two more Wisp deaths on her conscience.

She frowned suddenly. *As soon as the Shipmaster and Koffren came around that leftmost stone bluff . . .*

"Hold it," she said, grabbing Iosif's arm as he half rose to his feet in preparation for the mad sprint ahead. "They're not here for the Sibyls."

"Like hell they're not."

"They're not," Nicole insisted. "Trust me."

Iosif looked at her, then back down at the Koffren as they disappeared from sight around the bluff. "How do you know?"

"Because there's another hidden door over there," Nicole said, pointing to the side wall to their left. "Much closer to the Sibyls' hive than the one they presumably came in through. If they were heading for the hive, they would have taken that one."

"Not necessarily," Iosif said. But he lowered himself back into his crouch.

"Besides, they need the Sibyls alive," Nicole reminded him. "They can't afford to just slash their way through the group and hope one of them survives. But you can see they're not here to take prisoners—no spider guns, no nets, no restraints."

"And they probably should have brought more guys, too," Iosif said, still sounding unconvinced. "So why are they here?"

"I think they're checking out tomorrow's battlefield," Nicole said. "Picking their spots, and trying to figure out what I've got planned."

Iosif shook his head. "I hope you're right. If they see those Wisps, they're toast."

"Wisps," Nicole murmured, nodding as something else suddenly hit her.

"What?"

"Wisps," Nicole repeated. "The Koffren didn't bring restraints; but the really best way to capture and immobilize the Sibyls would be . . . ?"

"Yeah," Iosif said, nodding. "Wisps. A whole raft of Q1 Wisps. Only they didn't bring any." He raised his eyebrows. "Maybe because they can't?"

"That's what I'm thinking," Nicole said. "Look—they're heading back."

The Shipmaster and two Koffren had reappeared between the bluffs, now heading toward the right-hand side of the arena.

Walking more briskly now, too. Apparently, whatever the Koffren had been looking for, they'd found it.

"What now?" Iosif asked.

"We give them another couple of minutes to get fully clear," Nicole said. "Then we head down—*quietly*—pick up Firth and Hagert, and head back."

She smiled tightly. "And with any luck, we'll run into a couple of Q1 Wisps along the way."

They ran into three pairs of Wisps on their way back to the crosswise heat-transfer duct. All three pairs obeyed Nicole's order to step aside out of their way.

The Shipmasters had come through on their part of the deal. Now it was up to Nicole to deliver her half.

They crossed the duct into Q3 without incident, then the duct into Q4, and were soon back to the relative safety of the hive.

To find that Jeff hadn't come back.

"They've taken him, haven't they?" Levi muttered, tapping his fingertips restlessly on the dining room table. "Damn it. Damn it, and damn them." He looked at Nicole as if he wanted to add *and damn you.*

Nicole didn't blame him.

Iosif didn't say anything, but she could tell from his expression that he was thinking the same thing. She didn't blame him, either.

"He may still be on his way back," she said. "It might have taken longer than he'd expected to find one of the Koffren and deliver his message."

"Maybe," Iosif said. "So what now?"

"As I said before, they'd be foolish to kill or hurt him," Nicole said. "You saw them scoping out the arena. That proves they can think and plan ahead. They'll bring him to the meeting tomorrow as extra leverage against me."

"I hope to God you're right," Levi said darkly. "Bad enough we lost Bennett and almost lost Allyce. I'm getting tired of losing people this way."

"So am I," Nicole said. Bennett, Allyce, *and* the two Ponngs.

She looked at the door. Kahkitah was supposed to meet her here . . .

No. Kahkitah could wait. "Do me a favor, will you?" she asked Levi as she stood up. "I told Kahkitah to meet me here, but I need to go check on something. If he comes while I'm gone, can you ask him to wait?"

"Sure," Levi said. "I got nowhere else to be right now."

"Thanks," Nicole said. Nodding to Iosif, she left the room.

Allyce was lying on one of the recovery beds when Nicole arrived at the medical center. Beside her, on their own beds, were the two Ponngs.

Standing beside the Ponngs, to her surprise, were the four Thii.

"Hello, Nicole," Allyce said. She sounded tired. "Glad to have you back. Leaving the hive is so risky these days."

"I know," Nicole said, wondering if she'd heard about Jeff's absence. "How are your other patients?"

"We're recovering quite well," Moile said from his bed. "Dr. Allyce is a gifted healer."

"I and the *Fyrantha*'s medical magic," Allyce said. "But yes, they're doing well."

"Do you need us to do battle for you?" Teika asked hopefully. "We're recovered enough to do whatever you need."

"Thank you for the offer," Nicole said. "But can you even walk right now?"

"Of course," Moile said with quiet determination. "We can walk, or we can fight. Whatever you need us to do, we will do."

"I appreciate that," Nicole said. "But what I need right now is for you to finish recovering. There may be more battles down the road, and we'll need you there."

"If the Ponngs cannot serve," Nise spoke up from the group of Thii, "then perhaps you will permit us to fight in their stead."

Nicole winced. The Ponngs and Thii had started their lives aboard the *Fyrantha* trying to kill each other. Since then their animosity had faded into a sort of polite rivalry. But if the Thii were now trying to rub the Ponngs' noses in their current state of uselessness—

"Don't worry, Protector," Moile said. "We've discussed the situation at length. Since Teika and I cannot serve you at the moment, we've asked Nise and the Thii if they will take our place at your side."

"A request we were honored to accept," Nise said.

Nicole blinked. She'd figured the Thii would be happy to comply, but she'd thought there'd be a lot more gloating on their part and a lot more chagrin on the Ponngs'. "I'm . . ."

"You expected us to battle among ourselves for supremacy of honor, Protector?" Nise asked, a hint of humor in his turntable-scratching voice. "Once, perhaps, we would have."

"No *perhaps* about it," Moile put in. "Once, we were bitter enemies, as you well know."

"But we have grown in wisdom during our time aboard the *Fyrantha*," Nise said, half turning and bowing his head briefly toward the two Ponngs. "Whether Ponng or Thii, you, Protector, are leader of us all. We seek to serve with our hands, our hearts, and our talents, as you see best."

"Thank you," Nicole said quietly through a sudden lump in her throat. "That means a lot to me. A lot to all of us." She nodded to Nise. "And as it happens, I do indeed have an important task for you." She shifted her gaze to Moile and Teika. "And an important task for you, too," she added. Cooperating or not, allies or not, she'd seen enough wounded pride in Trake's gang to know how it felt. "I think I've got the Koffren figured out, but they may still decide the way to hit me is to hit my hive and anyone who's still here."

"You mean me?" Allyce asked quietly.

"Some of the others are around here, too," Nicole said. "The point is that I need you, Moile and Teika, to protect her if anything happens."

"She also has her Wisp," Moile pointed out.

"Cambria? Sure," Nicole said with a shrug. "But a Wisp and two Ponngs are a lot better than just a Wisp."

"Even when the Ponngs are injured?" Iyulik asked doubtfully.

"Especially when the Ponngs are injured," Moile said with grim pride. "There is nothing more dangerous than a Ponng in pain."

"Thank you," Nicole said, turning to the Thii. "Now, what I need from you—"

"A moment," Moile cut in. "Can we talk safely in here?"

Nicole frowned. "Why not?"

"Because of me," Allyce said, a wave of pain and self-reproach crossing her face. "Because of my betrayal in the arena."

"Allyce—" Nicole began.

"No, it's all right," Allyce said. Bracing herself, she got up from her bed and walked unsteadily toward the door. "I'll never do that again, but I know I can't ask you to believe me."

"It's not a problem—"

"No, let her go," Nise said. "She'll feel better knowing that, whatever happens, she won't be blamed."

"He's right," Allyce said over her shoulder. The door opened—

She jerked backward, nearly losing her balance, as Kahkitah charged in.

"Oh!" the Ghorf gasped, snapping out his hands and catching her shoulders to steady her. "I'm so sorry, Allyce. Are you hurt?"

"No," Allyce assured him. "Excuse me; I was just leaving."

Kahkitah stepped aside, letting Allyce pass, then stepped into the room. "I'm so glad I found you," he said eagerly. "Levi—I went to the dining room as you asked, but you'd left."

"And you figured I'd be here?" Nicole asked.

"Yes." The door closed behind him, and Kahkitah took a breath.

And with that breath, the eager, stupid Ghorf was suddenly gone. "Here, with the rest of your most loyal and trusted allies," he finished, his bird whistles taking on a grim, confident tone.

"Thank you, Kahkitah of the Ghorf," Nise said, equally gravely. "Thank you for your words of honor."

"And for your trust," Moile added. "We've long suspected you're more than you appear. It's good to finally add another to our side."

"Not just one, either," Nicole said. "Okay. Kahkitah's report first. Then I'll tell you what I've got in mind for the rest of you."

twenty-three

Nicole slept poorly that night. Every hour or so her nightmares were interrupted by an imagined knock on the door, or an imagined appearance of Jeff in her room. Each time she peered into the darkness until she was awake enough to realize it had all been a dream, and that she was still alone.

Oddly enough, while many of the dreams involved attacks and horror from the Koffren in the Q1 arena, none of them suggested attacks on her here in her room. Probably because Kahkitah had promised to spend the night outside her door, and her subconscious knew that nothing dangerous could get past him.

Two hours before the scheduled meeting with the Koffren and Shipmasters, she was back in the arena.

The Ghorfs had been busy while she'd been sleeping. The small, quarter-ring platform she'd requested had been attached about halfway up the right side of the leftmost rock bluff, extending from a spot over the river between the two stone pillars all the way around to the front of the bluff where she could look out across the ocean. With Nise's and Sofkat's help she climbed to the platform, while Misgk and Iyulik climbed the other bluff to the similar platform the Ghorfs had set up there.

"Are you all right?" Nise asked, holding her arm to steady her as she settled onto the platform.

"I'm fine," she assured him, peering across the river through the early-morning gloom. The other platform, as she'd requested, extended from a spot facing her around the bluff in the opposite direction from hers, the far end of it facing upriver instead of toward the ocean.

"Are you sure?" Nise persisted. "You seem nervous."

"No, I'm fine," she repeated, suppressing a wince. The platform was barely wide enough for her to stand on, and the sight and sound of the water churning past twenty feet beneath her was a little intimidating. "Do you want to stay here until the Koffren arrive? It'll be easier on your arms and legs than hanging on to the rock."

"Thank you, but this platform is for you," he said. "Sofkat and I will choose our own positions." He touched her arm. "But one of us will be watching you at all times. If you need us for anything just signal."

"All right," she said. "Be careful."

"We will." He pulled himself off the platform and started climbing up the bluff, using both feet and all four hands. Sofkat was right behind him, and Nicole flinched a little as one end of the bow strapped across the other Thii's back twitched toward her. Another look across the river confirmed that Misgk and Iyulik had settled onto their own platform and had unlimbered their own bows and arrow packs.

Now, with everything as ready as Nicole could make it, there was nothing left to do. Carefully easing down into a seated position with her legs dangling over the edge of the platform, she settled down to wait.

Ninety minutes later, a full half hour before the schedule she'd sent with Jeff, Misgk gave the warning crackle that announcing that the enemy had arrived.

They came through the hidden door on the right-hand side of

the arena, the side yesterday's scouting party had taken. The door was hidden from her view by the trees, but the swaying treetops as they passed was enough indication. A minute later the first ones in line emerged from cover as they crossed into the strip of reeds, then passed the reeds and slogged onto the dry sand.

At which point the leading edge again passed out of Nicole's sight as the other bluff blocked her view.

She breathed out a curse. The arena's lighting was still at early-morning level, though it was steadily growing stronger, and at her distance she could barely tell which figures were Koffren and which were Shipmasters.

More importantly, she couldn't tell if any of them was Jeff.

But if she couldn't see them, Misgk on the back side of his platform could. Even better, Iyulik had climbed to the top of the bluff, where he should have a clear view of the entire arena. Peering up the side of her own bluff, Nicole caught Nise's eye and gestured to him.

A moment later he was on the platform beside her. "Yes?"

"Can Iyulik see what they're doing?" she asked.

"Yes," Nise said, slinging his bow again across his back and making a rapid series of gestures toward Iyulik with three of his hands. Across the river, Iyulik answered with his own set of gestures. "They've reached the wet sand and have turned," Nise translated. "They're walking toward us along the edge of the ocean. Two Koffren lead the way, followed by two Shipmasters and more Koffren."

Nicole braced herself. "And Jeff?"

More gestures from Nise, more gestures from Iyulik. "He sees him now," Nise said. "Jeff and the two Wisps you sent with him are near the center of the line."

"How did he look?"

"He and the Wisps appear to be bound together across their

torsos," Nise said. "They're walking on their own, without tether or leash, though two Koffren walk on either side of them."

"How are they bound?" Nicole asked. "Is it spider gun goo?"

"Iyulik cannot be absolutely certain in this light," Nise said. "But it appears to be so."

Nicole took a deep breath. "Can he tell if Jeff's been hurt?"

"I'm sorry," Nise said. "They're still too far for Iyulik to see such detail."

"Understood," Nicole muttered, gazing out at the rolling white-caps. She knew Jeff better than Iyulik, and her eyes might be better than the Thii's. If she moved around to the front side of the bluff she might be able to see better what kind of shape Jeff was in.

No. That would also make her more visible to the approaching Koffren, and at this point she needed to stay partially hidden as long as possible. She'd know what they'd done to Jeff soon enough. "You said there were some Shipmasters near the front," she said. "Can he see if the Koffren have brought all the rest, too?"

"Many are there," Nise said. "The last of the invaders has joined the line, and the light is getting better. Iyulik is doing a count now, and will soon know whether the Koffren obeyed your orders."

And if they haven't? Nicole could hear the unspoken question in his tone.

Right now, she didn't have an answer. If she was lucky, she wouldn't need one.

She lowered her eyes to the other platform. Misgk was standing there, two of his hands holding a pair of quivers, the other two holding his bow and a nocked arrow. He was facing upstream, his head slowly moving back and forth as he scanned the riverbanks behind the little group.

She turned back to the ocean. It hadn't receded quite as much as it would have if the Koffren had been on their proper schedule, with maybe thirty feet of beach between the bluffs and the highest rise of the water. Briefly, she wondered whether or not that would work to her advantage, but there were too many variables and she gave up the speculation. Anyway, much of what happened next would depend on the Koffren and how suspicious they were of this meeting.

Which meant more waiting. She looked up at Iyulik, who could see everything, wishing she was up there. If the Shipmasters weren't here—or worse, if not all the Koffren had come—

"The final group is within clear sight," Nise reported. "Along with Jeff and the Wisps, there are fifty-two Shipmasters and thirty-six Koffren."

Nicole tensed. "Thirty-*six*? Not thirty-eight?"

"Thirty-six," Nise said, his tone going a little grimmer. "Two are absent."

Nicole threw a quick look over her shoulder at the hill and river and trees behind her. So were the missing Koffren up here, trying to sneak around behind her or pulling some other stunt? Or were they in the *Fyrantha*'s main Q1 command center with a few Shipmasters still as hostages?

It was a crucial question . . . and she didn't have an answer because, like an idiot, while she'd been concentrating on the Koffren's numbers she'd somehow forgotten to ask the Caretaker and Oracle how many Shipmasters were aboard.

And unfortunately, right here and now, there was only one way to get that number. Swearing again under her breath at her stupidity, she dug into a pocket and pulled out her inhaler. "Caretaker: tell me how many Shipmasters are aboard the *Fyrantha*," she called toward the arena's ceiling.

"What are you doing?" Nise asked, snapping out a hand as if to grab the inhaler away from her. "That device contains *poison*."

Nicole twitched it out of his reach. "Caretaker: tell me how many Shipmasters are aboard the *Fyrantha*," she repeated. Warning Nise off with a raised hand, she put the inhaler to her mouth and gave herself a blast.

There are fifty-two Lillilli aboard, the voice said in her mind.

"Iyulik said there were fifty-two Shipmasters?" Nicole asked.

"Yes."

"Then they're all here," she said, putting the inhaler away. Briefly, she wondered how much more of her life she'd just blown away, then put the thought aside. If this didn't work, the rest of her life would soon be lost, anyway. "What about weapons? Can Iyulik see how the Koffren are armed?"

"They have their swords." Nise hesitated. "He also counts eight greenfire weapons."

"Terrific," Nicole said, hissing out a breath. Eight weapons. Twenty-four shots. A potentially devastating advantage for their side.

Still, the plan she and Kahkitah had worked out had accounted for this likelihood. And it was highly doubtful that either the Koffren or the Shipmasters had the slightest idea what she could do with the river currently flowing along beneath her.

"Tell Iyulik he'd better get ready," she told Nise. "If all the Shipmasters are here, all the Koffren presumably are, too."

"Understood," Nise said. "Don't worry. The missing two shall be found before they can make trouble."

"Just be careful," Nicole warned. "They can't afford to shoot *me,* but you're open game."

"Let them try," Nise said, his voice dark with grim anticipation. Pulling out an arrow and nocking it into his bowstring, he headed back up the bluff.

A moment later, the front of the line of Koffren came into Nicole's view.

Not just came into view, but *marched* into view, like high-school bands she'd seen in parades or like soldiers she'd seen in movies.

Behind the two Koffren at the head of the line were the two Ship-masters Iyulik had mentioned, their shuffling gait looking weak and pathetic compared to the stride of the bigger aliens. Two more Koffren followed them, followed by three more Shipmasters, then two more Koffren.

On it went. They seemed to be taking their time, and after a couple of minutes Nicole stopped counting—Iyulik had already done that, after all—and focused her attention on the Koffren carrying the greenfire weapons. So far all of them had the slen-der black tubes slung across their backs, but she knew the weap-ons could be swiveled around and brought up into firing position pretty damn quickly.

And then, walking between a pair of greenfire-armed Koffren, Jeff and the two Wisps came into sight.

Iyulik hadn't been able to see whether Jeff had been hurt at all. But even at her height Nicole could see that his face was red and bruised, and that he was walking with an odd limp that didn't seem to have anything to do with the fact that he was strapped to two Wisps.

In fact, as they crossed the sand together, Nicole had the eerie sense that the Wisps were mostly carrying his weight.

What the *hell* had the Koffren done to him?

"Where is she?" came a Koffren voice from somewhere along the line.

From the Koffren standing next to Jeff, actually, she decided from the movements of that particular alien's chest.

And even through the river noise, she was pretty sure it was the voice of Justice, the Koffren who'd accosted her and Sam outside the Q1 teleport room.

The Koffren the Thii had slapped with multiple spider gun shots. The Koffren that Nicole had humiliated.

And if there was one thing she'd learned from Trake, it was how long and how hard people could hold grudges.

"*Where is she?*" Justice demanded again.

Nicole filled her lungs. The rest of the line hadn't made it past the other bluff yet, but it was time to get them all grouped together. "I'm here!" she shouted down to them.

The whole line stopped dead. Justice swiveled around, his helmet facing the river—

"No—up here." Nicole waved a hand.

Justice's helmet tilted back, and it seemed to her that the muscles in his bare torso flexed a little harder. "So," he said.

"Yeah," Nicole said. "So. You're Justice, aren't you? Justice and Revenge and Fire, if I remember right. How about I just call you *Justice?*"

"You said you'd repair the teleport," he said, ignoring the question. "Come down and do so."

"Not so fast," Nicole said. "I have something to say first. Actually, before I start I need to know if you brought all the Shipmasters like I asked."

For a moment Justice didn't move. Then, abruptly, he stepped back and to the side, snatched his sword from its sheath, and snapped its edge up against Jeff's throat. "Come down now," he said, biting out each word.

Nicole braced herself. *Grudges.* "Take it easy," she warned. "If you hurt him, you can kiss the teleport good-bye. Put the sword away, and gather everyone around the river mouth where I can see them. I have a proposition to offer."

"I don't wish to hear it."

"Then step aside and let someone with more sense listen," Nicole retorted. "Your leader, for instance. I assume you *have* an actual leader?"

"*I* am the leader," Justice said. "I am Justice and Revenge and—"

"And Fire," Nicole cut him off. "Yes, fine. I still need everyone to hear. And I mean both the Koffren *and* the Shipmasters."

"You will come down and repair the teleport," Justice said. "When that's been accomplished, we may perhaps listen to you."

"Then I guess we're done here," Nicole said. "If no one wants to listen, then you can all leave. Go back to the teleport and fix the damn thing yourselves."

"You are a fool, Protector of the *Fyrantha*," Justice said, his voice somehow both bitter and triumphant. "Now watch your arrogance betray you."

Nicole's heart seized up inside her. The two missing Koffren—

"Thii—get clear!" she barked.

But it was too late. Even before she finished the frantic warning a pair of green beams flashed at the bluffs from somewhere up the river.

Nicole spun around, wanting to drop to one knee, afraid that the move would send her toppling off the narrow platform. A second pair of shots lanced out, once again targeting the Thii, who were now scrambling for cover, and she could see now that the fire was coming from a clump of bushes along the riverbank.

"Iyulik!" Nise shouted.

Nicole swore viciously. If the young Thii had been hit—

But there was no time to think. No time to worry about Iyulik, no time to consider the possible disastrous consequences of changing the timetable of her plan. Each of the hidden Koffren had one shot left—or more if they'd each brought more than one greenfire weapon—and unless she did something right now more of them might die.

She filled her lungs. "*Fyrantha!*" she shouted as loudly as she could. "Protector says: full shock flood of the Q1 river!"

And suddenly the roar of the river became a bellow as, at the top of the hill, the dormant jets she and Iosif had found came to life, erupting with massive horizontal geysers that sent a wall of water sweeping down the riverbed, rolling over and through everything in its path. The flood reached the snipers, and she caught a glimpse of a pair of Koffren bodies being thrown into the nearest trees before being swallowed by the flood.

She spun back around, holding her breath. Justice and two of the others had their greenfire weapons in firing position now, clearly ready to take out the remaining Thii if they moved around the bluffs into range. If Nise had been taken by surprise by Nicole's sudden shifting of the plan's timeline—if he and Misgk weren't ready to act—

And then, even as the Koffren on the beach spotted the oncoming wall of water and scrambled to both sides to get out of its way, Nicole saw the two Thii lean out from their positions and fire their arrows at the group below.

Misgk's arrow caught one of the greenfire-armed Koffren beside Jeff squarely in the center of his chest.

Nise's arrow, in contrast, jabbed into Jeff.

A second later the flood reached the bluffs and roared past, the churning water splashing the underside of Nicole's platform and sending spray as high as her chest. The Koffren and Shipmasters below who hadn't gotten out of the way were slammed backward, tumbling to the ground and skidding across the sand toward the ocean.

The wall of water had been devastating inside the confines of the riverbed. But now, as it rolled past the bluffs and spread out onto the beach, its power and fury quickly faded. The Koffren who'd been right in the center were pushed back no more than a dozen feet, while most of those farther to the sides didn't even lose their footing.

The Shipmasters weren't nearly so lucky. Smaller and more

delicate than their massive captors, many of them found themselves tumbling helplessly backward across the beach, some directly into the ocean surf, the rest coming to rest in the line of foam. Jeff and the Wisps had also been thrown backward, toppling over and sliding along the water until the force dissipated.

"Was *that* your plan?" Justice shouted up to her, getting to his feet as the burst of extra water that Nicole had set up ran dry and the roar of the flood subsided. "To try to drown us?"

"My plan was to talk to you," Nicole said. "It still is." Steeling herself, she walked around the platform to the ocean side of the bluff.

It was as intimidating a sight as she'd ever seen. Thirty-five of the thirty-six Koffren down there had drawn up into a battle line facing her, standing well back from the river mouth and any attempt Nicole might make to send another flash flood in their direction. The thirty-sixth Koffren, the one Misgk had shot with the paralyzing liquid they'd taken from the drones, lay motionless and probably unnoticed on the sand behind the battle line, the edges of the now quiet river swirling around him. His greenfire weapon, also unnoticed by the rest of the Koffren, lay in the wet sand beside him.

Not that the enemy needed it. The other seven greenfire weapons were pointed straight at Nicole, and several of the Koffren had also drawn their swords, though what they thought they could do with them at that distance she had no idea. The Shipmasters, for the most part, were lying or kneeling at the ocean's edge, still shaken from Nicole's attack.

The whole thing was like a bad dream from all the gang confrontations she'd witnessed back in Philly. Two rivals trying to intimidate and threaten each other for whatever stakes of honor or territory or revenge were the day's reason for fighting. In nearly all of those clashes, the threats and bravado had eventually given way to violence and death.

Once, such standoffs had been terrifying. Later, Nicole had come to see them as pointless and even a little sad.

Here, somehow, it mostly seemed just plain sad.

Such a waste.

"You don't have to fight me," she called to them. "You don't have to fight any of us. You want to take over the *Fyrantha.* I get that. But it's not going to happen. The flight mechanisms, the Wisps, the Shipmasters, us—none of it is under your control. None of it will ever be under your control. Accept that, let me send you home, and it'll be over."

"You're a fool, so-called Protector," Justice said, spitting out the words. "You think *that*"—he jabbed his sword toward the river mouth—"is going to intimidate us?"

Nicole shook her head. *Just plain sad.* "No," she said. "I never thought I could intimidate you."

Justice's helmet tilted slightly. Trying to read her as he suddenly realized there might be more to her plan than just a flood?

He was still staring silently as the bindings tying Jeff to the two Wisps snapped open as the dissolving fluid Nise's arrow had delivered to the spider goo finished its work. Pulling away the last strands, Jeff rolled across the sand toward the greenfire weapon.

Maybe Justice heard something over the river noise. Maybe he caught a hint of the movement out of the corner of his eye. Abruptly, he spun around, snatching out his sword as he saw Jeff going for the weapon. "Koffren!" he snapped, twisting his arm into position to throw his sword.

Jeff got there first. Snatching up the greenfire weapon, he spun it around and pointed it toward Justice. "Freeze!" he snapped. "All of you—*freeze!*"

"All of you *die!*" Justice retorted. "Koffren—kill them all!" Ignoring the weapon pointed at him, he raised his sword a little higher. The other seven greenfire weapons twitched as the Koffren shifted their aim to the Thii and Nicole.

Justice might have seen it coming. Of all of the Koffren he was the only one facing the right direction. But he was focused on Jeff, and on vengeance, and his eyes and rage were directed elsewhere.

So it was that not a single one of them noticed the ocean suddenly boiling up with a line of monster waves, rolling majestically toward the shore. Even as Jeff sent a flash of brilliant green into Justice's chest, the wave broke, its top curling over in cascades of white foam and slamming down on the line of Koffren.

And behind the wave, rising from the depths of the water like sharks moving to the kill, were Kahkitah and his army of Ghorfs.

The Koffren never had a chance. A few were able to recover from the hammering waves fast enough to turn to the unexpected attack. But even those few were still stunned and off balance and fell quickly to the Ghorfs and their improvised weapons. Most of the Koffren probably never even knew what had hit them.

Thirty seconds later, it was over.

By the time Nise and Misgk got Nicole down the bluff and onto the beach the Ghorfs were moving systematically among the bodies, collecting swords and greenfire weapons, pulling off helmets—the Koffren were ugly and startlingly baby-faced at the same time, Nicole noted—and checking for survivors. A few Ghorfs were working the water's edge, rescuing Shipmasters who'd been dragged out to sea by the huge wave and bringing them to safety. Most of the latter seemed shaken but unhurt: the wave the Ghorfs had carefully engineered had expended most of its force along the Koffren line and had less effect on the inward area where the river had pushed most of the Shipmasters.

Kahkitah himself brought Jeff in from the waves.

Jeff was sitting up when Nicole reached him, Kahkitah kneeling beside him with a supporting hand behind his back. The two Wisps, Jessup and Lehigh, had taken up positions nearby.

"Hi," Jeff said as Nicole hurried up. "Nice job. Always great when those one-two punches work out."

"I'm glad you liked it," Nicole said, trying to force a casualness she didn't feel. There was something wrong with Jeff's right leg . . . "Sorry I couldn't tell you about it ahead of time."

"No, no, that was the right thing to do," he assured her. "We all knew there was a good chance I'd be taken hostage, and a prisoner can't tell the enemy what he doesn't know. I was supposed to grab the greenfire gun after you got me loose, right?"

"You were supposed to live through all of it," Nicole said, dropping down on one knee beside him. Up close, the bruising on his face looked far worse than it had from the bluff. "Anything else was just bonus."

"Good," Jeff said. "I really wanted to nail that bastard."

"Well, you did," Nicole said. "Come on—Kahkitah and I will help you up."

"No, don't," Jeff said, waving her back. "Standing up hurts. A lot. Sitting up isn't as bad."

"Oh, God," Nicole breathed. "What did they do?"

"Well . . ." He paused, a flicker of pain crossing his face. "There's this thing some people do to horses called hamstringing. The muscle and tendon in the back of the knee . . . well, we don't need to go into details. Let's just say walking is going to be a problem for me for a while."

"Can it be fixed?" Nicole asked. "Wait—you were walking earlier, weren't you?"

Jeff shook his head. "Jessup and Lehigh were carrying me. I only moved my legs so that . . ." He shrugged.

"So that I'd think you were okay and wouldn't go berserk," Nicole said. "Oh, Jeff. I'm so sorry."

"It's okay," he assured her. "Allyce can probably fix me up. If not, hey, I always wanted to sit around all day doing nothing. Now I've got the perfect excuse."

"Glad I could help," Nicole said, blinking away sudden tears. "Let's get you back to Q4. Jessup, Lehigh? Come here."

"A moment," a voice called as the two Wisps started forward.

Nicole turned. Wesowee was walking toward them, half pulling, half supporting one of the Shipmasters. As they got closer, the alien turned his head and she saw it was Fievj.

"This Shipmaster has urgent news for you," Wesowee said.

"Fievj," Nicole said, keeping her voice steady as she thought back on her earlier conversation with Kahkitah. The Shipmasters had done horrible things, and if Fievj was looking to make a deal he'd come to the wrong place. "What do you want?"

"You're in danger," Fievj said, his voice even weaker than his unsteady legs. "The Koffren—more Koffren—are coming."

"They're going to have a job of it," Jeff said. "The teleport's out of service, remember?"

"Not by Wisp and teleport," Fievj said. "They're coming by ship. They're coming by warship."

Nicole's breath froze in her chest, her mind flashing back to the space battle she'd seen from the top of the *Fyrantha*. "When?" she asked.

"Six hours," Fievj said. "Perhaps sooner."

"Can the *Fyrantha* withstand their attack?" Jeff asked.

Fievj closed his eyes. "No."

twenty-four

For a long moment the only sound was the soft roar of the ocean waves. "Okay," Jeff said. "Sounds like a good time to run like rabbits. How fast can we get this thing moving?"

Fievj sighed. "We cannot," he said. "The Koffren . . . they ordered us to this spot in space and then disabled the stardrive."

"Wait a minute," Nicole said. "You saying we can't move at *all*?"

"We can move through space-normal," Fievj said. "But even at maximum thrust six hours would barely suffice to move us even part of the way across this solar system. The approaching warships would find us at their ease."

"Then we fix the stardrive," Jeff said. "What did they do, pull a few components?"

"No," Fievj said. "They removed an entire bank of asymmetric capacitors. Even if you discovered where they hid it, it would need to be completely rewired back into the system."

"And we can't do that in six hours?" Jeff persisted.

Fievj shook his head. "Not even in twelve."

"Fine," Nicole said, marveling at how calm she sounded. "If we can't run, then we'd better get ready to fight."

"Did you not hear me?" Fievj said nervously. "I said the *Fyrantha* cannot withstand such an attack."

"We'll see," Nicole said. "Okay. First item of business is to get

Jeff back to the Q4 medical center so Allyce can take a look at his leg. Second item—"

"Whoa," Jeff put in. "First item of business is to gather our people together for a council of war. And if you think I'm leaving before that happens you're sadly mistaken."

"Jeff—"

"No, he's right," Kahkitah said. "We need a conversation, and he needs to be part of it."

"Agreed," Nise said, coming up behind Nicole. "He is one of the *Fyrantha*'s few truly experienced warriors. We need to hear his words and advice."

"All right," Nicole said, feeling a fresh twinge of pain as she looked at Nise. Of the four Thii only Misgk was walking alongside him. "Iyulik and Sofkat?"

"Iyulik gave his life for the Protector and the *Fyrantha*," Nise said. His voice was steady, but she could hear the quiet pain beneath it. "Sofkat is tending to him. Who else do we need?"

Nicole took a deep breath. There would be a time to mourn the young Thii. But not yet. "Wesowee, get the other Ghorfs over here," she said. "And find Nevvis and any of the other Shipmasters who are in any shape to talk. Kahkitah, do you know where Iosif is?"

"Beneath the ocean with Levi and Tomas, monitoring the wave equipment," Kahkitah said.

Nicole felt her eyebrow twitch. Levi had told her earlier that Tomas was still mad at her and had decided to sit this one out. Apparently, he'd changed his mind. "Are Firth and Hagert still with them?"

"The two Wisps? Yes."

"We can fill them in later when we fine-tune the plan," Jeff said. "Right now, we need to hammer out the basics." He jabbed a finger at Fievj. "You. What kind of weapons and defenses does the *Fyrantha* have?"

"I know nothing of weaponry," Fievj said, shrinking back from Jeff's glare. "When we . . . obtained . . . the ship from the others it had already been converted to the zoo you see around you. I assume any remaining weapons were removed."

"You'll forgive us if we don't take your word for it," Jeff said. "Nicole, would the Caretaker or Oracle know?"

"I'll ask," Nicole said, pulling out her inhaler.

"Whoa," Jeff said. "No inhaler. We can go up later and ask them in person. What about defenses?"

"There's a shield," Fievj said. "It's . . . mostly functional."

"How mostly is mostly?" Nicole asked.

"There've been some problems." He gave Nicole a sharp look. "In fact, I believe it was you who fixed a section once, wasn't it?"

"When was that?" Jeff asked.

"When you'd been taken prisoner by the Cluufes in the Q4 arena," Nicole said. "When I ducked out on you. A Wisp caught me and took me up to the top of the ship."

"And you fixed the *Fyrantha*'s shields?" Jeff asked.

"I was lucky," Nicole said. "It turned out to be a bad component. I swapped out a few of them, and the shield came back on line. Fievj, do you have a list of the sections that aren't working?"

"I can obtain one."

"From where?"

"The main control room."

Nicole nodded. It was about time someone from their group got a look in there. "Good. Kahkitah, take Fievj and go take a look. Grab Levi and Iosif on your way."

"Should I also take a Sibyl?" Jeff asked.

Nicole had almost forgotten about the Sibyls locked away in the arena hive. "Not yet," she said. "Once you all head out I'll go talk to them and tell them what has to happen. Wesowee, I need you to send the Ghorfs back to their work teams and do the same."

"They won't believe us," Wesowee warned. "We've all played the clown for a long time."

"I think I can fix that." Nicole looked up at the ceiling. *"Fyrantha:* Protector says to send me fifty—no, make it a hundred—send me a hundred Wisps. Send them to the Q1 arena."

"Good idea," Jeff said. "Nothing spells *authority* like having Wisps do what you tell them."

"Are you going to turn control of the Wisps over to us?" Kahkitah asked, his bird whistles sounding surprised.

"Why not?" Nicole countered. "Anyway, I pretty much have to. The damaged sections are likely to be spread out all over the ship, which means the repair teams will have to be, too. You might need a Wisp to fiddle with power levels or get more modules or something, and you'll certainly need them to ferry you across the heat-exchange ducts."

"Yes, but—" Kahkitah looked at Wesowee. *"You're* the Protector, Nicole. Shouldn't ultimate authority be yours?"

"It will be," Jeff said firmly. "We—all of us here—will make damn sure she stays the one in charge."

"We'll certainly try," Kahkitah said, still sounding uncertain.

"If I'm not worried about it, you shouldn't be," Nicole said. "Topic closed. Okay. First step is to get the shield fixed. For that we need a list of jobs we can hand out to the repair crews and Sibyls. So that's covered. Second step—" She looked at the line of Koffren, a few of whom were dragging themselves up to sitting positions under the watchful eyes of the Ghorfs. "Actually, first step is to put the Koffren and Shipmasters somewhere out of the way where they won't give us trouble."

"All the Shipmasters?" Jeff asked.

"That's what I was thinking," Nicole said. "Why, do you think we'll need them?"

"I think it wouldn't hurt to keep a couple of them around to show us how everything works," Jeff said.

"I don't know," Nicole said, looking at Fievj. "I get the feeling they'd be more trouble than they're worth."

"Not at all," Fievj assured her. "Our lives are at risk, too. It's in our best interests to work with you, not against you."

"Okay," Nicole said. "But not all of you. You, Fievj, and one other. Let's make it Ryit."

"Nevvis is our commander," Fievj said. "He knows the most about the *Fyrantha*."

Nicole raised her eyebrows toward Jeff. "What do you think?"

"I like the second part of that," Jeff said. "The part about knowing more. Not so crazy about the part where he's the commander. People like that can be very bad about handing over power to someone else. Let's go with the other Shipmaster you said."

"Okay," Nicole said. "Fievj and Ryit it is, then. Take it or leave it."

Fievj muttered something. "Very well."

"Good," Nicole said. "Now about the rest of them. Do you have a—what's it called, Jeff?"

"A brig," Jeff supplied. "If you don't, maybe those animal treatment cages up on level 10 might work."

"We have no brig," Fievj said. "There was one once, but it was repurposed and can no longer be locked."

"Then we'll go with something that can," Nicole said. "Wesowee, before you send the Ghorfs back to their teams, gather up all the Koffren that survived and lock them in the Q2 arena. I'll get you the code to get in. Just make sure none of them sees you punch it in."

Wesowee gave a low rumble. "They're our enemies," he said. "They've already brought death to the *Fyrantha,* and hope to bring more. Shouldn't we just dispose of them?"

Nicole hesitated. First Bennett, now Iyulik . . . "If you'd killed them in battle, that would be one thing," she said. "But we can't just kill them in cold blood."

"They're our enemies."

"Doesn't matter," Nicole said. "If one of them makes a move against you while you're taking them to Q2, you're welcome to beat his brains out through his ears. But not until and unless that happens. You hear that?" she added, gesturing to the nearest Koffren. "You're either prisoners, or you're corpses. Your choice."

For a moment the Koffren sat silently. Then, he inclined his head. "You will pay for today's carnage," he said. "But not yet. Soon, but not yet."

"Fine," Nicole said. "Just bear in mind that the Ghorfs aren't going to give any of you a second chance."

She looked back at Wesowee. "Okay, that takes care of the Koffren. I think we'll put the Shipmasters in the Q3 arena."

"Just a second," Jeff said. "These are Q1 Wisps. You sure they can see into Q2 and Q3?"

"Good question," Nicole said, scowling to herself. For a moment she'd completely forgotten about the Wisp perception problem. "How about it, Fievj? Now that they're all under my control, can they see the whole ship?"

"They can," Fievj said. "No part of the *Fyrantha* is dark to them anymore."

Nicole reached up and touched Jessup's arm. *Is that true?*

Yes, Protector. The blindness has lifted. For that, and more, we thank you.

You're welcome. "Jessup confirms it," she told Jeff, letting go of the Wisp's arm. "Any other questions?"

"We may not have enough Ghorfs to transport both groups together," Kahkitah pointed out.

"You won't need to." Nicole pointed over his shoulder as the

first group of Wisps glided into view around the bluff. "Our reinforcements are here. Wisps? Come here. Gather around."

Nicole had never seen a hundred Wisps all moving purposely
together. It was an awesome and rather intimidating sight. From
the suddenly stiffened backs of the surviving Koffren, it seemed
that they agreed.

"Wisps, who am I?" she asked when they were all standing
around her and the others. She touched the closest one's arm—

You are the Protector.

Right, Nicole confirmed. *These creatures here are the Ghorfs.
They and the humans aboard are going to be performing tasks vital
to the* Fyrantha's *survival. I'm therefore giving them command over
you. You will obey them as you obey me.*

*Do you order us to obey the humans as well as the Ghorfs? Or do
you order us only to obey the Ghorfs?*

Nicole hesitated. The Ghorfs had proved themselves reliable, and
she trusted them. She wasn't yet willing to go out on that same limb
with all the humans. *For now, just the Ghorfs. Is that understood?*

It is. The Wisps and the Fyrantha *welcome the Protector's army.*

An eerie tingle went up Nicole's back. She'd never thought of
her group as an army. But apparently it was. *Thank you. I also
need the entry codes for the Q2 and Q3 arenas. Can you contact the
Caretaker for those, or do I need to talk to him myself?*

*No need. The Q2 code is three seven two six two two four. The
Q3 code is eight four six nine two four six.*

Thank you. Nicole released her touch, pulled out her notepad,
and scribbled out the numbers. "Here are the entry codes," she
said, handing the notepad to Wesowee. "The Wisps will obey you
and the rest of the Ghorfs, so grab however many you need and
get moving. Once the Koffren and Shipmasters are tucked away,
you can split up and go talk to your work crews."

"Understood," Wesowee said. He studied the notepad a moment, then handed it back to Nicole. "What about food? Those arenas aren't stocked with the proper nutrients."

"If we survive the next few hours we'll redo the dispensers," Nicole said. "For now, they can make do with water."

Wesowee nodded and gestured to the nearby Ghorfs. "We're leaving," he announced. "Bring the Koffren and the Shipmasters."

"So," Nicole said quietly, touching Jeff's hand as the arena began shuffling itself all around them. "We'll get you to Allyce and see what she can do for you."

Jeff shook his head. "Allyce can wait. So can I. There's one other thing we need to get on right away. Remember what the Caretaker and Oracle said about the Core?"

"Damn," Nicole muttered. She'd all but forgotten about that.

"Damn and a half," Jeff agreed. "Fixing the shield is nice and all, but I'm thinking that getting the *Fyrantha* fully up and running might be a hell of a lot better."

"Agreed," Nicole said. "But I saw how the shield works. If we lose even one piece of it there'll be an opening the Koffren ships can shoot through. We need to fix all of it."

"Sure, but I wasn't suggesting we take a team off shield duty," Jeff said. "You heard what the Caretaker said about the Core: densely packed with narrow access corridors." He gently touched his right leg. "I'm not going to be running around the *Fyrantha* anytime soon. But I can lie on my back in a corridor and swap out components with the best of them."

"Yes, but even there you're going to need to move," Nicole said. "Remember how big he also said it was."

"The Wisps can carry me."

"What if the access corridors are too narrow?"

"Then we will carry him wherever he needs to go," Nise spoke up.

"You?" Nicole asked, surprised. "But don't you . . . ?" She broke off.

"There will be a time for remembrances for Iyulik," Nise said quietly. "But for now, there is vital work to do. He wouldn't have wanted his sacrifice to be in vain."

"Of course he wouldn't," Nicole agreed. "All right. We'll unlock the Sibyls and explain what's about to happen. Then the two of you will come to the Core with Jeff and me and see how much work it's going to take to fix it."

"Okay," Jeff said. "Don't forget I'll need a Sibyl."

"You've got one." Nicole tapped her chest. "Me."

"Absolutely not," Jeff said flatly. "You're the Protector. We can't risk you hurting yourself any further with that damn inhaler."

"I'm about to ask *them* to use theirs," Nicole countered, gesturing back toward the arena hive. "I can't ask them to take a risk I'm not willing to take."

"Sure you can," Jeff said. "Generals do it all the time."

"I'm not a general." She lifted a hand as he started to speak. "Subject closed. I'm going. You want to come, or should I have Jessup go get Levi instead?"

Jeff glowered, but reluctantly nodded. "Fine."

"Good," Nicole said, gesturing to one of the Q1 Wisps still grouped around them. "I want you to go back to Q4 and tell Allyce to join us at the Q1 section of the Core."

"She can't walk," Jeff reminded her. "She's still injured, remember?"

"Of course I remember," Nicole said huffily, turning back to the Wisp. "Also tell Cambria to give her a lift. Got that? Allyce and Cambria to the Q1 side of the Core as fast as you can." She looked back at Jeff. "You good with that? Or do I send you back to get fixed up first?"

"No, I'm good," Jeff said again. "Anyone ever tell you you're a hell of a hard-assed general?"

"All the time," Nicole said, eyeing him closely. He was putting up a good front, but she'd seen men who were in pain and trying not to show it. Jeff's face and neck muscles looked exactly that way. "Do you need some painkillers before we go? I can send a Wisp to see if any of the tool closets nearby have a first-aid kit."

"No, I've still got a couple left," Jeff said, digging into one of his pockets. "They took my kit away, but I'd figured they would and put the painkillers in my pocket." He winced as he moved his hand around. "I'm pretty sure I've got a couple left."

"You sure it's in that one?" Nicole asked, easing a hand into one of his other pockets. "No—just ease back. I've got this."

The two pills were indeed in the pocket Jeff had thought they were in, partially hidden in a fold of the pocket's lining. She gave him one, along with a drink from her water bottle, and a minute later he nodded. "Okay," he said. "*Really* like the way those things work so fast. We ready?"

"Yes," Nicole said, standing up and looking around. While they'd been focusing on getting his painkillers all but a dozen of the Q1 Wisps had disappeared, along with the Ghorfs, Koffren, and Shipmasters. The Wisp she'd ordered to get Allyce was also gone. "Jessup, Lehigh: pick up Jeff—*gently*—and follow me. The rest of you Wisps, come with us."

They waded through the ankle-deep flow from the river and headed back toward the hive. As they passed the bluff Sofkat joined the other two Thii, and the group continued through the reeds and bushes and trees until they reached the hive door.

Nicole had told Iosif to make sure the door was really and truly locked. He'd taken her at her word, and possibly a little more. It took nearly ten minutes, and a lot of Jeff's expertise, to finally get it open.

One of the Sibyls, Nicole remembered, had been wildly and loudly furious at being locked in. She'd hoped that the subsequent day of idleness would cool down the woman's anger.

It hadn't.

"What the *hell* did you think you were doing, you *bitch*," the woman stormed, stomping out of the hive at the head of the group of other women. "You think you can just throw us in here and lock us up—?"

"That's enough," Nicole said. "I need to talk to you—"

"*Who* are you to tell me to shut up, *girl*?" the woman snarled. "If you think I'm going to sit here and let you crap all over us this way—"

"She said she needs to talk to you," Sofkat said. There was the creak of a bowstring.

The woman broke off, her eyes going wide at the sight of the three arrows suddenly pointed at her.

The moment passed. "You trying to scare me, girl?" she said mockingly. "I used to go around my neighborhood dropping bricks on cockroaches. You got three cockroaches? Well, you just give me a brick and we'll see who wins."

"This isn't the fight," Nicole said. "Sofkat, Nise, Misgk—put down your weapons."

"You expect me to thank you?" the woman demanded sourly.

"I expect you to listen," Nicole said. "Like I said, this isn't the fight. The fight is coming." She pointed at the ceiling. "From out there."

She told them everything: about the Koffren, the Shipmasters, and the role the *Fyrantha* had been playing in their schemes for way too long. She warned them about the danger to Earth, and to the ship itself. She told them there was hope, and that there was time, but that they had to move quickly and together.

They listened in silence. All of them, even the loudmouth. Nicole watched their faces as she talked, seeing doubt become cautious belief become fear become equally cautious hope.

Finally, she ran out of words. "So what I'm saying—"

"I know what you're saying," the loudmouth cut her off. Alone of all of them she showed no sign of either belief, fear, or cooperation. "You're saying that because you've got these things"—she waved dismissively toward the Wisps—"you're the queen bee around here. Well, honey, that's not how it works."

"That's exactly how it works," Jeff said. "One word from her and the nearest Wisp picks you up and locks you in a tiny room somewhere."

The woman snorted a laugh. "So it's slavery, huh? We do what we're told or Queenie gets her drone bees and *makes* us? And you said the *Shipmasters* were the problem?"

"Fine," Nicole said, suddenly viciously tired of this. "You think all I've got is the Wisps? Fine." She raised a hand. "Wisps: from now on you will also obey orders from the Sibyls."

"Right," the woman scoffed. "Like you really just did that."

"I really just did that," Nicole assured her. "Go ahead, give it a try."

For a long moment the woman just stared into her eyes. Then, her lip twitched in a smirk. "Wisps, take those bows away from the big cockroaches."

Three of the Wisps glided forward. "Protector?" Nise whispered urgently.

"It's okay," Nicole soothed. "Let them."

Nise muttered something under his breath. But none of the Thii resisted as the Wisps took their bows and arrow quivers.

"Bring the weapons to me," the woman ordered.

The Thii started to move; again, Nicole gestured them to stay where they were. The woman took one of the bows and an arrow, peered at it a moment—

"And now grab *her*," she said suddenly, pointing the arrow at Nicole.

The Wisps didn't move.

"Did you hear me?" the woman snapped. "Grab her. Grab her *now*."

"They won't," Nicole said softly. "I'm the Protector. I protect the ship, and the ship protects me."

"She told you to *obey* me!" the woman shouted. "*Obey* me, damn you. *Grab* her!"

"You still don't get it, do you?" Nicole said. "You wanted power. Fine; you've got it. But *I* have authority."

For another moment the woman glared with the sort of hate Nicole had seen far too often on the Philly streets. Then, spitting a curse, she lifted the bow and arrow.

She was still fumbling, trying to get the arrow lined up with the string, when two of the Sibyls detached themselves from the group and silently took the bow and arrow away from her.

"Enough," the older of the two said. "We're with you, Protector. Tell us what we need to do."

Nicole nodded in silent thanks. "The Ghorfs will be coming back soon," she said. "They and the Wisps will return you to your work crews. About that same time, hopefully, we'll get a list of the defense systems that need to be repaired before the Koffren warships show up. Your job will be to guide your crews, just like you've always done."

"Only faster?" someone suggested.

Nicole smiled as a nervous twitter ran through the crowd. "If any of you have been dogging it, this is the time to stop," she agreed. "Any other questions?"

"What about her?" someone asked, pointing to the loudmouth.

Nicole focused on her. "You want to help?" she asked. "Or you want to sit this out?"

"I don't work for you," the woman bit out.

"Sitting out it is," Nicole said, nodding. "Wisp?"

A Wisp glided forward. "Hold her here until the Ghorfs are back and everyone's left," she ordered. "Once the arena is empty, you can let her go and come join everyone else. Lock the arena door behind you, of course."

"You can rot in hell," the woman snarled. "You will—" Her final words froze in her mouth as the Wisp wrapped its arms around her.

"The plan is to avoid rotting at all," Nicole said grimly. "Okay, Sibyls. You good here?"

"We're good," the older Sibyl said as the others returned the bows and arrows to the Thii. "How can we contact you if we need you?"

"You can give any messages to the Wisps," Nicole said. "They should be able to get word to me. Good luck."

The Q1 section of the Core was on level 51, nineteen levels below the arena access doors. Nicole led the way aft to the crosswise heat-exchange duct and, leaving the three Thii behind, ordered Jessup and Lehigh to take her and Jeff down. She got Jeff settled on the corridor floor, then sent the Wisps back up for the Thii.

"I'll need a tool kit," Jeff reminded Nicole as the door closed behind the Wisps, cutting off the flow of hot air.

"I'll go find one," Nicole said. "Do you want any food or water?"

"If you spot some, I wouldn't turn them down," he said. "But tools first."

By the time Jessup and Lehigh returned with the Thii—Lehigh carrying Nise and Misgk, Jessup carrying Sofkat—Nicole had found and collected tools and food. She waited while Jeff gulped down a food bar and a bottle of water, then directed the two Wisps to again pick him up for the thirty-foot walk down the corridor to the heavy door that marked the Q1 section of the Core.

"A formidable barrier," Nise commented as the Wisps again set Jeff down on the deck.

"Like the doors into the teleport rooms," Nicole agreed, eyeing the door. Ryit had used some kind of remote-control door opener to get them through that door. Unfortunately, she hadn't thought to ask Fievj if she would need something like that to get into the Core.

On the other hand, Ryit had also needed the remote to open the panels into the heat-exchange duct, which the Wisps could do without any such devices. "Jessup, can you open this door?" she asked.

"Don't bother," a familiar voice said from behind her. "You're not going in."

Slowly, her pulse suddenly pounding in her ears, Nicole turned.

Bungie and Trake were standing there, Bungie grinning, Trake glowering. Behind them, an open barracks room door a few yards down the corridor marked the spot where they'd been hiding.

And in Bungie's hand was the gun he'd brought aboard when he and Nicole had first been snatched from Philadelphia. The gun he'd taken from one of Trake's rivals after killing him.

The gun that was now pointed at Nicole's chest.

"We're not going in there," Trake repeated. "We're going to the teleport room . . . or you're dying where you stand."

twenty-five

And in the space of a single heartbeat, Nicole was back in Philadelphia.

Back to the gang, and Trake's absolute rule over it. Back to facing down guns and angry men, trying to stay safe and knowing she was anything but. Back to her life being held in Trake's hands, her future balanced on whatever whim he felt like exercising that day or whom he wanted to watch being abused or humiliated or crippled. Back to Trake's utter confidence as he stood back, letting other people hold the guns, protecting himself from legal consequences with the knowledge that none of those underlings would betray him.

Knowing that at one word from him, Bungie would kill them all.

"I was wondering when you'd crawl out into the sunlight again," Jeff said calmly. "Rest of your crew not crawling so good?"

Nicole tensed at the sudden hardening of Bungie's smirk, the whitening of the hand gripping the gun. "Give me an excuse to kill you right now," Trake said, his tone quietly vicious. "Just one excuse."

"Hey, the Koffren are *your* friends, not mine," Jeff protested. "Not *my* fault that they're stupid. Anyway, you can't kill me. You need me for leverage."

"I just need you alive," Trake countered. "And not by much."

"You need all of us alive and well," Nicole said. The brief panic attack had passed, and she was back on balance. Once again, Jeff's ability to sense her meltdown, and his willingness to draw enemy attention and anger to himself, had bought her the time she needed to recover. "Whatever mechanical stuff you want me to do, I need Jeff to help me."

"Bull," Bungie said flatly. "I've seen you do stuff by yourself. You don't need Pretty Boy or anyone else."

"You'd know better if you'd done any actual work," Jeff said.

"One more word and you lose your other leg," Trake said. For a moment he continued staring at Jeff, silently daring him to step over the line that had just been drawn. But Jeff remained silent, and almost reluctantly Trake turned his eyes to Nicole. "We're going to the teleport room," he said. "You're going to fix it, and you're going to send us back to Philadelphia. Work with me, and you can come back with us." His eyes narrowed. "*Screw* with me, and you die."

"And Pretty Boy here dies first," Bungie added.

"Take it easy," Nicole said, dropping into the voice and face and body language that had always been her best hope of talking Trake and the others out of something horrific they wanted to do to her. "You'll get what you want. But not yet. The ship is in danger. Earth—Philly—is in danger. The Koffren have battleships on the way, and we need to stop them." She gestured over her shoulder at the Core door. "To do that we need to fix something in there."

"Sure you do," Trake said. "You go in there and shut the door, and we're screwed? Yeah. Not a freaking chance."

"I'm telling the truth," Nicole insisted, frowning. Something here wasn't adding up. "But I don't understand. We had you locked in the hive, and the Koffren got you out and gave Bungie back his gun. But then they just let you wander around loose?"

"Who says we're wandering around loose?" Bungie countered. "This is a big job—"

"Shut it, Bungie," Trake growled, cuffing him across the back of his head. "You wouldn't know a big job if it tore your face off. It's simple. The Koffren said you might send someone here, and they told us to watch and kill whoever showed up."

"Keeping the rest of your gang as hostages," Nicole said, nodding. "I guess that makes sense. But then how do we get them back after I fix the teleport?"

"We don't," Trake said. "They're dead."

Nicole felt her eyes widen. "They *killed* them?"

"They're not dead," Jeff put in. "They're—"

"They're *dead*," Trake snarled. "That's how it is on the freaking streets. You're not useful, you're dead."

Nicole looked at Jeff. "What happened?"

Jeff's lips compressed briefly. "The Koffren didn't know much about human physiology," he said, his voice now as dark as Trake's. "Took them a little practice to figure out how to inflict just the right amount of disabling damage."

A chill ran up Nicole's back. "And that practice was on the other four?"

"Yeah." Jeff made a face. "Like I said, the Koffren are stupid."

"Yes," Nicole murmured, looking back at Trake. "Okay. Well, here's a news flash. The Koffren are done, all of them dead or captured. So there's no rush on this. Let us fix the Core, and then I can put the teleport back and we can get the others and send all of you."

"You weren't listening," Trake said. "*I don't want them.* Keep them, or feed them to your bugs there or whatever you want."

Nicole glanced at the three Thii. They were standing rigidly, their bows still slung over their backs, their quivers still at their sides. "Fine. Whatever you want. I'm just saying the teleport can wait. First we need to fix the Core so that—"

"You'll fix the damn teleport!"

Reflexively, Nicole flinched back. "Trake—"

"Kill him," Trake said, pointing at Jeff. Bungie lifted the gun—

"No!" Nicole gasped, taking a long sideways step, trying to get between the gun and Jeff.

The Thii were faster. Nicole had barely started moving before Nisc and Sofkat stepped squarely into the line of fire, Misgk right behind them.

"Trake?" Bungie asked uncertainly.

"I wouldn't," Jeff warned before Trake could answer. "That's a Colt 1911, with a maximum load of eight rounds."

"And it's already used up at least one of them," Nicole said, her mind flashing back to when Bungie had stumbled into her room in Philadelphia, holding the gun in his bloodstained hand. "That's the gun you took from Jerry, and you told me you took it away from him because his next shot might have hit something."

"Do the math," Jeff said. "Three Thii, two Wisps, one me. Leaves you one round max, maybe even completely dry. Not a good shape to be in when Levi and the Ghorfs come charging up behind you." He craned his neck, peering down the empty corridor behind Trake and Bungie. "As a matter of fact . . ."

"Cute," Trake bit out, giving Bungie another head cuff as he reflexively started to turn to look. "And *you.*" He cuffed Bungie again. "I swear, Bungie, if I'd had the choice I'd have kept Sticks and let them cut *you* up instead."

"Trake, I'm sorry—"

"Shut up," Trake cut him off.

"You know, Bungie, you don't have to take this kind of crap," Jeff said. "*You're* the one holding the gun. All he's got is a bloated sense of his own importance."

"And a death wish," Nicole said. "If we don't beat the Koffren here, even if you get back Earth won't be safe for long."

"Bungie, if you're even *thinking* about listening to this freaking pile of crap, I'll slice your gut open and feed you your own liver," Trake warned, his voice a low, threatening rumble.

"I'm not listening, Trake," Bungie hastened to assure him. "Really. I'm just—"

"Bungie, if I need to knife you right now I'll do it," Trake said, his voice going even deeper.

Bungie flinched. "No, Trake, you don't have to do that. Really. You don't."

"Good," Trake said. "Good soldiers obey their general. You're a good soldier, aren't you, Bungie?"

"Sure," Bungie said. "Always."

And with that, Nicole saw with a sinking heart, the small embers of doubt and self-preservation Jeff had been trying to breathe life into had gone out. Bungie was back squarely under Trake's thumb, and he would never even think of leaving that spot again.

"Good," Trake said. He smiled at Jeff, a smile of smugness and triumph. He'd seen what Jeff was trying to do, but he also knew Bungie. A little abuse, a little kicking of the dog, and the dog had gone whimpering back into line.

Nicole had spent a lot of time afraid of Bungie. She'd felt a lot of that same time hating him.

Now, all she had left was pity.

"So where were we?" Trake continued. "Right. We were going to kill Pretty Boy if Nicole didn't get her ass in gear and take us to the teleport." He raised his eyebrows. "Or maybe we should just blow his kneecap off. Lot of damage you can do with seven bullets."

And then, with a sudden blast of hot air, the door into the heat duct in the corridor behind Trake and Bungie slid open.

Bungie reacted instantly. He spun around, hunched his shoulders, and fired a shot into the opening.

Nicole flinched as the thundercrack hammered into her ears. A second later, Bungie went sprawling onto the deck as Trake snatched the gun out of his hand and slapped him hard across the back of his head. "You *damn* freaking idiot," he snarled as he turned to face into the wind. He lifted the gun into firing position . . .

And through the opening floated Cambria, its wings spread, its body already turned toward the group gathered by the Core door.

Wrapped securely in its arms was Allyce.

"Don't shoot!" Nicole shouted. In front of Jeff, the Thii were grabbing for their weapons—

Trake spun back around. "Drop 'em," he snapped.

"Do it," Nicole said, feeling her last flicker of hope fade away. She'd hoped it was Kahkitah or Wesowee or one of the other Ghorfs, or even a whole swarm of Wisps. But Allyce wouldn't be of any help at all.

In fact, her arrival just made things worse. Bungie's gun was down to six shots, but now he and Trake had an extra hostage to hold against Nicole's cooperation.

The vent door closed, cutting off the flow of hot air, and Cambria opened its arms. Allyce's feet settled onto the deck, her body slumping a little as the paralysis disappeared. "I'm here, Nicole," she called as she walked slowly and carefully toward the group at the Core door. "Cambria said Jeff needed a doctor."

"Yes," Nicole said with a sigh. "He does."

"You know this bitch, Bungie?" Trake demanded, glancing once at Allyce, then turning back and pointing his gun again at Jeff and the Thii. "Bungie?"

"She's a traitor," Jeff snarled before Bungie could answer. "She's the one who betrayed us back in the Q1 arena."

"But she—" Nicole clamped down on her tongue as she belatedly realized what Jeff was doing. If he could convince Trake that Nicole hated Allyce, he might not try to use her as a lever. "But she didn't succeed," Nicole continued. "We won, and I kicked her out to go live with the green work crew. I thought I told you I never wanted to see you again, Allyce."

A look of surprise and hurt crossed Allyce's face, quickly replaced by understanding as she realized what Nicole and Jeff were trying to do. "I'm sorry," she said stiffly. "But I told you then what side I was on. The reasons for that decision haven't changed."

"Bungie?" Trake prompted.

"Yeah, she helped us," Bungie said, pulling himself into a half-sitting position, as if afraid to stand all the way up in case Trake decided to hit him again.

"So what's she doing here?"

"I came because Nicole said Jeff needed me," Allyce said. "But never mind him. Do *you* two need anything?"

"Not from *you*," Trake said. "No, wait. Come here and pick up these toy bows and arrows. I don't feel like getting any closer to those freaking bugs than I have to."

"She's injured," Nicole said. "Your Koffren friends beat her up."

"So?" Trake countered.

"So it's going to take forever for her to walk all the way here," Nicole said as Allyce began limping toward them. "Be faster if I have Cambria pick her up again and bring her."

"You think I'm stupid?" Trake said scornfully. "This place is already too crowded with these damn overgrown butterflies. Tell the damn freaking thing to stay right where it is."

Nicole sighed to herself. With three Wisps close at hand, she might have been able to launch an attack that wouldn't get too many of the creatures killed. No chance now. She looked at Cambria, still standing just inside the heat duct where it had landed, its gloriously colored wings nearly filling the corridor.

She caught her breath. *Its wings filling the corridor?* But Wisps never spread their wings except when they were floating in the ducts, teleporting someone somewhere, or under orders from Nicole to do so. And when they were out of the ducts they always closed them down.

Only Cambria hadn't done that.

Nicole focused on Allyce, still making her slow way along the corridor, halfway now to Trake and Bungie. She'd told Cambria to obey Allyce, so presumably it was Allyce who'd ordered the Wisp to keep its wings up.

But why?

And then, abruptly, Allyce gave a little gasp and stopped. "Bungie, help me," she said, wobbling like she was ready to fall. "I can't—my knee—"

"Trake?" Bungie asked, starting to push himself to his feet.

"Did I tell you to move?" Trake snapped. With a last look at the Thii he swiveled his gun to point at Bungie. "I swear to God—"

Without warning, Allyce's legs collapsed beneath her, sending her sprawling to the deck. "Agony!" she screamed.

Trake spun the rest of the way around, shifting his gun from Bungie to Allyce. "Get up, you damn freaking bitch. Get *up!*"

In the corridor thirty yards behind her, Cambria finally folded its wings.

Revealing Moile and Teika standing behind the Wisp, their bows bent and ready in their hands. The butterfly wings were barely clear when both Ponngs fired, sending a pair of arrows flashing through the air to slam into Trake's cheek and forehead.

Trake bellowed with pain and rage, his head jerking back from the impacts, the gun in his hand barking out a round that sizzled past Teika and ricocheted off the corridor wall behind him. Cursing, he slapped the arrows off his face with one hand as he swung back around toward Nicole and the others. His gun settled onto Jeff and the Thii, and Nicole saw his finger start to tighten on the trigger.

Abruptly, he staggered, the gun sagging in his hand. He tried to bring it up.

And collapsed to the deck, the weapon dropping from his hand and clattering onto the floor.

For a moment Bungie stared at Trake, his eyes wide with disbelief. His gaze shifted to the gun lying on the deck—

"Don't," Jeff warned quietly.

Bungie looked at him, lying helpless on the deck. He looked at the two Ponngs walking stiffly toward them, their own walk as unsteady as Allyce's, toy arrows nocked into toy bows. He looked up at Nicole, gazing down at him.

And with that, all the stiffness and anticipation drained out of him. "What the *hell*?" he muttered.

Nicole looked at Allyce as Cambria glided forward and offered her a supporting arm. "Your cyanide mixture?" she asked.

"Yes," Allyce said, her voice weary. "I told you Moile and Teika had asked for some."

"I remember," Nicole said, eyeing the Ponngs as they limped forward on their half-crippled legs. "I'm just surprised . . ."

"That we were able to make the journey again to the treatment room?" Moile asked. "We weren't." He nodded toward the Thii. "Fortunately, our allies were both willing and able to do so."

"Ah," Nicole said, looking at the Thii as they retrieved their own bows and arrows. "Thank you."

"We were pleased to serve," Nise said. "We understood that the Ponngs wished to take the battle back to the enemy."

"Yes," Nicole murmured, turning back to the Ponngs and their damaged legs. Damage that Trake and Bungie and the others had inflicted on them.

The leader of that attack lay dead in front of them. But Bungie was still alive.

And the arrows nocked in the Ponngs' bows were undoubtedly also poisoned.

Unconsciously, she held her breath. If the roles had been reversed, Bungie would probably have taken revenge. Trake certainly would have. Would the Ponngs?

To her relief, Moile and Teika passed Bungie without a second look. "But how did you know we needed you?" she asked. "We didn't even know ourselves that Trake and Bungie were here until they jumped us."

"We didn't know," Moile said. "But you had given us the task of protecting Allyce. When Cambria suddenly came into the medical room and picked her up, we feared she was under attack. We hurriedly gathered our weapons and followed."

"But your *legs*."

"We told you we could walk as much and as far as you required," Teika said.

"I didn't know they were back there until Cambria opened the vent door," Allyce said. "They jumped in right behind us, landing on Cambria's back and hanging on to its wings." Her throat worked. "Did you know that if there are three people connected to a single Wisp they can hear each other's thoughts?"

"No, I didn't," Nicole said, looking at Cambria with new eyes. "That could be very useful."

"It's also rather . . . unpleasant," Allyce said, a shadow of something crossing her face as she let go of Cambria's arm. "I told the Ponngs I hadn't been abducted, that you'd just called for me to treat Jeff and ordered Cambria to carry me. They apologized for intruding, but by that time we were in the duct and there was no way they could leave me until we landed." She looked down at the gun. "And then Cambria said you were a prisoner."

"*Cambria* said that?" Nicole asked frowning. "How did it know?"

"There's some kind of telepathic communications system the Wisps can use," Allyce said. "I don't know if it's just this area or ship-wide. But they can use it to talk back and forth." She nodded toward Jessup and Lehigh. "One of them told Cambria, and Cambria told us." She hunched her shoulders. "But we didn't know they had a gun until one of them shot at us."

"No, the Wisps probably wouldn't recognize it," Nicole murmured. The *Fyrantha* had told her that the Shipmasters' communications setup had been added in after they took over the ship. Did this mean the Wisps had been the original system?

Maybe. Running all the ship-wide communications through the Wisps would explain why there were so many of them aboard the *Fyrantha*.

"We quickly formulated a plan," Moile said. "We would all come in and Allyce would find out what was going on while we stayed hidden behind Cambria's wings. At the right moment, she would call out the signal—*agony*—and Cambria would drop its wings."

"Simple and elegant," Jeff said.

Moile bowed his head. "Thank you."

"But why did you wait so long?" Nicole asked, turning to Allyce. "They must have had their arrows ready as soon as they were safely on the deck. Why didn't you signal them faster? What if Trake had decided to shoot Jeff?"

"We hoped that wouldn't happen," Moile said. "Perhaps we were indeed a little slow."

"I don't think so," Jeff said. "Nicole—"

"It's of no importance," Moile interrupted.

"I think it is," Jeff said. "Nicole, did you notice what happened just before Allyce gave the signal?"

Nicole thought back. "She dropped to the deck, right?"

"I'm talking before that," Jeff said quietly. "Trake's gun had been pointed at you, the Thii, and me. And you saw that even cyanide doesn't act instantly." He nodded at the Ponngs. "I think they'd specifically told Allyce to wait until the gun was pointed at them."

Nicole felt her stomach tighten. "Allyce?" she asked.

Allyce hesitated. "I—"

"It's all right," Moile said. "You're correct, Jeff." He inclined his head. "We also swore her to silence on that point. We didn't want . . . a warrior should not receive special gratitude for merely doing his job."

"Yet those who gain from their risk should not be denied the privilege of offering such gratitude," Nise said, bowing low. "Thank you, warriors of the Ponngs. The Thii stand in your debt."

"True warriors do not keep such books," Moile assured him. "We serve the Protector, as we serve each other."

"Thank you," Nicole said. "Thank you all. For everything."

"Meanwhile, there's a battle coming up that all the cyanide-tipped arrows in the universe won't help," Jeff said, reaching up and touching Lehigh's hand. "You want to see if the Wisps can open this door?"

"Yes," Nicole said, wincing. "Cambria, Jessup, Lehigh: Can any of you get the Core door open?" she asked.

She touched Cambria's arm. *No one of us can do so,* Cambria's voice came in her mind. *But three of us together can, if the Protector wishes it.*

I do, Nicole said. *Open the door.*

And with a kind of old, creaking sound, a sound Nicole had seldom heard on the *Fyrantha,* the door slid open.

"Well," Jeff muttered. "*That* was easy."

"That part was, anyway," Nicole said. The room beyond was as tightly packed with consoles and displays as Ushkai had warned it would be. The access passageway leading inward was narrow, but with the slight outward flare of the consoles the gap was wider at deck height. "Can you get through there, Jeff?"

"Sure, no problem," Jeff assured her. "Told you I'd be lying on my back. Okay. Sofkat and Misgk: you're on litter duty. You'll be moving me back and forth in there wherever I need to go. If you get tired of carrying me, help me crawl. Nise: you'll be the runner, going and getting whatever parts I need that aren't already in there."

"And we need to tell the others about the Wisp communication system," Nicole added.

"Already done," Jeff said, pointing up at Lehigh. "I sent a message to all Wisps to touch the nearest Ghorf and let them know how it works."

"Great," Nicole said, wincing. "I just hope the Ghorfs don't see it as an attack."

"I don't think Ghorfs scare that easily," Jeff said. He touched Lehigh's hand again and nodded. "No problem—they're already starting to check in. A few more minutes, and everyone should be with the program."

"Good." Nicole took a deep breath and pulled out her inhaler. "Then we'd better get busy."

"Hold it a second," Jeff said, holding out a hand toward her. "I still think you need to stay on top of things. We can call in one of the other Sibyls to help me."

"They all have their own jobs to do," Nicole said. "Until someone else gets free, I'm on this one."

"What about me?" Bungie asked.

They all turned to look at him. "What about you?" Jeff asked.

"I can help," Bungie said. His eyes were still on Trake as he got to his feet. He looked once at the Ponngs and their poisoned arrows, then turned to Nicole. "I can help you here."

Jeff snorted. "Like hell."

"I mean it," Bungie said. "I was part of the team, remember?"

"Part of the *team*?" Jeff shot back. "Not even once."

"It's all right, Jeff," Nicole said. Suddenly, with a clarity she'd never known before, she understood. "Don't you get it? Bungie needs to belong to something. Trake's gang, or the *Fyrantha*— he doesn't know who he is unless someone tells him what his place is."

"That's not true," Bungie protested. But there was a look in his eyes that told Nicole that he, too, now understood. "It's *not*."

"Yes, it is," Nicole said. "But you can change. You know that, right? You can make something new for yourself. Make a new life."

"Does that mean you're going to let me help?" Bungie asked.

Nicole smiled tightly. "Like Jeff said: hell, no. We need competent and trustworthy people. Right now, you're neither."

She lifted a hand. "Cambria? Take Bungie to Q3 and put him in the arena with the Shipmasters. He'll keep there until this is all over and we can figure out what to do with him."

"Nicole, you need me," Bungie said, a hint of a snarl creeping into his voice. "You've always needed me."

"I've never needed you, Bungie," Nicole said. "I never needed any of you." She waved a hand that encompassed Jeff, Allyce, the Thii, and the Ponngs. "*These* are the people I need."

"You ungrateful—" The rest of Bungie's insult was cut off as Cambria glided up behind him and wrapped its arms around him. The Wisp turned back toward the heat duct, cutting off Nicole's view of Bungie's frozen, angry, hopeless expression.

"It's really kind of sad," Allyce murmured.

"So is a wounded snake," Jeff said.

"I mean it," Allyce insisted. "We all need to belong to something. Or to someone."

"That's where choice and decision come in," Jeff said. "We doing this?"

"We're doing this," Nicole said, pulling out her notepad and turning her back to the burst of hot air as Cambria took Bungie into the heat duct.

Into the duct, and out of her life. Forever.

"And while I get the first list of repairs," she continued, "Allyce will do whatever she can to fix you up."

twenty-six

Six hours.

Nicole could remember times, usually late-night parties, when six hours had gone past in the blink of an eye. There'd been other times, usually when Trake had her on lookout duty, when those same six hours had dragged out forever. And there'd been far too many times, especially after a bash of heavy drinking, when six or more hours had been lost forever from her memory and her life.

Now, six hours were going to spell the difference between life and death.

By all rights, Nicole knew, she should be on the edge of panic. But to her own vague surprise, she wasn't. There was simply too much to do for her to stop long enough to think about the horrible task she and the *Fyrantha* were facing.

She'd expected the Koffren and Shipmasters to resist the imprisonment she'd ordered for them. But the brief battle by the ocean, along with the sudden revelation that the Ghorfs were far more powerful and dangerous than any of them had suspected, had apparently knocked the fight out of them, at least for the moment. She and Jeff were just getting started on the Core when one of the Wisps arrived with word from Wesowee that both groups had been safely locked away and that he, Iosif, and Levi were heading to the Q1 command center with Fievj and Ryit for a crash course in how to fly the *Fyrantha*.

Another message a few minutes later informed her that the rest of the Ghorfs were returning to gather their work teams, taking a few Wisps with them for support, communication, and transport. A few minutes after that, Kahkitah quietly joined Nicole and Jeff at the Core, clearly intending to be their assistant and guard.

And with that, the race had begun.

The Q1 Core section, as Nicole had feared, needed a *lot* of work. She and Jeff quickly settled into a pattern: she would use the inhaler to get the *Fyrantha*'s list of repairs and scribble as much of it as she could onto her notepad. Then she would hand the notepad to Jeff and stand back, feeling helpless and useless, while he got to work pulling and replacing the necessary components and restringing various bits of wiring. Occasionally he needed to tear off some sealing plastic, jobs he could pass off to Sofkat and Misgk while he worked on something elsewhere in the chamber. Mostly, though, he worked alone.

Over and over, Nicole had to fight back an almost overwhelming urge to offer her help. Each time, she stifled the impulse. Even the short, slender Thii had trouble finding room to work together in the cramped space. Two humans would have no chance at all, and she knew that even just bringing up the subject would do nothing but distract Jeff from his work.

Instead, she concentrated her thoughts on the work being done across the ship to restore the *Fyrantha*'s defense shields. Every few minutes Cambria came up behind her and touched her shoulder, and her mind would echo with a progress report from one of the work teams. It was a new experience, hearing someone else's voice coming into her mind instead of the familiar flat Wisp voice, and it took a little getting used to.

In some ways, it was also maddening. These were thoughts

coming across the telepathic network, not ordinary speech, and while the Ghorfs were pretty good at holding to a straight line of mental conversation, many of the humans were rotten at it.

Nicole had known people back in Philadelphia like that, people who blathered away without any verbal organization, their words tumbling over each other as stray thoughts bounced up and down bunny trails until whatever they were trying to say was completely lost in the weeds. This wasn't *that* bad—the people here were at least *trying* to stay on track—but the end result was still sometimes hard to sift through. The fact that the voices sounded like they were coming from down a long, echoey hallway didn't help.

Even stranger, the communication itself was surprisingly slow. Nicole would think a question or comment to the person at the other end, and it would be a good four or five seconds before she got a reply. Some of the delay might have been due to the other person having to organize his thoughts, but the rest apparently had to do with the whole Wisp/Oracle connection system. Even when she was talking to the Ghorfs, who had better mental organization, the delay was only a little shorter.

Still, she could hardly complain. Talking through the Wisps was a hell of a lot faster than having to send messengers everywhere or making the Ghorfs use their private tap-code system. And once she had the voices identified she knew each time who it was she was talking to, and could better sort through that person's own particular style of mental chatter.

Slowly, progress was made. One by one, the defense nodes Fievj had identified became operational, and their work crews were sent to the next one on the list. Levi and Iosif handled all of that from the control center, leaving Nicole free to monitor the progress and keep an eye on Jeff's work.

Occasionally, one of the crew foremen asked for a rest or food break. Iosif's invariable response was five minutes for the first, food bars and water for the second.

Four hours into the marathon, one of the foremen apparently got tired of that answer. He insisted he and the others weren't doing slave labor and threatened to pull his team off the job if they weren't given a full hour's break. Neither Levi's cajoling nor Iosif's threats had the slightest effect on his defiance, and he wouldn't even listen to Nicole's attempts to remind him of the threat facing them.

It wasn't until Kahkitah stepped in and spoke personally with the Ghorf assigned to that team that the foreman relented. Even then, the foreman and Ghorf were halfway to the Q3 arena, where the foreman would be forced to hang out for the rest of the day with the Shipmasters, before he finally agreed to go back to work.

They had fixed all but fifteen of the defense nodes when, twenty minutes ahead of schedule, the Koffren warships appeared.

Looks like twenty of them, Iosif's voice came through Cambria's touch on Nicole's shoulder. *Big suckers, too—about the size of* Nimitz-*class carriers.*

Nicole winced. *But we're still bigger, right?*

She waited through the interminable five-second pause. *Oh, a hell of a lot bigger—we're three thousand meters long to their three hundred,* Iosif replied. *Problem is, size isn't the biggest factor here. We've got a bunch of gaps they can shoot through. As far as I can see, they don't have any.*

Can *we shoot at them?*

Another pause. *I don't know. Fievj says they never found a working weapon anywhere on this thing. He still thinks the people who turned it into a zoo scrapped them at the same time they took the fighters out of the arenas.*

That's what he told us, too. Do you believe him?

Not necessarily. Just because they couldn't find any weapons doesn't mean there aren't any. I know that each of the defense nodes has a bunch of consoles that don't seem to do anything. Maybe they operate the guns.

Nicole thought back to the first time she'd been in one of the nodes. Two concentric rings of consoles, with only the one console that seemed to activate that section of the ship's shield completely dark. *If there are any guns, anyway. Maybe I should go take a look.*

Too late, Iosif said. *Right now, you need to come up here and talk to them.*

Nicole felt her eyes go wide. *Me?*

You're the Fyrantha's *Protector,* Iosif reminded her. *Anyway, someone has to. They've been hailing us for the past three minutes, and I'm sure as hell not letting Fievj near the mic.*

No, of course not, Nicole agreed reluctantly, peering into the Core room. Jeff looked like he was finishing up the last list she'd given him. *Let me give Jeff one more set of instructions. See if you can get one of the other Sibyls down here to take over for me.*

Make it fast, Iosif warned. *Fievj showed us how to put the shields up, but I don't want to do that until we absolutely have to. No point showing them where the holes are in advance.*

Agreed. I'll be there as soon as I can.

She pushed Cambria's hand aside. "They're here," she announced to Jeff as she pulled out her inhaler. "Give me back the notepad—I can get you one more set before I go."

"Never mind the notepad," Jeff said. "Just reel off the instructions. I'll remember them."

"You sure?"

"Positive," Jeff said. "We've got to be getting close to the end, anyway."

Which was, to Nicole's way of thinking, the absolute worst time to start missing things or getting sloppy. But there was no time to argue the point. "I hope so. Here we go." She took a full whiff from the inhaler, and as the *Fyrantha's* voice whispered through her mind she rattled off the instructions.

A minute later, she was done. "You sure you got all that?" she asked.

"No problem," Jeff said. "Go."

"Right." Nicole pushed herself up off the floor—

And nearly fell as a wave of dizziness washed over her.

"Are you ill?" Kahkitah asked anxiously, catching her arm before she could fall.

"I'm okay," Nicole said, leaning against his bulk. "Just a little dizzy."

Jeff swore under his breath. "Too much of that damn inhaler," he ground out. "Sofkat, Misgk—get me to the door."

"No," Nicole told him. "You stay there and keep working. Kahkitah and Cambria can get me to the control center."

"Nicole—"

"That's an order, Jeff," she said. "Kahkitah?"

"I have you," Kahkitah said. Shifting his grip, he picked her up in his arms and turned back toward the heat duct door. "Wisps? We need two of you for transport."

The control center was on level 56 in the *ecsisia* section of Q1. By the time Nicole and the others arrived her dizzy spell had passed.

The room was smaller than she'd expected, not much bigger than the defense node room near the *Fyrantha's* roof. But while there had been a double ring of consoles in the node, here there were four rings, the consoles set low to the floor with chairs facing each of them. Levi and Iosif were seated in two of the chairs in the inner ring, with a Wisp on either side of them. Fievj and Ryit were seated in front of them in the next ring outward, under the watchful eyes of a pair of Ghorfs. The consoles in the two inner rings were fully lit and active, while the third ring had several dark consoles and the outer ring was completely dark.

And here, instead of the thick glass of the node that had first showed Nicole the starry sky outside the ship, the walls were covered with displays.

Floating in six of them were twenty large, nasty-looking spaceships.

"About time," Iosif said, glancing over his shoulder as Kahkitah lowered Nicole's feet to the deck. "He's starting to get a little surly."

"I'll talk to him," Nicole said, working her way through the outer rings and coming to a halt behind Iosif. "Do we have a name?"

"Near as we can figure, it's *Djit-vis-ees,*" Levi said handing her a small mic. "I suggested we call him Djit, just to save time. He didn't seem to like that. The slider there on the side mutes it."

Nicole found the slider switch and put her thumb on it. "Got it."

"Ready to key the transmitter," Iosif said, his hand hovering over a switch.

Nicole braced herself. This was it. "Yes. Go."

"Good luck," Iosif said, and threw the switch.

"—will answer me *now,* or I swear to you your death is at hand," a harsh Koffren voice came over the speaker and through Nicole's translator.

Nicole took a deep breath and unmuted her mic. Back in Philadelphia, her health and safety had too often depended on her ability to talk people into things or talk them out of things. Here, she was about to put those hard-earned skills to their final test. "Hello, Djit-vis-ees of the Koffren," she called. "This is Nicole Hammond. What seems to be the trouble?"

"What are you, human slave?"

"We're not slaves," Nicole said. "I'm not, anyway. I'm a Sibyl."

"You're all slaves," Djit-vis-ees said flatly. "End this nonsense and bring me the ship's master."

"Yes. That's me."

"I refer to the ship's *master*. Bring me Vjiu-fusi-suut."

"Sorry, but there's no one here by that name," Nicole said. "Oh, wait. Are you talking about the Koffren who likes to call himself *Justice, Revenge, and Fire*?"

"Speak no more nonsense, slave!"

"Not a slave, and not nonsense," Nicole said. "See, I'm afraid Vjiu-fusi-suut is currently locked up. So are the rest of the Koffren."

"You will speak no more—"

"I think there are, what, sixteen of them left alive out of the original thirty-eight?" Nicole continued. "Kahkitah?"

"Sixteen is correct," the Ghorf confirmed.

"Right," Nicole said. "The other twenty-two didn't make it. They were—I think the term is *casualties of war*."

"You lie," Djit-vis-ees bit out. But it seemed to Nicole that some of the fire had gone out of his tone.

"If I'm lying, how come I'm the one talking to you instead of Vjiu-fusi-suut?" Nicole countered. "Oh, and just in case you're interested, we didn't lose any of our side at all. Anyway, the point is that we're holding sixteen of your people. Shall we discuss what you need to do to get them back?"

There was a short silence. "Who are you?" Djit-vis-ees asked.

"I already told you," Nicole said. "I'm Nicole. I'm a Sibyl." She paused. "I'm also the *Fyrantha*'s chosen Protector."

"Yes," Djit-vis-ees murmured, his voice gone dark and thoughtful. "Yes, I remember now. Vjiu-fusi-suut spoke of you. He promised you would be eliminated."

"Yeah," Nicole said. "I always hate it when people make promises they can't keep."

"His promise has not yet failed," Djit-vis-ees said calmly. "We may yet bring it to truth."

"I guess we'll see," Nicole said. "So about the prisoners?"

"Prisoners?" Djit-vis-ees made a sound like someone spitting. "You hold no prisoners. You hold failures. Embarrassments. The dead."

Nicole sighed. She'd been afraid that would be the Koffren attitude. "So you're saying you don't want them?"

"Their failure has brought shame on us all," Djit-vis-ees said. "Kill them and be thanked for it."

"Nice," Levi muttered.

"Fine, if that's what you want," Nicole said. "I just thought you might want to talk to them first. There are things you really should want to know."

"We already know all we need."

"I'm talking about stuff that would keep you from doing something stupid," Nicole said. "Like getting yourselves blown up. Maybe your whole world, too."

"It's *you* who is about to die, Sibyl, not us," Djit-vis-ees scoffed.

"Really?" Nicole countered. "I thought you wanted to take the *Fyrantha* intact. How do you expect to kill me without destroying the whole ship?"

"Once more you attempt a foolish bluff," Djit-vis-ees said. "I give you one chance. Surrender now, accept Koffren mastery over you and the ship, and you and your companions will live."

There was a breath of air on the back of Nicole's neck, and she turned to see one of the Ghorfs standing behind her, a Wisp at his side. "That sounds fair," she said. "Let me discuss it with my companions." She thumbed the mute slider. "What is it?"

"News from Q4," the Ghorf said, his birdsong whistles soft and intense. "One more defense node has been reactivated."

"Thank you," Nicole said. One down; fourteen still to go. This was going to take a *lot* more stalling. "We've got crews on all the others, right?"

"There are two crews working on each," the Ghorf confirmed. "Miron determined that more than two would add little in the way of speed, and likely get in each other's way."

"That was his evaluation, anyway," Iosif added. "I haven't seen the rooms myself."

"No, he's probably right," Nicole said. "What about the crews that have already finished?"

"I told them to stay at the nodes they'd just fixed," Iosif said. "Miron didn't have anything else for them to do, anyway, and I figured that nodes that broke once might break again."

In which case, it would save a lot of time to have a repair team already on hand. "Good idea," she said. "Do we know where the holes are?"

"Yeah," Levi said. "Ryit, pull up an overview."

At the console in front of him, Ryit keyed in a command, and one of the screens changed from a view of space to a schematic of the *Fyrantha*.

Nicole ran her eyes over it, wincing. She'd hoped the remaining shield gaps would be clustered together in such a way that they might be able to keep the ship between the Koffren ships' guns and the holes. But the openings were scattered all over the place, in all four quadrants. "Any idea when the rest will be fixed?" she asked.

"No," the Ghorf said. "They're working as quickly as they can."

"I know." Nicole studied the schematic another moment, then nodded. "Okay, Ryit, you can put it away."

The Wisp reached forward and touched the Ghorf's arm. "Carp also wishes to know if Tomas and Shantal arrived."

"Arrived where?" Nicole asked, frowning.

"I don't know," the Ghorf said. "Neither do the Wisps. Tomas said you wanted him."

"Yeah, hang on," Nicole muttered, pushing past the Ghorf and touching the Wisp's arm. *Where are Tomas and Shantal?* she asked it.

They are in the teleport room.

Nicole felt her eyes go wide. *The teleport room? How did they get in?*

Tomas ordered the Wisps there to open the door. He said you had told him to go in.

And no one bothered to ask me about that? Nicole demanded.

You gave the Sibyls authority to command us.

Nicole ground her teeth. Yes, she'd done that, all right. *Are the other Wisps still there? And how many are there?*

There were three. Three Wisps together can open security-sealed doors.

Yes, I know, Nicole said. *What's Tomas up to?*

I don't know. But he told Shantal he would need more Wisps when he was finished.

Nicole frowned. Tomas had wanted *more* Wisps? What the hell was he up to? *Well, you can tell all the Wisps—*

She broke off her order. Down in the *Fyrantha's* basement, after their raid into Q1, Tomas had bitterly argued that they should have killed the two Koffren when they'd had the chance. Then he'd stomped off, and had avoided Nicole ever since.

But before he'd left he'd said something. What had he said? Nicole strained at her memory, trying desperately to pull up the image of that moment.

Do you wish access to a memory?

Nicole started. *What?*

Do you wish access to a memory? the Wisp repeated. *Events involving the Protector are all recorded.*

There were a whole bunch of unpleasant implications of something like that, Nicole knew. But right now she had more important things to worry about. *Yes, let me see the memory of my last conversation with Tomas. It was in the Fyrantha's basement—*

And then, there it was. Tomas and Jeff and the others, talking and arguing after their escape down the heat-exchange duct—*Just the last part,* she told the Wisp. *The last thing Tomas said about the Koffren.*

Better yet, call me when you've got the bastards lined up against the wall.

A horrible certainty flashed into Nicole's mind. "Iosif, take over," she said, pushing past the Wisp and heading for the door. "If Djit-vis-ees calls back tell him I'm still talking to people."

"Where are you going?" Iosif called after her.

"He *knows* you're stalling, you know," Levi added.

"Well, stall him back," Nicole called over her shoulder. "Tomas is in the teleport room, about to do something stupid."

"What kind of stupid?" Levi asked.

"I think he's going to teleport all of the Koffren out there into the *Fyrantha* and kill them while the Wisps still have them frozen. *Line them up against the wall,* is how he put it."

"Damn," Levi said. "Yeah, that sounds like his brand of stupid. You want me to come with you?"

"No, Iosif needs you here," Nicole said. "I can handle it."

twenty-seven

The three Wisps were standing in the corridor outside the teleport room when Nicole arrived. She'd half expected Tomas to seal himself in, but the door was wide open. For a moment she wondered if she should bring a couple of Wisps in with her, decided she'd have a better chance of talking Tomas out of this if she was alone, and stepped through the door.

The door to the control room was also open, and Nicole could hear the murmur of voices coming from inside. She crossed the teleport room and went inside.

Tomas was sitting cross-legged in front of one of the consoles, a handful of tools laid out on the deck beside him, peering up into the console as he set aside the access panel he'd apparently just removed. "That was a forty-twenty back-flex modulator, right?" he asked.

"Right," the young woman beside him said, her fingertips restlessly tapping the inhaler in her hand. "Better hurry this up before Nicole finds out—"

"Speak of the devil," Nicole said casually. "How's it going?"

Tomas looked over at her, his expression darkening. "Yeah, we figured you'd show up sooner or later. You slumming? Or just tired of playing Big Boss?"

"I was never playing anything," Nicole said. "And this isn't going to help."

"How do you know?" Tomas countered. "You don't even know what I'm doing."

"I think I do." Nicole looked at the Sibyl. "Shantal, wasn't it?"

"Yes," the woman said.

"You can go back to Carp and his group now," Nicole said. "Tomas and I can handle things from here."

Shantal's eyes flicked to Tomas, back to Nicole. Then, with a silent nod, she headed out, crossing the teleport room and disappearing through the door.

"So what now?" Tomas asked. "You try to appeal to my higher instincts? Because those instincts died when the bastards killed Bennett."

"No, I'm going to appeal to your common sense," Nicole said. "There are twenty ships full of Koffren out there. Dozens, maybe even hundreds of the bastards."

"Yeah, I know," Tomas said. "That's the point."

"That's *not* the point," Nicole insisted. "You pull them in one at a time and it'll take forever. Even if they don't notice you doing it, which they probably will."

Tomas frowned. "What the hell are you talking about? Who said anything about teleporting Koffren back here?"

"I thought . . ." Nicole floundered. "What you said to me down in the basement. You're not looking to line them up against the wall?"

"Of course not," Tomas scoffed. "I'm going to take care of them a different way." He gestured in the direction of the Q2 arena. "Sixteen Koffren. I'm going to send one each out to those ships. With bombs strapped to them."

Nicole felt her eyes go wide. "You're not serious."

"Hell, yes, I'm serious," Tomas bit out. "They killed Bennett and tried to kill the rest of us. They deserve to die. All of them." He scowled. "Course, there are twenty ships out there, so we can't get them all. But taking out sixteen would be a good start."

"Yeah, a damn good start," Nicole agreed, thinking fast. "But what about the Wisps? Do *they* deserve to die, too?"

"I'll bring them back before the bombs go off."

"You may not be able to," Nicole said. "The Koffren commander has already said he doesn't care if our prisoners live or die. And they know all about the Wisps and the *Fyrantha's* teleport system. If a bunch of Koffren suddenly appear with big bombs strapped to them they'll probably open fire and try to stop the bombs from exploding."

"Not if we build them right," Tomas said. "But so a few Wisps die. Isn't that better than *all* of them dying? Along with all of us?"

"I don't think anyone has to die," Nicole said. "If we can get the *Fyrantha* up and running—"

She broke off, jumping, as a hand unexpectedly touched her shoulder. She had just enough time to look back and see it was one of the Wisps from the corridor—

Nicole, this is Allyce, the doctor's voice came in her mind. *Jeff's gone woozy—I think he's got internal bleeding. I need to get him to the closest medical center.*

Nicole clenched her teeth. *Yes, of course,* she replied. *Get the Wisps to carry him. What about the Core?*

I don't know. I think he's almost done, but I don't know.

I'll get someone else there to finish up, Nicole said. *You just worry about Jeff.*

I will.

"I've got to go," Nicole said to Tomas. "Jeff's in trouble—he needs to get to a medical center, and I need to find someone to finish his work on the Core."

"Yeah, good luck," Tomas said. "I'll keep working my side of the—"

Abruptly, the deck seemed to jerk under Nicole's feet. She started to turn—

"Attention, everyone," Iosif's voice came from somewhere in the ceiling. "We're under attack. Repeat, we're under attack. Nicole, get the hell back here."

"Damn," Nicole snarled, grabbing the Wisp's arm. *Iosif, I'm on my way,* she thought, hoping one of the Wisps would relay the message. "Tomas, you need to get back to Carp in case that node goes down again."

"I'm working *here.*"

"Yeah, whatever," Nicole gritted out. "We'll try to let you know when the ship starts getting blown apart around you." She turned to the door.

"Wait."

She turned back. Tomas was staring at the console in front of him, his lips compressed into a hard line. Then, abruptly, he started gathering up his tools. "Never mind," he said as the deck rocked again. "You need the Core fixed? Fine. How do I get there?"

"The Wisp will take you," Nicole said, feeling a flicker of relief. *Wisp, take Tomas to the Q1 Core.*

I obey the Protector.

"Good luck," she said to Tomas. "I've got to get back to Iosif. Maybe there's still time to stop this."

"Yeah," Tomas ground out. "If you can't, don't forget we've still got Koffren. And bombs."

The deck was bouncing like a truck over city potholes by the time Nicole reached the control center. "What's happening?" she asked as she made her way through the outer darkened console rings to the center. On the wall displays, the twenty Koffren ships had broken their earlier formation and were buzzing around the *Fyrantha* like a group of hornets, their weapons blazing away.

"They got tired of waiting for you," Iosif said tightly. "I had to raise the shields, which naturally showed them where the gaps were. So now they're trying to shoot through them."

Nicole winced. "And succeeding?"

"Yes and no," Levi said. "Their lasers—or whatever those are—are getting through just fine, but they aren't doing much against the hull armor. Their missiles seem to be a lot more powerful, but they take a few seconds to get here and so far we've been able to roll or pitch the hole out of the way in time."

"The shields we *do* have are working okay against them?"

"So far," Iosif said. "But they've figured out our strategy, and they're starting to coordinate their attacks. We're a hell of a lot more maneuverable than anything this big should be, so at the moment we're still staying ahead of them. But sooner or later they'll get a shot through."

"Any idea how many shots the hull can take?"

"Not a clue," Iosif said. "But I'm guessing we'll find out a lot sooner than we'd like."

"What's happening at the Core?" Levi asked as the screens shifted in response to another *Fyrantha* maneuver. "Allycc said Jeff was in trouble?"

"Internal bleeding or something," Nicole said, picking up the mic. "Tomas has gone to finish his work. Let me talk to the Koffren."

"Okay, but they won't want to talk back," Iosif warned. He keyed a switch. "You're on."

Nicole thumbed on the mic. "What the hell is *this*?" she snapped. "I told you I was going to talk to my people."

"The time for talking is finished," Djit-vis-ees said. "Do you surrender? Or do you die?"

"Neither," Nicole said. Ryit lifted a thin hand and pointed to one of the screens, and she saw that two more of the shield gaps had been filled. Still twelve to go. "I warn you again: if you persist in this attack you'll regret it."

"Vjiu-fusi-suut said you spoke such vague threats and nonsense to the Lillilli who once controlled the ship," Djit-vis-ees said scornfully. "Perhaps they were intimidated by such words. We are not."

On the schematic, two new gaps suddenly appeared. Nicole thumbed the mute and pointed. "Iosif?"

"Yeah, I see it," Iosif said grimly. "Wisp?"

One of the Wisps stepped closer to him, and Iosif touched its outstretched arm. There were the usual few seconds of silence— "Kointos and his people are on it," Iosif reported. "If you've got more stalling up your sleeve, this is the time to do it."

Nicole looked at the screens, feeling helplessness and panic bubbling together in her throat. The Koffren ships were zooming back and forth, firing their lasers and missiles as they glided gracefully like the ducks on Concourse Lake.

She frowned suddenly. *Glided gracefully as they fired . . .*

She thumbed the mic back on. "Okay, fine," she said. "I didn't want to do this, but I guess there's no choice. We'll be sending our prisoners back to you shortly."

"You think to bribe us?" Djit-vis-ees scoffed. "I already said we don't want them."

"Too bad," Nicole said. "They're coming, anyway." She paused. "Wait a second. Sorry—I said that wrong. Not *shortly;* we'll be sending our prisoners back to you *briefly.*"

"Your words are translating improperly," Djit-vis-ees said. "You say *briefly?*"

"Yes," Nicole said. "Actually, you probably won't even have time to say hello before you all hit the road for hell together."

"You speak nonsense."

"No, you just don't understand," Nicole said. "And since there's nothing you can do to stop it, there's no harm in explaining it to you. You know about the *Fyrantha*'s teleport? Of course you do—that's how Vjiu-fusi-suut and his crew came aboard in the first place, isn't it? Well, we're going to deliver the prisoners back to you the same way." She smiled tightly. "Only each of them is going to be carrying an extra package. A package that goes boom on delivery. We've got the first two ready. Do you want to point out the two least important of your ships?"

She thumbed the mute back on, holding her breath. If there'd been a flaw in Tomas's plan—if the teleport couldn't handle ship-to-ship transport, for instance—then the next sound she heard would be Djit-vis-ees laughing in her face.

But no one was laughing. And on the screens—

"They're pulling back," Levi said disbelievingly. "They're actually pulling *back*."

"And they're jinking," Iosif added, pointing. "Breaking up their vectors and curves." He looked over his shoulder at Nicole. "Trying to make it harder for you to hit them with the teleport."

"And making it harder for them to hit us, too?" Nicole asked.

"Looks like it," Iosif confirmed. "At least they've stopped firing."

"Great," Nicole said, exhaling a sigh of relief. The bluff had actually worked.

At least, for now. "Let's see if we can keep them at it." She activated the mic. "You've got to be kidding me," she said, putting as much scorn into her voice as she could. "The *Fyrantha*'s teleport can hit a planet a gazillion miles away. You really think backing off a couple of miles is going to be a problem?"

Djit-vis-ees didn't answer. The Koffren ships were still retreating, Nicole saw, but now the jittery movements Iosif had pointed out were increasing.

"So do we really have bombs to send across to them?" Levi asked quietly.

Nicole muted the mic. "Not that I know of," she said. "That was Tomas's idea, by the way."

"So he was planning on delivering instead of picking up," Levi said. "Yeah, that sounds like him."

"Let's just hope we can keep them off balance until we can get the rest of the shield gaps fixed," Iosif warned. "If they call our bluff, we might have to actually throw together some kind of bomb."

And sacrifice a Wisp to deliver it? Nicole's throat ached at the thought. But it might well come to that.

She touched the Wisp beside her. *I wish to access to a memory,* she said. *What Jeff said to me about choices and generals after the Shipmasters killed four Wisps.*

There was a moment's pause . . .

I know you're hurting about the Wisps. So am I. But we're in a war, and war requires choices. No general worth an honest salute likes making the decisions that will cost people their lives. But they keep making the choices, and the sacrifices that go with them, because if they don't a lot more people will die.

Nicole didn't want to be a general. She'd told Jeff that. All she'd ever wanted out of life was to be safe and not afraid and to have enough to eat.

But the *Fyrantha* had chosen her as its Protector, and the people and Ghorfs aboard had accepted her in that role, and she no longer had a choice.

And if it came to sacrificing a few Wisps to save everyone else, she knew she would indeed do it.

"Uh-oh," Iosif muttered.

"What?" Nicole asked, looking back at the displays.

"New strategy," Iosif said. "Nineteen of the ships are still doing their jump-and-twitch dance, but the last one is coming straight at us. Big, slow, and fat."

"Calling our bluff," Levi said tightly. "Offering us a clear shot if we actually have one."

"Only we don't," Nicole said, looking at the schematic. There were still thirteen gaping holes in the *Fyrantha's* shield. "I guess we've just got one option left."

She thumbed on the mic. "I see you're sending in a transport," she said. "Good, because I was just about to ask for one. I think it's time we had a face-to-face."

Levi threw her a shocked look. *"Nicole?"*

She motioned him to silence. "I assume there's a way to dock a smaller ship with the *Fyrantha*, but I don't know how to do it," she continued. "So I suggest you just wait outside the shield—hover or float or whatever it is ships do out there—while I get a spacesuit and come across. Then we can talk this out together."

"Once again, you speak nonsense," Djit-vis-ees said. "We have nothing to talk about."

"I think we do," Nicole said. "Are you going to just throw away the chance to maybe get the *Fyrantha* without any more damage to it or yourselves?"

There was a short silence. Levi and Iosif were looking at her with widened eyes, Nicole saw, and she again gestured a warning to them to keep silent.

"Very well," Djit-vis-ees said. "I accept. My ship will await your arrival. You have ten minutes."

"Make it thirty," Nicole said. "It's a big ship, and getting into a spacesuit is a pain."

"You have twenty."

"Twenty minutes," Nicole agreed.

She thumbed off the mic and gestured for Levi to cut the connection. "Figured he'd take me up on it," she said, handing Iosif the mic. "He was already willing to sacrifice that ship. Might as well let it hang around and see if he could get a good hostage out of the deal."

"You're not seriously thinking about going over there, are you?" Levi asked.

"That depends on whether we can get the rest of the shield fixed in the next twenty minutes," Nicole said.

"And if we can't?"

Nicole took a deep breath. "Then I go to see them. And buy you as much extra time as I can."

"And if we say no?" Iosif asked.

"I'm the Protector," Nicole said. "No one says *no* to me."

"*No!*"

Nicole jumped violently as the sudden voice echoed through the control center. Through the control center . . . and inside her mind.

What the *hell*?

"No!" the voice said again, deep and rumbling and powerful.

And suddenly, between the dark outer console ring and the display screens on the wall the holograms of Ushkai and R'taas appeared. "You will not leave me alone, Protector," they said, speaking in unison, their voices somehow blending into this new voice. "You will *not*."

With an effort, Nicole found her own voice. "Who are you?" she asked. The two holograms drew themselves up, again in unison.

Then, to her amazement, the images flowed into each other, swirling and twisting and sparkling together, until they'd formed a new image, an image utterly unlike either of them, an image like one of the golden Greek gods from Nicole's old mythology reader.

And suddenly she knew. "You're the *Fyrantha*," she breathed.

"I am *Leviathan*," the new figure said in the same sonorous voice. "I am training ground. I am ark of refuge. I am peacekeeper.

I am war-bringer. I am scourge of the Arm. I am strength and resolve and purpose.

"I am *death*."

And suddenly, the consoles in the two outer rings came to life, flicking on with lights and controls and images. On the big ship schematic, the gaps abruptly filled in, and the light blue haze of the shield deepened and thickened. Beneath the blue shell, a hundred orange spots appeared at points scattered all across the hull.

"Protector!"

Nicole took a deep breath. "I'm here," she called.

"I rise against this attack," the voice said. "Guide me."

Nicole looked helplessly at Levi and Iosif. *Guide me?* "I don't understan—"

Without warning, a flood of images filled the room and her mind. Faces, thoughts, fears, hopes. Images of women, mostly young, all of them surrounded by other people and consoles with glowing lights and controls. All of them feeling helpless, all of them abruptly aware of Nicole and of each other.

It was the Sibyls. *All* of them, their minds linked to Nicole and to the ship.

And the last piece of the puzzle that was the *Fyrantha* finally fell into place. The ship's builders, the ones who'd first brought in humans as partners in their work, had never intended them to need the slow poison of the inhalers to hear the ship. That had only become necessary when the *Fyrantha's* mind and soul were fragmented. Tomas had finished the work Jeff had started in the Core, and the ship was once again whole.

And now, for the first time in perhaps centuries, the *Fyrantha* was at its full capabilities.

No. Not the *Fyrantha*.

Leviathan.

Maybe the Koffren commander guessed what had happened.

Maybe he was just reacting to the ship's newly strengthened shields. But suddenly the distant ships stopped their defensive jinking and swung back to their attack, their lasers and missiles filling the sky.

"Guide me."

Nicole took a deep breath. *Sibyls, this is the Protector,* she spoke to the images in her mind. *The weapons control consoles are in front of you. Find them, and each of you stand in front of one.*

There was a brief moment of doubt and fear as the Sibyls reacted to the flood of thoughts within their minds. But they'd spent years listening to the *Fyrantha,* and the confusion surrounding the new voices quickly disappeared. The mental images shifted as each of them obediently moved in front of the proper console, and on the schematic nearly half of the orange spots brightened to show which weapons clusters were now active and ready.

The ship is under attack, Nicole said. *We're going to help it defend itself. Consoles—*

She'd already seen there were no numbers on the orange spots. Yet somehow she knew which cluster was which.

—fourteen, thirty, twenty-seven: target the nearest Koffren ships and fire lasers.

How? someone asked.

But even as the question formed in Nicole's mind it vanished into understanding. *Leviathan* was guiding the Sibyls just as it was guiding Nicole, and just as she knew which cluster was which so they knew how to aim and fire the weapons as Nicole had ordered.

The sky was filled with blazing light as the Koffren continued their attack, their weapons not even denting *Leviathan*'s shields. They got five more seconds before the Sibyls got their own weapons lined up.

And *Leviathan* returned fire.

Nicole caught her breath. She'd thought the sky was as brightly lit up as it could be. She was wrong. *Leviathan*'s weapons were sheets of blazing green, the Shipmasters' greenfire weapons scaled up a million times, slicing through the Koffren ships like they were cardboard. The targeted ships disintegrated, a few of them bursting with secondary explosions as their remaining missiles blew up.

Consoles eleven, eighteen, fifty-six, seventy: target and fire.

Four more blasts of greenfire weapons. Four more Koffren ships destroyed.

Consoles fifteen, twenty-two, ninety-one, forty: target and fire.

Four more blasts. Four more disintegrated Koffren ships.

Nicole gazed at the screens, awe and disbelief mixed together with horror. In the space of a dozen seconds, half the enemy force had been utterly destroyed. A dozen more seconds, a couple more salvos, and the rest would be turned to dust.

And the Koffren commander knew it. The remaining ships abruptly broke off their attack and turned to flee, flying desperately away from the unexpected disaster.

Finish them, Leviathan ordered.

Nicole watched the Koffren ships another moment. *No.*

I am Leviathan. *I am scourge of the Arm. You will guide me in destroying them.*

No, Nicole repeated. *At least, not yet.*

"Levi, let me talk to them," she said aloud, reaching to the console and picking up the mic.

She focused on Levi. He was gazing at the screens, his eyes wide. "Levi?" she prompted.

He seemed to shake himself. "Right," he said, reaching to the controls. "You're on."

"This is the Protector," Nicole called. "I have a message for the leaders of the Koffren. Promise to deliver it, and I'll let the rest of your ships leave. Otherwise, we'll just have to find another way to deliver it. Probably directly to your home world. Personally."

There was a short pause. "Speak your message," Djit-vis-ees said, his voice tense.

"You've been using the Shipmasters' data to steal war slaves from other worlds," Nicole said. "That stops now. Any beings you're still using are to be removed from whatever battlefields they're on and returned directly home."

"Many of the recruits now serve others," Djit-vis-ees said. "We cannot simply demand them back."

"Oh, I think you probably can," Nicole said. "If not, we'll just have to go to them directly, get their attention like we just did with you, and deliver the message. Of course, if we have to do that we'll also make it clear that the Koffren knew what was coming after them and didn't bother to tell them what they needed to do to avoid it."

"I'll deliver the message," Djit-vis-ees said. "The Koffren leaders will do all they can."

"I hope so," Nicole said. "Because we've got all the Shipmasters' records here, including the names and locations of every world they sold to you or others. We'll be checking all of them, so the faster and wider you can spread the word, the better. Understood?"

"Understood," Djit-vis-ees said. He was still angry, Nicole could tell, and refusing to acknowledge his defeat. But he *did* understand.

"Good," Nicole said. "And just in case you forget anything, we'll be sending Vjiu-fusi-suut and the other survivors home with the same message. Probably without any bombs attached, but you never know. Now get out of here, before we decide that Vjiu-fusi-suut can handle the message without you."

She muted the mic and signaled Levi. "You think they've had enough?" Iosif asked.

"I don't know," Nicole said. "Let's find out."

They had. On the displays the remaining Koffren ships continued to fly away, accelerating as they went. As Nicole watched they did a little flickering sort of jump, like something out of a movie, and vanished.

Why did you not let me destroy them?

Nicole took a deep breath. The Sibyls, she noted, had disappeared from her eyes and mind. Apparently, this new conversation was between just her and the ship. *Because that's not who you are anymore.*

I am scourge of the Arm.

That's what you were once, Nicole said. *That was when your job was to punish. But that changed. Someone else took over, and you weren't there anymore to punish people who deserved it. You were just a warship.*

I was the most powerful warship.

Maybe, Nicole conceded. *But you didn't care about why you were doing what you were doing. You were fighting whoever your masters told you to fight. You didn't care whether they deserved it or not.*

Leviathan seemed to think about that. *No,* it said. *I always cared. It was the masters who did not.*

I know, Nicole said, her throat aching. How many times had she done something just because Trake had told her to? Did any of the people she'd helped rob or hurt really deserve it?

She didn't know. She would never know.

Because she'd never wanted to.

But then things changed again, she went on. *You were damaged in battle, or maybe your masters broke your Core into pieces on purpose, and you weren't a warship anymore. Someone else took over and made you into a zoo.*

Not a zoo, Leviathan said, its voice thoughtful. *I was an ark of refuge. A sanctuary. Animals were brought aboard to live until their home worlds could be rebuilt and reinvigorated.*

Really? Nicole asked, frowning. The Caretaker had told her the

Fyrantha was a zoo. Had Ushkai been wrong then, or was *Leviathan* wrong now?

Maybe it wasn't either of them. Maybe the ship had been made into a sanctuary, and also a viewing place so people wouldn't forget why it was important that the animals' habitats be put back together.

For that matter, maybe *Leviathan* had been the cause of that destruction in the first place. Maybe the *Fyrantha's* job as sanctuary had been an effort to help atone for *Leviathan's* wars.

And that was good, she said. *But then the Shipmasters came— Nevvis and Fievj and the others. They took out the animals and turned you into a place where people fight each other.*

So that once again I was a warship?

Yeah, I suppose, kind of, Nicole said. *But here's the thing. You rattled off a list of things you'd been when you first woke up. But between being a warship and an animal sanctuary, you said you'd been a peacekeeper. Tell me about that.*

It was the Plimkatae, the ship said slowly. *The beings who created me, the people of the Oracle who names herself R'taas. They won me back, and made me once again their instrument of justice. But instead of a scourge against evil I was made a vessel of peace. I stood between aggressor and victim, forcing those who sought destruction or conquest to stand down or flee.*

Nicole nodded to herself. So R'taas's people had built the ship, lost it to someone, gotten it back, then lost it to the Lillilli. The first group of Lillilli had then lost it to Nevvis and his group. Like a bunch of gangs fighting over the same couple of blocks of territory. *So you know what it's like to stop fights,* she said. *How about we go back to that?*

We? Does that mean you're staying with me?

I don't know, Nicole said, frowning. Somehow, she hadn't thought that far ahead. *Do you want me to?*

I don't want. I need.

Nicole swallowed hard. Was she about to trade one imprisonment for another?

But really, why not? Trake was dead, and even if he were still around she had no interest in going back to her previous life in his gang. Here, she could do things that mattered, maybe even live up to the name *Protector* the ship had given her. Was there anything else she needed or even wanted back on Earth?

Actually, now that she thought about it, there was.

I'll need to go back for a day or two, she told *Leviathan. I have to see my grandmother and tell her I'm all right.* She winced. *And tell her how sorry I am for the way I behaved to her. She was right—she was always right—but I was too sure of myself to understand. Can you do without me that long?*

I can, Leviathan said. *You will return quickly?*

I will, Nicole promised. *Don't worry, I have plans for us.*

She smiled tightly. Yes, she had plans, all right.

Big plans.

twenty-eight

"I have to say," Nicole said, "that I'm really getting tired of visiting you in medical centers."

Jeff smiled wanly. "I could get behind never meeting like this again," he agreed. "Allyce says I'll be walking again soon."

Nicole nodded. "She told me that, too."

Though she'd also warned Nicole that he might never walk properly again. She'd done everything she could, but it might not be enough. They would just have to wait and see.

"Nise told me that you had Iyulik's memorial service while I was still under," Jeff said quietly. "I'm sorry I wasn't well enough to attend."

"It's all right," Nicole assured him. "Everyone understood. Iyulik's people hold specific time periods for remembrance, memorial, and interment, and Nise wanted to honor those."

"He's with the humans in Q4?"

"That was the original plan," Nicole said. "But we decided instead to make his memorial the first of a new group in Q2. We're not slaves anymore. We're free people, *Leviathan*'s friends and allies."

"Yeah," Jeff said, his eyes narrowing slightly. "I'm still a little unclear about how all this is working now."

"So am I," Nicole admitted. "But we've got time to figure it out.

Before we do anything else we need to sort out everyone who wants to leave and send them home."

"That's most of them, I assume?"

"Surprisingly enough, it isn't," Nicole said. "About two-thirds of the workers are staying, including most of Miron's green team—including Iosif—and most of our blue team." She felt her throat tighten. "Tomas is going home, though. He says the ship has too many bad memories for him."

"I figured if anyone left he'd be the one," Jeff said, nodding heavily. "Who else?"

"The Q3 gray team's sticking around," Nicole said. "And like I said, about two-thirds of the rest."

"Green, blue, and gray," Jeff said, nodding. "Interesting."

"What is?"

"Our team, Miron's team, and Kointos's team," Jeff said. "People who'd actually met you."

"That has nothing to do with it," Nicole protested. "They just like what they see here and want to keep going."

"Right. Like I said."

"Jeff—"

"What about the Ghorfs?" Jeff asked.

Nicole gave him another half second of glare, just to make it clear that she still wasn't agreeing with him. "Surprisingly, they're all staying. Kahkitah said they decided *Leviathan* needs a good internal security team, and that they were the best qualified for the job."

"I wouldn't argue the point for a minute," Jeff said. "I presume the Thii and Ponngs are heading out?"

"Actually, no," Nicole said. "Well, okay, they are, but only so they can alert their governments as to what's going on out here. Nise set up a return Wisp rendezvous for next week, while Moile figures it'll take two weeks to work his way up to the people who need to hear him. But both Ponngs and all three Thii will be back before we finish with the rest of the teleport work."

"Again, people who've met and worked with you." Jeff held up a hand. "I know, I know—I'm imagining things."

"Whatever." Nicole eyed him. "You didn't ask about Allyce."

Jeff's amused half smile faded. "Don't need to," he said. "She told me two days ago that she was leaving."

"Yes," Nicole confirmed. "She left yesterday morning." She paused, just long enough to watch his expression droop a little more. "And came back this evening."

Jeff sat up a little straighter in his bed. "She's *back*?"

"Uh-huh," Nicole said, enjoying his surprise far more than she probably should have. "And with a surprise: her husband, Tad."

"Okay, you've lost me," Jeff said. "I thought she betrayed us in Q1 because she wanted to go home."

"She wanted to go home to her *husband*," Nicole corrected. "And I guess he missed her as much as she missed him. Twelve years since she disappeared and he hadn't remarried."

"So did she bring him here to explain why she didn't come home that night?"

"I think she's hoping to persuade him that this would be a good home for both of them, at least for the next few years," Nicole said. "He's a doctor, too, it turns out. I only talked with them for a couple of minutes, but from what he's seen already it sounds like he's three-quarters of the way to agreeing to stay."

"Great," Jeff said. "So we've got Ponngs, Thii, Ghorfs, work crews, Sibyls, and now a couple of doctors. Sounds like we're set." He eyed her closely. "The question is, set for *what*?"

Nicole looked away. "You know what the *Fyrantha* was all about," she said. "Finding useful fighters and selling their worlds to people who wanted battle slaves. We've stopped the Koffren . . . but I've seen the records. Nevvis wasn't shy about selling to anyone who had money, and there were a *lot* of people out there with money."

"You want to free all the slaves."

"For starters, yes," Nicole said. "But the fact that there are so many battle slaves out there also means there are a lot of battles. Battles, wars, people fighting and killing and dying. Like the streets where I grew up. It's a horrible, horrible waste."

"It's also stupid," Jeff agreed, his gaze steady on her. "So . . . ?"

"So we have *Leviathan,*" Nicole said, waving a hand around her. "The biggest, nastiest warship around. And my experience is that the person with the biggest, baddest gun usually scares everyone else so much that he almost never has to use it."

"So *Leviathan* becomes *Peacekeeper?*"

"Why not? That was its role once. Why can't it fill the same role again?"

"I'm not arguing," Jeff said. "But *my* experience is that people who like to beat on other people are pretty stubborn. They don't give up easily. You're looking at a long, uphill climb."

"I know," Nicole said. "But really, I've got nothing else planned."

"I figured."

"Yeah." Nicole braced herself. "I'd really like to have your help. Unless you were planning to go home?"

"Actually, home sounds great," Jeff said.

Nicole nodded heavily. She should have known he would want to leave. His life aboard the *Fyrantha* had been nothing but work and boredom before she arrived, and afterward had been nothing but danger and pain.

"Which is the funny part," he continued. "A long time ago I realized that I was a slave who would spend the rest of my life here. Once I accepted that fact, life became reasonably pleasant. Now that I'm not a slave, the place is even more comfortable."

Nicole frowned. "Are you saying *this* is home for you?"

"It's better than that," he said, smiling. "I joined the Marines because I wanted to stand between the evil and the innocents. Then I was injured, and that dream went away."

He waved a hand around the room. "Now, you're giving me the chance to do that on a scale I'd never have imagined. So, bottom line: damn straight I'm staying."

Nicole huffed out a relieved sigh. "Thank you," she said quietly.

"No problem." He reached over and squeezed her hand. "So I suggest you haul Allyce and Dr. Tad up here and get them back to work on my leg."

He smiled. "And then let's take the biggest, baddest gun in the neighborhood and find some bad guys to scare."

about the author

TIMOTHY ZAHN is the Hugo Award–winning author of more than fifty science fiction novels, including *Night Train to Rigel, The Third Lynx, Odd Girl Out,* and the Dragonback sextet. He has also written the all-time bestselling Star Wars spin-off novel, *Heir to the Empire,* and other Star Wars novels, including the recent *Thrawn: Treason.* He lives in coastal Oregon.